FOR WHAT IT'S WORTH

FOR WHAT IT'S WORTH

Lynda Page

headline

First published in 2006
by HEADLINE BOOK PUBLISHING

1

Cataloguing in Publication Data is
available from the British Library

ISBN 0 7553 0884 0

Typeset in Stempel Garamond by Palimpsest Book Production Limited,
Polmont, Stirlingshire
Printed and bound in Great Britain by
Clays Ltd, St Ives plc

Headline's policy is to use papers that are natural, renewable and
recyclable products and made from wood grown in sustainable
forests. The logging and manufacturing processes are expected
to conform to the environmental regulations of the country of origin.

HEADLINE BOOK PUBLISHING
A division of Hodder Headline
338 Euston Road
London NW1 3BH

www.headline.co.uk
www.hodderheadline.com

For Mary Inchley

I thought it was about time to acknowledge what a truly wonderful friend – in every sense of the word – you are to me.

To describe your qualities and what a good impact you have had on my life would take more words than in this book, so all I'll say now is that if you were a man I would marry you without hesitation!

With all my love
Lynda x

For John Chaplin

In grateful appreciation for the time you spent with me reliving your experiences and imparting information from your forty years in the taxi business.

CHAPTER ONE

Charles Tyme froze rigid as the length of cheese wire throttling him tightened round his neck, cutting into his flesh. He could feel the warm trickle of blood running down to pool in the well of his throat. The nauseating stench of foul breath assailed him as a low throaty voice in his ear warned: 'Hand over yer takings! And no funny business or it's a six-foot hole they'll be digging for you.'

His assailant left Chas in no doubt he meant business. He hadn't liked the look of the scruffily dressed man when he'd appeared out of the shadows and before Chas could stop him, slipped into the back of his vehicle. He'd just dropped off his last fare in a deserted, dimly lit street on the outskirts of the city. The new fare had gruffly indicated 'town' as his destination.

Chas had been earning his living by taxi-driving barely a month, was still in fact a novice compared to the old stalwarts who'd been in the game for years and knew all the tricks of the trade inside out. Nevertheless he was well aware that it was illegal for private-hire taxi companies to pick fares up off the side of the road unless they'd previously booked through the firm's office – a fare accepted off the street was known as a flimp or flimping in the trade. This law, and many more besides, was flouted shamelessly by most other private-hire drivers. Chas, though, was the conscientious sort. To him the law was the law, made for a purpose and to be abided by regardless of the cost in lost business.

He'd informed the man twice that he wasn't for hire but it was obvious the passenger was not going to budge. His response on both occasions had been a curt, 'I said, town.'

As Chas saw it he was faced with two options. Either he dragged the man bodily from the vehicle or else he turned a

1

blind eye to the law and delivered him to his destination. Chas struggled with his conscience. He didn't like the thought of knowingly breaking the law but balancing that was his reluctance to leave anyone in an area of Leicester that was known to be a criminal haunt. Should any ill befall the man there, Chas would never forgive himself. His better nature gave him no option but to take the unwelcome fare where he demanded to go. As a sop to his conscience about breaking the law, Chas decided that he would put his cut of the fare in the box for the blind in his local corner shop and those unfortunate people would receive the benefit of it.

'All right, mate,' he'd eventually agreed. 'I'll make an exception just this once, but next time – no official booking through the office, no ride. Not in my car.'

He'd tried to appraise the man huddled in the back seat through his rear-view mirror as he'd driven along but the night was a dark one, a blanket of thick cloud masking the moon. Besides that the man had kept his head down. In his present dire predicament Chas realised why: to avoid any possible later identification.

Chas hadn't been fazed initially when a few minutes after they'd set off the man had suddenly demanded he should stop, having apparently changed his mind about his destination. Chas had been told on his sketchy induction to the job that people frequently did this and most were disgruntled that, regardless, they still had to pay for the distance already travelled. But Chas hadn't been given the time to calculate what was owed him. Immediately he'd stopped the thin length of wire was slid around his neck, the man issuing his murderous threat to make sure Chas complied with his demand.

When he had decided to take this job, it had never crossed his mind that he'd one day find himself having his life threatened for a meagre amount of money. Making matters even worse for Chas was the fact that the money in the takings bag belonged to his employer, so in truth was not his to hand over to the thief.

In an effort to reason with his attacker he began, 'If you'd let me explain that the . . .'

The wire was yanked tighter and a fresh trickle of blood ran down his neck. 'I said, hand over yer takings. And mek it quick,

2

I ain't got all night. Any more shilly-shallying and I'll finish you off here and now and help meself to 'em.'

Despite Chas's own aversion to violence in any form, he felt that in this case he was being given no other option.

Despite the pounding of his heart and his restricted breathing, he managed to say matter-of-factly, 'Me takings bag is under me seat. You'll have to release me if yer want me to pass it over.'

Silence prevailed for several long seconds before Chas felt the tension on the wire relax enough for him to lean as far forward as he needed to. 'Don't try 'ote stupid 'cos I meant what I said,' the man snarled, 'I will finish you off.'

Chas felt under his seat for the canvas takings bag. Grabbing the end of it and gripping it tightly, he then sat upright again and, taking a deep breath while praying his aim would be accurate, with a quick flick of his wrist he brought the bulky bag of coins back to land forcefully smack against his attacker's temple. A surprised yelp rent the air as the man let go of the cheese wire, slapping his hands to his head. Simultaneously, Chas made a grab for the car door, levered the handle open and leaped out. Next he yanked the back door open and hauled out his still-stunned assailant. Thrusting him forcibly away, Chas snatched up the length of wire that had fallen out of the taxi. He twisted the ends around his huge hands, flexing it in a threatening gesture. 'You picked the wrong cabby to fleece tonight,' he hissed. 'Now, unless you want a taste of yer own medicine, I'd make a run for it while you can if I was you.'

Sprawled across the pavement, the gash on his head pouring blood, the man stared up at Chas wild-eyed, stunned senseless by this sudden reversal of roles. Chas could tell his mind was flailing around, seeking for a way to turn the situation back in his own favour. As Chas stared down, wondering if the man was going to risk another attack and preparing to defend himself, he felt a sudden rush of pity. He wondered what had brought about this situation where a man would threaten grievous bodily harm on another human being for the sake of a few pounds? Any number of things could have caused him to become desperate enough to resort to such measures. A hungry wife and children perhaps? A sick relative needing expensive care? Being the man he was Chas could not help but extend a show of compassion.

'Look . . . er . . . I don't condone what you've just tried but if you're that desperate for money, desperate enough to threaten murder, I could give you a few shillings. It's not much but, you see, the money in the takings bag isn't mine. If you did try to relieve me of it again, well, I'd have to try and stop you and one of us would come off the worse. I have to tell you straight that I would do my damnedest to make sure it wasn't me.'

The man looked up at him, stupefied, wondering if he had heard right.

Chas smiled kindly. 'Would a few shillings help? Enough to buy you a hot meal at any rate.'

The mugger scrambled up to stand staring at Chas as though he was mad. 'Er . . . you on the level, Gov?'

Chas untwisted the wire and thrust one of his hands into his pocket, pulling out a half-crown which he held out towards the man. 'I should march you down to the police station as any other cabby would after what you tried. Just count yourself lucky it was me you picked on and not one of my colleagues 'cos, I can assure you, they wouldn't have let you off anywhere near so lightly. Now take this and scarper before I change my mind. Oh, and . . . er . . . I'd get that cut on your head seen to urgently in case it turns nasty.'

The man made a sudden snatch for the money then, spinning on his heels, stumbled off into the night.

Chas stared after him until the sound of his footsteps had died away. Forming the wire into a tight ball, he shoved it deep into his trouser pocket then rubbed his big hands wearily over his face. He had just had a close call. If that desperado had carried out his murderous threat, Chas could now be well on his way to whatever lay in store for him in the after-life. He hoped vehemently that his attacker had learned his lesson and in future would choose more legitimate ways in which to earn a living. He also knew that should this incident become common knowledge amongst his fellow workers they would never understand why he had chosen to act the way he had and he would be mercilessly berated. So as far as Chas was concerned, no one else needed to know. No harm had come to him, well, no serious harm, and it was he himself who was out of pocket and not his employer.

A crackling sound over the car radio alerted him. Slipping

back into the driver's seat, he unhooked the hand-mic and pressed down the receiver button. 'Romeo with you.' How uncomfortable his call handle made him feel! If he had been Adonis-like then it might have been apt, but as it was he was more the unremarkable, gentle giant sort. He hadn't been given any choice, though. It was the boss who had allotted his call handle to him when his employment began so Chas was stuck with it.

A shrill response in the thick Leicester accent of Marlene Cox, evening-shift radio operator back in the firm's office on Blackbird Road at the other side of town, sounded like gobbledegook to Chas.

'Repeat, base?' he requested.

Irritated, she responded, 'Oh, yer should wash yer lug 'oles out, Chas Tyme, then you'd hear me proper! I asked if you were free to do a pick up on Beaumont Leys? Bloke needs ter get to the station to catch the six-twenty to Nottingham.'

Her disrespectful attitude towards him was not lost on Chas but now was not the time to reproach her for it. He flashed a quick look at his watch. It was a minute to six, in actual fact his knocking off time. Even in a speeding car with no traffic on the road, he'd still be hard pushed to collect the client and get him to the station in time to catch the train. 'I'm at the top of Welford Road at the moment. Traffic permitting, it'd take me fifteen minutes at least to get to the Beaumont Leys. The train would be halfway to Nottingham by the time I got the customer to the station.' If Marlene took more interest in her job instead of forever preening herself to attract the eye of any man who came through the firm's door, or of one driver in particular, then she should have known exactly where Chas was and that he couldn't possibly do the job to the satisfaction of the customer.

'Eh? Wha' did yer say?'

Taking a deep breath, Chas slowly repeated himself.

'So yer won't do it then?' came her shrill reply.

He groaned. After what he'd just been through tonight he was in no mood for dealing with the likes of Marlene who only exhibited a spark of intelligence when the mood took her. In fact, it was Chas's private opinion that she didn't actually have any as he hadn't witnessed any evidence of it so far during the two weeks she'd been at Black's Taxis. He knew from the

grumbling of the other drivers too that although they appreciated her physical attributes, they were not at all impressed by
her radio-operating skills He snapped down the switch on the
mic. 'I didn't say I wouldn't do it,' he sighed. 'Only that it's not
humanly possible for me to do it in time. What about one of
the other drivers?'

She whined, 'Can't gerrold of no one else. Bloody ignorant
sods are ignoring me!'

Regardless of the fact that she had had it explained to her
several times, Marlene still didn't seem to appreciate that the
radio didn't work in some areas of the city if in the vicinity of
tall buildings and, depending on the terrain outside the city
boundaries, only sporadically over a ten-mile radius. Meanwhile,
Chas was aware that a customer was awaiting his arrival and
that precious time was being wasted. 'Tell the bloke I'll be there
as soon as I can and I'll do me best to get him to the station on
time, but I ain't making any promises.'

'Eh? Wha' did yer say?'

His mind already fixing on the best possible route through
the back streets of Leicester to help him achieve this seemingly
impossible task, he uncharacteristically snapped: 'I said, I'll do
me bloody best!' Replacing the mic in its cradle, Chas roared
off.

CHAPTER TWO

In the snug back room of a two-up, two-down rented terraced
house a few minutes' walk from the premises of Black's Taxis,
a sprightly, neat seventy year old with iron-grey hair, Iris Imelda
Tyme, dropped her darning and got to her feet as soon as she
heard the back door open. Arriving in the kitchen she smiled,
relieved to see her son home safe and sound.

'Yer very late tonight,' she said, moving towards the stove.
She picked up a worn tea towel then bent over to open the door
and remove a piping hot chipped enamel dish. 'I was starting to
worry you'd met with an accident or summat.' Straightening up,
she smiled warmly at Chas. 'Well, yer dinner's all ready for yer
and it's nice and hot.'

Hanging his working jacket over his arm, he looked quickly
into the dish. The contents, whatever they were, were so shriv-
elled it was hard to tell what she'd cooked but he loved and
respected his mother far too much to say anything that would
hurt her feelings. 'Looks great, Mam,' he said enthusiastically.
Sniffing appreciatively he added, 'Smells good too.'

Iris looked up fondly at the huge man who dwarfed her. At
thirty years old, six foot two and a well-muscled fifteen stone,
no would ever guess what a struggle for life her son had had
when he'd arrived in the world six weeks' premature. He'd been
a scrap of humanity, not expected to live by the medical profes-
sion. The first few weeks of his existence had been touch and
go as his underdeveloped body fought to cope. His survival was
like a miracle to Iris. By the time she had learned of her pregnancy – a 'change-of-life baby' the doctors had termed him –
she had long ago resigned herself to the fact that the large family
her beloved husband Charles and she had longed for was not
going to materialise. They had reluctantly resigned themselves
to remaining childless.

Then, at the age of forty, in the space of a week Iris had lost her soul-mate in an accident – on his way to work a runaway horse and cart had ploughed into Charles's push bike, killing him instantly – and while still coping with the trauma of her devastating loss, had discovered to her utter shock that she was expecting their much longed-for child. During a time of otherwise desperate sadness, the life growing inside her had become a source of deep comfort and Iris had vowed to her dead husband that she would raise their child as best she could, labour hard not to let it suffer from the loss of the loving father he would have been.

All these years later she still shuddered at the memory of her vigil by her son's hospital cot, willing the tiny scrap within to fight to live, constantly terrified she would lose him. Her gratitude towards the hospital staff when her six-week-old son was finally pronounced to be out of danger knew no bounds, but deep down and despite others possibly labelling her a crank Iris was convinced it was the spirit of her dead husband that had helped their son through his first difficult weeks. From the hereafter Charles had reached out and given her the one thing she desired most in the world, the one thing he had known would help her through the rest of her days without her husband by her side. Thirty years later, every night before she settled down to sleep, Iris thanked him for what she was convinced was his last bequest to her.

With her love and determination to help him on his way, the scrawny child she'd named after his father grew into a strapping lad, possessing a kind and caring nature, eager to help his mother in any way he could to bring money into the house. Iris herself took any work open to her – mostly cleaning for ungrateful people who treated her like a slave, rewarding her labours with as little as they could get away with. Chas run errands for the neighbours, and as soon as he was old enough took a Saturday job with the local garage cleaning cars, despite her protests, always insisting every penny he earned was hers to spend.

Much to her regret, Iris became aware that due to his concern for her and his naturally shy nature, her son had been labelled by the other local children of his age group as a 'mummy's boy'. He was ostracised and ridiculed mercilessly by them at every opportunity. Iris knew that this state of affairs had resulted in her beloved boy finding it difficult even now to trust anyone long enough to forge a close friendship with them. That hadn't stopped him from taking up interests of his own, though. Listening to the wireless as a child had developed his great love of music. He owned an ever-increasing record collection and many people would have envied his selection of rare imports, Chas having a penchant for songs by the likes of Sam Cooke, Harry Belafonte, Nat King Cole, and a variety of black American Rhythm and Blues artists. An avid reader also, the bookcase in his bedroom groaned under the weight of the paperbacks he had amassed over the years, both fiction and non-fiction. He had taught himself the basics of plumbing, electrics and motor mechanics, something the neighbours were well aware of. They often called upon him to help them out in emergencies. Chas always obliged, never accepting payment for his time, just glad to be of help. He enjoyed speedway too, and when the mood took him would pay a visit to the local stadium for a night at the track when certain riders he favoured were appearing.

Her son was handsome in Iris's eyes though she was clear-sighted enough to realise that, pitted against other men, he did not possess the kind of physical attributes that turned women's heads. That in itself, she felt, was not the real reason why he'd never plucked up the courage to ask a girl out. His crippling lack of self-confidence was. It saddened her to think of the missed opportunities he'd suffered because of the constant barrage of unwarranted callous remarks and nasty tricks, some of them potentially dangerous, that he'd suffered at the hands of his tormentors. Iris knew what a wonderful husband and father he would have made, and for Iris herself having a daughter-in-law's companionship would have been a delight. She lived in hope, though, that one day a good woman would present herself, manage somehow to break though her son's reserve, and then when the time came Iris could join her beloved husband, happy in the knowledge that she hadn't left their child alone in the world.

'Yer just like yer dad was, God rest him. He loved my cooking too. Ate 'ote I put before him and never complained once. I should apply to be one of those chefs on the telly, shouldn't I? Show the women of Britain how it's really done. It was yer grandmother, God rest her, that I've to thank because she taught me all I know. "Never be afraid to use yer imagination in the kitchen, Iris," she constantly used to say to me as I stood beside her, watching her throw this and that into a bowl and mixing it all up. "Always make sure all yer meat is cooked well through so it's no germs left in it." So I always have and I've never poisoned yer, son, have I? Or yer dad neither.'

Chas pressed his lips together. In truth her cooking skills left much to be desired. She couldn't follow a recipe to save her life. If the directions said three ounces of flour, Iris would add another 'just in case'. She thought nothing of substituting something else if she hadn't got the exact ingredient the recipe stated, such as nutmeg for cinammon in a cake. She liked to make up her own concoctions too. Chas had often finished a meal with no idea of what exactly he'd just eaten. Regardless, he would never hurt her feelings by making even the slightest complaint, eating everything she put before him with relish and complimenting her after for her efforts, whether he had enjoyed it or not. His mother always made sure he'd a hot meal waiting for him when he came home, and what she produced, she produced with love.

Iris was just about to tell him she'd serve up while he went to change out of his working attire when she spotted dried blood on his shirt collar and then the thin red weal circling his thick neck. Her face creased with worry. 'What on earth happened to you?'

Chas looked at her blankly. In his desire to get his last passenger to the station on time to catch his train, which he'd achieved with only seconds to spare, he'd forgotten about his encounter with the thief and subsequent injuries. The office had been empty when he'd gone in to sign off his shift, apart from Marlene, varnishing her nails, and if she had noticed, she certainly hadn't bothered herself to enquire about it. Considering the circumstances of his father's death on his way to work, he couldn't risk alarming Iris with the truth. As far as he was aware his mother had no inkling of some of the types he encountered during his working hours, was under the impression all his passengers were polite, nice people who were thoroughly appreciative of the service he was doing them. He wanted to keep it that way. Covering the weal on his neck with his hand, he said lightly, 'Oh, I . . . er . . . walked into a washing line. It looks worse than it is.'

She scowled disbelievingly. 'Do I look as though I was born yesterday? That cut was caused by summat thin like . . . like . . . wire. It looks to me like someone tried to throttle yer!'

Chas stopped himself from laughing out loud. He should have known his lame excuse would not fool his mother. She might be in her twilight years, not quite as nimble on her feet as she once used to be, but there was nothing wrong with her faculties. 'Yeah, yer right, Mam. It was a thin wire-type washing line. I . . . er . . . couldn't make a customer hear I'd arrived at the front so I went round the back. The idiots who lived there had hung their washing line across the yard instead of down the length of it like most people do and, well, before I knew it I'd walked into it and it somehow got wrapped around my neck.' Before she could question him further, Chas added, 'I'd better get changed before my dinner goes cold.'

With that he hurried off to his bedroom.

A while later, his injury having been bathed using cold water from the jug on the stand in his room and now concealed by a black polo-necked sweater, he pushed away his empty plate and smiled appreciatively over at his mother. 'That were grand, Mam, thanks.'

She looked pleased as she gathered up the dirty dishes. 'Glad you enjoyed it. I've fruit pie for yer pudding.'

Fruit pie? Now that could mean anything. Apple. Blackberry. Pear. Blackcurrant. Apricot. Tinned fruit salad. Pineapple. Peaches. A mixture of two or three or even the whole lot.

Putting the overflowing dish of pie in front of him, smothered in thick custard so he was unable to determine just what fruit it contained, Iris sat down opposite nursing a cup of tea and looked at Chas hard. 'Yer look tired, son. I thought the idea of you changing yer job was to make it a lot easier on yerself? You worked all hours driving that lorry around all over the country. Now it seems yer working even longer hours, ferrying folks in and around Leicestershire. I suppose the only good side to yer changing yer job is that yer home every night so I can at least be certain you've had a home-cooked meal and can sleep in yer own clean bed.'

'Tired' wasn't the word for what Chas was feeling. His close brush with death was just beginning to register with him. What he'd gone through wasn't uppermost in his mind, it was what his mother could have been facing should the worst have happened to him at the hands of that mindless thief. When his father had had his life cut short through a senseless accident it was only the arrival of her son that had given Iris something to live for. If he had met his end tonight, she would have been left all on her own in the world in her twilight years, when love and help from her family were of paramount importance. Iris would never admit it but everyday tasks she once used to take in her stride, such as shopping and getting in the coal, took their toll on her now. Chas did his best to make sure he tackled this heavy work while endeavouring to make sure her pride was not dented.

From the best of intentions he had not been entirely honest with his mother about his decision to change his job. In fact, he hadn't been honest at all. He had loved his job as a lorry driver, delivering loads around the shires and up and down the country for a boss who was a decent man to work for and who had been sorry to lose such a conscientious worker. The only downside of that job had been spending several nights on the trot away from home every other week. But after his mother suffered a tumble in the street several weeks previously, turning her ankle on slippery cobbles while she was struggling with heavy bags of shopping, Chas was forced to acknowledge that the years were telling on Iris and he needed to be constantly on hand to avoid anything similar happening again.

At the age of thirty and with no experience of anything else but driving for a living, most local occupations paying a live-able wage were closed to Chas. Just about resigned to the fact that his only option was to take a labouring job in a factory, something he would have detested doing, after his years on the open road, he chanced to overhear a conversation in the pub. A local firm was on the lookout for a taxi driver, apparently. Vacancies for such jobs were few and far between, very much sought after, in fact. Surely he wouldn't stand a chance of securing it, matched against those with experience who were bound to apply. A job such as that, though, would suit Chas perfectly. It was driving which he liked, local which meant it was near at hand to where he lived, but more importantly it meant no nights away from home so he'd be able to do all the heavy chores for his mother. He wasted no time in making an application and couldn't believe his luck when Jack Black, the owner of Black's Taxis, liked the sound of what Chas had to offer and took him on.

Knowing his mother realised how much he had loved his lorry driving, Chas had fobbed Iris off with a tale that slack orders at work meant a cut in the workforce and he had felt morally obliged to put himself forward as one of the first to be let go, since he'd no wife and children as dependants like all the other drivers had. Iris had balked at his reasoning, pointing out that his wage was as important to him as it was to any of his work-mates, but Chas had stuck firmly to his story and she had had no choice but to accept his decision. His mother, Chas knew, would have been mortified had she ever found out the real truth. He just prayed she never did.

Now, his filled spoon poised in mid-air, he smiled at her. 'A couple of the part-time drivers called in sick so we were short-handed. It would've been daft of me to turn down the chance of earning a bit extra to put in the house-buying fund, wouldn't it? And besides, with what's going on at work, the least I can do for the boss is pull my weight as hard as I can to keep his business going until ... well ... hopefully he returns.'

Iris gave a disdainful click of her tongue. 'I see the need to do what you can for your boss but, oh, you and this house-buying lark! I keep telling yer, I've lived here all me married life and I've me friends roundabouts ...'

'Yes, Mam, I know that,' Chas cut in. 'But a modern house would be so much easier for you.'

'The way you talk, you make it sound like this new house you want to move me into when yer've saved up enough will just look after itself.'

'Oh, Mam, you know it won't. But don't tell me you don't like the thought of modern conveniences helping to make your life easier? Think about it seriously, Mam. A water heater would mean no more boiling up pans for a wash. And having a proper bathroom ... well, if *you* don't like the thought of that, *I* most certainly do. For a man my size, sitting in the tin bath ain't no fun, Mam. And look how the twin-tub and the Hoover changed your life. You went mad at first when I got you those, saying I should have spent the money of meself.' He looked at her tenderly. 'I just want to make life easier for you. You worked yourself half to death raising me on your own. Now you should be gracious enough to let me return the favour by doing what I can for you. Dad would have wanted that, I know he would. Forgive me for saying it but you're not so young as you were and I want you around for many years to come. If what I do to make your life easier helps achieve that, then it makes me happy.'

Iris pulled a shamed expression. She knew she was a fortunate woman to have a son who possessed such a generous nature. Chas could easily have turned out like so many of her neighbours' offspring whose priorities were strictly centred on themselves, the possible needs of their aging parents not figuring at all in their scheme of things. They even begrudged paying over their board money which in reality was not enough actually to keep them. The rest they earned went on entertainment and sporadic repayments of hire purchase agreements for clothes, cars and other frivolities they in truth couldn't afford and would take years to pay off.

Not that she was ungrateful for all Chas did for her and would do in the future, Iris just felt strongly that his efforts were all centred on what he could do for her, with little or no thought for his own well-being. She realised he was talking to her. 'Eh, what did yer say, lovey?'

'I'm just saying, I'm sorry I never got a chance to get the heavy shopping for you today but I'll make sure I do it tomorrow.'

She leaned over and patted his hand. 'I did gather that as yer came in empty-handed. Look, if yer can't manage tomorrow . . .'

'I will manage tomorrow,' he cut in, knowing what she was about to suggest. 'I'm not having you lugging bags of heavy groceries up the street at your age.'

'Oh, that's it, lad, remind me how old I am.' It was a scolding tone Iris used but her eyes were twinkling mischievously.

He laughed. 'Your body might be failing you a bit, but inside you're still a young girl. Isn't that right, Mam?'

She chuckled. 'That's about the size of it. Getting old is no fun, son. I wouldn't wish it on anyone. Mind you, I suppose it could be a lot worse. At least I ain't crippled with arthritis and

I've n'ote wrong with me hearing or eyesight.' Her eyes settled on him tenderly. 'And I never forget what a lucky woman I am, having the likes of you for a son.'

'It's me that's the lucky one, having you for a mam.'

Although delighted by his compliment, she said dryly, 'Ah, well, I agree with yer there seeing's you could have ended up with one like Clarice Dewhurst.'

Chas shuddered at the very thought. Clarice Dewhurst lived next-door-but-one. Whether she was a widow or her husband had deserted her was not known, but either way it was the opinion of the rest of the neighbours roundabouts that her spouse had had a lucky escape. Clarice and her three thread-bare children, two boys and a girl, six, five and four respectively, had arrived in the neighbourhood on one balmy evening twenty years previously, their assortment of shabby belongings carried between them since there wasn't a penny to spare for a cart or barrow. The children immediately took it upon themselves to shatter the peace of the street, becoming personally responsible for causing as much trouble as they possibly could, and no one ever dared complain for fear of a foul tongue-lashing or possible black eye from their hard-faced mother who, as far as she was concerned, was not responsible for what her offspring got up to outside her four walls. How exactly Clarice afforded to pay her way had never been fathomed, but it wasn't from respectable work. It was the general opinion of the neighbours that she lived off the proceeds of her own and her children's misdemeanours.

Of all the other children in the street it was Chas who had suffered worst at the hands of the Dewhursts. Immediately they'd moved in, they had decided this pleasant-natured boy with the widowed mother would be a prime candidate for their own particular brand of fun and had made it their business to make sure all the other local children followed their lead – or risked the nasty consequences.

After years of their torment, much to Chas's relief adulthood saw the Dewhurst children turn their attention further afield. As a result the eldest son met his end falling off a roof while in the process of robbing a factory; the other was serving a life sentence for holding up a bank with a sawn-off shotgun, killing a bank clerk who refused to open the vault for him; the girl, now twenty-five, had married an unsavoury sort who saw providing for his family as an optional extra and she was now living in worse squalor than she had with her mother, four children of her own hanging on her skirts. Clarice herself was housebound, suffering from the degenerative disease of elephantiasis, dependent for the most part on the long-suffering home help who came in daily to see to her needs. Local rumour had it recently that Nadine, Clarice's daughter, had left her husband, and she and her children were now back with her mother. Chas fervently hoped this rumour had no substance to it. If Nadine's children were anything like she had been when young, then he pitied all the other youngsters in the vicinity.

Iris was looking at her son with concern. 'Any news on Jack Black? Bad luck that state of affairs, ain't it? A fortnight into your new place and the boss suffers a heart attack. Now everything's up in the air about yer job, depending on the outcome.'

Chas had to admit it was but unlike Iris, who saw the bad luck as her own son's, his sympathies lay with Jack himself. From what he had gleaned of the sixty-four-year-old man during the two weeks he had worked under him, Jack had come across as a thoroughly decent man, very focused on keeping his business profitable against constant competition, not only so as to keep a roof over his own head but to keep his workforce employed as well. Trouble was, in doing so he'd worked eighteen hours a day and taken no holidays for the last twenty years. That practice had taken a heavy toll on his health from which he was now suffering.

Chas heaved a sigh. 'I've not heard anything one way or the other, Mam.'

She pulled a face. 'So he's still in hospital then?'

'As far as I know.'

Iris sighed. 'Doesn't look so good for him then, does it? No mild heart attack that wasn't, not if he's still in hospital. My heart goes out to his wife, it really does. Just at a time when she could start looking forward to her husband retiring and to seeing more of him, this has to go and happen. Still, it's my opinion Mrs Black is lucky insomuch as there's still a chance her man could pull through, whereas . . .' Her voice trailed off as she remembered that terrible morning thirty years ago when she was left with no hope of ever seeing her husband again. She mentally shook herself and added, 'Still, that's life, ain't it, son? How's the new day operator panning out?'

Chas put his spoon back in the dish and loudly sighed. 'Ralph Widcombe is doing his best. As a retired driver himself, he at least has a good idea of what the job entails, but as he's never operated the radio before it's all new to him. He's very forgetful too so he gets us drivers in a right pickle sometimes, giving us wrong addresses, etcetera. But after all, he is in his eighties. When all's said and done it's good of him to come out of retirement to help out Mrs Black in her time of need. As for Marlene Cox, the evening girl, well, she's not a clue, Mam, and the trouble is, I don't think she's really that interested. I can only think that when she was interviewed she blagged her way through it as I can't see any other reason why the boss's wife would take her on. Mind you, in fairness to her, Mrs Black did have other things on her mind at the time.'

'Mmm, rather a lot, I'd say,' mouthed Iris sympathetically. 'I suppose she was just glad to find someone who'd work such unsocial hours at short notice so she could get on with caring for her husband. My heart goes out to her, it really does.' A look of sadness filled her face. 'Such a shame about Jack Black. From what you told me about him he seemed to be the rough-around-the-edges sort, but also a fair-minded man.' She smiled warmly at her son. 'A man like yerself, in fact. I'm praying he recovers and that hopefully this has delivered a warning to him to take things easier in future 'cos no one is immortal, however much we might think we are.' She pursed her lips thoughtfully. 'If he doesn't make it . . . well, I wonder what Muriel Black will do about the business?'

'That's something that's concerning quite a few of the drivers. Some of them are putting out feelers for work with other companies should Mrs Black decide to close us down. But getting work with other outfits is touch and go, depending how many, if any, plates they have free at the time.'

Iris looked aghast, thinking of her son's job. 'Oh, surely she wouldn't close the business down?'

Chas gave a shrug. 'As far as I understand it she's never before had anything to do with running the firm so it's not like she's equipped to take over. They have no children so there's no son or daughter to assume the reins. She could appoint a manager,

I suppose, and keep it running that way. Or she could decide to cash in on all the plates. Most cabbies who own their own plates look on them as their retirement fund. That might be what Jack Black had it in mind to do when the time came. Black's have fifteen private-hire plates acquired over the years. Between them ABC Taxis, Highfield's and Swift's have the rest of the eighty the council issued. I overheard one of the drivers debating whether he could raise the money to buy one should Mrs Black decide to sell them off and then go into business for himself. But then, it's like he said. Where does someone like him get a spare couple of hundred or so quid at the drop of a hat when on a good week he only earns about thirty-five to forty? 'Course, should ABC, Highfield's or Swift's want the plates by way of expanding their own businesses then they'd be in a position to offer stupid money just to get their hands on them. Anyway, this is all speculation, Mam. Hopefully, Mr Black will pull through.'

Iris vigorously nodded her head. 'Oh, yes, let's hope so, son.' Then something he had said struck her and she frowned quizzically. 'You said that cabby who was wishing he could afford to buy a plate earns about forty quid on a good week? You don't earn that much. Not that what you earn is my business, even though I am yer mother, but you've never hidden yer pay slip from me so that's how I know.'

'Mam, some cabbies can earn that much because of what they're prepared to do for it.'

'Prepared to do? What do you mean, son?'

He took a deep breath. 'Let's put it this way. I don't fancy a term in jail, and neither do I feel it right to blatantly fleece the boss. I know I'm still a greenhorn as far as the drivers' scams go. After all, I've only been in the job a short time. Haven't really had the chance to find out all they get up to so as to boost their pay packet, but one thing I do know is that although it's against the law for private-hire cabbies to pick up straight off the street same as Hackney cabbies, they still do it.'

Iris looked perplexed. 'But I don't understand how they make extra money by doing that?'

'Well, the company hasn't any record of the fare as it's not been booked through the office. That way the cabby can pocket all of it.' Chas could tell his mother still didn't understand so he added, 'Look, Mam, say I have to take a chap to the station, and when I drop him a man coming off the train asks me to take him back into town. Well, I'm going back through town anyway on my way to the office to wait for my next job, or even if I'm radioed through with my next job, I can still detour through town on my way to pick up my next fare so as to cover my mileage that way. As long as a copper doesn't spot you, or a beady-eyed member of the public, then a few of these daily adds up over the week to a nice tidy sum and no one back at the office is any the wiser.'

'Oh, I see what you mean. I hadn't a clue that it was illegal for private-hire firms like you work for to pick up off the street. But then, I suppose I wouldn't as I've never had cause to flag down a taxi. I've always wanted to, just to know what it feels like, but my money would never stretch farther than the bus fare or Shanks's pony. Mmm, well, yes, I'm glad you don't condone such practices as I'd sooner live on fresh air than have to visit you in prison.' She gave a laugh and added, 'Mind you, a slice of my bread pudding would make a handy tool for helping you dig your way out, wouldn't it? You nearly broke your teeth on the last one I made.'

An idea suddenly struck Iris and she grew silent for a moment while she pondered it. It was a good idea, she reckoned. Chas might scoff at it at first but even he would see the wisdom of it when he thought long and hard. 'It's just a thought, son, but should the worst happen to Mr Black and Mrs Black decide to sell up then . . .' She was interrupted by a knock on the back door and a voice calling out, 'It's only me.' She turned her head towards the door leading into the kitchen. 'In here, Freda.'

A tall, thin, shabby but scrupulously clean elderly lady entered. 'Oh, just the person I was hoping to see,' she said, addressing Chas.

'Oh, and yer didn't want to see me?' Ivy asked her, feigning a hurt expression before the woman who had been her friend and next-door neighbour for so many years now both women had lost count.

Freda's aged face looking serious, she replied, 'Unless you've suddenly found yer've a talent with a spanner like your son possesses, then it was him I was hoping was at home rather than you.' She gave a sudden grin, showing tombstone-like, badly fitting dentures. 'Though as you make a better cuppa than yer son, I will let you mash one for me while I ask him me favour.'

'Yer a cheeky beggar, so you are, Freda Lumley. What's this favour yer want from my Chas?'

'You want me to have a look at your mangle, don't you, Mrs Lumley?' Chas piped up.

She looked at him, startled. 'How did you know that? Soothsayer now, are yer?'

He laughed. 'I heard you swearing at it as I went down the yard on me way to work this morning.'

She looked indignant. 'Swearing! I might have been cussing at it but I wasn't swearing.'

'"Bugger" is swearing, Freda, in anyone's language,' said Iris.

Freda flashed her a disparaging look. 'I thought you was mashing a cuppa?' She turned her full attention to Chas. 'So will you look at it for me, ducky? The rollers are jammed.'

'I don't know why you didn't take up your Rita's offer to buy you a twin-tub like the one my Chas got me. I know I hummed and hah-ed for ages before he finally had one delivered but, my goodness, it almost makes me weep now when I think of all those hours I used to spend boiling up the copper! Then after that the backbreaking work of washing it all and mangling it after, 'specially sheets and towels. I couldn't do without my twin-tub now, I really couldn't. It's cut my wash day down to less than half which means I have more time to spend having a cuppa and a natter with you.'

Folding her arms under her flat chest, Freda said haughtily, 'I like me things washed proper.'

'They are washed proper,' Iris scoffed. 'The machine does it for yer instead of you doing it, yer daft ha'p'orth. And I hope you're not insinuating my whites ain't as white since I started using me twin-tub?'

''Course I ain't. It's just that I don't trust motorised things. Vi Newly got a terrible shock off her electric iron.'

'That's 'cos her clot of a son-in-law wired the plug up wrong.'

Freda looked thoughtful. 'Yes, and I have my suspicions about him proclaiming it was an accident. It was rather coincidental that only the week before Vi had confided in me she was going to ask her daughter if they'd consider letting her move in with them as she was finding it difficult managing on her own since her husband died. Funny how after her brush with death she suddenly found she could manage on her own, in't it? Anyway, a copper and a mangle was good enough for me mother so it's good enough for me. I don't like those Hoover contraptions neither. They make such a racket. And ain't you feared yours'll blow up on yer, Iris?'

She had been for a while after Chas had presented the labour-saving device to her a couple of years back, having saved for it to help ease her work load. She had been very grateful for the sentiment behind his generous gesture, but all the same these machines had represented a step into the unknown for her. Chas had patiently maintained that both were safe if used properly and would cut down her housework time dramatically, as well as the aches and pains she suffered as a result. She felt the least she could do was to try them out and, within a short space of time, should anyone have dared try to take these machines away from her, they would not have done so without one hell of a fight.

'Well, if it did blow me to kingdom come, to me it'd be a better way to go than lingering painfully in bed for years, having the embarrassment of yer nearest and dearest attending to yer personal needs. Oh, I couldn't go back to the old ways, not now I've got used to me machines. I'm sure you'd be the same, Freda, if yer'd just get off yer high horse and give 'em a try out. I've offered, I don't know how many times, for you to try out mine.'

'Yes, I know, and I'm grateful. But as I said, I prefer to stick to what I know.'

Chas scraped back his chair. 'I'll go and get me tool box.'

'What about yer apple pie?' asked his mother.

Oh, so it was plain apple? No guessing what the filling was tonight then, like he'd to do most times. 'Keep it hot for me, Mam, and I'll look forward to it when I get back. Hopefully I won't be long. Oh, and on me way back I'll fill the coal buckets for tomorrow.' This offer was meant as a warning for her not even to consider tackling the job while he was gone.

'He's a good lad,' mused Freda as Chas departed for her house next-door. 'Pity my Rita was so much older than him as it's my opinion she'd be a darn' sight happier married to a man like him sooner than the one she did plump for. Oh, not that she's miserable by some standards, and not that Kelvin's a bad lad as men go, but he could help a lot more with the kids and around the house.' She looked at Iris enquiringly. 'Any sign . . .'

Pre-empting what Freda was going to say as she asked the same question every other day, Iris cut in, 'Chas will bring a nice girl home when he's ready to and not before. You'll be the first to know when he does. After me, of course.'

'Huh, well, for all the size and age of him, he's too shy to ask a gel out, that's his problem.'

'Yes, well, I'd sooner me son be of the temperament he is than like some I could name around these parts. Nancy's son treats women like they've been put on this earth just to do his bidding, and he treats her no better.'

'And worse still, those silly women let him.'

'Mmm,' agreed Iris. 'I looked after my husband like he was a king but, bless him, he never took advantage of me.'

'Nor Henry of me neither. We were lucky with our men, weren't we, Iris? God bless 'em.'

She smiled and sighed. 'I can't believe it's thirty years since my Charles passed on. There ain't a minute goes by that I don't miss him. It's my lad I feel most for, though. That 'oss and cart denied him a chance of ever knowing his father and those two would have liked each other so much and got on well, that I know for a fact. Still, it's no good brooding on the past, is it, me old ducky? It's the future we have to get on with.' Iris smiled warmly at her friend. 'Make yerself comfy and I'll get yer that cuppa.'

CHAPTER THREE

An extremely good-looking bleached blonde, wearing a shabby short skirt and tight blouse over her voluptuous curves, was leaning against her back door-frame, smoking a Park Drive cigarette. Her mouth formed a sneer as she spotted Chas enter through the back gate of the house next-door. She silently watched as he located the mangle beside the wash house, put his tool box down beside it, lit a paraffin lamp which he placed on top of the crumbling garden wall so it cast light over the area he was working in, then proceeded to open his tool box to select the ones he needed.

'Still at yer do-gooding I see, Quasimodo,' she called across, her voice heavy with sarcasm.

Not having noticed her presence, his head jerked in surprise as he looked up. 'Oh, hello, Nadine,' he said finally. She looked very much at home on her mother's dilapidated doorstep in the cluttered, weed-filled yard and he wondered if the rumour about her return was indeed true. 'How are you?' he asked automatically, out of politeness.

'D'yer think I'm stupid enough to think you really care how I am after all me and me brothers did to you when we were young? But then, you're that nice a bloke you'd ask Hitler how he was if yer bumped into him in the street,' she snorted sardonically. 'So what has the old duck got you doing for her now? I bet she ain't paying yer. Always was a sucker, weren't yer, Quassie? And it's obvious age ain't wised you up none.'

His back stiffened at this use of the derogatory nickname given to him by the Dewhurst children years ago. This reference to the Hunchback of Notre Dame had caused him much inward grief, though in truth he knew it was unfair. He was definitely not ugly and neither did he have a hump on his back. He would not, though, give Nadine the satisfaction of letting her see that her reminder about his old nickname still managed to upset him all these years later. She was a very good-looking woman but her nasty attitude and cynical view of life badly let her down. 'We all need a helping hand now and again, Nadine, and I'm only too happy to oblige when I can,' Chas replied evenly.

'Yeah, but what you don't seem to realise, Quassie, is that a helping hand now and again in dire emergencies is one thing. Allowing yerself to become the local odd job man without payment for your services is called *the neighbours taking the piss.*'

He smiled tightly at her. 'You may see it that way, Nadine, but I happen to know Mrs Lumley hasn't the money to pay for her mangle to be fixed by a proper tradesman who'd more than likely charge her well over the odds. I receive ample payment for what I do for other people.'

She looked quizzical. 'How? They give yer goods in return you can sell on?'

He looked reproachfully at her. 'Have you never heard the saying, "You don't give to receive"?'

Nadine pulled a scornful face as she took a long drag from her cigarette. Smoke billowing from her mouth, she said, 'Eh, and have you ever heard the saying, "No one helps those that don't help themselves"?' Flicking the butt of her cigarette over on to a pile of discarded rusting objects by the dividing wall, she added, 'I much prefer that one meself.'

'Nadine!' a voice bellowed.

She swivelled her head to look back inside the house. 'What?' she snapped.

'Get yer arse back in here and get yer bleddy kids ter bed, they're driving me daft.'

Childish squabbling could be heard and Nadine turned back to lean wearily against the door-frame. 'Pity my mother's illness affects her legs and not her big gob.' Then she shouted back, 'Just coming.' She made to go back inside then stopped as a thought struck her. She looked expectantly over at Chas. 'You being such a Good Samaritan to the neighbours, yer don't fancy a bit of babysitting so I can escape for a couple of hours and restore me sanity down the local? The kids wouldn't be no bother to yer, honest. Yer can have 'em round your house and it'll give yer mam a taster of what having grandkids is like. Well, a taster's all she's going to get, ain't it, as it ain't likely you're ever going to give her any.'

Her mother's bellowing voice cut through the air like a fog horn on full volume. 'Nadine, get the fuck in here – now, I said! I might be slow on me pins but I can still walk, yer know, and if I have to come and get yer, you'll be paying a visit to the hospital and it won't be to visit *me*.'

Face scowling darkly, Nadine bellowed back, 'Hold yer horses, Mother, I'm bloody coming.' She looked back at Chas. 'I musta bin mad coming back here thinking it'd be better than where I was. So you up for it then?'

He stood staring her, frozen. He would help anyone out if it was in his power to do so but the thought of entertaining Nadine's children for one minute, let alone a couple of hours, terrified him. Plus the fact that his mother, although very fond of most children, would surely draw the line at having Nadine's four rampaging through her house. 'Sorry, Nadine, I'm . . . er . . . well, it could take me a while to fix Mrs Lumley's mangle and we're short-staffed at work so I could get called in to help out.'

She looked disappointed. 'Oh, another night then.' As her mother bellowed for her again she screamed back, 'All right, Mother, I'm fucking coming!'

With that she turned abruptly and stormed back inside the house, slamming the door behind her.

Chas sighed with relief as he resumed his task, knowing that was the second lucky escape he had had that day.

Back inside the Dewhurst house, Nadine grabbed her children by the scruff of the neck and pushed them in the direction of the stairs, warning them she would be up shortly to check they were in bed, and leaving them all in no doubt what she'd do if they were not. They were all well aware of what their mam could be like in a temper, even the youngest at two years old, and without further ado they scarpered.

Nadine raised her children in the same way her mother had raised hers. For the most part they fended for themselves.

'Your young 'un's got ringworm on his bum,' Clarice told her daughter as she flopped down into the manky armchair opposite.

Nadine's eyes were already glued to an episode of *Emergency Ward 10* which was showing on the flickering, scuffed and dirt-smeared black-and-white television set.

Clarice picked up a filthy threadbare cushion and threw it at her daughter. 'Oi, you ignorant bleeder! I said, yer youngest needs some boracic powder slapping on his arse before it gets any worse.'

Dragging her eyes away from the television set, Nadine gave her a scathing look. 'Oh, and you're suddenly the doting gran, are yer?'

'Ringworm's catching and I don't want to get infected. I've got enough ailing me without having to cope with 'ote else.'

'Well, I don't see how you could catch anything from me kids, being's yer don't exactly show much grandmotherly affection towards 'em. Mind you, you was never much of a mother to yer own so what else can I expect?'

'You done all right,' Clarice hissed through clenched teeth, insulted even though she knew her daughter spoke the truth.

'No thanks to you though, eh, Mother? Many a night we'd have starved if it wasn't for what we managed to find in the neighbours' dustbins or else nicked from the corner shop.'

'A mother's job is to mek her kids resourceful,' Clarice snapped defensively.

'Well, don't bother congratulating yerself that you achieved that, Mother, 'cos if you had then our Simon wouldn't be dead, nor our Jamie serving a life sentence for murder, nor me in the predicament I'm in.'

'Yer can't blame me for what you all got up to outside my four walls. I never asked Simon to rob that factory, or our Jamie to blast that bloke to kingdom come, or you to marry the slimy toad yer did and be stupid enough to have four kids by him, one after the other. What's happened to you all is yer own fault. When are you and yer brood going home anyway?'

'Don't get yer hopes up, Mother, 'cos I ain't. The punching that fucker gave me the other night for catching him in the act was the last one I'll put up with. Yer might as well get used to the fact we're here for a while until summat better comes along.' Nadine cast a sardonic glance around the room. 'Mind you, anywhere is better than here, ain't it?' Bringing her eyes back to rest on her mother, she added, 'Steptoe and Son's scrapyard is a palace compared to this.'

Clarice snatched up her walking stick, thrusting it out to whack it down on her daughter's arm, but it fell short, hitting the arm of the chair instead.

Nadine laughed. 'Your illness has at least done me a favour, 'cos yer can't beat us like you used to anymore, can yer, Mam? Yer've never done much for me so it won't hurt to make up for it by letting us stay for a while.'

Clarice knew that her illness had rendered her powerless to throw her daughter and her brats out bodily so until Nadine decided to move herself she had little choice but to accept their presence. That didn't mean to say she had to give her daughter an easy time of it. 'If yer staying, then keep yer kids quiet. Their screaming and yelling is driving me daft. Eh, and yer can pay yer way. I ain't feeding you all on what bit I get from the Social. And I want something towards the gas. It's not like I can earn 'ote meself any longer, is it?'

Nadine gave her mother a glare. 'How am I supposed to earn a living with four kids to look after? Tell me that, eh?'

'You should have thought of it before you upped and left that excuse of a husband of yours. I told yer the day yer married him he'd lead you a merry dance and it wouldn't be long before you rued the day you wed him.' Clarice gave a sneer before adding gloatingly, 'But would you listen?'

'Oh, and I'm expected to take advice from the woman who married a man like me dad, am I? Some father he was, scarpering, leaving you with three youngsters and not a brass farthing to yer name, and not one word from him since. Mind you, I can't say as I blame him after it hit home just what he'd married. Lucky escape me dad had, didn't he?'

Clarice's face darkened thunderously. 'Shut yer fucking trap! I *am* yer mother.'

'My bad luck, that.'

'Well, I didn't exactly win the top prize landing up with you for a daughter, did I? Let's say we're quits. I heard yer talking when you was outside. Who was yer talking to?'

'Oh, and 'cos I'm back living with you for the duration I ain't allowed to talk to no one, Mother, unless you give me the go ahead?'

A murderous light flared in Clarice's eyes. 'If I was more able you wouldn't dare speak to me like this, for fear of yer life. I only asked who you was talking to. I know what a gob you've got on yer and I don't want none of the neighbours knowing our business.'

'We ain't got any business no more for the neighbours to gossip over. If yer must know, I was talking to Quasimodo.'

'Eh? Who?'

'Him next-door-but-one. He's fixing Ma Lumley's mangle.'

Clarice realised who her daughter was referring to. 'Oh, Lady Tyme's son. I forgot you called him that.' She looked at her daughter through narrowed eyes. 'Now if you'd half the brains you were born with and learned by yer mother's mistakes, you would have gone after a man like Chas Tyme instead of the cretin you did saddle yerself with.'

'Oh, yer admitting you do make mistakes then, are yer, Mam? And there was me thinking you was under the impression you was perfect.'

'Yer sarky cow,' Clarice spat at her. Then gave a haughty sniff. 'Yes, I do admit I made the biggest mistake of my life in marrying yer dad. The second biggest mistake I made was giving birth to *you*.' She leaned over in her chair, picking up one swollen leg, then another, and settling them as comfortably as her illness allowed on a threadbare low stool whose greying stuffing was protruding in parts. Settling back in her chair again, she folded her arms under her skinny chest and looked at her daughter snidely. 'If I had my time over again, I'd do things very differently, very differently indeed. When I met yer dad I had several lads after me who all wanted to marry me, let me tell yer,' she boasted.

Nadine let out a bellowing laugh. 'Pull the other one, Mother! As if I'd believe that.'

'It's bleddy true, I tell yer. You can scoff all yer like but I was a looker in my day. I could name at least five men who were falling over themselves to win my affections, including a chap called Harry Ingles. Worshipped the ground I walked on, did Harry. No matter how I treated him, he always bounced back. Harry wasn't a looker by any means, not set against someone like yer dad he wasn't. He wore glasses, didn't dress in what we called fashion back then and he was on the beefy side. We used to call him Billy Bunter. He could have been the last man on earth, I still wouldn't have been seen dead with him because of how much me mates would've ridiculed me. But if only I'd had me brains in gear, I would have snapped him up. He might have been shy and had a boring job as a clerk for a man who owned several off-licences, but I was daft enough to judge a book by its cover. I never bothered to find out that Harry had ambitions.

'Yer dad now, he wouldn't have known what the word "ambition" meant, let alone how to spell it. Nowadays Harry owns those off-licences he once clerked in, and more besides, and him and his wife live in a big house up Lutterworth Road and have two cars and holidays abroad. I could have had all that if I'd not been so blinded by yer dad's handsome face and fallen for his gift of the gab, which in fact turned out to be empty words.

'You, my girl, could have had the life of Riley married to someone like Chas Tyme if yer was half as clever as yer try and mek out you are. I hear he's not lorry driving any more but works for Black's Taxis on Blackbird Road. Taxi drivers earn quite a good living, I understand, good enough to pay the bills each week and afford a few luxuries anyway. I bet him and his mam don't have Echo marge on their bread but best butter.' A smug expression spread across Clarice's lined face and her spiteful piggy eyes were fixed stolidly on her daughter. 'Still, you made yer choices . . . wrong 'uns as it turns out, like I did. So, like I did, now you have to get on with it. Turn that telly up, I can't hear it.'

Nadine sat staring at her mother. It wasn't often she said anything worth listening to but this latest announcement had set Nadine's brain into overdrive.

When she had set her own sights on Phil Rider he'd been the local heart throb, swaggering around in his trendy Beatles jacket and tight-fitting trousers, and she'd been beside herself that he'd chosen her above all the other women fighting to claim his attention. Her mother was spot on, Nadine hadn't thought to consider what kind of life she could expect when they had been forced up the aisle because she was expecting their first child. She'd thought she had landed on her feet, not only in snaring Phil himself but also in moving into the tiny one-bedroomed flat over a fishmonger's on Fosse Road. It might have been damp and direly in need of renovation, the windows never opened to help stem the fishy stench filtering up from below, but it was still a damned sight better than the home she had come from.

At first it had been fun playing the housewife, but the rot had very quickly set in when it became apparent to Nadine that Phil begrudged handing over any more than a few shillings of his building labourer's pay towards keeping his wife and new baby, much preferring still to play the part of the single man with his mates. Nadine soon had no choice but to resort to her old ways of shoplifting in order to pay the bills and keep herself and her baby fed and clothed. Regardless of not wanting a husband's responsibilities, Phil still expected his conjugal rights and another three children followed in quick succession, although the way he ranted when each pregnancy was revealed to him it appeared he thought Nadine had created their children completely by herself.

Life as a single woman living under her mother's roof had been far from cosy. As a married woman with four constantly hungry children and mounting bills, it was living hell for Nadine. The final straw had come several evenings previously when she found herself with not a bean in her purse, nor even a dry crust in the flat to give her children for their tea. Their hungry misery grating on her already fraught nerves, knowing Phil called into the local on his way home from work every night, she had bundled all the children inside a huge rusting coach pram and gone around to shame him into handing over some money to enable her to buy food. Being a known tea leaf in the area, she was banned from the local corner shop and larger Co-op Society unless she could prove to them as she entered the shop that she had money to pay for what she wanted. It was too late in the evening now for her to find someone to watch her kids while she went further afield to lift what she needed.

She had found her husband all right. Plate of meat pie, chips and peas growing cold on the table in front of him, he'd been draped over a tartily dressed, heavily made-up woman seated beside him, very obviously encouraging his attentions. Nursing suspicions of what her husband got up to were one thing, but having the confirmation staring her in the face was another. Nadine's temper mounting to volcanic proportions, she had flung herself on him, hammering her fists into him, yelling what a bastard he was to be filling his own stomach while his children went hungry and fornicating with another woman when he was a married man. In the ensuing fight tables had been knocked over, plates of food and beer glasses sent flying. The woman with Phil received a hefty punch from Nadine which knocked her out cold. When he had managed to restrain his wife, Phil had retaliated by dragging her outside by the hair. In front of their children and passers by who stared agog, he had blacked her eye and split her lip with his fists for humiliating him in front of his drinking companions. Then, leaving Nadine slumped on the dirty pavement, blood pouring from her cuts and bruises blackening rapidly, heedless of his children's screams of terror at what they had seen, he had stormed back inside the pub, but not before warning her that if she ever did anything like this again she would not live to regret it.

With her children still wailing and distraught, she had dragged herself back to their tiny flat. As far as Nadine was concerned, her tempestuous marriage was over. Phil could do what he liked with whom he liked in future, she didn't care any longer. In fact, truth be told, she hadn't cared for her husband as a man for as long as she could remember.

Collecting what little she possessed of her own and her children's belongings which she stuffed inside brown carrier bags, she slammed the door shut on her marital home, vowing that under no circumstances would she ever return, and headed straight for her mother's house. That place, as bad as it was, was preferable to the accommodation the council offered homeless mothers and their children.

Since the moment of their arrival back in Nadine's childhood home, something Clarice had made very clear she did not welcome, Nadine had worried that somehow she had to find a way of supporting herself and her children. She realised it was no good hoping that Phil would stump up even a paltry amount towards their keep. She knew without asking also that her mother would balk at babysitting while she went out to work, but then Clarice really wasn't in a position to mind four lively youngsters while suffering the debilitating illness that had claimed her, and paying for childcare was out of the question. Nadine wasn't skilled at anything that would pay anywhere near a liveable wage. She'd only been a shop assistant in a grocery store when she had married Phil, and had been on the verge of losing that job because it had only been a matter of time before the owner discovered how much of his profits went missing via her quick-fingered hands. She received her Family Allowance but the bit that there was would only cover a couple of days' worth of food a week and then only if she was careful with it.

As she had stood on the doorstep, tonight, smoking a cigarette she had stolen out of her mother's packet, she had been so at a loss to know what to do that she had come to the reluctant conclusion that she had no choice but to return to her former life, such as it was, until such time as the kids were old enough to fend for themselves, leaving her free to follow her own pursuits. Resigned to her fate, she had returned back inside to shut her mother up by sending her kids to bed.

Now Clarice's ramblings had given her an answer to her problems, one she would never have thought of for herself. Despite the fact that physical contact in any form with her mother made her stomach churn, Nadine could have kissed her for it.

Her mother broke into her thoughts. 'What?' Nadine snapped.

'You bloody deaf cow! I said, you could always dump yer kids on the Social and let them do-gooders tek care of them. Leave you free to pursue whatever yer wanted, wouldn't it?'

Nadine couldn't deny that thought had crossed her mind, but despite her lack of parenting skills she did have a certain affection for her children and the thought of never seeing them again should she hand them over for adoption was hard to take. She sneered her disgust at her mother for suggesting this option. 'Like you wish you had done with us, yer mean, when me dad left you high and dry? Mind you, Mother, it's my guess you never 'cos we kids were useful to yer in what we brought home. And of course yer couldn't queue down at the Parish Office without a pram full of kids to beg handouts for, could yer?' She cast her a mocking smile. 'Pity I can't hand *you* over to the Social and that way have some peace from your constant earache.' Nadine smiled secretively. 'If it'll put yer mind at rest, we won't be here for long 'cos I've a plan that's gonna give me and my kids a comfortable future.'

'A plan!' Clarice scoffed. 'You couldn't plan yer escape out of a brown paper bag. So what is this brilliant plan that's gonna bring you fame and fortune then, eh?'

'If yer think I'm telling you so you can ruin it, you've got enough think coming. You'll just have to be content knowing that I want out of here much more than you want me out, so I'll be putting me plan into operation as soon as possible.' Nadine settled her eyes back on the television set but her mind was not on the programme, it was fixed firmly on her scheme. Her next husband would be Chas Tyme. With him providing for her and her kids she could live the life of Riley because his sort was too soft-hearted ever to retaliate. Smugness filled her. Poor Chas, she thought. As he laboured next-door fixing old Ma Lumley's mangle out of the goodness of his heart, little did he know what lay in store for him. But then, he should be grateful for what she was about to offer him. After all, a big oaf like him was never going to be given the chance by anyone else in his lifetime to become a husband and father.

CHAPTER FOUR

The next afternoon, as Chas delivered customers to their destinations, totally oblivious to the future Nadine was plotting for him in order to ensure a meal ticket for herself and her children, over in a plush solicitor's office on New Walk in the centre of town, Harriet Harris, an extremely striking twenty-five-year-old with a mane of thick titian hair flowing past her shoulders and blessed with an eye-catching figure which showed off to perfection the short fitted fashions of the day, was saying to her fiancé: 'Jeremy, I know this isn't the time or the place to mention such matters, but with only eight weeks to go to our wedding you still haven't asked me to go and view anywhere suitable for us to live. I'm not worried whether it's a house or a flat but I'll need time to sort out curtains and such like, and we'll need to look for furniture. I haven't mentioned it before because when we got engaged you told me not to worry about our living arrangements, to leave all that to you, but with time wearing on and nothing being said . . . Jeremy, you are doing something about finding us somewhere to live, aren't you?'

His mind fixed firmly on work-related matters, Jeremy Franklin, a boyishly good-looking, blond-haired, smartly suited junior solicitor, lifted his head and looked at his fiancée distractedly. 'Pardon? Oh, yes, everything is in hand regarding our living arrangements, Harriet. There's no need for you to concern yourself. Mother is having my room redecorated and moving an extra wardrobe in for your clothes. She's sure you'll like the colour scheme she's chosen.'

This news stunned Harrie rigid. 'We're . . . we're moving in with your mother when we get married?' she mouthed, aghast. 'But . . . oh, but I assumed we'd have a place of our own, Jeremy.'

Still distracted he said, 'I told you, didn't I, that we'd be living with my mother for . . . well, the foreseeable future? I'm so sorry

35

if I didn't but I really did think I had. It makes sense for us to live with her. The house is certainly big enough.' He raised his head, revealing the arresting deep blue eyes that always had the ability to turn Harrie's legs to jelly, and smiled briefly at her before returning his attention to his work. 'Mother is so looking forward to your moving in and to having a daughter-in-law to share her interests.' He slapped shut a leather-bound, sectioned binder and pushed it across his desk towards her. 'All those letters want sending in the evening post, and can you make sure Mr Podger's file is passed back to me when you have done the necessary as I have one or two things to clarify before his appearance in court next week? He's guilty as sin, of course, but I'm positive I can get him off.'

Harrie's mouth was gaping even wider in astonishment. She was positive no suggestion of living in his mother's house had been made before and wasn't at all sure that she liked the idea. Having a mother-in-law at a distance was one thing; living under the same roof, constantly under her watchful eye, was another. And it wasn't as though she knew Jeremy's mother that well, if at all in fact. She wasn't sure what to make of Daphne Franklin. Admittedly she had been politeness itself to Harrie on the occasions they had been in each other's company, but without being able to pinpoint exactly why Harrie strongly suspected that Daphne only pretended to approve of her in front of her son while in private she saw her future daughter-in-law as not nearly good enough for him.

The truth was Harrie wasn't naturally in her fiancé's social circle. Her own father's occupation before his retirement had been that of foreman in an engineering factory, while Jeremy's had been a prominent solicitor. Jeremy's family had always owned their own home and the one they lived in now was an imposing four-storey double bay-fronted detached house in a highly regarded area of the city. Inside it was tastefully arranged with very nice furniture, most of it antique, that you dare not touch or sit back on for fear of damaging it somehow. Harrie's widowed father had always paid rent on their two-bedroomed single bay-fronted terraced house with its small slabbed yard in the not-so-salubrious Blackbird Road area. Much of their furniture had been acquired from long-dead relatives or via second-hand shops.

Harrie hadn't attended a private school but a state one, gaining her secretarial qualifications at night school, while Jeremy was university-qualified and his mother had articled him to a small but respectable legal practice, fully expecting her son to follow his father and eventually open his own. Jeremy's father had died prematurely when he had been in his early-teens and the business had been sold, leaving his wife comfortably able to finance the life-style she was accustomed to for the rest of her days along with a separate fund to cover their son's education.

Harrie had started her working career as an office junior for the firm of Chatterley and Bigson on leaving school at the age of fifteen, progressing by way of hard work and dedication to senior secretarial level. Nine months ago she had fallen head over heels for Jeremy Franklin the minute she had been introduced to the new junior partner and told she was to be his secretary. Despite her attraction to him, which she had carefully kept hidden, she had never for one moment thought a man like him would look in her direction. She was wrong and got the shock of her life when, not long into his employment, Jeremy had asked her to accompany him to the theatre one evening.

Despite her busy social life and several boyfriends to her credit, Harrie had never been to the theatre before and never had a date with such a well-spoken, handsome escort. Nervous was hardly the word to describe her inward state when she turned up to meet him outside the De Montfort Hall, wondering if she was suitably dressed for such a venue in her cream suit with a pleated mini-skirt, navy blue platform shoes and matching leather shoulder bag. She was terrified she would not be able to converse with Jeremy on his own level in such a setting.

She need not have worried. Jeremy did not turn out to be a chatty sort of man though, despite lengthy lulls in conversation while they were having drinks during the interval and as he drove her home afterwards in his immaculate Rover 2000, he had proved pleasant company and was indeed very gentlemanly and attentive towards her. It was plain to her that he liked her but nevertheless Harrie was surprised when he asked to see her again, considering the difference in their backgrounds.

From then on it seemed she was swept along by his sophisticated pursuit of her which made a welcome change from the kind of relationships she was used to, those having mostly been conducted in noisy pubs and dance halls, usually surrounded by very animated friends, with Harrie having to fend off a young man's groping hands at the end of the evening. Jeremy did not have a large circle of friends, only three or four who she got on well with and who appeared to accept her. Nevertheless when he proposed marriage to her over dinner three months into their courtship, although stunned by the suddenness of it, Harrie was by then deeply in love and readily accepted him.

Moving in with his mother after their marriage had never entered her head, though. The thought did not appeal to her one iota. After all, she was marrying Jeremy, not his mother.

'Is it really the right thing for us to start our married life living with your mother, Jeremy?' she asked now.

He looked at her, bemused. 'Why, yes, of course.' Then scraping a hand through his hair, added, 'Well, of course, it's not ideal, I do admit. I would prefer it if we were starting our life together in a home of our own, but I'm not in a situation financially to afford the type of house a man in my position is expected to live in. Won't be until I receive promotion to full partner. Besides, Mother has no one else in the world apart from me and I cannot simply abandon her to rattle around in that big house by herself.'

But Harrie was having to leave her father all by himself.

'Mother is so looking forward to having your companionship after we're married,' Jeremy was saying to her as he flicked through paperwork to find the report he was looking for. 'She's going to introduce you to her afternoon Bridge Club and get you involved in her women's groups.'

Harrie didn't at all fancy playing bridge. She wasn't a fan of card games. It also sounded very stuffy, not her way of passing an afternoon at all. 'But I work, Jeremy, so . . .'

'Darling, solicitors' wives don't work. Anyway, you'll have more than enough to keep you occupied looking after your new husband and his mother. And, of course, there's all the entertaining I'll be starting to do to consolidate my position in the firm. I intend to become a full partner sooner rather than later before owning my own practice eventually like my father did. As soon as I'm married I'll be considered seriously for such a position by the hierarchy here. In this day and age it really is ludicrous that single men aren't considered for promotion! Can't understand why myself. Just because you're married doesn't mean you're going to do your job any better. Still, that's the way it is and to get on you have to play by the rules.

'I've already interviewed for your replacement as my secretary, by the way. I've decided on a Miss Abberington. She's not as pretty as you but she seems very capable. I've asked her to start at the beginning of next month so you can get her up to speed before finishing work yourself a week before the wedding. I thought you would need that time free to pack before moving and for any last-minute things you need to arrange before our big day.' He smiled winningly at her. 'See, I do think of you, dear. Now, was there anything else you needed to see me about? I must get on as my next client is due shortly and I've a couple of things to do before he arrives.'

She didn't want to leave her job. Her work situation on marrying had never been broached and Harrie had automatically assumed she would continue until such time as children came along. After all, she loved her job, deriving great satisfaction from her contribution towards solving the problems of the various clients who walked through the busy law firm's doors. But then she supposed she was marrying a solicitor and Jeremy had told her that their wives did not work. She had no choice but to get used to the idea that she wouldn't after she was married; in fact, it was remiss of her not to have realised this for herself. She was marrying a professional man and, like he said, legal practices still abided by the rules and regulations set down centuries ago. Hadn't she herself complained in private to her friends about some of the more antiquated systems and equipment she had to work with when she heard of the modern conveniences their workplaces boasted?

She would have liked a bit more warning so she could get used to the idea of her husband providing for her in the future and having no money at her disposal that she had earned herself. She supposed, though, that she would have a housekeeping allowance and some of that would be for her own use. Then a question posed itself. If they were to be living with Jeremy's mother, as it was her house, would Harrie herself actually be designated as being in charge of the household or would she have to take a back seat to Mrs Franklin while they were living with her?

Leaving her job to become a full-time housewife and seem-ingly companion to her future mother-in-law was not all that was bothering Harrie, though. 'Er . . . well . . . yes, Jeremy, there is something I need to discuss that's of concern to me. Where you live, well, it's two bus rides away from my house so me living there when we're married . . . well, I won't be able to pop in and see my father as regularly as I'd like to. I'd thought, you see . . . well, assumed . . . wrongly as it turns out now . . .'

He lifted his head and looked at her in exasperation. 'Harriet darling, could you get to the point? I've already told you that my next client is due any minute and I've a couple of things to do before he arrives.'

'Yes, I'm sorry, I'm rambling, aren't I?' She took a deep breath. 'Jeremy, I was under the impression that you'd be buying a place for us in an area that was between both our parents. Convenient for us to visit them and for them both to visit us. If we can't afford to buy a house at the moment, couldn't we consider renting one?'

'Renting?' He looked appalled at the thought. 'Rather a waste of money, don't you think, when Mother has so much space?' He frowned at her quizzically. 'How regularly do you propose to visit your father after we're married?'

'I had hoped daily.'

'Daily? That's a bit much, don't you think, darling? Your father isn't going to get used to living on his own if you're constantly on his doorstep, is he? It's not like he's infirm, is it? He can fend for himself.'

'But he's never had to look after himself before, Jeremy. After my mother died five years ago, I took over his care and suddenly to be on his own . . . it's going to be a big change for him. He has just turned seventy. He's never actually cooked a meal for himself, and until he gets used to doing things like that I would like to keep a regular check on him, to satisfy myself that he's faring all right.'

'I know you've no other relatives but he's neighbours and friends, hasn't he?'

'Yes.'

'Well, then, they'll pop in and see to him so stop worrying. Lots of people his age live on their own and are perfectly all right. If it puts your mind at rest we can always slip a few shillings weekly to a neighbour to cook him his dinner each day and do his washing, just until he's fully competent himself. Mother entertains her old friends to tea on a Tuesday afternoon so that would be a good time for you to visit your father each week. Oh, that reminds me, Mother is expecting you for dinner tonight. Please don't be late. She does get herself worked up if dinner is held up for any reason, as you've seen for yourself.'

'Well, I did apologise to her. It wasn't my fault the bus never turned up and I had to wait for the next! Anyway, I'm sorry, I can't make dinner tonight. I've already arranged to spend this evening with my father. I haven't spent much time with him recently, what with my dress fittings and all the other running around I've had to do towards the wedding, and he's so looking forward to me helping him with a new puzzle . . .'

'Mother really would like you to come, Harriet,' her fiancé cut in. 'She wants to update you on the table arrangements for the reception at the Belmont. She's also hoping you've finalised your guest list so she can decide where best to sit them.'

'The Belmont? But I thought we'd decided on the Assembly Rooms? My father's already paid a deposit and sorted out the music for the dancing.'

Jeremy looked shocked. 'Oh, gosh, didn't I tell you? I thought I had. I do apologise if not. Mother paid a visit to the Assembly Rooms the other day to go over her instructions with them and wasn't much struck by the standard of the decor or what they had to offer for the wedding breakfast. She would have discussed this with us but there really wasn't time, what with the wedding date being so close and her concern somcone else would book the Belmont and then she'd have a real job to find somewhere else suitable, so she had to make a snap decision. We'll get your father's deposit back. And before you start worrying, Mother told me she will settle the difference in cost as she's conscious your father might not be able to stretch to the extra. She just wants to do her bit towards giving us the perfect day, Harriet.'

The Belmont was a hotel frequented by the type of person who earned far more than her father had before he'd retired. Daphne Franklin might see it as a much more fitting place than the Assembly Rooms in which to entertain her family and friends at a wedding reception, but Harrie knew her father and their respective friends and close neighbours would not feel relaxed enough in a place like that to let their hair down and properly enjoy the proceedings. Besides that, Harrie knew her father saw it as his responsibility to finance her wedding day and she didn't know how he would take the news of all the arrangements he had made being cancelled and rearranged without his even being consulted, regardless of the reason behind it.

She made to voice her concerns but was stopped by the intercom sounding on Jeremy's desk and the receptionist announcing in her nasal tones the arrival of the next client.

As she left Jeremy's office Harrie felt a tight knot of apprehension forming in her stomach. She had been so excited at the prospect of her forthcoming marriage ten minutes ago. Now, after the bombshells Jeremy had dropped on her, she was beginning to feel very uneasy about it.

Percy Harris's face lit up when his daughter walked through the back door at just after six that evening. 'Hello, me old duck,' he said, going over to kiss her cheek. 'Get yer coat off and sit yerself down at the table.' He then announced proudly, 'I've cooked you dinner.'

Midway through taking off her coat she stopped to stare at him, stunned. 'You've cooked dinner, Dad?'

Eyes bright, he nodded. 'Well, with you getting wed and leaving home very shortly, I have to start fending for meself. You'll have enough on yer plate looking after your husband without worrying whether I'm eating properly, I know you will, so I thought I ought to get some practice in. Then, if I go wrong, you'll be here to put me right and so hopefully by the time yer big day dawns I'll be an expert.' His gaze grew tender and he said huskily, 'I shall miss you, yer know.' Percy sniffed away a tear and shook himself. 'Still, I should count meself lucky that you ain't left home before this, a pretty gel like you who could pick and choose who she settled for. I know you'll visit yer old dad often and I can always visit you, can't I?'

His eyes grew misty again and he said distractedly, 'I just hope you don't settle for a house too far away.' He coughed to clear his throat. 'When are you going to start house hunting, by the way? I mean, time is wearing on, isn't it? I could always help you out by visiting the agents and seeing what's for sale in your price range roundabout. Or maybe it's a rented place to start? Either way, I'll help if I can, you just have to say the word. I expect with a job like Jeremy has he can afford a nice place for you both.' Percy lapsed back into melancholy again. 'I do hope what you do settle for isn't too far away so I can come over regular and see to any odd jobs you might need doing. Well, Jeremy being a busy man like he is, he'll surely welcome someone giving him a hand with any repairs or whatnot that need doing around the place. That's the trouble with houses, there's always something wanting repairing . . .

'Oh, dear, hark at me, sticking me oar in! Wherever you decide to live, I don't care as long as yer happy. Just as happy as me and yer mother were, God rest her.' He gazed at Harrie tenderly again, the love he held for his precious daughter unashamedly obvious. 'Yer mother would have been so proud of you, yer know, lovey. Can you imagine what she'd have bin like if she was here now? Fussing and worrying over making sure yer big day was perfect . . . driving us all mad. Well, she can rest easy 'cos she's knows I'll do me best to send our daughter off proper.'

He realised he ought to get off this subject before he broke down altogether and begged his beloved daughter not to leave him, which was what he really wanted to do. 'Anyway, I looked through yer mother's old cookbooks and found a recipe for sausage casserole. It's been in the oven the amount of time the book said so it should be done by now. I've just got to mash the spuds. So, go on then, get yer coat off and settle yerself at the table and I'll bring it through.'

Harrie was choking back a lump in her throat. Her father loved her so much and was having great trouble coming to terms with the fact that very shortly he would be handing over the care and protection of her to another man. Bundling her coat on to the hook on the back door, she rushed over to him and hugged him fiercely. 'You won't have time to miss me when I'm married, Dad. I'll be popping round to check on you as often as I can.' She pulled away to look up at him with a wide grin splitting her face. 'I know how much you loved Mam, but, you never know, with me off your hands you might take up with some other nice woman.'

He gave a scornful grunt. 'And who'd d'yer reckon is going to want to take up with an old fossil like me?'

She slapped him playfully on his arm. 'Old fossil indeed!

You're still a very handsome man, and you leave me behind puffed when we run to catch the bus.'

'Ah, well, that's because you will insist on wearing those silly platform shoes. It's a wonder you ain't broke yer neck before now. And them short skirts . . . well, if yer mother was here I know for a fact she would insist you wore woolly drawers underneath to keep out the wind. Mini-skirts don't afford much by way of protection from the elements, do they? Mind you, you always look a picture in whatever you wear, in fashion or not. Right, let's get this dinner dished up before it's cremated. You are hungry, I trust?'

Harrie inwardly groaned. It was bad enough having to tell him that their planned evening together wasn't going to happen, she hadn't the heart to say her future mother-in-law was expecting her for dinner as well. She was so proud of him for making this attempt at independence and under no circumstances was she going to hurt his feelings. Harrie would have to eat two dinners tonight.

'I'll mash the spuds, Dad. It's the least I can do, being's you've gone to all the trouble to cook the actual meal. It smells absolutely delicious.'

He sniffed the air. 'Yes, it does, doesn't it? Hope it tastes as good,' he added a mite worriedly.

When Harrie tested the potatoes to check they were cooked she was dismayed to find that most of them had disintegrated into the water, obviously having been boiled for far longer than was required. She would do her best, though, to resurrect what she could. As she strained them off she said casually, 'Dad, potatoes this size only need to be boiled for twenty minutes at the most.'

Arriving back in the kitchen after putting plates and cutlery on the gate-legged table in the back room, Percy pulled a face and said, 'Oh, I put those on over an hour ago. That's too long, is it? Oh dear, are they ruined, lovey?'

She smiled warmly at him. 'They're just a little overcooked but I'm sure I can salvage them.'

He looked relieved. 'I'll not boil them so long next time.'

Seated at the table, filled plate in front of him, knife and fork raised, Percy said, 'Well, it looks good if I say so meself. Tuck in then.' With that he scooped up a forkful of the sausage casserole and put it in his mouth. Immediately his face contorted in disgust and, whipping his handkerchief from out of his cardigan pocket, he emptied the contents of his mouth into it. He then leaped up, knocking away the filled fork Harrie was just about to put in her mouth.

As food splattered over the table cloth, she looked at him in bewilderment. 'What on earth . . .'

'Yer can't eat that, lovey, it tastes horrible.' He looked perplexed. 'I don't know what I've done to it, I followed the recipe.'

'I'm sure it's not that bad . . .'

'Oh, it is, ducky. It . . . well, it's so peppery.'

'How much pepper did you put in, Dad?'

'Just like the recipe said. A tablespoon. And I added a bit extra just to be on the safe side.'

'How much!' Then as giggles exploded from her and tears of mirth spurted from her eyes, she spluttered, 'Oh, Dad, I think you'll find the recipe said a teaspoon, not a tablespoon.'

'Oh, really?' he exclaimed. 'I thought the abbreviation tsp stood for tablespoon. It never twigged with me it meant teaspoon. Oh, dear, no wonder it tastes so peppery.'

'Were you wearing your reading glasses?'

He shook his head. 'I had the house upside down but couldn't find them so I had to manage as best I could without them. Oh, I'm sorry, me darling,' he said remorsefully. 'I so wanted to prove to you I can cope by meself.'

'No need to apologise, Dad. You tried, that's the main thing. You were always telling me when I was a little girl that we must learn by our mistakes. Next time you definitely will be much easier on the pepper, won't you? By the way, your reading glasses are on top of your head.'

He took them off and tutted disdainfully. 'Well, would you credit it? There they were all the time.'

'We've a couple of sausages left over in the pantry. Shall I fry them up and do some chips for you?' she said as she scraped up the food from the table then rose to gather the plates.

'What will you have, lovey?' he asked her.

'Oh . . . er . . . well . . . I might have something later.' She decided to disguise the truth a little. 'I hope you won't be too upset, Dad, but I've to pop over to Jeremy's as his mother . . .'

She just couldn't bring herself to tell him right this minute that Daphne had ridden rough-shod over all his arrangements for the wedding. She had no idea how much the reception at the Belmont was going to cost but knew without a doubt it would be out of her father's price range and, regardless of the fact that Mrs Franklin had offered to pay the difference, he was going to be insulted, deeply hurt that she had taken it upon herself to do what she had without consulting him. Doubtless he'd still insist on paying the full cost and on a state pension there was no easy way he could raise that sort of money. In Mrs Franklin's endeavours to secure the very best for her son, she hadn't taken the time to consider the impact her change of venue for the reception would have on the bride's family. Harrie needed to think of a way to resolve this situation to the satisfaction of all concerned but at the moment the answer eluded her. Hopefully, it would come to her soon.

'. . . well, Mrs Franklin just wants to go over something to do with the wedding. I'll try and be as quick as I can. I'm looking forward to doing your puzzle with you.'

He smiled warmly at her. 'Harrie lovey, it takes you over an hour to get to Jeremy's house, that's if the buses are running on time and there's no traffic on the road. My puzzle isn't as important as dealing with your wedding arrangements. We want your day to go smoothly, don't we? We'll have a night in together another time.' His face suddenly lit up. 'Talking of yer wedding, the payment for the cashed insurance policy came through today so I can start to settle all the bills. That was a good decision of yer mother's to take out the sixpence-a-week policy when you were born to cover this eventuality. A hundred and forty-nine pounds the maturity figure came to! That amount should pay for a wedding fit for a queen,' he announced proudly. 'No front-room reception for you, me darlin', but a proper sit-down do with waitresses serving us. Might even be a little left over to put towards some furniture for your new place.'

Percy gazed at his daughter tenderly. He and Dora, his beloved late wife, had long given up hope of ever having the large family they'd both wished for when at the age of forty-four Dora discovered to her utter shock that she was expecting a baby – a 'change-of-life baby', the doctors had termed it. They had both worried that they were too old to be running after a youngster,

but they needn't have. Harriet, or Harrie as she was affectionately known by them, had brought such joy into their lives. She
had been a happy child, very content, and never caused either
of them a moment's worry. It was such a pity that Dora had not
lived long enough to witness her beloved daughter's success not
only at work but also in landing herself a future husband with
such good prospects. Married to a solicitor, Percy knew his
daughter would never want for anything and he himself could
join his dear, very much missed wife when the time came, content
in the knowledge that their girl was well provided for.

He had been anxious when the time came to meet Harrie's
future mother-in-law. Hadn't felt at all comfortable in the lounge
of the Bell Hotel, dressed in his best suit and with a stiffly
starched shirt itching his neck, them being served lunch by
formal waiters addressing him as 'Sir' and bowing courteously,
himself striving to make a good impression for the sake of his
daughter, watching his Ps and Qs, remembering to use his
napkin, and overpoweringly thankful when it was over and as
far as he was aware had all gone well.

Privately, he was surprised by his daughter's choice of future
husband. Oh, Jeremy Franklin seemed a nice enough man, very
well-mannered and obviously very taken by Harrie. But Percy
had found him too stiff for his liking, and he didn't seem to
have much of a sense of humour. His Harrie liked to laugh. Still,
she seemed set on marrying the man so she must know what
she was doing.

He wasn't sure either what to make of Daphne Franklin. He
hadn't been able to understand half what she was saying because
of her posh accent, sounding very like the Queen's in her
Christmas Day speech. He couldn't pinpoint exactly why, after
all it was nothing she had specifically said or in the way she had
acted, but he could not shake the feeling that beneath her bright
smile and words of welcome to Harriet, as she and her son called
his girl, the truth was that she was not at all happy with her
son's choice of future wife.

His own assumption was that Daphne Franklin viewed the
Harrises as being of a lower social standing. But then, according
to Harrie, Jeremy had told her his mother had been a tailor's
daughter working alongside her own father in his shop as a
seamstress when she had met her husband, so in truth it was

47

only through her good fortune in marrying a professional man and his hard work in building up his business, leaving her well provided for on his death, that she had risen in the world.

If it was indeed the case that she was looking down on the Harrises, then she had no right to. She should be glad her son had landed himself such a pretty, bright woman as Harrie, one any man would be proud to have as his wife and who would prove herself more than adequate to the role of solicitor's wife. Still, the most important thing to Percy was that his daughter was happy, and she did seem to be.

'I can see to me own dinner, lovey. You go and get ready and get yerself off.'

'Are you sure, Dad?'

'Eh, surely even I can't make two disasters in one day. There's n'ote to frying a couple of sausages. I've seen yer mam and you do it enough times.' He then added with a twinkle in his eyes, 'If you return home to find the house burned down, I'll be next door having a cuppa with Albert and Nell.'

CHAPTER FIVE

Harrie had just finished putting the finishing touches to her make-up when a tap sounded on her bedroom door and her best friend Marion Allcott came in. She was a tall, slim, attractive young woman of the same age as Harrie and they had been friends forever, it seemed to them both, having teamed up as youngsters playing in the street then attended school together and started their working lives on the very same day, Marion as a wages clerk in a shoe factory, Harrie as a junior for a solicitor's. They had supported each other through their daily ups and downs and each felt that a friendship such as they shared was indeed very special. Neither would relish the prospect of losing it.

'Your dad sent me up,' Marion said, shutting the bedroom door behind her. 'Oh, you do look nice,' she complimented Harrie who was wearing a dark grey maxi-skirt, split to her knees, with a silver-grey, short-sleeved jumper. 'I gather from what he said that you're in a rush to get to Jeremy's to discuss wedding details so I won't keep you a minute.'

Harrie beamed with delight on seeing her. 'Oh, sit yerself down, I can spare two minutes being's it's you.'

Sitting on the edge of Harrie's bed, Marion asked, 'What happened to you last night? I was worried, thought you might be ill or summat.'

Replacing her mascara brush in its case, Harrie snapped it shut and responded, 'Why would you think that?' She swivelled around on her stool, giving her friend her full attention. Then she slapped her hand to her forehead and exclaimed in remorse, 'Oh, goodness, Marion! I was going to come around after my dress fitting and have a catch up with you, wasn't I? I'm so sorry, I completely forgot. You see...'

'It's all right, I've been through it all, remember?' Marion cut in, grinning good-humouredly. 'The dressmaker kept you hanging around, pinning and tucking, and what should have taken ten minutes took three hours?'

'That's about the size of it.' Harrie gave a sigh. 'The dress I'm going to end up with isn't the design I originally asked her to make, but after all her expert advice on what she feels will suit me and what won't . . . Oh, I do hope the end result is going to look all right,' she added worriedly.

'You're going to look the biz whatever you wear, Harrie.'

'I just hope Jeremy likes what I'm wearing.'

'He will,' Marion said with conviction. 'You'll take his breath away when he sees you walking down the aisle to meet him. He'll be thinking you're the most beautiful woman he's ever clapped eyes on. Present company excluded,' she added with a giggle. 'I suppose we're lucky the know-all dressmaker hasn't tried to change the style of the bridesmaid's dress we decided upon. Mind you, I haven't told you this before. She *did* attempt to. I soon put her straight. "Oi," I said, "me and Harrie went to great lengths to choose this style and we want it kept this way." She muttered something under her breath but I couldn't make out what it was. I gather she felt insulted but I wasn't willing to listen to her opinions on what suits me and what doesn't – as if I didn't know well enough meself! Why do dress-makers always think they know better than their clients, eh, Harrie? I know I'm going to look smashing in my dress and Allen's going to want to marry me all over again when he sees me in it. Well, he'd better. Do you remember my wedding day, Harrie? Despite all the planning, what a disaster it turned into.'

'Oh, it wasn't. Everything was great.'

Marion gave a disdainful click of her tongue. 'Yes, it was, if that's what you call the bride having to walk to church because the hire firm forgot to send her car, half the guests ending up with stomach cramps because the fish course at the reception was off, and the icing on the wedding cake setting that hard that not only was it inedible unless you risked broken teeth, we had to smash the top with a hammer so we could at least have the cake bit inside to hand around – and that was dry. My mother wouldn't stop crying and my father disappeared during the afternoon for a couple of hours to listen to the football match on the radio back home. Yes, it all went great, didn't it?' she said sardonically. 'You're not having a fish course served at your reception, are you? I won't touch it if you are. I still have fond memories of spending most of my wedding night with my head down the toilet. Mind you, one consolation is the The Regency Rooms were closed down not long after our reception because of how many complaints the Health Department received about the standard of their cooking. Pity no one bothered to tell me *before* we had our reception there. Still, the Assembly Rooms have a good reputation so you should be all right.' She noticed the look on Harrie's face and frowned. 'Have I said summat wrong?'

'No, it's just that . . . well, it seems my reception isn't going to be at the Assembly Rooms any longer, Marion.'

'It isn't? But why? I thought your dad had arranged it all. He's booked that DJ I recommended to him who played at my cousin's twenty-first birthday do and he's ever so good. He's always booked solid, so yer dad was lucky to get him.'

'Dad had arranged it all but it seems it's now all been unarranged.'

Marion looked bemused. 'Unarranged? By who?'

Harrie gave a deep sigh. 'Look, you must promise to keep this to yourself because I haven't spoken to my dad about it yet and anyway I only found out myself late this afternoon, and then when I got home Dad was going on about the money arriving from the insurance policy that him and my mam took out when I was little to pay for my wedding, and he's so chuffed and thinking he's giving me just the best send off, which he was, and I was so happy with everything . . .'

'Oi,' Marion interjected. 'You're rambling on and not getting to the crux of the matter. Just who changed all your arrangements for the reception?'

'It was Jeremy's mother.'

'Jeremy's mother! But what business is it of hers? It's the bride's parents' privilege to arrange the wedding. 'Course, the poor sods get landed with the bill for the do but that's the joy of having daughters, ain't it? If we have any then we'd better get saving now as weddings ain't cheap, are they? By the time our kids get married, the way prices are rising it's a king's ransom we'll be looking at. Oh, sorry, now I've just done what I accused you of and that's rambling on. It's not Jeremy's mother's place to change the arrangements so why did she take it upon herself to do that?'

Harrie shrugged. 'Whether it is or isn't her place, she has. Jeremy said that she visited the Assembly Rooms and wasn't impressed . . .'

'What do you mean, she wasn't impressed?' Marion sharply interjected. 'There's nothing wrong with the Assembly Rooms. My Allen's firm had their Christmas do there last year and the food was great and plenty of it. The beer and spirits were cheaper than down the pub and plenty of staff on hand to serve so we weren't kept waiting, like what usually happens at these kind of occasions. Couldn't wish for better than that, could you?'

'No, you couldn't,' Harrie agreed. 'They don't charge extortionate rates either so the likes of us can afford to have a do there.' She looked worried. 'I dread to think what having the reception at the Belmont is going to cost, Marion.'

'The Belmont? Where's that?'

'It's a hotel on De Montfort Street.'

'But that's miles away across town. How the hell is your side going to get there after the church service? Jeremy's side might all have cars but we don't. What's this Belmont Hotel place like anyway?

'It's very nice but . . .'

'But what?'

'Well, it's a bit . . . let's put it this way, I don't think Mrs Brown will feel free to do her can-can when she gets drunk like she usually does, showing off her old-fashioned bloomers. I think if she did attempt it she'd pretty quickly be marched off the premises for unbecoming behaviour.'

'Oh, it's that sort of place, is it? Only waltzing allowed to a string quartet kinda place, where you sip Bristol Cream from schooner glasses with your little finger stuck out, served by stiff waiters who look at you like they've a bad smell under their nose 'cos they know you can't really afford to be in a place like that, and they have never heard of chicken in the basket, and they definitely don't serve pints of beer only bottles and all drinks at double the price of even the poshest pub 'cos yer paying for the privilege of being in their grand surroundings?'

'Mmm, yes, it is that sort of place. We're all going to be sitting looking at each other, not daring to move in case we show ourselves up by our ignorance of etiquette.'

Marion looked at her friend knowingly. 'Well, you're choosing to marry a man like Jeremy so you'll have to get used to places like that in future. No more sawdust and spittoon dives for you, gel. Eh, but your wedding day is your choice. You need to speak to Jeremy, get him to tell his mother she had no business going over your head like this and to change it all back to what you'd originally arranged.'

Harrie looked bothered. 'Yes, I know I'm going to have to do something. Oh, Marion, I just want everyone to feel comfortable at my reception and I thought they all would, but now I know that if it's in the Assembly Rooms then Jeremy's lot are going to feel uncomfortable and if it's at the Belmont our side is going to feel uncomfortable. And as for me ... Well, how can I enjoy my day, knowing half the guests aren't enjoying themselves?'

'Surely there must be a place that would suit everyone that your dad can afford?' She paused for a moment, looking at Harrie searchingly before adding, 'But then there's always the other option.'

'Oh, and what's that?'

'You could elope.'

Harrie flashed her a wan smile. 'That idea does sound very tempting at the moment, Marion, but I could never get married without my dad and my best friend being present at the very least.'

'I must admit I would feel upset if I wasn't there for your big day. You must speak to Jeremy and sort this out, sooner rather than later as time is wearing on. Oh, listen, I was offered a pair of curtains this morning at a good price. A friend at work bought them for her living room, only they're miles too big and she can't take them back because she got them in a sale. They're really nice. Top quality. Any good to you?' Then Marion frowned quizzically. 'Have you somewhere to live yet? You haven't mentioned even looking so what's going on in that respect? I can't wait to help you arrange your furniture and make the place look homely. You are going to let me help you, ain't yer?'

'I really don't want to talk about that.'

53

'Why not?' Marion glanced at her friend suspiciously. 'What's bothering you, Harrie? I know you better than I know meself and you've something on your mind that you're not happy about as well as this reception business, so come on, what is it?'

She sighed again and looked at her friend questioningly. 'You know when you were getting married, would it have bothered you if you'd been living with your mother-in-law for a while to start with, Marion?'

'No, not in the least. Allen's mother is a dear, you've met her and know for yourself I've been lucky in that respect. I get on with my mother-in-law better than I do my own mother. In fact, having been married to Mrs Allcott's son for four years and putting up with his habits, I wish I'd married *her* now,' Marion added, laughing. 'Oh!' she exclaimed as the penny dropped. 'So you're not moving into a place of your own but in with his mother. I'm right, ain't I?'

Harrie nodded.

'Oh, I see.' Marion's face clouded over. 'Oh, Harrie, Jeremy lives two bus rides away. I won't see much of you after you're married, will I? I won't be able to pop in for a cuppa and a chat like I do now, or you to me.' Then she looked remorseful. 'Oh, I'm sorry, I'm being selfish. I'm glad for you, really I am. Jeremy's house sounds lovely from what you've told me about it. And lots of people live with their folks until they can afford a place of their own.' She pulled a face. 'I would have thought, though, that with Jeremy being a solicitor he'd be able to afford a place for you both.'

'He says he can't afford the type of place that a man in his position is expected to live in until he gets promoted to full partner.'

'Oh, I see. Well, which of us can afford what we feel we ought to live in when we first start out? Look at the pokey flat Allen and me rented for the first year of our married life. You could hardly swing a mouse it in, let alone a cat. Even the little terraced place we have at the moment isn't the house I intend to live in for the rest of my life, but it does us for now. Huh, sounds to me like you're marrying a bloody snob!' She looked remorseful. 'Oh, I didn't mean that, Harrie. Jeremy's not the type I thought for a minute you'd settle for but I'm happy for you as long as you're happy. He loves you, anyone can see that, and you're mad about him. Mind you, they do say love's blind.'

'Does that mean you don't like him?'

''Course I like him, you daft clot! Well . . . I've only met him a couple of times, but what I know of him I like.' Marion paused and looked for a moment at Harrie, then giving a deep sigh said, 'Now yer asking, I have to say I wasn't exactly relaxed in his company the couple of occasions we went out in a foursome. Look, it wasn't Jeremy who made me feel uncomfortable, it was just the fact that with me knowing he's a solicitor and what kind of background he comes from, well, I felt like I'd to watch my Ps and Qs. So did Allen. We had to make sure we sipped our drinks, not knocked them back, that sort of thing, and the sort of things we talk about . . . well, he didn't seem to have much idea what we were going on about. And then when he asked what classics were our favourite, the look on his face when Allen said an open-topped Triumph TR sports and went into great detail about his dream of driving one around the Italian countryside! Well, of course, now I realise Jeremy meant books not classic cars but I felt so stupid at the time. I suppose I can't really blame him for thinking what ignorant friends you've got.' She tilted her head and looked questioningly at Harrie. 'I have wondered if you've ever sat back and really thought what marriage to a man like him is going to be like for you?'

Harrie stared at her, taken aback. 'What do you mean?'

Marion leaned forward, clasping her hands and looking at her friend intently. 'Look, Harrie, I love you and wouldn't want to hurt you for the world. I've wanted to talk to you about all this before but you seemed so . . . well . . . amazed by the fact you'd managed to land a man like Jeremy and so wrapped up in it all . . . I'm not putting this very well, but what I'm trying to say is that he's introduced you to things that you've never experienced before, like the theatre and going to nice restaurants for dinner, eating with silver knives and forks at his house on posh furniture with proper napkins to wipe yer mouth on, and I just think you've got swept up in the glamour of it all. I mean, it's all very well being wined and dined and going to nice places but I just wonder if you'll feel really comfortable when you're actually living that life day to day?'

Harrie was staring at her, open-mouthed. 'You mean . . . I'm not good enough for Jeremy, is that it?' she asked softly.

'You're joking! Far from it,' her friend responded with conviction.

'Well, what are you getting at then, Marion?'

She took a deep breath. 'I'm just concerned you don't know the man you're marrying as well as you should do before you marry him, if you understand what I mean?'

'But I do know him . . .'

'No, you don't, Harrie, not properly you don't,' her friend interjected. 'You've only been going out with him all told for nine months and for six of those you've been planning this wedding. You can't know someone well enough to judge if you can live with them just by going for evenings at the theatre or out for a meal or dinner at his mam's. You can't really talk personally with yer fella's mother sitting opposite, listening to everything you say. Harrie, you know me and Allen went on holiday to Great Yarmouth in that caravan together? Oh, bloody hell, what an experience that was,' she sidetracked as memories of that time blasted to the surface. 'Remember I told you what a pokey little tin can it turned out to be after we were expecting . . . well, something that at least had enough head room to stand up in and somewhere comfortable to lie on and a stove to cook our meals. Good job we had the foresight to take along sleeping bags we'd borrowed off friends and a primus stove or we'd not have had a night's sleep or a hot meal all week. We couldn't afford to eat out, and besides we were stuck in the middle of a field miles from anywhere so going out was an expedition.'

Harrie was giggling now. 'You both had fun that week, though, didn't you?'

'We certainly did. And besides that holiday, Allen and me spent loads of days together just doing things that couples do and really got to know each other before we were married. So although no marriage is without its off days – well, ours certainly isn't as you know because you're the one I turn to and have a good moan with when he's driving me daft – at least we both knew in advance we got on well enough for our marriage to have a chance of working out. Look, I could be wrong but Jeremy doesn't strike me as the type to sit cuddled up with on an evening, both watching the telly and giggling together like me and Allen do over jokes cracked by comedians like Tommy Cooper.' She paused and looked earnestly at her friend. 'Harrie, have you ever spent an evening like that with Jeremy?'

A worried expression clouding her face, Harrie slowly shook her head. 'No, I haven't.'

'Well, don't you think you ought to?'

'Well, it's not like I haven't wanted him to spend an evening at my house, it's just that . . . well . . .'

'You've been too embarrassed to ask Jeremy because your house can't compare with his?' Marion jumped in.

'No, that's not it,' Harrie responded sharply. 'I'm not ashamed of where I come from. It's not like I've hidden my background from Jeremy, and he has been to my house when he asked Dad for my hand in marriage so it's not as if he doesn't know what it's like. It's just that . . . well . . . it's always Jeremy who's decided what we're doing and when we're seeing each other.'

'He doesn't ask you what you'd like to do?'

'Not in the way you mean. It's always *"I'd like to take you for dinner tonight if you're free"* or *"I have tickets for the theatre if you'd like to go"* or *"Mother has asked us to eat with her tonight if you haven't other arrangements"*, that sort of thing. It's not like he takes me for granted, Marion, but going out with him hasn't been the same as going out with other boyfriends I've had. Jeremy is a busy man and lots of evenings he's tied up working on cases he's dealing with. He's explained to me he has to do that to prove his worth to his bosses, so that he's considered for promotion when the time comes. I have to have the patience to wait for him to tell me he's free, if you understand me.'

'Mmm, yes, I suppose I do. So when you're married and he's tied up in the evenings working, you'll be doing . . . what?'

Harrie frowned thoughtfully. Keeping his mother company, she supposed. They'd watch the television together. But then, come to think of it, she could not remember seeing a television set on the occasions she had visited Jeremy's house. There was a radiogram in the lounge, a very grand-looking piece of furniture that housed a radio inside as well as the record deck and racks for keeping a selection of records which Mrs Franklin had proudly showed to Harrie. None of the records had been to her own particular taste although she had been too polite to speak out. Would Mrs Franklin let her play her own records in the evening while Jeremy was otherwise occupied? She did not seem the type who would appreciate the likes of the black American artists Harrie had a weakness for as well as Cat Stevens, Bob Dylan and anything by the Rolling Stones.

She flashed Marion a brief smile. 'There's lots I can do in the evenings when Jeremy's working. I love reading and I can . . . can . . . Look, I realise life's going to change for me when I marry him and I have to be prepared for that if I want to be a good wife to him. And I do, Marion, I really do.' She flashed a glance at the alarm clock on her bedside cabinet. 'Oh, goodness, is that the time? I'd better hurry. Jeremy's mother doesn't like lateness at dinner and I want to avoid getting on the wrong side of her before I become a full-time housewife.'

'A full-time housewife! You're giving up work when you get married?'

'Solicitors' wives don't work, Marion.'

She looked affronted. 'Huh! Wives of lowly factory workers like my Allen do though, don't they?'

'Oh, don't be like that. I'm only repeating what Jeremy told me today.'

Her friend's face softened and she said graciously, 'Well, I suppose if we could afford for me to stay at home, I'd jump at the chance. What bliss that would be! I'd skim around my housework in the morning and have all afternoon to do whatever I wanted. Allen would be thrilled to have a proper cooked meal every night instead of some of the slapped together affairs I manage when we both get home 'cos I'm too knackered after a hard day's work to be bothered spending two hours cooking, and anyway Allen's usually that starving he can't wait long for his dinner. Mind you, unless I'd kids to look after, I think I'd soon get bored just being a housewife. I presume someone like Mrs Franklin has a char going in daily and maybe a cook, so while you're living with her you won't exactly be getting your hands dirty, will you? What will you be doing all day?'

'I'll have lots to do such as . . . such as . . . well, lots of things. Mrs Franklin is keen for me to learn to play bridge and join her women's groups.'

Marion laughed. 'Playing bridge?' she scoffed. 'That's an old fogey's game. And it's always fussy middle-aged ladies who go to these women's groups 'cos they've n'ote better to do with their time. Well, marriage is going to be a lot of fun for you, ain't it?' She looked seriously at her friend. 'If you're happy with what you're getting into, then all well and good. I know you're going to make Jeremy a smashing wife, Harrie, and he's lucky to have landed you in my opinion, but upsetting yer dad over this reception business is not really on, is it? You're going to have to at least get that sorted with Jeremy.'

'Yes, I know. I'm sure Mrs Franklin will understand when I talk to her about it and will be willing to change the arrangements back.'

Marion stood up, buttoning her coat and picking up her shoulder bag which she slung over her shoulder. 'I'll love you and leave you. See you soon, yeah?'

'I'm definitely having a night in with Dad tomorrow night to make up for tonight, and if Jeremy wants to see me he'll have to understand why I can't. I know he's got a Round Table meeting on Thursday so I won't be seeing him then. How are you fixed for me coming round to you and making up for not coming last night?'

Marion beamed. 'Suits me. It's Allen's darts evening down at the pub so me and you will have the house to ourselves. See you about eightish.'

CHAPTER SIX

All the way to Jeremy's house, Harrie worried how best to raise the matter of the rearranged reception without hurting Daphne Franklin's feelings. She wished she knew her future mother-in-law better so she'd have a clearer idea of how best to approach the subject, but she didn't. Finally she decided it would be best to speak to Jeremy about it first and take her lead from him.

'I was getting worried you weren't going to arrive in time, darling, it's just coming up for eight,' he said as he affectionately kissed her cheek then helped her off with her coat.

'I did mean to arrive earlier,' Harrie said lightly, kissing him back. 'But by the time I got home from work and got myself ready, and then of course I had two buses to catch . . .'

'Very soon you won't have all this travelling back and forth,' he interjected, smiling lovingly down at her. 'You'll be here waiting for me when I get home from work. It can't come soon enough for me.'

'Nor me,' she said sincerely. Then something Marion said came to mind and she asked, 'Jeremy, when we're married and at home together in the evening, will you sit with me cuddled up on the sofa watching the television?'

He looked surprised by her question for a moment before responding. 'We haven't got a television. Mother and I have always been far too busy with other things to have time to watch, that's why we've never bothered. I suppose we could see about getting a set and finding somewhere to put it so you can watch it if there is something of interest you really are keen to view.'

'And you'll sit with me and watch it, cuddled up on the sofa?'

'Darling, we're adults, not silly teenagers anymore to be cuddling on sofas.'

'Oh, well, yes, I suppose we are,' she said with mixed feelings.

Disappointed to find he felt that she at twenty-five and he at thirty were too old to be having a cuddle on the settee.

Jeremy glanced appreciatively at her. 'You look lovely.'

'Thank you,' she said graciously.

He circled his arms around her, pulling her close. 'The moment I set eyes on you in the office, I knew you were the one for me. Mother was beginning to despair of my ever meeting anyone suitable I'd want to settle down with. She thinks you're perfect for me.'

A warm glow filled Harrie then. 'I'm glad to hear that. I wasn't sure what your mother thought of me.'

'She thinks you've got great potential, Harriet.'

Locked in his arms, her head resting on his chest, she frowned. What did he mean by 'great potential'?

She wanted to ask him but before she could he had released her, hooked her arm through his and was saying, 'Shall we go through? Mother is waiting for us.'

'Yes . . . er . . . no. Er . . . Jeremy, could I have a word before we join your mother?'

'Can't it wait, darling, as dinner is about to be served? It's Mrs Rogers' day off today so Mother has cooked it herself. She's done her special in your honour, chicken in white wine sauce.'

'Yes, I suppose it can wait. Er . . . no, it can't, Jeremy. In case the subject is raised during dinner.'

He looked puzzled. 'What subject?'

She took a deep breath. 'This matter of the rearranged reception. My dad is going to be so hurt about this, I can't bring myself to tell him. I was hoping I wouldn't have to.'

'Hurt? Why?'

'Because he wants to give me the best send off his money can buy. He won't be able to hold his head up, knowing he didn't pay for that send off but his daughter's mother-in-law did.'

'Well, yes, I can appreciate that. My mother, though, wants the best for us too. Surely she has a right to contribute as she is my mother?'

'But shouldn't she have consulted my dad first before she went ahead with cancelling all his arrangements?'

Jeremy looked thoughtful for a moment then sighed. 'Yes, I agree she should have, but as I explained this afternoon at the office, we could have risked losing the date at the Belmont.'

'I was happy with the Assembly Rooms, Jeremy, and I thought you were too?'

'Well, yes, I said I was . . .'

'You weren't?' she cut in, shocked.

'Well, if you want me to be truthful, the Assembly Rooms didn't offer exactly the kind of venue I had thought to have when I got married. I didn't say anything as I didn't want to hurt your father's feelings.'

She eyed him, confused. 'But you're prepared to hurt them now?'

'I've no choice, Harriet.'

'What do you mean, no choice?'

'I simply can't hurt my mother's feelings after she's gone to all this trouble to do her best for us.'

'And I can't have my father hurt, Jeremy. I just can't, I'm sorry. I'm sure your mother will understand . . .'

'I'm sure your father will when he learns what the Belmont has to offer against the Assembly Rooms,' he cut in. 'And it's not as if Mother is expecting your father to fork out for the difference in cost, is it? She is being very generous, Harriet.'

'Yes, I know she is, but my father is a proud man and he's been putting money aside in an insurance policy each week since I was born to pay for this day for me. I'm happy with what he's arranged and . . .' She looked at her fiancé pleadingly. 'I really want to have our reception rearranged as it was, Jeremy. Will you please speak to your mother about it? I just hope the Assembly Rooms haven't filled that slot because if they have I don't know what I'm going to tell my dad.' And while she was at it she might as well take this opportunity of addressing another matter that was bothering her. 'I have to tell you, Jeremy, that I'm not happy about moving so far away from him. I won't be able to see him regularly until I'm happy he's coping on his own. I know you said we could pay a neighbour to do for him but he won't like that, Jeremy, I know he'll feel demeaned. Couldn't we rent a house near enough for me to see him regularly, and your mother too, of course, just until we can afford a suitable place to buy?'

'I've told you, I can't see the point when Mother has all this room. And besides, I've already explained that I can't leave her on her own. She has no one else but me.'

'But, Jeremy, you're expecting me to leave my dad on his own and *he* has no one else but me.' It came out in an accusing manner which was not what Harrie had intended.

Jeremy was looking at her askance. 'It seems you're suddenly not happy with a lot of things, Harriet. Why haven't you spoken up about any of this before?'

'But how could I when you only told me about them yourself today?'

'I've already told you that I thought I had, and apologised for my oversight if I hadn't. Now, please, let's go in to dinner.'

He started to guide her through into the dining room to join his mother but Harrie pulled him to a stop. 'Jeremy, you are going to ask your mother to change the reception arrangements back to what they were, aren't you?'

His answer was blunt. 'No.'

She stared at him aghast. 'No?'

'I've told you, Harriet, I can't hurt her feelings. And I really do think you're being most unreasonable about this.'

She wrenched her arm from his, stunned by his refusal. 'You think *I'm* being unreasonable? You don't think you're being unreasonable, Jeremy?'

Just then Daphne Franklin appeared. She was dressed for dinner in a long, loose aqua-green silk kaftan, a string of large pale pink freshwater pearls around her neck and matching drops in her ears. 'What on earth are you both standing out here for?' The large woman smiled warmly at Harriet. 'How nice to see you, dear. You have brought along your completed guest list?' She glanced enquiringly at her son. 'You did ask Harriet to, didn't you, dear? I know how consumed you become by your work and then you forget to do things I've asked you to do. The Belmont want our seating arrangements handed in to them as soon as possible so they can have the place cards printed up.

'Anyway, let's go through and get dinner over with. We have so much to discuss tonight, not only regarding the wedding preparations but also when you propose to start moving your belongings in, Harriet. Then when you return from honeymoon everything here will all be shipshape and Bristol fashion, ready for you to get on with your new life here with us.'

She clasped her large hands together, a smile lighting up her heavily jowled face. 'Oh, the three of us are going to be one big happy family, I just know we are.' She smiled warmly at Harriet again. 'You and I between us are going to be behind Jeremy's rise to great heights. It's true what they say, you know. Behind every great man is a great woman. Or in Jeremy's case, two. You are a lucky man, darling,' she said, beaming at him proudly before returning her attention to Harrie. 'By the time I've smoothed your rough edges, you are going to make a first-class solicitor's wife. I have great faith in Jeremy's judgement, my dear. Come along then,' she ordered them both as she headed back into the dining room. 'You know I'm not amused when food gets cold, Jeremy.'

Harrie's thoughts were whirling frantically. What did Daphne Franklin mean by saying she was looking forward to smoothing her rough edges? But beyond that was another glaring factor. Harrie had received the distinct impression that her future mother-in-law did not see their living with her on first marrying as purely an interim measure, until Jeremy's promotion afforded him the means to buy a house of his own. Harrie was positive that Daphne saw them living with her for good. Trouble was, did Jeremy also?

She looked up at her fiancé quizzically. 'Jeremy, how long do you think we'll be living with your mother after we're married?'

He gave a shrug. 'I don't know. How do you expect me to answer a question like that? It depends how long my superiors take to recognise my potential and offer me a full partnership.'

'Well, do you think that will be in six months? A year? Two?'

A flash of irritation glinted in his eyes. 'Oh, Harriet, for goodness' sake! I've already told you I can't be precise about the timing of my possible promotion.'

'But when you are promoted, you will be buying a house for just the two of us?'

'What on earth makes you ask that?'

She eyed him worriedly. 'Jeremy, I need to ask you a question. Am I marrying you or you and your mother?'

'What? Oh, now you're just being silly.'

'I don't think I am, Jeremy. I got the distinct impression just now that your mother thinks we will be living with her for good and that we'll be looking after you between us.'

'Harriet, what on earth has come over you? My mother was

just trying her best to welcome you into our family and extend the hand of friendship to you.'

Harrie couldn't deny that Daphne Franklin had been very nice to her and appeared to be very welcoming. It was true that she would need help in learning to be a good hostess at all the dinner parties Jeremy had warned her he would be having in order to gain his promotion, and who better to teach her than a woman who'd had plenty of experience during her own marriage to a solicitor? There was, though, still the problem of the reception that needed resolving to Harrie's satisfaction.

'Jeremy, I apologise. It's very nice of your mother to offer her wealth of experience to me and I welcome it, I really do.' She paused, taking a deep breath before adding, 'But I have to make a stand about the reception. It's the bride's family's prerogative to take care of that. You have to allow my father to do this for me. Please will you speak to your mother about putting it all back the way my dad arranged it all? Please, Jeremy?'

His face set tight. 'I've told you, I can't hurt Mother's feelings, Harriet.'

She couldn't believe that the man she was about to vow to love and cherish for the rest of her life was showing such unwillingness even to approach his mother about reversing the results of her interference.

Blinking back the flood of tears that threatened, Harrie asked him, 'Is it always going to be like this, Jeremy?'

He looked at her blankly. 'Like what exactly?'

'Your mother coming first, before me?'

'That's a very selfish attitude, Harriet. I've never seen this in you before.'

'I've never seen you like this before either, Jeremy.'

Suddenly something Marion had said to Harrie earlier that evening flooded back to her full force. Marion was right. Harrie did not really know the man she was marrying. She had been so swept up by his romancing of her that she hadn't stopped to consider whether he was actually offering her the kind of marriage she'd envisaged for herself. She did want someone who would sit with her in the evening, cuddled up on the settee, and Jeremy had shown her that she couldn't expect that from him. She agreed with him that they were adults, but just because they were it didn't mean they had to act grown-up all the time, even in the privacy of their own home. What else had she taken for granted about her marriage without spending lengthy periods of time with Jeremy just doing normal things together, to discover if they were compatible, as Marion and Allen had had the sense to do before theirs? She suddenly knew that if this marriage was going to be the long-lasting happy one she wanted it to be then they needed to spend plenty more time together getting to know each other better. A lot better.

Gnawing her bottom lip anxiously, she took a steadying breath and said, 'Do you think we've jumped into arranging our marriage a little too soon, Jeremy? Maybe it would be a good idea to postpone it for a while, until we get to know each other better.'

'What!' He looked at her, astounded. 'I know quite enough about you to be sure I want to marry you. Just what is it you feel you don't know about me?'

'Well . . . lots of things, Jeremy.'

'Such as? You know I've got good prospects. You know I'm offering you a fine home to live in. You know I love you. What more do you want to know about me?' His face suddenly filled with a knowing look and he said, 'I know what the matter is, darling. You have pre-wedding nerves. The big day's drawing close, it's all overwhelming you, isn't it? I'm sure Mother will know of a tonic that will help calm you. Come on, let's go through and ask her.'

She was looking at him, flabbergasted. 'Jeremy, did you listen to what I said?'

He looked hurt. 'Yes, of course I did, darling, and I've given you my response.'

'That I need a tonic?'

'Yes.'

She gave an exasperated sigh. How on earth did she get it through to him that she was serious about their spending more time together before they became man and wife? She didn't really want to postpone their wedding for long, just enough for them to spend some time together, doing things that she wanted to do as well as the things he liked. That way they'd have a better understanding of each other and could give their marriage the best possible start and chance of lasting. When it came to rearranging their big day again, maybe by that time a place to hold the reception could be found that Jeremy's mother approved of and which was also affordable for her father. And it would give her time to make sure her father was better able to care for himself, and also a chance to adjust to the fact that she would be sharing Jeremy with his mother until they could afford a place of their own, which she had a terrible feeling would be later rather than sooner if Daphne Franklin had any say in it.

Harrie slipped her arm out of his, stepped across to the coat stand and unhooked her coat which she placed over her arm.

'Where are you going?' Jeremy asked her, frowning in bewilderment.

'I need you to think seriously about what I've suggested so I'm leaving you to mull it over.'

Before he could respond, Harrie had unlatched the front door and hurried through it.

CHAPTER SEVEN

The next morning, looking far calmer than she inwardly felt and armed with the post for his attention, Harrie tapped lightly on Jeremy's office door and entered when she heard his response.

Her father had been most surprised the previous evening when she had returned home far earlier than he had expected. He'd had no reason not to accept her explanation that she was tired and wanted an early night, but was delighted that before she retired to bed she had spent over an hour with him, both of them sipping cups of drinking chocolate while attempting to find the right places for some pieces of the complicated two-thousand-piece jigsaw she had bought him for his last birthday. Harrie had enjoyed working alongside her father and this only reaffirmed for her that not only did she want a husband who was also her lover and friend, she wanted this sort of companionship with him, not necessarily spent jigsaw-making but to share the pleasure of joint pastimes.

Despite the way she had left Jeremy, she had slept surprisingly well, confident that her suggestion of delaying their nuptials was right and that leaving Jeremy to think about it would make him see that too.

As she laid the post on his desk, he raised his head to look at her. Locking his eyes on hers, he said, 'Well, I'm waiting.'

She was confused by this cool greeting. 'Er . . . waiting for what, Jeremy?'

He gave an exasperated sigh. 'Your apology.'

She stared at him, stunned. 'My apology?'

'It's the least I deserve after what you did last night. It really was unforgivable of you, walking out like that when Mother was waiting for us to join her for dinner, and especially after she had taken great pains to choose the menu and cook the meal herself.'

The last thing Harrie had been expecting was a demand for

69

an apology, but she supposed he did have a point. She shuffled her feet uncomfortably. 'Yes, I suppose I should not have left without making my excuses to her. I am sorry for that, Jeremy.'

'She was upset but I managed to cover your behaviour by telling her you had a sudden migraine and it was best you went home to take care of it. She's expecting you for dinner tonight so we can sort out the issues we were going to tackle last night. Please remember to bring your completed guest list with you.'

'But, Jeremy, did you not listen to what I suggested last night? That we postpone the wedding until . . .'

'Darling, it's as I told you then. You're suffering from a bout of pre-wedding nerves. It's too late in the day to cancel all the arrangements just on a whim that a simple dose of medication will resolve.'

'A whim!' She scraped her hand despairingly through her neatly styled titian hair, making it stick out wildly in places. Jeremy really was not listening to her. A rush of frustration washed through her and she snapped, 'It's not too late to cancel the arrangements and rearrange them after we've spent some more time getting to know each other better.' And added before she could check herself, 'Your mother has already proved that, hasn't she, by what she did?'

His eyes narrowed in annoyance. 'I will ignore that remark, Harriet, and put it down to your emotional state at the moment.'

He picked up the telephone and started to dial.

'What are you doing?' she asked him.

'I'm calling Mother to ask her to arrange a visit to our doctor so he can prescribe something for you. It seems to me that it's urgently needed.'

She couldn't believe he was totally dismissing her request to delay the wedding as if he was at a loss to understand why she had requested it, without even discussing it with her further, and instead diagnosing her as suffering from an ailment she definitely wasn't prey to. A tonic was not the answer. Getting to know each other better was.

Taking a deep breath, she clasped her hands tightly in front of her and announced, 'Until you take me seriously, Jeremy, I think . . .' She realised that he needed strong words to make him sit up and take notice of her as nothing else seemed to have that effect '. . . well, I think it's best we don't see each other.'

He was staring at her. 'You're calling off our wedding?'

'No, Jeremy, I'm not calling it off. I'm saying we should postpone it for a while and I've already told you why.'

'And I gave you my response last night.'

She gave a deep sigh of exasperation. 'We're getting nowhere, Jeremy. You're not listening to me. You're not even offering to make any sort of compromise . . .'

'How can I compromise? I want us to get married on the day we have arranged.'

'Well . . . well . . . you could offer to take us for a weekend away together before the wedding, and we could spend evenings doing . . .'

Before she could finish he jumped in. 'That's not compromising, Harriet, that's putting you in a compromising position by asking you to go away with me.'

She smiled. 'This is the Swinging Sixties, Jeremy. We haven't . . . well, done anything intimate together so far except kiss, so how do we know whether we are compatible in that department?'

He was looking completely shocked. 'Are you telling me you're not pure?'

'Pure!' She fought not to laugh at his old-fashioned terminology. 'Jeremy, I had other boyfriends before I met you and . . . I'm not a virgin, if that's what you mean. This is what I meant about us not knowing each other as well as we should before we commit ourselves to each other for life.'

He was looking at her as though she had a dreadful social disease. 'This admission from you has come as a great shock to me, Harriet. You should have told me that I wouldn't be your first.'

'But you never asked me. We've never discussed anything like this.'

'I was wrong to take it for granted then, wasn't I? I don't know how I feel now about introducing you as my wife to my colleagues while wondering if you've been with any of them.'

She was gazing at him, horrified. 'What! Oh, Jeremy, how could you insinuate that I've slept around? It was with one boy who I was very fond of but things didn't work out between us, that's all. I know girls who have slept with several men before they settled for their husbands.'

'Their husbands might not have minded that fact, I do. I don't know how I feel about getting into bed with you on our wedding night while knowing I'm not your first. Would you even have told me about this if it hadn't come out in conversation just now? What else about your past have you been keeping secret from me?'

Her face filled with hurt. 'Nothing, Jeremy.'

'Can I trust that you're telling me the truth?'

'Oh, Jeremy,' she uttered, 'how can you ask me such a thing?'

'Well, after all, it's not every day a man like me comes along for someone like you, is it? Perhaps you're not to blame for keeping secret from me something you had an idea I wouldn't like.'

She gasped at the implied slight. 'Oh, Jeremy, how can you accuse me of being a gold-digger?'

'I wasn't . . . or maybe I was . . . Oh, I don't know. You're right. I don't know you, do I?'

'Have you had girlfriends before me that you were close to, Jeremy? Ones you haven't told me about?'

'Yes, of course I have. I'm a man, and a man has the right to sow his wild oats before he settles down to marriage.' He stared at her thoughtfully. 'I'm wondering if I can overlook your indiscretion as long as I have your assurance there are no other skeletons in your closet?'

Her mouth dropped open at the audacity of his double standards. She knew then that he was not the one for her. This knowledge hit her so hard she actually took a step backwards and gasped. She knew more about Kate Lane's husband who lived next-door than she did about the man she was planning to marry. The Jeremy she loved was only the part of him he had allowed her to see. The side he was showing her now she certainly did not like. What else did she not know about him that would be just as unwelcome? It struck her that the equal partnership she had thought to have with him would never have been possible.

It was glaringly obvious to her now that Jeremy was the type who would see himself as the master in his own home and her as the little woman he expected to jump to attention at the click of his fingers. She hadn't seen this before because they had never been in any domestic situations for it to show itself. When he had ordered food in restaurants for her, she had seen this as a gentlemanly act on his part, an attentiveness she'd never received from a boyfriend before, and she had found it romantic. Now she realised that in actual fact it was Jeremy's way of taking charge, that he automatically considered himself the principal in this relationship, assumed he knew better than she did even down to what food she chose to eat or wine to drink when out dining. He would dominate any marriage, she had no doubt of it, and for it to be an amicable relationship his wife would have to become a woman who jumped unquestioningly whenever he clicked his fingers.

A sudden wave of sadness washed through Harrie. She felt bereft of what she'd thought she had, not the way things had really been. Thank goodness Marion had opened her eyes so she was able to see it clearly or else she dreaded to think what kind of subservience she would blindly have entered into.

With tears in her eyes, voice thick with emotion, Harrie said, 'I don't want you to overlook my indiscretion, as you called it, Jeremy.'

He looked taken aback. 'I beg your pardon?'

'You heard what I said. You accused me of not being the woman you thought I was. Well, you certainly aren't the man I thought you were. I can't marry you now I know your true character. What you really want, Jeremy, is a hostess for your dinner parties and a companion for your mother. A lapdog, in fact. I would have been a good wife to you. I would have done my best to make you happy. But a lapdog I'm not. I'm sorry if I gave you the impression I was something you and your mother could mould into the perfect little wife for you.' She flashed him a wan smile. 'I hope you eventually find what you're looking for, Jeremy, I really do.'

With that she spun on her heels and rushed from the office, leaving him staring after her confounded.

As Harrie arrived back at her desk a colleague sitting nearby stopped what she was doing to look across at her. 'You all right, Harrie? Only yer look like you've just been told a relative has died.'

'Pardon? Oh, yes, I'm fine, thank you. Just . . . er . . . have a lot on my mind, that's all.'

Resuming her task, the office assistant said, 'Well, yer bound to, what with the wedding looming so close. All us girls here are so envious of you, landing Mr Franklin. What a catch he is! I bet you pinch yourself every night, don't yer, Harrie, to make sure you ain't dreaming? Oh, you've never mentioned your hen night. Have you arranged that yet? I will be invited, won't I?'

Harrie stared at her, frozen. Oh, this was awful. All the staff knew of the forthcoming wedding, some of the senior staff even expecting invitations, and would have to be told it was off. What explanation could be given so as not to demean a man in Jeremy's position in front of the staff or, worse still, damage his promotion prospects in the eyes of the fuddy-duddy partners? Then a more worrying question presented itself. How could she continue working so closely with him now she had broken off their engagement? It was going to be extremely difficult for them both. Despite knowing without a doubt that he couldn't be the kind of husband she wanted, Harrie still had deep feelings for him and was in no doubt that he did love the part of her he had known and understood.

She knew then that the only fair thing for her to do was to resign from her job, leaving Jeremy free to decide what information about their break-up he divulged so as to save his own face. She refused to allow herself to think what effect leaving the job she enjoyed so much would have on her. Jeremy would not suffer through lack of secretarial support due to her departure. After all, he'd already chosen a replacement for her on their marriage so all that was needed was to ask Miss Abberington to bring forward her starting date.

Without saying a word to her colleague, very aware the woman was still looking at her, bewildered by her lack of response, Harrie quickly put a piece of paper into her typewriter and expertly tapped out a letter. After signing it, she folded it up to put in an envelope. She then hurriedly swept her desk of personal belongings and put them into her handbag. Grabbing her coat, she handed the envelope containing her resignation to her colleague.

'Would you please give that to Miss Rayner for me, Colleen?' Miss Rayner being the office manager in charge of all the secretaries and clerks.

The other girl frowned. 'What is it?' she asked, taking the letter.

Harrie flashed her the briefest of smiles. 'Please excuse me, Colleen, I have to dash.' She spun round to depart, then stopped to say, 'It's been great working with you all. I shall miss you.'

'But . . . but . . .' a bewildered Colleen stammered.

Harrie, though, had left.

CHAPTER EIGHT

Percy was most surprised to see his daughter walk through the back gate an hour later but he didn't need to ask if there was anything amiss. He instinctively knew there was, and something serious.

After hurriedly laying aside the brush he'd been using to sweep the yard, he rushed across to her. 'Oh, me ducky, what's wrong?' he demanded, taking her arm. 'Are you ill or summat?'

During the bus ride home Harrie had managed to keep her emotions under control. Now, safe in the confines of their back yard with her beloved father by her side, the dam broke and tears welled up to pour down her face. She fell into his arms. 'Oh, Dad . . . Dad,' she blubbered. 'I'm so sorry, I really am.'

The sight of his beloved daughter breaking her heart, the reason as yet a mystery to him, sent a chill of fear through Percy. 'Let's get you inside.'

Seating a still sobbing Harrie on a dining chair, he sat down next to her to take her hands protectively in his. His face creased in deep concern, he asked, 'What on earth are you sorry for, ducky?'

'Letting you down, Dad.'

'Now how could you ever let me down?'

She wiped her runny nose with the back of her hand before she answered, 'All the money it's cost you.'

He frowned. 'Harrie ducky, what are you going on about?'

'Oh, Dad, I can't bear to think that you've been putting by money every week all these years and now I've made you lose it! Do you think it's too late to get the deposits back if we tell them we're sorry we have to cancel?'

The penny dropped then and he looked stunned. 'Harrie, are you telling me the wedding's off?'

She nodded.

His face hardened in anger. 'He can't do this to you! It's that mother of his, it's her what's behind this, I bet. I had an inkling she thought you weren't good enough for her son. Well, we'll see about this.'

He made to rise but she stopped him. 'It's me that's called the wedding off, Dad.'

He lowered himself back on to the chair. '*You* have!'

She nodded. 'Please don't think badly of me, Dad. I couldn't marry Jeremy when I realised he wasn't the one for me.'

'Oh, I see. Well, in that case, I'm glad you've been sensible before it's too late.'

'You are, Dad?'

'Of course, me darlin',' he replied with conviction. 'Yer don't think I want you to marry someone you know isn't right for you, just to keep me happy, do yer? As for the money we might have lost, I'd sooner that than find out you married the wrong chap.' He patted her hand and looked at her, at a loss as to quite what to say and do for the best. It was upsetting him greatly to see his daughter so distressed. It was at times like this he really missed his wife. Times of crisis were when women came into their own. He hoped he was handling this catastrophe as well as Harrie's dear late mother would have done. His mind sought to identify what she would do if she was here now. Then the answer came. She would have done what all women do in situations like this: make a cup of sweet tea and offer a sympathetic ear.

A while later Percy gave a deep sigh. 'You've done the right thing, Harrie.'

'I did love him, Dad, or the Jeremy I knew I did. I'm missing that man so much. You don't think I could have been too hasty and . . .' Harrie's voice trailed off. She had seen Jeremy for what he truly was and it was no good thinking she could somehow change herself or him just to ease the pain of the loss she was feeling at the moment. 'Yes, I have done the right thing, haven't I, Dad?' she whispered.

'Oh, ducky, most certainly. When I married yer mam, God bless her, neither of us had any doubts at all. When you finally get married you mustn't have the slightest doubt either. Too many people have gone through with weddings knowing they were doing the wrong thing just because they felt they couldn't upset their families. And then lived the rest of their lives in misery.' He held out his arms to her. 'Come and give your dad a hug.'

She fell into his arms and he embraced her tightly. 'I know this is the last thing you'll want to hear just now, but there's someone else out there for you, a man just right for you. It's best you left yer job. Clean break all round You'll get another one easily with your skills. And, Harrie, we ain't that hard up yer can't take a little time to get yourself over this properly before you start working again.' In an effort to lighten the mood he said, 'Eh, there's one good thing come outta this.'

She pulled away from him and with tear-blurred eyes smiled and asked, 'What's that?'

'Well, call me selfish, me old ducky, but with you not leaving me so soon I can take a while longer to learn this cooking and washing for meself lark, can't I?'

Despite how wretched she was feeling, she couldn't help but giggle. She'd get through this, she knew she would. She had her wonderful father to help her. She did worry how Jeremy was feeling, mortally sorry for the fact that she must have hurt him as well as leaving him with the task of explaining to his mother that their relationship was over, but once he got over the initial shock and thought clearly, she felt sure he would appreciate that what she had done was for the best in the long run. One thing she had learned from this episode in her life: the next time she met a man and felt like getting serious with him, she would make sure she knew him well enough, and he her, to know without a shadow of a doubt that their relationship offered each of them what they were seeking.

CHAPTER NINE

While Harrie was being consoled by her father, at the front door of a smart residential property in an affluent suburb of the city Chas was depositing bags of shopping where his passenger indicated. He accepted the money the expensively dressed, middle-aged woman handed him.

'Keep the change,' she said in regal tones.

He respectfully tipped his forelock. 'Thank you. I hope you had a pleasant journey and Black's Taxis can be of service to you again.'

As he walked down the drive lined with neatly trimmed laurels he checked the money in his hand and didn't know whether to laugh or cry when he quickly calculated that his tip for this trip was the grand sum of twopence. He'd never become rich at this rate, he thought. Tips made up a good proportion of his wage and he was determined to save as much as he could towards the eventual purchase of a new house.

The boom of a voice over the radio alerted Chas. He made a dash for the car, quickly unlocked the door and leaned inside to unhook the hand-mic from its cradle. Snapping down the button, he spoke clearly into it: 'Romeo receiving.' As usual he cringed inwardly as he always did when having to announce himself by his call handle which he felt had been inappropriately assigned to a man of his plain looks.

Ralph Widcombe's gruff tones came back to him. 'Pick up for you from the Royal Infirmary to Wingate Drive. A Mr Chapman is waiting outside the main entrance on Welford Road. And as soon as you've dropped him off yer'd better come straight to the office. Mrs Black is here dishing out the wages and she's wanting to get back up the hospital as soon as she can to be with Mr Black.'

'Right you are, Ralph. Any news on the boss?'

'No . . .'

Ralph's voice was suddenly replaced by a loud crackle of inter-ference then a second authoritative voice came over the air. Chas knew this was the police whose radio transmissions often broke into taxi operators' as the wave bands used were so close together. It seemed by what was being relayed over the air that a motor accident had occurred on the Narborough Road and the sergeant operating the police radio was summoning all avail-able officers to the area. There was more interference and then Ralph's voice filtered back again. 'You there, Romeo?'

'You'll have to repeat, base, had police interference.'

'I said, no change as far as I know in Mr Black's condition.'

'Oh, dear. Thanks, Ralph. I'll do that pick up and see you back at base in about half an hour, give or take.'

As he put the mic back in its cradle and started the engine Chas grimaced, unsure whether no change in his boss's condi-tion was good news or bad.

A while later, as he waited for his next fare, Chas was taking a break in the drivers' rest area. Most unusually there was no one else present and he was enjoying his own company – for the short time he knew it would last. The once-white walls of the rest room were now stained khaki-yellow by cigarette smoke and the red Formica-topped table was faded, cracked and stained. The end of one of its legs had broken off and was held up by a tatty old telephone book. The matching red plastic-covered chairs had seen better days too. Old newspapers lay in toppling heaps, being added to on a daily basis by drivers chucking theirs on top when they'd finished with them; rows of dirty milk bottles, their contents in varying stages of rancidness, were stacked six deep under the table which held a gas ring, black-ened kettle and three grubby plastic containers holding tea, instant coffee powder and sugar, all clogged into lumps from having wet spoons dipped into them.

Taking a sip of stewed tea, Chas slit open his wage packet and counted the contents. Frowning, he pulled out his wage slip and studied it. Something was wrong. The money in his hand did not tally with the net figure on his wage slip. He'd a fiver too much.

He made his way to Jack Black's office which was next-door to the rest room. Tapping on the door, he walked inside. The decor of this room was no better than the drivers' refuge. Three over-flowing filing cabinets filled one wall, above them two shelves crammed with bulging ring binders and other paraphernalia to do with the business that Jack Black had never got around to clearing out over the years. The window looking out on to a small yard behind was filthy, preventing much light from filtering through.

Chas smiled politely at Muriel Black who was sitting at her husband's cluttered desk, a tray containing several brown wages envelopes in front of her.

The middle-aged woman looked harassed and distracted. 'Oh, it's you again, Chas. I thought it was one of the other drivers come to collect their pay. I hope the others hurry up as I really need to dish these out then get back to the hospital. Er . . . did you want to see me about something?'

'It's my pay, Mrs Black.'

'Oh?'

'It's not right?'

'Oh!'

'You've given me too much money.'

'I have?'

'A fiver too much according to my wage slip.'

'Oh . . . oh, I see. Oh, dear, you're the third one I've had back today because something wasn't right with their pay and not all the drivers have collected theirs yet so how many others are wrong?' She rubbed her hands wearily over her face, looking defeated. 'Oh, I'm no good at this making up wages lark. Jack saw to all that, you see. I've never had any office experience. Since he took ill I've had to battle through as best I can with just a bit of help from the daughter of a neighbour who works as a wages clerk at the British Shoe Corporation.' She gave a sigh and shook her head ruefully. 'To me the tax and National Insurance books Her Majesty's Tax Inspectors issue might as well be written in Chinese. I can't make head nor tail of them.' She smiled at him. 'I appreciate your honesty, Chas. Keep the fiver and get yerself drunk on it tonight – my treat.'

'Oh, I couldn't take advantage, Mrs Black.'

'Keeping quiet about the extra fiver in your pay packet would have been taking advantage of me, Chas.' She gave a resigned sigh. 'This has brought home to me that I'm on a fool's errand trying to keep the office side of the business ticking over 'til Jack's better again. I haven't touched any of the bookwork at all since he took ill 'cos in truth I ain't a clue how. If I don't want to end up bankrupting the business, I need to be sensible. I must get someone in to do the office work temporarily 'til Jack's back on his feet again.

'To be honest, I'm about on my knees with popping in here daily to make sure no disasters have happened, though God knows if something had I wouldn't know how to put it right, and then spending the rest of my time at the hospital sitting by Jack's bed willing him to get better. I haven't slept a wink hardly since he had his attack. If I carry on like this I'll end up in the bed next to him.' She gave a rueful shake of her head. 'I kept telling him this place'd be the death of him if he went on working the hours he did with no let up. I just hope to God I ain't proved right, Chas. I pray with all my might I ain't.'

He saw tears glisten in her eyes when she added, 'I'd be lost without that silly old bugger. We've been together forty years. We've only got each other 'cos we weren't blessed with family. It was always a dream of Jack's to own his own business and he scrimped and saved, begged, borrowed and . . . well, he never lowered himself to steal to my knowledge, although between you and me I wouldn't have put it past him if it meant he'd fulfil his dream. He got his first licence plate by paying over the odds for it from a taxi driver friend of the family who was forced to give up 'cos he lost his leg in an accident when he was driving home drunk from the pub one night and met up with a lamp post.

'For Jack, getting that plate was like being given the crown jewels. From then on he's lived and breathed this business, but then I can't complain 'cos it's bought me a nice house and stuff inside it and put good food on the table. But I was so looking forward to him retiring and us doing all the things we haven't done together since he started up the business over twenty years ago. A week away would be nice. I ain't fussy where. We haven't had a holiday since . . . well, I can't remember when.'

Muriel gave a sigh. 'Mind you, I've always known it's wishful thinking on my part that Jack will ever retire. He couldn't bear to part with this place. It's like his baby. He gave birth to it and since then he's nurtured it carefully. I suppose the most I can hope for is what's happened to him will bring home to him that he needs to slow down a bit.' Muriel gave a sniff and mentally shook herself. 'Forgive me, Chas, this is no way for the boss's wife to carry on in front of the staff, is it? It's just that . . . well, there's something about you that makes you very easy to talk to and that's a rarity in a man.' She looked at him hopefully. 'You don't know anyone who's looking for a job in the office line, do you? Someone who'd take all this lot off me hands so I can devote myself to being with Jack full-time? I dread the thought of him coming round in a strange hospital bed and me not being there. And of course I'll need to be on hand all the time when he's at home convalescing.'

He shook his head. 'No, sorry, Mrs Black.' Feeling he could not leave her without any hope of having her burdens alleviated, he added, 'I'm sure that there's someone somewhere who'd be willing.'

Muriel looked doubtful. 'Mmm. It's a case of finding them, ain't it? I mean, this ain't the most salubrious of places to work in, is it?' she said, casting her eyes around the room and wrinkling her nose in disgust. 'Any decent temp is going to turn their nose up at working here all day, and I can't say as I blame them. I got a big shock when I saw how bad it is, especially that rest room. Well, it's just a pig sty. Yer can tell no woman works here, they'd never have allowed it to get like that. I shall nag Jack to tidy this place up until I'm blue in the face when he gets better 'cos if the hours he works don't eventually kill him, the germs rife in here certainly will. But even finding office help is difficult for me. The time I have to spend doing it is time I could spend with him. Plus I wouldn't know the first thing about interviewing anyway.' She rubbed her hands over her face again. 'I'll just have to keep battling through as best I can, and hope that at the end of it all my Jack has a business to come back to.'

Just then Ralph's voice was heard outside shouting, 'Got a pick up for yer, Chas.'

He flashed a smile at Muriel Black. 'I'd best go. Er . . . please give my best to Mr Black. Everyone's best wishes, in fact.'

Before he turned and left he put the five pounds she had over-paid him before her on the desk and Muriel Black knew by the look he gave her that despite her offer to let him keep it he was not comfortable about doing so. Jack certainly had chosen well when he had recruited Charles Tyme, she thought. Whether his boss was around or not, his type would carry out his job to the best of his ability and be scrupulously honest into the bargain. She had a feeling, now she had met the drivers, that not all of them were in the same mould as Chas Tyme. She worried some might be taking advantage of their boss's absence. Still, there was nothing she could do about that. If they were up to anything untoward behind Jack's back, she was too inexperienced to do anything about it.

Later that evening, as Chas tucked into an overcooked pork chop and lumpy mashed potatoes, he said to his mother, 'I do feel for Mrs Black, Mam. She's having a tough time of it just now, trying to do what she can for the business while spending as much time as she can at her husband's bedside. She looks frazzled to say the least. She told me herself how much of a struggle the office side is for her, with her having no experience. She really needs help running it, but I fear it's like she said, she'd be hard pressed to find someone to do it temporarily with the facilities our office offers. It's not exactly posh.'

'Oh, I'm sure there's someone who'd cope, but she won't find 'em 'til she starts looking, will she? Is your pork chop tough?' Iris asked him, looking dubiously at the one on her own plate.

It was but only because his mother had fried it in far too hot a pan, for too long. 'It's fine, Mam, just how I like it,' said Chas diplomatically.

'Huh, well, it must just be mine then. I shall be having words with the bucher when I next go in.'

Just then a knock sounded on the back door.

Iris tutted crossly. 'Who can that be, just when we're having our dinner?'

'I'll get it, Mam,' Chas offered, making to lay down his knife and fork.

'You sit where yer are,' she ordered him. 'I don't want yer dinner getting cold.'

She went off to answer the door and Chas could hear the murmur of voices before his mother returned tight-faced to announce, 'It's Nadine Dewhurst, or Rider as she is now, for you.'

Chas looked surprised. 'Me? What does she want with me?'

'She wouldn't say. I told her you was having yer dinner but she said it was urgent.'

A horrifying thought struck him. Nadine couldn't be calling to ask him to watch her four children while she went to the pub, could she? He supposed there was only one way to find out.

'Oh, Quas . . . Chas,' Nadine quickly corrected herself when he went into the kitchen. 'I'm so sorry to bother you, yer mam said you was having yer dinner, but . . . well . . . yer the only one around here I could think of to call on, you always being so helpful to the neighbours like. *It* could go away I suppose, but if *it* doesn't and *it* bit one of me kids . . .'

'If *what* bit one of your children, Nadine?'

'The rat. Bloody great big black thing it is. I saw it with me own eyes shooting across the yard when I went to put some rubbish in the dustbin just now.' Tilting her head, she ran her tongue over her lips and pouted at him. 'Oh, Chas, you will come and see if you can catch it, won't yer? I'd be ever so grateful.'

The suggestive undercurrent in her voice made him squirm uncomfortably. All his wiser instincts told him he'd be best off telling her he was extremely busy and shutting the door on her, but his good nature dictated that he could not turn down anyone's request for help, and especially not when children could be in danger. 'I . . . er . . . think we've a trap somewhere in the outhouse that we bought a few years back when the dustmen were last on strike, just in case we had a problem like that. I'll dig it out and bring it round and set it for you. It's a case of waiting and hoping then. Best keep your children out of the yard meantime, though. I'll just finish my dinner and I'll be round.'

She smiled charmingly at him. 'Thanks. Proper knight in shin-ning armour you are, Chas Tyme.'

'What did the likes of her want with you?' Iris asked when Chas took his place back at the table.

Tucking into his dinner, he said, 'Apparently they've a rat running amok in their yard.'

'Huh, and why ain't I surprised? All that junk they have stacked in there. Rats' paradise the Dewhursts' yard is. I hope you told her to get the council in?' She saw the look on her son's face. 'Oh, yer never offered to go and try and catch it?' Iris clicked her tongue. 'You don't know the word "no", do yer, son? Still, I suppose I wouldn't have you any other way. But I don't need to tell you, do I, that them Dewhursts are n'ote but trouble so when yer've done what yer have to, make sure that Nadine knows you ain't at her beck and call or she'll be around here asking yer help all hours of the day and night. Them's the type that, given a yard of 'lastic, they'll not be happy until they've stretched it the length of a mile.'

'Don't worry, Mam. I'll be setting the trap and that's all I'll be doing.'

Nadine was leaning on her mother's open back door smoking a cigarette when Chas entered via the yard gate twenty minutes later, armed with the trap he had unearthed from the outhouse.

He was surprised to see her there. He would have thought she would be inside, the back door firmly shut, to stop the rat getting into the house.

Nadine smiled winningly at him, smoothing one hand down her short, tight-fitting skirt and flicking the other through her long blonde tresses. 'You really are a gem, Chas. I was just saying to Mother what a relief it was to be able to call on you.'

Just then a voice from inside boomed, 'Who you talking to, Nadine?'

She hurriedly pulled the back door to. 'As I was saying, it's really good of you to come and help us.'

'Where did you say you saw the rat running to?'

Nadine looked blank. 'Eh? Oh . . . er . . . in there somewhere,' she said, pointing to the outhouse whose rotting door was hanging off its hinges. It was packed full with an array of discarded items in varying stages of decay.

Chas blew out his cheeks. Several nests of rats could be thriving inside that little haven. 'Well, I'll set the trap near the entrance and then hopefully Bob's yer uncle.'

'Oh, I'm sure it will be. I have faith in you, Chas.'

He was very conscious she was watching his every move as he set the trap. When he'd finished, she said, 'You must let me buy you a pint down the pub by way of a thank you.'

'Oh, there's no need really.'

'But I insist. I'll see you there sometime, yeah?'

He gulped. 'Just make sure your children don't come into this yard until you're certain one way or the other whether you have a rat. If you have and the trap doesn't work you'd best get the council in. They're the experts at getting rid of vermin. I'll be getting back now as my mother is waiting to dish up pudding.'

As he hurried off back to his own house, a curl of satisfaction played around Nadine's lips. The first stage of her plan was off to a good start.

CHAPTER TEN

A few streets away in an identical style of terraced house to that where Chas and Iris lived, Marion was giving her best friend a comforting hug. 'Oh, Harrie, you and Jeremy breaking up? Well, it's the last thing I was expecting.' She pulled away and looked sympathetically at her. 'From what yer've told me yer've done the best thing, gel. It's nice for a woman to feel protected by her man, but dominated by him is another thing. Before long yer'd have felt stifled, Harrie, and deeply regretted tying yerself to him for life – and 'is mother too by the sound of it. I'm not saying Jeremy's a bad man, Harrie, I've no doubt he loves you, but it seems he's not the one to make you happy in the long run.'

Harrie issued a deep sigh as she sank down on a well-used chair by the drop-leaf table. 'If you hadn't come round last night and said what you did, I'd still be going ahead with the wedding, too wrapped up in it all to see what I was actually heading for.'

Marion's face filled with horror. 'Oh, Harrie, are you saying you deciding not to marry Jeremy is all my fault?'

'Yes, it is, but in a good way. You opened my eyes to the type of man he really is. Oh, Marion, I feel so stupid. I shan't ever be so blind again. I've no doubt, though, that Jeremy will find someone else who wants a man just like him and will enjoy the kind of life he's offering.'

'The doormat kind, you mean? You might be some things, Harrie, but the doormat type you ain't.' Marion sat down on a chair beside her. 'Have you told yer dad?'

She nodded.

'And how did he take it?'

Harrie gave a wan smile. 'He was great, Marion. As supportive as he always is. I couldn't wish for a better dad than mine. I could do with my mother, though, at the moment,' she added softly, her voice thick with emotion.

'You never grow too old not to need yer mam, do yer, Harrie? My mam drives me insane sometimes 'cos she's an argumentative old sod but I'd be lost without her.' It was very evident to Marion that her friend was fighting back an emotional outburst. She thought it would be a good idea if she tried to keep Harrie's mind on more positive matters, to give her a breathing space until she got into bed tonight and cried herself to sleep as Marion knew she would. 'So it's job hunting for you then?' she said brightly.

'Mmm, seems so, doesn't it?'

'I got the *Mercury* tonight on my way home from work if you fancy a look down the Jobs column?'

'Thanks, Marion, but I'm not in the mood just now. I haven't given my job situation much thought because as I'm sure you can appreciate I've had other things on my mind, but I thought I might try temping for a bit. I fancy a change from a solicitor's office and I expect you can see why.'

'Yes, I can. Until you're fully over this it's best you avoid as many reminders as you can. Er . . . just a thought, Harrie. Do you think yer've seen the last of Jeremy?'

'What? You mean, you think he'll sue me for breach of promise, Marion? You can't do that any more.'

'No, I mean . . . well, men don't think the way we do. I should know, I've been married to one for long enough. You might think you've made it clear it's best you go your separate ways, but what I'm getting at is that he might not have accepted what you've told him and . . . well, think you're still suffering from pre-wedding jitters and didn't really mean what you said.'

'Well, I *did* mean what I said. He'll know I mean it too after he's found out I've left the firm, which he's bound to have done by now. I don't like the thought of him suffering, I really don't, but Jeremy's an intelligent man. I'm sure in time he'll thank me for what I did.'

Marion wasn't at all sure he was going to take Harrie's rejection of him as quietly as she thought he would, but decided not to voice her thoughts.

Harrie stood up. 'I'd better let you get on with making Allen's dinner. I just thought I'd come round and tell you what was going on.'

Marion smiled warmly. 'Look, don't go. Stay and have dinner with us. I've a chicken pie that Allen's mam made us, it'll stretch to three. I'll send him down the pub after and I'll pop down the offie and get us a bottle of cider. Help you drown your sorrows.'

'That's a nice offer, Marion, but I'll give it a miss, if you don't mind. Dad's fussing around me. I've left him peeling spuds for chips to go with the bit of frying steak he got from the butcher's this afternoon in an effort to cheer me up. He knows steak and chips is usually my favourite dinner. Actually I'm afraid any food will choke me at the moment but I'll have to force it down somehow or I'll hurt his feelings'

'Ah, bless him,' said Marion. 'Yes, I understand, you must get home.' She rose to put her arms around Harrie and gave her a bear hug. 'Remember, no matter what time of day or night, if you need a shoulder to cry on or just a chat, I'm here for yer, gel.'

Harrie smiled appreciatively. 'Yes, I know you are, and thank you, Marion.

CHAPTER ELEVEN

The following Monday morning Harrie found it strange that she needn't leap out of bed to ready herself for work. As well as losing Jeremy it seemed she'd lost the familiar routines of a job she'd loved, and the comradeship of her workmates.

Percy, who was in the process of mashing his daughter a cup of tea, having heard her moving around upstairs, took one look at her when she came down and suggested she go straight back to bed as it didn't look to him like she'd had much sleep.

'I did sleep well, Dad,' Harrie fibbed. 'It's just I'm not quite awake yet, and no woman exactly looks her best when she's just rolled out of bed, does she?'

'You look to me like yer've been rolling around it all night. Darlin', you don't have to cover things up, I know you haven't slept. Go back to bed and I'll bring you up a cuppa.'

'No, Dad. I've spent all weekend wallowing in self-pity and even you must be fed up by now with all the pots of tea you've mashed me and the wet patches on your shirt where I've been crying on your shoulder. I have to start getting my life back together, and the best way I can do that is by getting myself back to work. I'm going to throw some clothes on now and pop down to the telephone box to make an appointment with a temp agency. Chatterley and Bigson used a firm called Ace Employment. The girls they sent along to help us out always seemed to be up to the job so I'm going to approach them first. Hopefully they'll see me soon and be able to get me something for next Monday.'

Percy smiled warmly at her as he put a pot of tea on the table. 'I'm glad to see you're thinking positively, lovey. But before you start on this new episode in yer life, will you at least have a cuppa and slice of toast to keep yer stamina up? Just to please yer old dad.'

*　　*　　*

Meanwhile, a few streets away in the Tyme household Iris was frowning as she scanned the contents of the pantry, wondering what she could do Chas for his dinner that evening. Left over from the weekend was a slice of corned beef, a noggin of cheese, a couple of potatoes sprouting eyes, one rasher of streaky bacon and one sausage which had burst its skin. There was also a small piece of dried up-looking beef from the Sunday joint which was supposed to have been big enough to provide leftovers for today but had shrunk so much while cooking – possibly because Iris had the oven set too high – it had just about been enough to feed them for the one meal.

She sighed. It seemed she had a bit of everything and not enough of anything. She needed to provide a substantial meal to satisfy her son's healthy appetite when he came home this evening. Chas deserved a good meal after labouring all day and she would have to be on her death bed not to provide him with one. She hadn't done liver and onions for a while. If she hurried she'd catch the butcher before he shut for lunch.

Then a sudden desire to go into town overwhelmed her. Since her tumble in the street a few weeks ago and the resulting injury she had honoured Chas's request for her not to venture too far without someone, preferably himself, accompanying her, just to be on the safe side. Since her accident she had felt redundant to a certain extent as Chas now did the heavy shopping each week on his way home from work at the large branch of the Co-op on the bottom of the Groby Road. The other bits and pieces she might need during the week were obtainable just a short distance away from the local shops and he'd reluctantly conceded after a sharp exchange with his mother that she could manage to get those herself. But Iris missed her window shopping in the big stores and her bargains from the market; a milky frothy coffee and sticky bun from Brucciana's café on Horsefare Street; the hustle and bustle a visit to town afforded her.

A mischievous twinkle lit her eyes. Well, what Chas didn't know wouldn't hurt him.

All ready for the off, she was just about to leave when a tap sounded on the back door. As it opened Freda's voice called out, 'Cooee, it's only me! Got the kettle on, I hope, 'cos I'm parched.' She was fully inside now and immediately spotted her friend dressed for outdoors. 'Oh, you off out? Where yer going?'

'Er . . . just up the shops.'

Freda cocked an eyebrow at her. 'No, you ain't.'

'What do you mean, no I ain't? If I say I'm going to shops then that's where I'm going.'

Her brow still cocked, Freda folded her arms under her skinny chest and took a stance. 'No, you ain't.

Iris scowled at her. 'You calling me a liar?'

'Yes, I am. You're off up the town, ain't yer.' That was not a question, more a statement.

Her friend looked shocked. 'How the hell did you know?'

''Cos yer wearing yer best coat, which you always do when yer going to town. When you go to the shops you just throw on yer old gabardine mac. And yer've got yer best shopping bag on your arm. For the local shops you just take your old string bag.'

'Bloody Sherlock Holmes you, ain't yer?' Iris hissed at her accusingly.

'I just know yer, Iris. I should do, we've been friends long enough. Anyway, I can't let you go up the town.'

'You can't? You can't bleddy stop me!'

'Oh, I can. I promised Chas that when he wasn't here I'd keep me eye on you and make sure you didn't do 'ote daft like what yer trying to do now. He said if I ever caught you, I was to barricade you in and get him fetched from work.'

'Oh, so you're me jailer now, are you? And as for that son of mine . . .'

'Now get off yer high horse, Iris,' Freda cut in. 'Chas only has yer best interests at heart. We both have. I'd come with you if I'd time but I've not as I've our Rita and me grandkids coming for tea tonight so I've baking to do this afternoon. If you're hell-bent on going to town, I can go with you tomorrow.'

'I am quite capable of getting meself up the town and back. I had one silly accident a few months back and my Chas and you seem to think that from now on 'til the end of me days I'm to be reined like a toddler. I'm as fit as a fiddle and raring to go. Now listen, Freda, and listen good – I'm going up the town and I'm going right now.'

'Your Chas won't like it, Iris.'

'He's my son. It's me that tells him what to do, not the other way around. Anyway, I'll be back long before he gets home

93

from work so he'll be none the wiser. Now do you want me to bring you 'ote back?'

'Well, if yer going through Lewis's you could get me a pound of their loose assorted biscuits.'

'Yes, 'course I will. Now I'd best get off or I'll miss the eleven-forty-seven bus.'

Back in the Harrises' house, Harrie was checking her appearance in the mirror hanging above the 1930s tiled fireplace in the back room.

Her father eyed her appreciatively. 'You look the business, me duck. The top-notch secretary that you are. If that agency don't snap you up, then they ain't what they're cracked up to be.'

Harrie turned and smiled at him. 'Thanks, Dad.' She glanced at the mantel-clock. 'Oh, I'd best hurry or I'll miss the eleven-forty-seven into town.'

'What time is your appointment with the agency?'

'Twelve-forty-five. I was quite surprised when they said they'd like to see me this morning. I got the impression they've lots of temp work in at the moment and not enough staff to cope with it.'

'Have you got your typing certificates to show them?'

She patted her handbag. 'All in here. I still have to do a typing and shorthand test for them, though.'

'And you'll pass with flying colours,' Percy said with conviction. 'I'll walk with you to the bus stop, lovey. I could do with a blow of fresh air. And I'll get a Lyon's sponge from the shop and we can have a slice of that and a cuppa when you get back while you tell me all about the new job the agency has offered you.'

Harrie smiled at him tenderly. The encouragement he was giving her was just what she needed to keep her mind focused, not dwelling on what might have been but only what could be in the future.

The three people waiting at the bus stop were glad to see a bus approaching in the distance.

Iris was relieved it was on its way because Black's Taxis' office was just across the way and the last thing she wanted was for her son to spot her waiting. He'd immediately know what she was up to and challenge her, and she didn't want an altercation in the street with him regardless of his concern for her welfare.

Harrie was relieved to see the bus on its way because it was eight minutes late and she was cutting it fine to get to the agency. The last thing she wanted was to arrive late. That wouldn't create the right impression at all.

Her attention was fixed too firmly on the bus, willing it to hurry, for her to notice the car that overtook it and passed the bus stop only to come careering to a stop a little further down the street. The driver leaped out and came striding towards the bus stop.

Harrie jumped and spun around as she heard her name being called, immediately recognising the voice. 'Jeremy!' she exclaimed.

He was advancing on her with a most annoyed expression on his face. 'I've just been round to your house and was surprised to find no one in,' he said, heedless of the interested onlookers. 'Are you on your way to see me?'

She shook her head. 'No.'

'Oh! I trust you're on your way to see the doctor then?'

She shook her head again. 'No, I'm not.'

'Well, where are you off to?'

'Where I'm going is really none of your business any more, Jeremy.'

'Not my business! Of course what you do is my business, I'm about to become your husband, Harriet.' He gave an aggrieved sigh. 'This has gone on long enough. After your display of dramatics in the office last Friday I thought it best to leave you alone for a couple of days, let you come to your senses. I did think you'd have paid me a visit by now to offer an apology, though. Obviously your condition isn't getting any better. I really must insist you see a doctor and get medical help.' He took her arm and made to guide her towards his car as he continued speaking. 'I have an hour before my next client is due so I have time to take you to my family GP and . . .'

'I'd be obliged if yer'd take your hands off my daughter.'

Jeremy turned his head to look at Percy in surprise, not having noticed his presence. 'Oh, er . . . Mr Harris. Good morning. I didn't see you, I do apologise. Please excuse us but I must get Harriet to the doctor.'

She pulled her arm free. 'I do not need to see a doctor, Jeremy, I'm not ill.'

'Oh, but darling, you are,' he insisted, retaking her arm. 'There's no other explanation for the way you're acting.'

She tugged her arm free again. 'Jeremy, for the last time, I am not ill. If anyone has a problem it's you.'

He looked stunned. 'Me?'

She sighed. 'You have to accept that it's over between us. We're not right for each other. I can't make you the sort of wife you want, and you won't make the sort of husband I want for myself. That's why I thought it best to hand in my notice at work and leave immediately, give us both a clean break.'

'We *are* right for each other. I won't accept that you think we're not. I knew you didn't really mean to give in your notice. You just did it in the heat of the moment because you weren't thinking straight due to pre-wedding nerves, so I retrieved it and explained to Miss Rayner that you're sick.'

'You did what? Jeremy, you had no right to hold back my notice or tell Miss Rayner that I'm ill when I'm not.'

'Listen here, lad,' piped up Percy, stepping between Jeremy and Harrie, 'I know it must be a shock for you, Harrie calling the wedding off, but you're going to have to accept my daughter's decision that it's over between yer.'

'I will never accept that,' he said resolutely. 'I love Harriet and I know she loves me. As far as I am concerned we're still getting married as we planned to do in seven weeks. Once she's been given the right medication by the doctor she'll soon be back to her normal self, you see if I'm not right.'

He made to step round Percy and take Harrie's arm again but his shoulder caught the older man a glancing blow, sending him tumbling backwards to land against the concrete post of the stop.

Iris, who hadn't been able to stop herself from taking an interest in this saga being played out before her, couldn't believe her eyes at what she had just witnessed. Before she could help herself, she'd swung back her handbag and launched it at Jeremy, shouting as she thrashed her bag repeatedly against his arm, 'Oi! And just who the hell are you to be pushing an old gent about?

Shame on you! Shame on you, you hear? And trying to drag this young lady off to the doctor when she doesn't want to go . . . well, that's kidnapping, that is.'

Jeremy, shocked himself to realise what he had done to Harriet's father, albeit accidentally, was holding up his hands, trying to fend off the blows from the handbag of his mysterious assailant. 'I didn't mean to do it. It was an accident. Now stop hitting me, will you? Stop it, I said.'

Harrie was over by her father now, arm around him protectively. 'You all right, Dad?' she demanded urgently.

'I'm fine, me ducky.' He could tell she wasn't convinced and added, 'I'm fine, really. I was just taken off guard, that's all. I need to catch me wind.'

Fatigue getting the better of her, Iris finally stopped her attack and stood with hands on hips, glaring at Jeremy. 'Bloody bully, that's what you are, a bloody bully.'

Rubbing his throbbing arm, Jeremy was glaring back at her. 'How dare you accuse me of being a bully?' he snapped at her, outraged.

'Well, from your performance just now there's no other way I or anyone else could describe yer,' she answered him back. 'I heard that poor gel say it was over between yer, but just 'cos you don't want it to be, then as far as you're concerned it ain't. If that ain't bullyboy tactics I don't know what is. Look, lad, you might think that you can browbeat this young lady into doing what you want, but do you really think by forcing her to be with you it'll all end up happy ever after? If yer do, then yer want yer brains seeing to. You'd be best to put this down to experience and find a woman who wants you for who and what you are. Leave this gel here free to do what she wants.'

'This lady is right, Jeremy,' chipped in Percy. 'My daughter knows her own mind and she's made it up that you and she ain't right for each other. Best you say your goodbyes before this turns nasty.'

Jeremy was staring at them both, opening and closing his mouth fish-like. He looked at Harrie and she could plainly see the hurt he was suffering. 'Are you sure you want to call the wedding off? Really sure, Harriet?'

She nodded. 'It's for the best, Jeremy, really. We wouldn't

make each other happy, I know we wouldn't. If it's any consolation, I do still care for you very much.'

He heaved a long resigned sigh and his shoulders sagged. 'Mother is going to be so upset when I break this news to her. She really liked you, Harriet, and was so looking forward to having you as her daughter-in-law.' He leaned over and kissed her cheek. 'I hope you find what you're looking for. I'm just sorry it wasn't me. Goodbye, Harriet.'

With his head hanging, he walked back to his car and drove away without a backward glance.

Harrie watched him go, her bottom lip trembling, then a trickle of tears ran down her face. 'Oh, Dad,' she faltered. 'I'm so sorry I hurt Jeremy, I really am.'

'Better this way, ducky, than living for years trapped in a marriage you didn't want to be in,' said Iris, putting a comforting hand on her arm.

'You know, this lady is right. That's why you finished with Jeremy in the first place,' said Percy, sliding his arm around his daughter's shoulders and giving her a comforting hug.

'Are you all right?' Iris asked him.

He flashed a smile at her. 'I feel a bit foolish having a lady come to my rescue but I'd like to thank you all the same.'

Iris was just grateful not to be accused of interfering in something that was nothing to do with her, which in truth was what she had done. 'Your daughter needs a cup of sweet tea,' she suggested. 'Best tonic for an upset.'

'That's what my dear late wife would have prescribed. I'll take her into the café over there and get her one. Er . . . would you care to join us?' Percy asked out of courtesy.

Iris looked down the street to see the bus disappearing into the distance. In the excitement of the scene at the bus stop, none of the onlookers had thought to wake it to a halt. There was at least another fifteen minutes to wait for the next, longer if it was late which was usually the case. The incident had fatigued her and a sit down with a welcome cup of tea to revive her before her trip to town would be a good idea. She would also like to satisfy herself that this lovely young girl, who was still clearly upset, was none the worse for her ordeal.

'I'd love to,' she replied, smiling warmly.

*   *   *

Later that evening Iris put Chas's plate of dinner before him and sat down opposite. 'Sorry it's such a mishmash of leftovers, son, but I never got to the shops 'cos I . . . er . . . was busy today.'

From under her lashes she cast a quick glance at her son. Despite the fact that she would dearly have loved to divulge her escapade of today and the promising results, she sincerely hoped he did not ask her just what she had been busy doing because then her intended trip into town would come out. He would not be happy to learn about that despite the fact that in the end she had never actually made it, nor would he like to hear of the way his mother had acted like a fishwife in the street, launching an attack on a perfect stranger, albeit coming to the defence of someone else.

Chas had had a day of it himself. It had seemed to him that everyone suddenly needed a taxi and it had been non-stop. He hadn't even managed to snatch a lunch break but had had to eat the sandwiches his mother had packed him up that morning as he'd driven between jobs.

Now he scanned the contents of his plate. Heaped on it was a mound of cheesy, lumpy mashed potato, a more than well-done burst sausage, slice of corned beef, the remains of the over-cooked roast from yesterday, all swimming in a sea of baked beans. Considering that this was a woman who had once decided to make a chicken and leek pie, but not having chicken thought chunks of belly pork would do the job just as well, and leeks being out of season substituted Brussels spouts, today's offering looked fine to him.

'I hope you haven't been overdoing things, Mam?' he said as he piled his fork with food.

'Oh, no, definitely not,' she said lightly, and thinking it best she change the subject before she told him any more lies to cover up her misdemeanours, asked the first thing that came to mind. 'Fancy a stroll with me down the pub after dinner?'

He looked across at her in surprise. 'I've never known you ask me to accompany you down the pub, it's usually the other way round.'

'Well, yes, but . . . you never went last Friday,' she babbled. 'You're not one for going out but you do like a couple of pints on a Friday after work, and being's you never went last week 'cos you said you was too tired and there was summat good on the telly you wanted to watch, well, I thought you might fancy going tonight instead? And if so I would go with you 'cos I'd quite like a half meself . . .' and she added before she could check herself '. . . after the afternoon I've had.'

He eyed her sharply. 'Why, what happened this afternoon?'

'Oh, nothing, nothing, son, just a turn of phrase, that's all. I had a boring afternoon, if you must know. Yes, extremely boring. So boring in fact it's not worth talking about. Well, eat up before yer dinner gets cold and afterwards I'll wash up while you get changed to go out.'

Chas inwardly groaned. He'd not been entirely truthful with his mother about his reluctance to partake of his weekly two pints down at the local last Friday evening. He'd feigned tiredness and a desire to watch a programme on the television just in case Nadine happened to be there and forced him to accept the drink she had promised him for laying the rat trap. He'd worried that any further conversation between them might lead to her abusing his good nature, thinking she could call on him for anything and everything at any time of the day or night, as his mother had warned him there was a good possibility she would do. Still, Monday wasn't a popular night for a visit to the pub as most people hadn't the spare money for drinking after the weekend. More than likely Nadine would not be in there tonight so he felt safe to go. He quite fancied a pint to wash the day's dust out of his throat and it would do his mother good to have a natter over a glass of stout with any of her old cronies who happened to be in there.

A while later, having washed and changed, Chas arrived in the back room to find his mother settled in her armchair by the fire, engrossed in a programme on the television.

'You ready then, Mam?' he asked her.

She looked at him blankly. 'Eh?'

'You wanted to go to the pub.'

Despite the excitement of the day having taken its toll on her, Iris had never had any intention of accompanying her son. 'Oh, er . . . I've changed me mind, son. I'm all settled now. I forgot *Take Your Pick* was on tonight. Now off you go. It will do you good to get out and socialise instead of sitting here of an evening with yer old mam. I'll see you when you get back.'

Fred Bales, the portly landlord of The Blackbird, greeted Chas with a friendly smile when he arrived at the bar. 'Not your usual night. Everything all right with you and yer mam, is it?'

'Yeah, fine, thanks, Fred. Yourself?'

'Oh, can't grumble, ta. Although maybe I can. There's rumours in the trade that the Government intend sticking another penny on the price of beer and fourpence on a bottle of spirits in the next budget, and of course we landlords will bear the brunt of it with the punters. But apart from that my main worry is this new money that's coming in next year. What's it called . . . decimication?'

'I think you mean decimalisation.'

'Do I? Oh, well, whatever it's called, it's still gonna cause chaos. We've had pounds, shillings and pence since the year dot. Why do we need to suddenly go all foreign? I'm gonna have a job getting my head around it myself as well as keeping an eye on my bar staff to make sure they're giving the right change. If it's too much they'll eventually bankrupt me. Too little and I'll have the punters threatening murder 'cos we're fleecing them. My work is going to be more than cut out for me when it comes in, ain't it? But it's the old dears I really feel sorry for, I fear they'll never get the hang of it. At their time of life they're starting to forget things as it is. How the hell are they gonna learn summat as mind-boggling as this new money lark? Usual?'

Chas nodded. He felt Fred was right to be concerned about the new coinage that was being introduced the following year. It was going to cause pandemonium while people got used to it. Regardless, though, it was coming in whether they liked it or not so they'd better get used to it. It would be a sad day, he thought, when the old coins that had been a part of British life forever, it seemed, disappeared in aid of the country's becoming part of what was known as the Common Market. Whether this was a good thing or not, and whether the change of coinage was a prelude to other changes they would have to endure in future, remained to be seen.

As Fred poured out his pint of bitter, Chas glanced around. 'Not very busy tonight.'

'Never usually are on a Monday, Chas. Get a few in just after ten when the twilight shift finishes at the Marconi factory.' He put a frothy pint of Everard's best bitter in front of Chas and took his money. After putting it in the till, he picked up a cloth and as he dried glasses asked Chas, 'Any news on Jack Black yet?'

'He's still very poorly, his wife says.'

Fred pursed his lips. 'Shame to be cut down like that at his age. I have to say I don't think it looks good for him. Jack wasn't what I could call one of me regulars so I don't know him as well as I do some of me punters but personally I found him a pleasant sort of man. I admire the way he built his business up from nothing, working all the hours he did to make it what it is now. All right, so Black's Taxis ain't in what yer'd call the big league compared to the firms based in town, running twice as many cars as Black's, but it's my guess Jack's profit's are enough to keep his wife in stockings. When yer see Mrs Black next please tell her that all of us at the pub are rooting for her husband. Yes, mate?' he said to a man who had just arrived at the bar.

Leaning on it, sipping on his pint, Chas did not see the outer door open and a woman pop her head inside to scan the drinkers. When she spotted her quarry she gave a satisfied smile before stepping in and trotting over to the bar.

'Why, Chas,' said Nadine, arriving to stand beside him. 'How nice to see yer. I've just popped in to buy some ciggies, but while we're both here let me buy you that drink to say thanks for helping me out the other night.'

It seemed to Chas that she was more dressed up for a night out dancing than popping out quickly to get a packet of cigarettes, and he wondered why she hadn't gone to the corner shop to buy them as it was much nearer and considerably cheaper than Fred's pub prices.

'Oh . . . er . . . Nadine . . . How . . . yes, how nice to see you too. I've got a drink, thanks.'

'Which is nearly finished,' she said, observing his near-empty glass. 'I'll get a refill for you.'

'Nadine, there's no need to repay me for what I did the other night. It was my pleasure and I don't expect any recompense.'

She looked at him coyly. 'Oh, Chas, I can assure you the pleasure was all mine.'

The way she was looking at him made him feel mortally uncomfortable. 'Er . . . did . . . you catch anything?'

She looked at him blankly. 'Eh?'

'In the trap?'

'Oh, I dunno, I ain't looked. I was wondering if you would come around and do that for me? I'm scared of rats, living or dead. They wouldn't scare a man like you though, eh, Chas? So you will, won't yer?'

'Er . . . yes, sure. I'll pop round when I get a minute.'

She tilted her head. After running her tongue over her top lip, she said suggestively, 'I'll look forward to it.' Then she clicked her fingers at the landlord. 'Another of what Chas is drinking and I'll have a vodka and black.'

'No drink for me, Fred. Nadine, thanks for the offer but I was just going.'

'Oh, yer can't,' she cried urgently, then hurriedly added, 'I mean, you must let me honour me commitment to say thanks.'

He sighed. 'All right, but just a half.'

She slapped him playfully on his arm. 'Oh, a proper man like you doesn't drink halves. Chas will have that pint, Fred,' she called across to him.

She put her handbag on the counter, opened it and rummaged around for her purse. 'Oh,' she finally exclaimed as Fred put the drinks in front of them. 'Would you believe, silly bugger me has come out without me purse. Oh, what am I like? I hope I didn't forget to put on me drawers,' she added, laughing raucously.

Chas was already fishing in his pocket for his wallet. 'I'll get them. How much, Fred?'

'Oh, you are a proper gent, Chas Tyme, you really are,' said Nadine, batting her eyelashes at him. 'That'll be another favour I owe you. We'll have to have a chat about how I can pay yer back. Maybe . . .'

'No need, really,' he cut her short. 'It's my pleasure, honestly it is.' In a way he was relieved that Nadine had forgotten her purse as he did not feel at all comfortable about a woman buying him a drink, whether it was repaying a favour or not.

'One good deed deserves another, Chas. Er . . . would yer stretch to getting me a packet of Woodbines?'

Chas obliged, then picked up his pint and downed it in one. 'Well, I really must be going.'

'Oh, but won't you have another?' she said, disappointed. 'It's still early.'

'I have an early start in the morning. Well, good night, Nadine. 'Night, Fred,' he called to the landlord.

Nadine snatched up her glass and knocked back its contents. 'Hold up, Chas, I'll walk back with yer.'

He had no way of refusing.

Outside on the pavement she linked her arm through his. 'Oh, a nice big man like you does make a woman feel protected,' she said as they began to make for home, Chas striding and she tottering on her high heels to keep up with him. 'Oh, slow down, will you, Chas? Anyone would think you was in a rush to get home and be rid of me.'

That was exactly what he was trying to do. Never having had a girlfriend, he had never walked down the street before with a woman on his arm and understandably it felt strange to him, but especially strange when it was Nadine whose arm was linked with his, a woman who until very recently had never missed an opportunity to show her scorn of him.

Chas was relieved when they arrived at his entry. He unhooked his arm from hers and said, 'Goodnight, Nadine.'

'Oh, ain't yer going to see me to me door, Chas?'

'Pardon? Oh, well, it's only just there.'

'It might be but it's dark and anything can happen to a woman on her own in the dark.'

She had a point, he supposed. 'Come on then.'

He stepped the several paces with her to her entry then made to take his leave but she got in first with, 'Thanks for tonight, Chas. I really enjoyed it. We must do it again, I'll look forward to it. Oh, don't forget you're going to pop round and check the trap. See yer.'

With that she disappeared off down the entry.

As Chas made his way home, a happy Nadine let herself in by the back door of her mother's house. She had been disappointed every night since she'd first put her plan into operation not to have caught Chas down at the pub, but patience had paid off and tonight she had.

It was a mystified Chas who let himself back inside his house to join his mother. He couldn't understand why Nadine was suddenly acting the way she was with him. She didn't have to be so familiar to get him to help her with the alleged infestation of her yard, she knew enough about him to know that. He would check the trap, he decided. Hopefully it had done its job and that would be the end of it.

CHAPTER TWELVE

The next day, just after twelve-thirty, Chas was making his way into the drivers' rest room to eat his lunch while he waited for his next fare when he stopped short, spotting a young woman backing out of the boss's office, pulling along a bulky sacking bag.

Having no idea who she was but regardless about to offer to help her with the bag – whatever she was doing with it – he was stunned suddenly to be shoved aside by three other drivers charging out of the rest room and across to the woman, all proclaiming, 'I'll help yer with that bag.'

Chas heard her say, 'Thanks, very much appreciated. It's rubbish to go in the dustbin.' Still with her back to Chas she watched the men vying with one other to do the job for her. She suddenly seemed to sense his presence and turned to look across at him. Her face broke into a bright smile. 'Hello, I'm Harriet Harris. My friends call me Harrie though,' she said as she stepped across to him, holding out her hand. 'I'm the temporary office help.'

He smiled back at her. 'I'm Charles Tyme. Chas. Another of the drivers.'

As their hands clasped and their eyes locked, Chas experienced a peculiar sensation shooting through him. His heart started to race, a rushing sound filled his ears. Time suddenly seemed to stop. Nothing else around him existed but this woman whose hand he was clasping, whose magnetic emerald-green eyes his own unremarkable blue were staring into.

Simultaneously Harrie was thinking that there was something about this big man whose bear-like hand was clasping hers that seemed very familiar to her, but there couldn't be as she had never met him before. Then suddenly she had the overwhelming feeling that he was important to her, that this meeting was a significant milestone in her life, but she had no idea why or what part he was going to play or how she could know this. Then one reason why he was familiar to her registered. His mother had talked so much about him yesterday in the café that in truth Chas Tyme wasn't a stranger. Then she realised he was looking at her strangely and seemed to be frozen to the spot. Besides that he was holding her hand so tight he was cutting off the blood supply and it was beginning to hurt her.

'Are you all right?' she asked in concern.

Through the wind-like rushing that was filling his ears, Chas heard her voice and was jerked out of his trancelike state. 'Sorry,' he blurted.

'I asked if you were okay?' Harrie repeated.

'Eh? Oh, yes, I'm fine. Absolutely fine. Couldn't be better.'

She looked relieved. 'Good. Er . . . do you think I could have my hand back, only you're crushing it.'

'What!' he exclaimed, mortified. He dropped her hand as if it was suddenly burning him. 'I . . . er . . . sometimes don't know my own strength, I'm so sorry. I haven't hurt you, have I?' he asked worriedly.

Thankfully feeling was returning and she smiled. 'No damage done. It's nice when a man's got a firm handshake, shows he's got strength of character.'

The loud commotion the men were making as they vied with one other to help attracted Chas and Harrie's attention then. Harrie chuckled as Darren, the victor of the three, slung the sacking bag over his shoulder and gave her the thumbs up sign as he made his way towards the back door that led into the yard, the losers making their way back into the drivers' rest room.

'As payment for me help, I'll settle for a drink with yer down the pub tonight,' Darren called out to her.

'You'll settle for a cuppa here in the office and like it,' she bantered back. Harrie then turned her attention back to Chas. 'How's your mum?' she asked him.

He looked taken aback. 'My mum?'

'She did seem fine when she left us yesterday but . . . well . . . no disrespect to her, she's not as young as she used to be and after what she did . . . well, I was concerned it could have an adverse effect on her. I must find some way of repaying her for coming to our rescue – more than the cup of tea in the café we had after-wards. After all, if it wasn't for your mother I would never have found out that Mrs Black needed temporary help here and gone round to see her to apply. I just thank goodness your mum decided to catch the same bus as I did yesterday. Apart from the fact that the situation with Jeremy might have become worse than it did without your mother's intervention, I'd never have found out about this job here and could be starting one I might not be as happy in. I know I'm going to like being here while Mr Black gets better.

'I am sorry, though, that because of what your mother did and the amount of time we spent talking in the café afterwards it was too late for her to go into town, but she did say I wasn't to worry about that as she could go another day. Oh, does Mrs Tyme like chocolates?'

Chas was feeling decidedly hot under the collar. The feelings he had experienced on their initial meeting were returning, doing things to his insides that he'd never experienced before. His heart was thudding in his chest again and he felt light-headed and couldn't think straight. What Harrie was saying to him wasn't quite registering. He stuttered, 'Me mother . . . er . . . well . . . er . . . yes, she is my mother. Er . . . I mean, I think she likes chocolates.'

Harrie frowned at him. 'You don't know for sure?'

'Er . . . yes, of course I do. Yes, she loves roast beef. Er . . . chocolates.' Oh, God, what must this woman be thinking of him? He was making a fool of himself. He needed to get away from her before he made even more of an idiot of himself in front of her. Just then the voice of Ralph taking details of a pick up from a customer on the telephone filtered through to him. 'I'll do that,' Chas called across.

'But you're just starting your lunch . . .'

'No matter, Ralph. Not hungry. I'll do it.'

Without even excusing himself to Harrie he leaped over to Ralph and waved his hand in front of him for the slip with the details of the job.

Ralph gave him a grin and a wink and in a low voice said, 'Well, Miss Harris is certainly gonna ruffle a few feathers, ain't she, and one person's in particular methinks. Marlene ain't gonna like competing for Darren's attentions, no siree, she ain't.' His grin broadened. 'You liked her an' all, didn't yer, Chas? An old veteran like me can tell.'

'Just give me the details of the pick up, Ralph,' he demanded, snatching the note on which they were scribbled. Before Ralph could pass further comment Chas had gone.

As he set off, part of the conversation he'd just had with Harrie flooded back to him. She had told him she'd met his mother at the bus stop yesterday. Why had his mother been waiting for a bus? Then the rest of what Harrie had relayed to him came back. His mother had told him last night that she had spent a very boring afternoon, so boring in fact that it wasn't worth repeating. Now it seemed her afternoon had been anything but boring. In fact, distinctly eventful. Oh, Mam, he inwardly groaned. Was that trip into town more important than the possible risk to your health? Well, he'd make sure she didn't attempt anything so stupid again after he'd had strong words with her tonight when he got home.

For the rest of the day Chas was thankfully kept busy on the road and had no reason to return to the office except at clocking off time. Before he went inside to sign off, hoping that Harrie had left for the evening, he spent longer than usual tidying the inside of his vehicle ready for work the next morning. It was kept in the compound at the back where taxis not in use on the night shift were kept secure and Terry Bragg, the maintenance mechanic-cum-night security guard, carried out his work.

Having finished his task, Chas was just locking the car securely when he heard a noise close by and turned his head to see Terry lifting the bonnet of the car he'd parked next to.

Terry's job was to deal with any mechanical problem the firm's vehicles were suffering from. He worked during the night in order to keep cars off the road for as short a time as possible. Problems beyond Terry's abilities to cope with on site were dealt with by the local garage just down the road, quickly and satisfactorily. If not too busy with his maintenance duties he would valet the cars inside and wash them outside for which the driver of that particular vehicle gave him a backhander for his trouble. The appearance of their car was in actual fact their responsibility. The drivers were well aware that Terry's promise to share with them any loose change he found down the back of the seats was a hollow one, but if they'd had a good day they didn't begrudge him the chance of making a little extra for himself.

Terry secretly held a deep-seated rancour against the latest driver employed at Black's. Life had been far from fair to him so far, he felt. Having lost both his parents thanks to the German bomb that landed on the Freeman, Hardy and Willis factory during the war, the young boy had been grudgingly taken in by his widowed grandmother, a sour-faced old woman who had not hidden her resentment at having to take in her only grandchild and never ceased to remind him at every oportunity how grateful he should be to her for her benevolence.

Thanks to her lack of encouragement Terry had left school barely able to read and write, and as a result the only work he could secure was low-paid unskilled labouring on building sites. Most of what he earned his grandmother took from him as her attitude was that now she was too old to work any longer as a cleaner, he should be responsible for paying the bills on the damp one-bedroomed flat they shared over a baker's shop next to the notorious Robin Hood pub on the Woodgate. His sleeping quarters there were in the recess in the grimy kitchen-cum-living room, on an ancient flock mattress that stank disgustingly from when he used to wet himself as a child. There was nothing Terry could do about this. Despite his being desperate to escape, the money he was earning did not afford him the means to get a place of his own so he was stuck.

Thirty-year-old Terry was neither short nor tall, fat nor thin. His hair was fine and mousey, features arranged pleasantly enough but not the sort to set girls looking twice – he was thoroughly mediocre, in fact. Regardless, he'd had several girlfriends but once they learned of the existence of his grandmother, and viewed for themselves what possibly lay in store for them in any permanent relationship with her grandson, they had soon beaten a hasty retreat.

His only saving grace was that at the age of eighteen he'd learned about a job cleaning cars at a garage on Frog Island. Thinking it had to be better than what he was doing, he went along to apply for it, despite his grandmother's ridiculing him, saying that he was wasting his time. The owner's limited choice being between Terry or an elderly man who appeared very much on his last legs, a jubilant Terry was set on. During the course of his ten years' employment there, Terry picked up the rudiments of car maintenance by watching the skilled mechanics as they went about their work. Eventually he was trusted by them to carry out some of the easier tasks when the apprentice was otherwise occupied. This gave Terry the necessary skills to apply for the job at Black's just over a year ago when he heard through local gossip that the maintenance mechanic who'd been in the job since Jack had started had finally succumbed to retirement at the grand old age of seventy-five.

Thanks to the unsocial hours it was only Terry who applied for the position. He was eager to get the job not only because the remuneration was a pound a week better than he was getting before, but more importantly because it gave him the excuse to be far less in his cantankerous grandmother's company, listening to her constant nagging. He could sleep through the day and was out at work from six in the evening until six in the morning.

When the driver's job had become vacant just over a month ago, Terry had been desperate to get it, seeing it as his only means of escaping his grandmother's clutches and leaving his miserable existence with her far behind him. In fairness to Jack Black, he had given the application due consideration before explaining to Terry that the person he had picked brought with him years of driving experience which Terry hadn't got. Despite understanding the wisdom of Jack's choice, nevertheless Terry could not help but view big kindly Chas as being solely responsible for locking the door to his escape. His resentment against Chas was not helped by the fact that vacancies for cabbies did not come up very often and it could be years before he got another chance to apply for the job that would give him his only opportunity of bettering himself.

'Nothing serious, I hope?' Chas said to him now.

Terry cast him a nonchalant glance. 'Don't know 'til I have a gander,' he said shortly.

Chas could not understand Terry's brusque attitude towards him. As far as he was aware he'd given the maintenance man no reason to treat him in such an off-hand way. From what he had observed Terry wasn't like this with any of the other drivers. Chas, though, saw an opportunity here of building bridges between this man and himself. Despite his need to get home, he offered, 'Want a hand?'

To Chas's surprise Terry cast him a scathing glance and said, 'Oh, want to do me out of this job too?'

'Sorry?'

'I can manage, ta,' he muttered, pulling out a dipstick and giving it a wipe with an oily rag he'd taken out of his grubby working overalls.

'Oh! Oh, right you are. Good night then.'

Chas received no reply.

Marlene, who had by now taken over from Ralph for the evening shift from six to ten, appeared not to hear the telephone ringing and was thumbing through a magazine when Chas walked in. She glanced up momentarily to see who had come in. As it was no one she considered important, she returned to her magazine.

As he put his car keys into the key box on the wall at the back of her desk Chas said to her, 'Aren't you going to answer the telephone, Marlene? Marlene, I said, aren't you going to answer that phone?' Just then it stopped ringing. 'Marlene, that customer will have gone elsewhere now and Black's has lost a fare.'

She lifted her head and looked at him blankly. 'Couldn't do whatever run they wanted anyway as the three night-shift drivers are already out.'

'I'm still here and I would have done it,' Chas said.

'Oh, well, it's too late now. They've rang off, ain't they?'

Chas couldn't believe her attitude and wondered if Mrs Black had any idea that the evening-shift operator was losing the business money. The poor woman, though, had enough to cope with already without more worry heaped on her. As he walked around the desk to leave he noticed a bulky brown paper bag with a note on top with his name written on it.

'Oh, is this for me?' he said, picking it up and wondering what it was.

'Has your name on it so it must be,' she said dismissively and added in a bored voice, 'That new office woman asked me if I saw you to tell you it was for your mother.' Marlene gave a haughty sniff and flicked back her head. 'She thinks she's summat, she does, telling me to make sure I log in all the jobs properly tonight so she can update the books tomorrow. Bloody cheek! Saying I didn't write down the jobs I handled clearly, and insinuating I can't spell proper. And another thing . . . I saw the way all the drivers went in to say good night to her before they left. Fucking tart, she is! Well, she needn't think she's gonna get her claws into Darren by flashing her eyelashes at him 'cos I saw him first and he's *mine*. He's the only reason I stay in this poxy job. As soon as I finally get him to ask me out, I'm off to summat better than this.'

Just then the telephone started ringing and she snatched it up, announcing bluntly into it, 'Black's. We've no vehicles available at the moment,' then slamming the telephone back down in its cradle. Finally she noticed the way Chas was looking at her. 'What you staring at?' she demanded. 'Shouldn't you be getting off home if yer shift's finished?' Her eyes narrowed then and a nasty smirk played round her lips. 'Oh, I get it, you've got the hots for me, ain't yer? Well, sorry to disappoint yer, but I'm keeping meself for Darren, so piss off and leave me alone.'

Chas couldn't be bothered to point out to this conceited woman that she possessed nothing whatsoever that evoked within him any feelings other than pity. Turning from her, he left the office to make his way home.

Iris greeted him in her usual enthusiastic way, glad to see him home safe and sound. After kissing his cheek, she ordered him to sit at the table and said she would bring his dinner through. It was liver and onions tonight. As usual Chas was ravenous and was glad of anything his mother had taken the trouble to cook him.

They were halfway through the meal, the liver being surprisingly tender for a change and the gravy not too thick or thin, just right in fact, albeit the potatoes sported the usual lumps. They'd been chatting away happily until Iris spotted the brown paper parcel Chas had laid on the table when he arrived home.

'What's in the bag?' she asked.

'What bag?'

'The one you brought home with yer. That one,' she said, pointing to it.

'Oh, yes, I'd forgotten about that.'

Before he could explain how he had acquired it an impatient Iris had leaned over to pick it up, untwist the top of the paper bag and taken a peek inside. 'Oh, it's a half-pound box of Cadbury's Milk Tray. Oh, Chas, thank you, what a lovely thought.' Then she frowned quizzically. 'What are these in aid of? It ain't me birthday, is it?' She looked suspicious. 'These are a peace offering, ain't they? What you been up to, son?'

The reason behind the giving of this box of chocolates came flooding back to the forefront of his mind. Laying down his knife and fork, Chas looked at her meaningfully. 'It's not me who's been up to something I shouldn't, but you certainly have, haven't you, Mam?'

She suddenly realised who the chocolates were from and how

Chas must have come by them. 'Oh, she got the job then, did she?' Iris exclaimed, pleased. 'And these are by way of thanks for the part I played? Well, I wasn't expecting any reward, I'm just glad she's got set on after the way she was made to miss her appointment with that agency yesterday. I'm so glad Mrs Black liked her enough to take her on, but then I knew she would. I'm a good judge of character and I found Harrie such a nice girl . . .'

'I want to know what Harrie meant by saying you'd come to her dad's rescue, Mam?'

'Eh?' She looked alarmed for a second before she gave a nonchalant shrug and said, 'Oh, I don't know what she's going on about, I'm sure. Eh, what do you think of Harrie yerself, Chas? She's a nice girl . . .'

'Quit the matchmaking, Mam.'

'I'm not . . .'

'Don't try and deny that you are,' he interjected. 'Even if I did find her attractive, which I don't,' he added hurriedly before continuing, 'I'm not stupid enough to think that a woman like Harrie is going to look twice at a man like me.'

'Oh, don't be silly,' his mother scolded him. 'It's only you who thinks that because you don't see what a good catch you are. There's gels out there that'd give their eye teeth for a man like you, if only you'd give 'em the chance. I know this is all down to them Dewhurst kids and how they made you the butt of their jokes for all those years you was growing up. I hope they're proud of 'emselves, I really do. But then, folks like them have no conscience.'

His mother was right. It was due to one of the wicked pranks the Dewhursts had played on him that Chas had lost any last shred of confidence he might have had about approaching suitable girls.

He'd just turned sixteen, was starting to notice girls properly for the first time, and earning just about enough money from his job as a lorry driver's assistant to take a date to the pictures and treat her to a bag of popcorn. A new family called the Vines had taken over the corner shop and Sylvia was the younger of their two daughters, the same age as Chas himself. She was not the prettiest of girls roundabouts, quite ordinary-looking and reserved in fact, like himself, but he thought her beautiful. Immediately they met, when she served him with a packet of

Bird's custard powder his mother had sent him to fetch, Chas was smitten. It was obvious to him that she returned his feelings from the way she acted towards him whenever their paths crossed.

How the Dewhursts found out about this budding relationship Chas had no idea but they most certainly did.

After weeks of building up his courage he finally made a decision to ask Sylvia out before his chance passed him by.

Making sure he went into the shop at a time when he knew she'd be helping to serve, and fighting down a bout of nerves, he asked if he could have a private word with her. It was obvious to him that she had a good idea what he wanted to see her about from the way her eyes lit with excitement. She said she would meet him in an hour just inside the entrance to the jetty at the side of the shop, under the lamp-post. Fifty minutes later he was there waiting for her, nervously pacing up and down. When she arrived they stood staring at each other for several long moments.

'Well, what did you want to ask me, Chas?' Sylvia finally prompted him.

'Oh, yes, er . . . well . . .' Then he blurted out, 'I wondered if you'd go to the flicks with me on Friday night? I'd really like that, Sylvia.'

Her reply froze him rigid.

With a look of scorn on her face she said, 'Me go to the flicks with you? Why, you've got to be joking, ain't yer? I wouldn't be seen dead out with you, Chas Tyme.'

With that she spun on her heels and ran off.

It was then he heard sniggering coming from behind a yard wall close by. Bewildered, he went across and stood on tiptoe to look over it. Crouched behind it were all three Dewhursts along with their teenage cronies, convulsed with laughter.

It was Jamie who spotted Chas looking down at them. 'Oh, Quassie, that's the best laugh I've ever had! Ain't it, you lot? Just the best laugh ever. Fancy you thinking any gel is ever gonna be seen out with the Hunchback of Blackbird Road.'

'Yeah,' one of the others piped up, wiping tears from his face with the back of his hand. 'Worth waiting for that was.'

It was then Chas knew he'd been set up for this. He couldn't believe he'd been so wrong about Sylvia. Consumed by humiliation and devastating hurt, the sound of cruel laughter ringing in his ears, he ran for home. In the safety of his bedroom he vowed that he'd never put himself in a situation like that again, and he never had. He never went into that shop again either, but whenever his mother wanted anything made a detour to a shop several streets away instead.

'Mam, the reason I haven't had a girlfriend is because I've never yet met one I fancy enough to take out,' he fibbed to her. 'Now, stop avoiding my question. What did Harrie mean by saying you came to her dad's rescue?'

'It was nothing,' his mother said evasively. Despite the fact he'd only half eaten his plate of dinner, she asked, 'Ready for your pudding?'

'Mam?'

She stared at him. Chas was not going to give up until she had come clean, she could see. Iris sighed and explained, 'There was a bit of an altercation between Harrie and her fiancé... well, ex-fiancé as that was what the altercation was about. The fact that he couldn't accept it was over between them. Things got a bit out of hand and I just stepped in to calm them down before it all turned really nasty, that's all.'

Chas wasn't surprised to hear that an attractive woman like Harriet Harris had been engaged. Her sort could pick and choose who they wanted. He wondered what had caused her to want to break off the engagement? Then he wondered if she'd already got someone lined up to replace her ex-fiancé? He realised with a sense of shock that he hoped she hadn't. Then mentally checked himself. It was no good his even thinking a woman like her would look in his direction, and even if by any remote chance she did, he would never summon the courage to take any action. His only concern should be that while she was covering temporarily for Mr Black, their working relationship was a harmonious one. Unlike the one he shared with the lazy and conceited evening-shift radio operator.

'What do you mean by "stepping in", Mam?' Chas asked her.

'Just ... er ... offered some advice like we old ladies are renowned for doing. Now can we drop this subject?'

'We will after you tell me what you were doing at the bus stop in the first place. Don't bother, I already know. You were going up the town, weren't you?'

Iris's face set defiantly. 'Now look here, son. I appreciate that you worry about me, and look out for me more than any mother could expect a son to do. I had a silly accident a few weeks ago which could have happened to anyone and which I'm fully recovered from now. If you expect me to live the rest of me life going no further than the corner shop unless I've got someone holding me hand, then you can think again. I'm quite capable of catching a bus into town and taking care of meself while I'm there or anywhere else I choose to go. It's me that will know when the day comes that I ain't. All right, Chas?'

He looked at her hard for several long moments. Suddenly it struck him that in his need to protect her after her accident he was actually treating her like a child, insisting she was accompanied everywhere she went. His mother was not a stupid woman and was well aware of the limitations her advancing years placed on her. She would not have risked going into town unaccompanied if she didn't think she was up to it. There would come a time in the future when she would need much more from him but that time was not here yet, despite a silly accident making him think it was. One thing he dare not divulge to her was that he had actually changed his job to make sure he was close to her, only a telephone call away and not the vast distances he'd been when a lorry driver. But then he was still glad that he had done what he had, despite knowing she would be most annoyed should she find out. The real reasons for his job change would remain Chas's secret.

'I'm sorry, Mam,' he said sincerely. 'I have been treating you like a child and it was wrong of me. I know we've all got to go someday. It's just that I want you around for as long as possible, not to lose you through some silly avoidable accident.'

She smiled warmly at him. 'I know it's what happened to yer dad that's behind this. But you can't let fear ruin your life. Anyway, I intend leaving this world from the comfort of me own bed at least another twenty years in the future. Now finish yer dinner and I'll get yer pudding then afterwards we can settle down to watch the telly.' A wicked twinkle in her eyes she added, 'If yer a good boy I'll let you choose the first chocolate out of the box Harrie kindly bought me. So long as it's not the orange cream.'

An hour later a few streets away Marion was staring at Harrie agog. 'No? No . . .' she was interjecting now and again as Harrie relayed the events of the last two days to her. 'No . . . Really? . . . Well, I never.'

When Harrie had finally brought her up to date she sucked in her cheeks then exhaled loudly. 'Life certainly is eventful for you, ain't it, gel? Must be the star sign you were born under.' Her face creased into a broad grin. 'Oh, what I'd have given to be there when that old lady launched herself at Jeremy. I bet he got such a shock.'

'I don't actually think Jeremy meant to push my dad. After realising what he'd done, he was probably more shocked by that than by Mrs Tyme battering him with her handbag.'

'Well, I did try and warn you that I had a feeling he might not have accepted you finishing with him and you should be prepared for some backlash. At least he knows now, so he can get on with his life and you with yours.' Marion's eyes lit keenly. 'So this new job. That was a turn up for the books how you got that. Well, you wouldn't have known about it without . . . what was her name . . . the old duck anyway, telling you about it. That's what I call fate. It was meant to happen, you going to Black's Taxis.' She gave a thoughtful frown. 'I wonder what the reason is?'

'Couldn't it simply be that Mrs Black needs someone to take over the office duties until her husband recovers enough to return, and I'm in need of a job?' Harrie tutted. 'You've never been the same since you had a sitting with that gypsy on the front in Skeggie when you went there for the day with Allen a few months ago.'

'Ah, well, are you forgetting that she told me then I had a friend who was going to meet the love of her life through the break-up of one relationship being responsible for bringing about another?'

Harrie pulled a knowing face. 'That could be aimed at any of your friends, Marion.'

'The gypsy said close friend, and I've only got one close friend and that's you. So have you met all the drivers yet 'cos it could be one of them?'

'Most of them I have, and most are already married. The ones that aren't didn't exactly sweep me off my feet.'

'That old lady who came to your rescue . . . She told you about her son who works there, that's how she knew Mrs Black was looking for someone temporary in the office. Did you meet him?'

'Yes.'

'And?'

'And what?'

'Was he handsome?'

'Not what you'd call handsome, but he's certainly not ugly.'

'Athletic body?'

Harrie shook her head. 'More the cuddly bear type.'

'What, small and fat?'

'No, tall and well-made. I meant the grizzly bear type not the teddy bear. But then not a nasty grizzly bear but a gentle one, that type. I'm sure you know what I mean.'

'Not your sort then?'

'I don't know what my sort is, Marion.'

'I'm sure you'll know when you meet him. I did immediately I met my Allen. Well, maybe not immediately but I soon realised he had possibilities as I got to know him better.'

Harrie looked at Marion thoughtfully. 'When you first met Allen, did you feel funny inside?'

'Not inside I never, but my foot certainly hurt me! He stood on it when he was pushing past me to get to the bar. You should remember, you were there when I met him. Anyway, why did you ask me that?'

'Oh, no reason,' Harrie replied evasively.

'I don't believe you. Tell me?'

She sighed. 'When I first met Jeremy, quite honestly it was his looks that attracted me to him. I was shocked to find out he fancied me too and, well, you know what happened next. When I met Chas . . . that's Mrs Tyme's son's name, well . . .' Her voice trailed off and she fought for words to describe how she had felt when they shook hands.

'Well, what?' snapped Marion.

'It's hard to describe, Marion, but it was like I already knew him. I just have this feeling that somehow he's going to be important in my life though I have no idea why. What would make me feel like that? I've never met him before, I know I haven't.'

'What was he like with you then?'

Harrie pulled a face. 'Well, I have to say I got the impression he wasn't very comfortable with me but I can't think what I did to make him feel like that.'

'Is he married? Engaged? Courting?'

'Not according to his mother. Actually, now I come to think on it, she was rather going on about all his good points to me.'

Marion laughed. 'Seeing you as a possible daughter-in-law, do you think?'

'Well, if she is then she's wasting her time because whether Chas is my type or not, judging by the way he was with me I don't think I'm his cup of tea. Anyway, Marion, I'm still getting used to what's happened between me and Jeremy so men aren't my top priority at the moment. I do like my new job, though, and feel I'm going to be happy there.'

'Well, it'll give you a breathing space until you find something you want to take on permanently.' A thought struck Marion then and her face lit up. 'Eh, maybe it's through Chas introducing you to someone he knows that you'll meet the great love of your life, and that's why you got the feeling he was going to be important to you when you met him.'

'Oh, yes, maybe that explains it. But I hope he doesn't introduce me for a while. It's as I said, I'm not in the mood to meet any new man yet, great love of my life or not.'

Just then Allen popped his head round the door. 'Is it safe to come in?'

'What do you mean, is it safe?' his wife shot at him.

'Well, I didn't know whether you were talking about me,' he said, a cheeky grin splitting his face.

A look of scorn filled his wife's. 'As if we haven't got better things to talk about than you. What's so important you need to disturb us?'

'Well, being's I know you two well enough to realise that you'll be sitting in here gossiping for hours, I thought I'd pop down the pub . . .'

'And you haven't any money,' Marion pre-empted him. 'Help yerself to the loose change in me purse. That's if you don't mind pot luck tomorrow night instead of the pork chop I was going to get you.'

He looked at Harrie, feigning sorrow. 'I get pot luck every night, Harrie. My wife saying she was going to get me a pork chop tomorrow is for your benefit only so you'll be under the false impression she feeds me proper.'

Allen laughed as he dodged the teaspoon that was thrown at him by Marion, which clattered against the wall.

'Keep some of that change back and bring us home a bag of chips,' she told him.

After he had left and Marion had made them both a cup of Nescafe and opened a packet of custard creams for them to munch on, she asked Harrie, 'This job at the taxi place – what does it involve?'

'Keeping the office running smoothly, I hope. There is something I need your help with though, Marion.'

'Oh?'

'Well, the office work itself doesn't pose me any problems as such. Of course, from the mess I've been wading through today I'd say Mr Black doesn't seem to have a very structured system so I'm going to have my work cut out sorting through it all and trying to make sense of it. I'm very glad now that when I did my secretarial course, I also did book-keeping. Although I wasn't all that keen on doing it at the time it will serve me in good stead now.' She paused and looked at her friend expectantly. 'I do need to ask you a favour, though. Rather a big one.'

'Oh?'

'Will you teach me how to do wages, Marion? I've never done that before. Well, you being a wages clerk, who better to ask for help? I need to learn before Friday as that's when I have to make the wages up. It can't be that hard, can it? I thought if you could spare me an hour for the next three nights then I should be able to cope all right by myself on Friday.'

Marion was gawping at her. 'You're asking me to teach you in three hours what it's taken me years to learn?' She shook her head in disbelief. 'Oh, Harrie, you never cease to amaze me. Did you tell Mrs Black you hadn't done wages when she interviewed you?'

She nodded. 'Yes, 'course I did, but all she said was that I can't make any more mistakes than she has since she's been trying to do them. I did tell her I had a friend who would show me all I needed to know and I can't tell you how relieved she looked when I said that.'

'Then all I can say is, it's a good job you have me as your friend then, ain't it?' Marion said sardonically.

CHAPTER THIRTEEN

A few streets away from where Marion lived, Clarice was looking at her daughter suspiciously. 'Are you hoping your prat of a husband is gonna come round and proclaim himself a changed man – beg you and the kids to go back to him?' Which was what she herself was secretly hoping.

From her position by the kitchen window where she was keeping watch, Nadine turned to look across at her mother, framed in the back-room doorway, leaning heavily on her walking stick. 'Not on your nelly! I wouldn't care if that man turned himself into the Angel Gabriel, me and him are over.'

'Huh! Well, what are you up to then?'

'Wadda yer mean?'

'Eh, don't treat me like I'm the village idiot. No sane woman dolls herself up to stand staring out the kitchen window. You're waiting for somebody,' Clarice said accusingly.

Nadine was, and this waiting game was frustrating the hell out of her. Chas had said he would come round to check if anything had been caught in the trap. Two nights later he still had not shown. What was the matter with the man? Was he too thick to notice she was taking a great interest in him and now it was up to him to move matters on?

Nadine wanted the new life she had planned for herself and wasn't prepared to play the normal courting game, months passing while the relationship deepened. Her aim was to pass on all the preliminaries, going straight to the final stage. She needed to come up with something else to give that dim-witted idiot Chas Tyme a shove in the right direction. The rat idea had been a great one, knowing how helpful Chas was. She knew he would eventually come round to check it like he'd said he would but he obviously didn't think there was any great urgency. She was fed up with dolling herself up just in case he should show. She'd already used the pub as an excuse to bump into him, couldn't use that again so soon. Besides, he didn't go down there that often and she herself hadn't the money to spend on drinks in the hope that he would.

Trouble was, she knew, Chas didn't believe someone as good-looking as her would glance at the likes of him twice when she could have any man she wanted. After all the years she had spent convincing him at every opportunity that he was worth no more than something she'd scrape off her shoes, her task wasn't going to be easy, that she did know. Nadine was angry with herself now for siding with her brothers to make him the butt of their cruel fun. She hadn't had the foresight then to see the likes of Chas as her eventual saviour. Still wouldn't have unless her mother had pointed it out to her. She realised it was more than likely he was not going to ask her out on a date so it was up to her to manipulate him into taking her out. But how?

She realised her mother was shouting at her. 'Eh?' Nadine snapped back, irritated.

'Fucking deaf cow, you are. For the third time, who are yer waiting for?'

'Oh, Mam, give it a rest, will yer? You're getting on me nerves.'

Her mother's face darkened thunderously. 'Don't you speak to me like that, you nasty-tongued bleeder!' She raised her stick and stepped forward, meaning to strike her daughter with it, but forgot she was standing on the step that led down into the kitchen. Before she could stop herself she had toppled forward to land with her head thudding against the hard floor.

Nadine stared frozen at the still figure of her mother sprawled before her, her grotesque legs looking like thick gnarled tree trunks. Oh, God, she's dead, she thought. Next part of her thought, Thank God. Then panic reared. Whether she liked the woman or not this was her mother after all, and although Nadine was desperate to get herself from under Clarice's roof she didn't wish her dead. She bent down and put her ear to her mother's mouth. She was still breathing. She really ought to get medical help. The kids were all in bed upstairs but they'd be all right while she ran to fetch a doctor. Then a thought struck her and Nadine smiled. God had answered her prayer and sent her this golden opportunity to call on Chas. What better excuse could she have than this? As she rushed around to the Tyme house, she was muttering under her breath, 'Don't you dare be out, Chas Tyme. Don't you dare be.'

She almost hugged him with relief when he answered the door to her. Before he could ask what she wanted, she cried, 'Oh, Chas, Chas, thank God you're at home! It's me mam.'

'Your mother? What about her, Nadine?'

'She's had an accident. She fell and bashed her head in the kitchen and she's out cold. I thought she was dead but she's still breathing. I don't know what to do. Can you help me, Chas, please?'

Iris appeared in the doorway then, squeezing herself in beside the bulk of her son. She did not look pleased to see who their caller was. 'What can we do for you, Nadine?' she asked stiltedly.

Nadine's eyes narrowed darkly. Chas's mother interfering was the last thing she wanted. 'It's Chas whose help I need, Mrs Tyme.'

'It's Mrs Dewhurst,' explained Chas. 'She's had a fall in the kitchen and knocked herself out.'

Iris was not at all happy that this young woman had started to call on her son for help. Nadine and her brothers had caused him much grief in the past, the effects of which he was still suffering. Just because this woman seemed to have forgotten her own appalling past behaviour didn't mean that Iris could. 'I don't see how my Chas can help as he's not a doctor,' she said stiffly. 'Do what we'd do in the circumstances and call an ambulance.'

Chas shot a look at his mother, shocked by her uncharacteristic sharpness and reluctance to help, though also appreciating why she was acting as she was. Pulling her out of earshot of Nadine, he said to her, 'Mam, I know the Dewhursts aren't your favourite people, they're not mine for that matter, but Mrs Dewhurst needs help.'

'There's other neighbours they can ask, so why us?'

'Now's not the time to argue the toss, Mam. Mrs Dewhurst could be in serious trouble and we need to act.'

She looked shamefaced. 'Yer right, son. You go with Nadine and see what's what and I'll pop over to Fran Parker and ask if I can use her telephone to call an ambulance. She's funny about people using it but in the circumstances I'm sure she'll let me if I bung her the pennies to pay for the call.'

Nadine clung to Chas's arm all the way back to her house where they found Clarice in a dazed state, struggling to sit up.

'What the fuck happened?' she said, voice slurred as though she was drunk.

Chas squatted down on his haunches beside her, putting his arm around her back to help her sit up. 'How do you feel, Mrs Dewhurst?'

She looked at him, befuddled. 'What the hell are you doing in my kitchen?'

'You've had a fall, Mrs Dewhurst. Nadine fetched me to help. My mam's telephoning for an ambulance.'

'Fall? I had a fall?' Her face screwed up as she tried to remember. She looked past Chas to Nadine hovering behind him. 'Did you push me?'

'No, I never bleddy pushed yer,' she cried indignantly. 'You was standing on the kitchen doorstep and went to hit me with yer bleddy walking stick and lost yer balance.'

Clarice looked unconvinced. 'Huh! You sure you never tried to do me in?'

'You wouldn't still be breathing if I had, I can assure you.'

'All right, ladies, that's enough,' said Chas, sensing World War Three about to erupt. Do you feel all right, Mrs Dewhurst?'

'Oh, fucking great,' she sneered. 'Ready to dance the Gay Gordons.'

'Mother,' Nadine scolded her.

'Well, what a stupid question! This bloody kitchen floor is hard and me head feels as though me brains are pouring out where I bashed it.'

'Well, the ambulance men should be here soon and they'll advise us what to do now. I don't think it's advisable to move you until they've checked you over, Mrs Dewhurst,' said Chas politely.

'I don't need no ambulance. I think we should call the police and have her questioned,' she said, glaring up at Nadine.

'Give it a rest, will yer, Mam? I won't tell you again, I never tried to kill you.'

Chas stood up and went across to Nadine. 'The ambulance shouldn't be long.'

'You're not going?' she cried, grabbing his arm.

'Well, I don't see what more I can do . . .'

A miracle had happened to get him here and Nadine had no intention of letting him leave until she had at least furthered her plan a little. 'Oh, please don't leave me! What if the knock to me mam's head is more serious than it looks and . . . well, I don't know. I can't cope, not on me own with her. Please stay 'til the ambulance men get here, Chas . . . please?' she begged.

He sighed. 'All right, I'll stay. I'll put the kettle on and mash you a cuppa,' he offered, glancing around the cluttered, filthy kitchen for a sign of any clean cups. Clean anything, in fact.

'I could murder a gin,' piped up Clarice, hands cradling her head where she had hit it on the floor.

'I don't think that's advisable, Mrs Dewhurst,' said Chas, looking worried.

'Listen here, Sonny Jim, if I say I want a gin then I want one.'

'We ain't got no gin, Mam, so you can't,' Nadine told her.

Just then a tap sounded on the back door and an ambulance man appeared.

'See, I told yer I didn't need no ambulance fetching,' snarled Clarice ten minutes later, now sitting in her shabby armchair in the back room, swollen legs resting on the stool. She glared suspiciously at her daughter. 'But I still ain't convinced it was an accident I had.'

Chas was desperate to make his escape. He said to Nadine, 'Your mother needs peace and quiet so I'd better be off. Oh, by the way, I popped over and checked that trap on my way to work this morning and it's empty. I let myself in by the back gate as quietly as I could so as not to disturb you all. If you have got a rat it's a clever one. I will keep my eye out, though.'

So Nadine's vigil at the kitchen window every evening since he'd laid it, all dressed up and hoping to catch him, had been a total waste of time. She couldn't let him go tonight without making some sort of arrangement for him to take her out. Her mind was working feverishly as she followed him to the back door to see him out. As they passed through the kitchen her eyes caught the stack of dirty dinner plates piled in the sink and an answer miraculously presented itself.

As she opened the door for him she said, 'Thanks, Chas.' And before he knew what was happening she had reached up and kissed his cheek. 'You really are Mr Wonderful, ain't yer?' she huskily uttered, batting her eyelashes at him. 'I don't know what I'd have done tonight without yer.'

'Oh, er . . . it was the least I could do for a neighbour,' a mortally uncomfortable Chas blustered back.

'We're more than neighbours now, ain't we, Chas? Things like this happening bring people close together.'

He swallowed hard. 'Well . . . er . . . best you get your mam to bed like the ambulance man suggested.'

Nadine purposely waited until he had walked through the back door and was halfway down the yard before she called after him, 'Oi, Chas, I could thank you by taking you for a curry one night down that new Indian place that's opened on Woodgate. I'll book a table for us and let you know when for. Goodnight.'

He froze in his tracks and spun back to face her, mind racing for an excuse to refuse her unwelcome invitation, but she had already closed the door.

Standing with her back to it Nadine was smiling, very pleased with herself. This was the second time since returning home she'd had cause to thank her mother. First for opening her eyes to Chas's potential, and now due to her accident tonight in pushing forward her plan to entrap him a little more. All she had to do was get him to the restaurant. Friday night would be best, she felt, only two nights away. She was confident that with a few pints and hot curry down him, a quick shag in a dark corner of the jetty afterwards, they'd practically be engaged. She really ought to start proceedings to get out of her marriage to Phil as quickly as possible because she wanted to be free to marry Chas as soon as she'd manipulated him into asking her.

CHAPTER FOURTEEN

The next evening a weary Chas was driving back to the office after dropping off his last fare – hopefully his last anyway if he wasn't radioed to cover a job the night-shift drivers could not tackle because they were late clocking in. One driver in particular of the three employed to cover nights had taken to doing that since their boss had been ill, and no one was actually monitoring their arrival times at the moment or their actual finishing times either.

The night itself was promising to be a cold one. Frost was already forming on the damp pavements. Winter always proved a trial for anyone connected to the transport business. As a lorry driver, sitting for the most part of his working day in a freezing, draughty cab, constantly scraping the icy windscreen, Chas had found it no fun. Now he'd have the task of scraping down a car on frosty mornings ready for use as well as keeping his windscreen ice-free as he drove around, something he was not looking forward to. He wished someone would invent some sort of heating system that worked inside cars rather than merely requiring the driver to open a vent in the dashboard to allow warm air to filter up from the engine. It was a very feeble heating system and didn't really make that much difference. When it rained – and Leicester and the Shires were renowned for their frequent winter deluges – his car's inadequate window wipers struggled to cope and often the motor failed under the pressure. It was constantly in need of repair. It was common practice amongst the taxi drivers at Black's to steal each other's blades in the event that they needed a new one. It was not unusual to arrive for work in a morning and find one or both missing, leaving that unfortunate driver with the task of helping himself to another car's blades or else managing without until the mechanic dealt with the problem.

A brightly lit festive display in a chemist's shop window caught his attention as Chas was driving past. There was an assortment of gift-boxed soap and bath-cube sets, perfumes and men's aftershave. He started wondering what to buy his mother for Christmas which would be upon them in several weeks. He usually bought her slippers and a pound box of Terry's All Gold chocolates, but having spotted the gift sets thought she'd like one of those too. There was a particular brand of soap Iris was fond of. He couldn't quite recollect its name but knew her favourite fragrance was Lily of the Valley. He could ask Freda Lumley the next time he saw her, she would know.

Chas didn't need to wonder what he would receive from his mother. There was always a knitted pullover she'd spent the months between the previous Christmas and the one they were celebrating making up; a box of handkerchiefs with the initial C embroidered in one corner; a pair of slippers; two pairs of socks in black and brown; and a box of Blue Bird assorted toffees. Despite being very grateful for what his mother put together for him, and knowing everything was chosen with love, he would have liked a change, something to surprise him. Realising that made him see that his mother might like a surprise too. Well, this year he would make sure she got one.

As he sat at a junction waiting for a line of cars to pass he glanced quickly at his watch. It was just after six. Hopefully Harrie would have left the office by the time he arrived to sign out. He still wasn't ready to face her after what he felt had been his own idiotic behaviour yesterday. Today he had thankfully been kept busy with a continual run of fares and hadn't needed to find an excuse not to go into the office. He knew he couldn't avoid coming into contact with her for much longer, though, as come Friday he would have to go and collect his wages.

He was vehemently hoping that Harrie hadn't noticed his reaction to meeting her, but should she have, then hopefully by Friday other matters would have taken her attention and she would have forgotten all about it. Chas considered himself nothing special so there was no reason why she should remember him in particular anyway.

The traffic thinned enough for him to manoeuvre safely into the road ahead but as he turned he spotted a hold-up further down where a stream of vehicles was queuing to pass what seemed to be a broken-down lorry, almost blocking the road. He quickly indicated to turn down the next road on the right which would lead him through a maze of backstreets but regardless save him the wait while the lorry was dealt with to allow the traffic through.

He was halfway down a dimly lit, deserted street when something ahead caught his attention. A large object was lying in the gutter. As he got closer he realised it was a person, a man judging by the huddled shape. It was probably a drunken vagrant. But drunk or not, the man was a human being and would freeze to death if he stayed where he was all night. Maybe Chas could rouse him and persuade him to get himself along to a shelter for the homeless, give him the couple of shillings for a bed for the night. Take him there himself if necessary.

As he stopped the car opposite the bundle in the gutter, to his absolute horror a man approaching from the opposite direction thrust out his foot as he passed the tramp, giving him a weighty kick. The tramp issued a low groan.

Chas leaped out of the car, shouting at the attacker, 'Oi, what do you think you're doing?'

The man stared over at him. 'Fucking filthy vermin littering our streets,' he shouted back. 'We don't want that sort round here.' Then, sticking two fingers up at Chas, he strode off.

Chas hurried over to the tramp and knelt down beside him. It immediately struck him that this wasn't the normal kind of vagrant. His clothes, although caked in mud, were far from the rags he'd expect a man of any fallen station in life to be wearing. Nor was there the stench emanating from him that Chas had expected either.

'Hello, mate,' he said kindly, gently shaking the man's shoulder. 'You can't stay here all night, you'll freeze to death.' He gently shook the shoulder again. 'Come on, mate, let me help you up and we can decide what's best for you to do.'

The man gave a soft groan and as Chas looked closer at him he saw bruises forming on his clean-shaven face. It was then he realised with a sense of shock that this was no tramp he was trying to help but a man who had had some sort of accident.

The man's eyes flickered open. After moaning a little he asked painfully, 'Did he get . . . my wallet?'

Chas was horrified to realise that this was an elderly man

who'd been attacked and robbed, not the drunken vagrant he'd assumed. 'Can you sit up?' he asked.

'I . . . I think so.'

With Chas's help he sat up. Cradling his head in his hands, he uttered, 'Thanks.'

'Do you need help getting to the hospital?'

The man lowered his hands and shook his head. 'No, I'll be fine in a minute.'

Chas took a closer look at the abrasions on his face. Thankfully they didn't seem serious. 'Is there somewhere I can take you?' he asked. 'I've a car, I can drive you.'

The old man looked at him appreciatively. 'I'd be obliged if you could take me to me daughter's, if it's not too much trouble. She will see to me. It's just a few streets away. I was on my way there as she's expecting me for me dinner. I was taking a short cut when a man jumped out of the alley and set about me. It all happened so fast.'

'You'd better check your wallet,' Chas told him.

The man felt in his breast pocket and, sighing heavily, nodded.

'Oh, dear,' said Chas, aggrieved that a mindless thug could attack an old man who it was readily apparent wasn't the well-off sort. Immediately his own impulse to help the underdog asserted itself. 'I could help with a few shilling to tide you over?'

The man gratefully patted his hand. 'Thank you, son, you're very kind, but I've a bit put past at home so I'll manage. Thankfully I didn't have that much on me, just a couple of shillings to treat my grandkids with.'

Chas carefully helped him up and over to the car, settling him comfortably inside. The man's daughter was distraught at hearing what had happened to her father and thanked Chas profusely for coming to his aid and getting him to her so she could see to him. Happy in the knowledge that the old man was safe and his injuries only superficial, he politely refused the cup of tea that was being pressed on him. He needed to get home himself before his mother starting worrying about his whereabouts.

He forbore to mention the incident to her on arriving home as he did not want her worrying unnecessarily about her own safety when out and about. She only rarely ventured out alone when it was dark so the chances of something like this happening to Iris were very remote.

CHAPTER FIFTEEN

Friday afternoon found Harrie feeling pleased with herself. All but a couple of the day-shift employees had collected their pay, and none had returned with any queries so far. Hopefully that meant she had worked them all out correctly, and that was thanks to Marion for patiently explaining to her over the last two nights how to calculate the stoppages on each individual's earnings, taking into account their tax codes and marital status using the books issued by the Inland Revenue. Harrie was still far from fully adept, and as she had beavered over her task that morning, had constantly had to refer to the notes she had made during Marion's tutorials. One thing this had brought home to her was that she had never before fully appreciated her friend's responsibilities in her job as payroll clerk. Along with the payroll supervisor, between them they made up the weekly dues for nearly a thousand factory employees and dealt with all the associated problems that arose along the way. Harrie had only twenty-three employees, including herself, to deal with and their pay had seemed to be straightforward, or she hoped she hadn't overlooked anything.

Unlike Marion, though, making up wages was only part of her duties at Black's Taxis. Harrie's eyes fell on the open ledger book in front of her and the piles of paperwork she needed to enter to bring it up to date, making sure that what she entered was in the right column. The book-keeping had fallen behind since Mr Black had been taken ill, and been left undone. As she had gone over the books, though, it had become glaringly obvious that Jack Black himself was haphazard in his book-keeping. She was constantly finding mistakes he'd made which she had to put right in order for her own figures to tally. It seemed to her from what she had uncovered that when Jack Black couldn't get his columns to balance, he just altered figures willy-nilly to achieve it. To Harrie that was no way to run a business.

Her job as secretary to a busy solicitor had not been easy. She'd been constantly on the hop as she had dealt with all the queries and problems that arose, along with all the administration associated with individual clients' problems. Managing the office of a busy taxi firm was no cushy number either and she was having to draw on all her skills and quickly find some she hadn't yet acquired so as to carry out her work to the high standard she always set herself. She was confident, though, that what she had done so far would confirm to Mrs Black that she hadn't made a mistake in taking her on. And when Mr Black did return to take over the reins, Harrie felt she would hand over to him properly accounted books, showing a true picture of how his business was doing and not how he thought it should be doing.

Before she set about the ledger books again, a cup of tea was called for. Harrie picked up her mug and made her way to the drivers' rest room to make herself one. As she passed Ralph at the radio-operator's desk, she asked him, 'Want a cuppa?'

He looked at her appreciatively. Jack had been a very good boss to work alongside but he'd drawn the line at mashing tea for the employees, expecting them to furnish him with one when they brewed up for themselves. 'Oh, ta, ducky, I could murder one. I've been too busy to do the honours.'

Having noticed they were getting low on tea and sugar and making a mental note to add them to her list, Harrie made her way back to her office, stopping en route to give Ralph his mug of tea.

He thanked her, adding, 'You're a breath of fresh air in here, Harrie ducky. Judging by the way the other lads are around yer I'm not the only one that thinks . . .' He was cut short by the telephone ringing and, after excusing himself, started to answer it.

She was just about to enter her office when the outside door opened and she saw a pleasant-faced, middle-aged woman approach the counter. Knowing Ralph was busy and not wanting to keep a potential customer waiting, Harrie went over to see what she could do.

'Hello, welcome to Black's Taxis. Where would you like to go?' she asked the woman, smiling welcomingly at her.

'Well, actually, I don't need a taxi. I'm after one of your drivers. Unfortunately I never got his name but thankfully my dad remembered the name of your firm. It was painted on the side of the car. The driver I'm after is a big man, a very pleasant sort. Obviously a very kind man too after what he did. Sorry I can't be more helpful but do you know which of your drivers I'm referring to?'

To Harrie, there was only one driver this description fitted. She wondered what it was he had done. 'The driver you're after is Chas Tyme. I don't think he's in at the moment. Well, I know he's not, none of the drivers is. Can I give him a message?'

The woman looked terribly disappointed. 'Oh, I'm sorry I've missed him personally as I would like to have thanked him more than I did at the time, but if you could give him this,' she said, handing Harrie an envelope in which she could tell there were coins. 'I just hope it's enough to cover the fare, and also for a pint.' She noticed the quizzical expression on Harrie's face. 'I'd better explain. A couple of nights ago my father was robbed in the street and left in the gutter. Mr Tyme came to his aid.

'I dread to think what would have happened to my dad if your driver hadn't done what he did. My father isn't a young man and the evening was a very cold one. Mr Tyme kindly drove Dad to my house, and when I realised he was a taxi driver and offered him the fare he wouldn't take it, said it was the least he could do and he was just glad my dad was all right. After he'd gone and I'd seen to Dad, I realised that Mr Tyme must have covered the fare himself out of the goodness of his heart. I didn't think it fair he should be out of pocket from coming to my dad's rescue. And Dad wanted to show his appreciation for what Mr Tyme did by buying him a drink, which we hope he'll accept.'

As the woman's tale unfolded, Harrie was thinking that Iris Tyme's fulsome praise of her son was not as exaggerated as she herself had thought. Harrie had worked at Black's for not quite four days but already she knew from what she had overheard the drivers saying that they relished nothing more than telling stories to each other about incidents that happened to them while out on jobs. She had not heard one mention of this, either from Chas's own mouth or via any of the other drivers, so that meant Chas had kept it to himself. There was something special about a man who did not court praise from others for the good deeds he had done. Chas Tyme really was a very nice man, she thought.

'I will make sure Mr Tyme gets this,' she said to the woman. 'I have an elderly father myself so I can imagine how upsetting this was for you. I hope your father has recovered from his ordeal?'

The woman smiled. 'Yes, thank goodness. My dad's attitude is that it's nothing to what he faced on the battlefields in France during the First World War.' She ruefully shook her head. 'I can't think what this country is coming to, though, when old people are being attacked in the street for what bit they have on them.'

Neither could Harrie.

The woman took her leave and Harrie made to return to her office but was stopped by another woman coming through the outer door. Ralph was busy on the radio relaying instructions to a driver about the fare he'd just taken so Harrie asked if she could help the new arrival.

'Is Chas Tyme in?'

She shook her head. 'No, I'm sorry, he isn't.'

Nadine already knew Chas was not because she had checked before she had come in to make sure the car he drove was not parked outside. The last thing she wanted was to ask Chas directly to meet her and for him to find an excuse not to accept her invitation. Knowing the sort of man he was, she realised he would never be able to leave a woman sitting waiting for him. She put a disappointed expression on her face. 'Oh, I was hoping to catch him.' She then noticed Harrie properly for the first time. In a male-dominated environment she had not expected to find a good-looking, smartly dressed woman. For a moment she worried that she could have competition for Chas's affections here, but her fears quickly vanished as it struck her that a woman like this one would not look in Chas's direction so Nadine herself had nothing to fear from her.

Harrie meanwhile was wondering if this was another woman Chas had helped in some way who had come in to thank him. 'Can I give Mr Tyme a message for you?' she asked politely.

Nadine smoothed her hands down her tight short skirt and flicked back her long bleached white-blonde hair. 'Yeah, yer can. Tell him Nadine is expecting him at the Rajah's Palace tonight at eight. I've booked a table for us.'

Harrie fought not to show her surprise. She would never have put a man like Chas and this woman together as a couple. She wondered if people had thought the same of herself and Jeremy when they had learned they were together. But what was more of a surprise to her was the fact that she actually felt a stab of jealousy for the fact Chas was spoken for.

'Yes, of course I'll tell him for you.'

Nadine fixed her with her eyes. 'Make sure yer do,' were her parting words.

Harrie stared after her as she flounced out. There had been no please or thank you and Harrie did not like rudeness in any guise. That woman was mannerless. She wondered what a man like Chas was doing with someone like her. Love was indeed blind, she thought.

Returning to her office, she immersed herself in her work. An hour later there was a tap on the door and Chas entered. She smiled at him warmly. 'You've come for your wages then?'

Prior to coming in Chas had given himself a stiff talking to reminding himself that Harrie would have forgotten all about his making a fool of himself on their introduction. She probably hadn't even noticed. Why would she? He was nothing to a woman like her. He returned her smile. 'Yes, I have.'

She handed them to him. 'I hope they're all correct but I'm sure you'll let me know if not.'

'I'm sure they're fine. Thank you.'

He made to depart but she stopped him. 'Oh, a lady came in and asked me to give you that,' she said, picking up an envelope and holding it out to him.

Chas looked puzzled. 'Oh?'

'She told me you helped her father and they wanted to make sure you weren't out of pocket for the fare, and also to buy you a drink to say thank you.'

Chas looked embarrassed and shuffled his feet uncomfortably. 'Oh, they needn't have done that.'

'People like to say thank you when someone has helped them. Your mother helped me and it gave me pleasure to repay her with a box of chocolates.'

'Yes, well, I suppose so.' Then he remembered a message his mother had given him which he hadn't been able to pass on yet since he'd been avoiding the office.

'Er . . . my mother asked me to thank you only I haven't seen you since.'

Harrie beamed, delighted. 'She enjoyed them, did she?'

He laughed. 'I'll say she did! The way to my mum's heart is through chocolates.'

'Me too, I have to say.'

Harrie suddenly realised that on the occasions Jeremy had bought her chocolates they had been the expensive hand-made kind. They had been very nice and she had felt spoiled by the extravagance of the gift but in truth she would have been happier with a box of Rowntree Dairy Milk. Jeremy hadn't known her preference because he hadn't asked her, had just assumed her taste. It was a little thing, she knew, but this realisation only reaffirmed to her that breaking off their engagement had been the right thing to do.

It also struck her what a refreshing change it was to be having a conversation with a man who wasn't chatting her up. Even the conversations she'd had with Jeremy before he'd asked her out had been peppered with insinuations that left her in no doubt how attractive he found her. Despite being flattered by these, nevertheless they'd had a tendency to make Harrie feel uncomfortable. She also realised that she wanted to know more about this man in front of her. There was something about Chas Tyme that was drawing her to him. She was seeing past his plain looks, his burly build, to the real man who lay underneath, and she found herself liking what she was discovering about him.

From under her lashes Harrie glanced at him, up and down. He was very well presented. He might not dress exactly in the latest fashion but what he was wearing was smart, the colours of shirt, jacket and trousers co-ordinating. Most of the drivers seemed to throw on anything to wear for work, heedless of the fact that they were representing the company in the eyes of the general public, and to Harrie a scruffy appearance didn't make for the kind of impression Black's should be striving for. She wondered if this lapse in dress code had come about since Mr Black had been off ill or if it hadn't crossed his mind that he could be losing business by not insisting his drivers presented themselves smartly for work, as Chas Tyme obviously did.

'I noticed from the wages records that you've only worked with Black's a month. What did you do before that?' Harrie asked, interested. Then added hurriedly, 'Oh, I hope you don't think I'm being nosey?'

He hadn't felt she was prying into his private life at all. The way she had asked the question had left Chas in no doubt that she was genuinely curious about what had brought him to Black's Taxis. He smiled at her. 'Not at all. I was a lorry driver. I did some local runs but a lot of my job was deliveries and pick-ups all around the country.'

'Oh, really?' She rested her chin on her hand before adding, 'I've hardly been out of Leicester myself so I do envy you, having visited all those different places.'

'Unfortunately most of what I saw of each town I visited was their goods yards. The firm I worked for operated to tight schedules so there was no time for sight-seeing.'

'Oh, that's a shame. I suppose, though, you didn't like it that much, considering you left it to take this job as a taxi driver.'

'Oh, I did enjoy it, very much.'

'Really? But you still left that job to come here?'

'Oh, well . . . I was worried about leaving my mother on her own for days on end. She won't admit it, but she's not getting any younger and can't do as much as she used to.'

So he'd given up a job he enjoyed to be on hand should his aging mother need him. Only a man of great integrity would do something so unselfish. Harrie wondered if Jeremy would have. But then she hadn't known Jeremy well enough to be able to answer that question. Yet she had been on the verge of marrying him.

Chas was realising that his initial awkwardness had gone. Instead he was feeling very much at ease in Harrie's company and enjoying chatting to her. In the short time he'd been talking to her he'd revealed more about himself than he ever had before to a woman. Harrie was different from any one he had come into contact with. The feelings he had experienced on their first introduction began to manifest themselves again and he hurriedly pushed them away. He must not read too much into this. Harrie was just being pleasant to another work colleague. More than likely she chatted to all the other drivers like she was doing to him.

Just then Darren breezed in to sit on the edge of her desk. 'Hello, gorgeous,' he said suggestively, looking her in the eye.

'I've come to collect me wages and I can't think of anyone I'd sooner be collecting them from. So what do yer fancy doing tonight then?'

Chas politely excused himself, not wanting to get in the way of them making arrangements with each other to go out this evening. He didn't like the stab of jealousy he was experiencing at the thought either.

As Harrie watched him leave the office she felt annoyed by the way Darren's rude interruption had cut short her conversation with Chas. She fixed Darren with her eyes and said lightly, 'The same as I told you I was when you asked me the same question yesterday.'

He looked downcast. 'Can't you wash your hair another night?'

'No, unfortunately I can't. I've other arrangements every night.'

'He's a lucky fella,' said a disappointed Darren as he stood up. 'You know where I am when you get fed up with him. I can assure you, you'll not want another man after being with me.'

As she watched him saunter out Harrie was very aware Darren wasn't the type who was used to being turned down by women and realised he wouldn't give up on her, certain his charms would eventually win her over. More than likely he felt she was just playing hard to get. Oh, well, she thought, he would eventually get the message. Darren might be good-looking but he didn't appeal to her in the slightest. Neither did he possess the qualities that she now realised she wanted in a man.

She immersed herself in her work and so engrossed did she become in it that it was with a shock that she looked at her watch, expecting the time to be around four o'clock, only to see that it was in fact approaching six. She hurriedly began to tidy her desk. Her father would have been expecting her by now and would be starting to worry where she had got to.

Ready for home, she was just leaving the office when she remembered the message from Nadine that she hadn't given to Chas.

She made her way across to the radio-operator's desk to find that Ralph had gone home and his place had been taken by Marlene for the evening shift.

'Good evening, Marlene,' Harrie said politely. 'Has Chas signed out for the night yet?'

Marlene was not in the best of moods. She had come in early to catch Darren before he signed out for the night, having dressed herself very alluringly she felt in a short white smocked dress, matching white tights and white ankle boots. She had been pleased to see that Darren was still on the premises, in the drivers' rest room chatting to one of the other men, but despite her going in and making a great show of making herself a cup of coffee and endeavouring her best to get herself included in their conversation, which had been about football, she'd only received blank stares in return. It wasn't what she had aimed for and she knew she had made herself look stupid in Darren's eyes.

Without lifting her head from the magazine she was reading, she replied off-handedly, 'How should I know? I've only just come in. Check for yerself in the comings and goings book.'

Marlene's attitude towards her was not lost on Harrie. She hadn't been long in this job and their hours of work had not brought them much into contact with each other, but she had not formed a favourable opinion of the evening-shift operator.

Going over to the table that held the book in question, Harrie was just looking through it when Darren came out of the rest room. On spotting her he sauntered across. 'So what do you think of how City performed last night, Harrie?'

She gave a shrug. 'Have no idea. I know nothing about football.'

'Well, I'd take great pleasure in teaching you all you need to know,' he said meaningfully.

Both of them were unaware of Marlene glaring murderously at Harrie.

She smiled graciously at Darren. 'Thanks for the offer but football doesn't interest me in the slightest.' She walked back to the radio-operator's desk. 'Chas hasn't signed out, Marlene, and I have an urgent message for him which I'd be obliged if you would give him when he comes in.'

The girl scowled darkly at her. As far as she was concerned this temporary office upstart was blatantly flirting with the object of her own desire and Marlene was not in the slightest bit amused. An idea of how to get back at her then presented itself. The message was urgent, was it? Well, if it was that urgent

Harrie should have made sure she passed it on personally instead of landing others with the problem. When the message wasn't received by its intended recipient Harrie's reputation would be blackened and Marlene would make sure her lapse was known to the other drivers who all thought her Miss Wonderful.

Smiling sweetly she said, 'Write it down and if I'll do my best to make sure he gets it.'

'Thanks, Marlene.'

Harrie said her goodnights and left. Much to Marlene's displeasure Darren followed moments later, not even saying goodnight to her.

Chas arrived back soon after. 'Good evening, Marlene,' he said cheerily as he signed out from his shift in the book. 'I'll be glad to get home today. It's been a long one.'

She didn't bother to acknowledge him.

Realising his attempt at polite conversation was totally wasted, Chas hung his keys on the key board and left.

He was surprised when he arrived home to find his mother dozing in her armchair by a dying fire. He couldn't ever remember returning home to find her sleeping.

His arrival roused her and, yawning, Iris struggled to sit up, then gawped when she realised the time. 'Oh, goodness, son. Oh, dear, I haven't dinner started yet.'

'Sit where you are, Mam, I can see to dinner.'

'Oh, but you shouldn't have to, being out at work all day.'

'It won't hurt me for once.' Having taken off his top coat which he temporarily draped over the back of a dining chair he crossed over to her, looking down at her with concern. 'You all right, Mam?'

'Yes, why shouldn't I be? An old duck like me is allowed a nap in an afternoon, isn't she?'

Her defensive tone was not lost on Chas. It wasn't the afternoon, though, it was getting on for seven in the evening. 'Yes, of course you are. It's unusual, that's all.'

'Ah, well, maybe it is. I've had a busy day, that's why.' Before he could ask busy doing what, she levered herself out of her chair, saying, 'Right, let's get the dinner cracking. You must be starving. See to the fire, will you, lovey?'

As she bustled off to the kitchen Chas stared after her. His mother had been up to something, and wasn't prepared to tell him about it. Then he knew. She'd been into town and obviously on her own. He stopped himself from having a go at her, remembering her scolding him for treating her like a child. She was home safe and sound, and as long as she had enjoyed herself Chas should be glad.

'You off for a pint tonight being's it's Friday?' Ivy called out to him from the kitchen.

He was kneeling by the hearth now replenishing the fire. A pint after dinner sounded good to him. A vision of Nadine danced before him then and her announcement that she was booking a table for them as a thank you rang in his ears like a threat. Despite appreciating her intentions he nevertheless couldn't understand her insistence on repaying him in such a way when he had told her a simple thank you was more than enough. The thought of them staring at each other across a table in a restaurant for hours on end did not appeal to him at all. What would they talk about? They had nothing in common. And what if she was waiting to pounce on him in the pub tonight to make the arrangements? How could he refuse her invitation without hurting her feelings? Best he avoided the pub tonight just in case. Hopefully, as other things in her life took over, her offer to him would be forgotten about by next Friday and he could resume the weekly ritual he enjoyed. He was tired anyway and what he would be far better doing was fetching a bottle of stout for his mother and beer for himself from the off-licence, and having a cosy evening by the fire with her as they watched television. An early night would see him refreshed for work in the morning as Saturday was always the busiest day of the week for Black's Taxis.

Harrie arrived home that evening to find her father bustling around the kitchen in the process of preparing a meal for them both. The fact that he was cooking was not what struck her most as he'd taken to doing this frequently when the menu was one he felt capable of tackling. Harrie might not be leaving him for Jeremy but someday she would want to marry and move out. Percy intended to be prepared for that. It was the seeming vigour with which he was going about things that had Harrie looking at her father quizzically. He seemed to have an air of excitement about him that she had never noticed before. She wondered what the cause of that excitement was.

'You won the pools, Dad?' she asked him as she went over to kiss his cheek.

'I wish,' he replied. Then asked, 'What made you say that?'

'You seem to be cock-a-hoop about something,' she replied, stripping off her coat and hanging it on the peg on the back door.

Percy gave a disdainful tut. 'People my age don't get excited, Harrie ducky. There's n'ote left in life we ain't experienced to excite us.'

'That I don't believe. There must be lots of things you haven't done but would love to.'

He turned and grinned at her. 'Yes, there are. Like cook an edible meal for once.' He pulled a face. 'I think you'd better look at this gravy. It's got big lumps swimming around in it.'

She went across to inspect it. There were huge lumps in it and Harrie had a suspicion it was actually on the verge of setting like custard as he'd obviously added too much cornflouer. Adding boiling water and whisking vigorously with a fork in an effort to resurrect the gravy, she asked him, 'So are you going to tell me what's put this spring in your step?

He had his back to her, was mashing the potatoes at the kitchen table. 'Don't know what yer getting at, lovey, I'm sure. Maybe I'm just glad to be alive. When yer've done that can yer set the table, dear, as it won't be long? I put the faggots in the oven for the length of time you said, I've now mashed the spuds, so all I need to do is heat the tin of garden peas and Bob's yer uncle.'

Her father was being evasive with her. Something had tickled his fancy, of that Harrie was positive. Whatever it was he was keeping it to himself. They didn't usually keep secrets from each other, being the close father and daughter they were, so she supposed he would tell her what had happened when he was good and ready.

They had not long cleared the dinner away when Marion arrived.

'Allen's working overtime tonight so I've popped around for a natter with you,' she told Harrie as she took off her coat and settled herself at the kitchen table. 'I'm miffed 'cos he was taking me out for a drink, but then I suppose we could more than do with the extra money for Christmas. If you're wondering what to buy me this year, Harrie, then I wouldn't mind the latest Walker Brothers LP. I heard a track from it on the radio at lunchtime in the factory canteen and it's ever so good. That Scott Walker is some good-looking man, ain't he?'

Harrie flashed her a look as she shook the kettle to check for water and put it on the stove, lighting the gas underneath. 'Who said I was thinking of buying you a present for Christmas?'

'Well, you usually do. And besides, you owe me an extra big one this year considering all the help I've given you this week out of the goodness of me heart. How did you get on, by the way?'

She was putting leaves in the pot. 'All right, I think. Well, no one returned with any queries. My wages money balanced.'

'Did it? That's great, Harrie. More than I can say I managed the first time I did the wages on my own, when my manager was off on holiday and I was left in charge. You wait, though, when it doesn't balance and you have to go through all the packets to find out where you made the mistake. Or when you start having to change tax codes or calculate rebates when someone gets married. I could go on, but that's when all the fun starts.' She saw the look on Harrie's face and giggled. 'Don't worry, I'll always be there for you to pick me brains.' Her eyes sparkled keenly. 'Did you see your bear man today?'

As she put the pot of tea on the table Harrie looked at her blankly. 'Pardon?'

'You know, the rescue biddy's son?'

'Oh, you mean Chas?'

'Yeah, that's him, I just forgot his name. I'm still intrigued to know all about the important part he's going to play in your life.'

Having put two mugs and milk and sugar beside the tea pot, Harrie sat down opposite Marion. 'Well, he's not going to do it in the way you think he is.'

'What do you mean by that?'

She began pouring out the tea. 'I'm sorry to disappoint you but there isn't going to be any romance. He's already got a girl-friend.' And pushing Marion's filled mug towards her, Harrie added tartly, 'At this very moment they're about to have a romantic meal together at that new Indian place on Woodgate.'

'Oh! Oh, I see.' Her friend looked at Harrie enquiringly. 'I didn't hear a hint of jealousy in your voice when you told me that, did I?'

'Jealousy? Don't be silly,' she replied scornfully.

'I ain't stupid, Harrie, and there's something you ain't happy about.' Marion eyed her friend knowingly. 'You've taken a fancy to this Chas, haven't you? Go on, admit it?'

'I like him as a person, Marion, that's all.' She proceeded to relate to her friend the story of his coming to the aid of the old man who had been attacked in the street and ended by saying how commendable she felt it was of him not to have broadcast his good deed in order to heap praise on himself. Didn't Marion agree that there was something special about a man who didn't feel the need to do that?

It was very obvious to Marion by the way Harrie's eyes had sparkled, and her tone of voice when relating this tale, that Chas Tyme had made a big impression on her.

'You sure you just *like* this man and it's nothing else, Harrie?'

Harrie stared at her, taken aback. Was it just *liking* she felt? Why did the thought of Chas being spoken for disappoint her? Why had she felt rankled when Darren had cut their conversation short that afternoon? Oh, this was absurd, she hardly knew the man. 'Yes, I'm sure, Marion. How can I be fancying someone else when only a week ago I was in love with Jeremy, on the verge of spending the rest of my life with him?'

'You were in love with the side of Jeremy you knew, Harrie,' Marion reminded her. 'You now know a marriage between you two would never have worked. You would have ended up as miserable as sin, playing the part of the dutiful solicitor's wife and companion to his mother, cut off in that house miles away from your dad and your friends until such time as you got a place of your own, and that could have been years in the happening. There's women out there ripe for that kind of role but not you. I just thank God you realised and did something about it before it was too late. I admire you, Harrie, 'cos lots of women would have just put up and shut up, too cowardly to speak up for themselves.'

She smiled warmly at her friend. 'Thanks for being so supportive, Marion.'

'That's what friends are for, Harrie. I do n'ote for you that you don't do for me. Do I need to remind you that it's thanks to you that me and Allen are happy together now. I was prepared never to see him again after that stupid row we had when I sent him packing. I can't even remember what it was about now, but I was adamant I wasn't going to apologise even though I knew it was my fault we'd argued. You spent ages talking to me, made me see that if I didn't get off my high horse then I could spend the rest of my life regretting it.'

'Well, I knew that you and Allen were meant for each other.'

'Like I strongly suspected you and Jeremy weren't.' Marion took a sup of her tea, then, cradling her mug in her hands, looked at Harrie keenly. 'So what do you feel for this Chas?'

'I told you, I just like him. He's a nice man.'

'Oh, you can tell me you just like him 'til yer blue in the face, Harrie. There's something about him that's attracting you, I can tell.'

'You're making too much of this.'

Marion cocked an eyebrow at her. 'Am I? We'll see.'

CHAPTER SIXTEEN

At just before eight that evening Nadine swanned through the door of the Rajah's Palace.

Rich dark red and cream flocked paper lined the walls and vibrant ethnic paintings adorned them. Gilded statuettes of four- and six-armed goddesses, ornate alabaster elephants and brasses, were positioned around the room in strategic places along with potted plants. All the waiters were smartly dressed in colourful traditional dress.

Nadine, in her ignorance of Gujarati custom, thought their chooridars were pyjama bottoms and wasn't impressed.

Without waiting for the majestic owner of the establishment to seat her, she barged her way over to a table in a secluded corner and, dumping her coat on the chair next to her, sat herself down.

A waiter who had rushed after her to pull out her chair instead picked up her coat. In her lack of knowledge about restaurant behaviour, she called sharply to him, 'Oi, you, where yer going with that?'

But he appeared not to hear her. With narrowed eyes she watched him weave his way through the occupied tables to the back of the large room and into a corridor behind where he hung her coat on a rack along with other customers' outerwear. Her astute eyes scanned the rack. Several coats looked to be in far better condition than her own and, if luck was on her side, by the time she and Chas left then one of them would be hers.

Another waiter appeared and without a please or thank you she took the proffered menu. After saying she was expecting her boyfriend to join her, she ordered herself a double vodka and black. At home she'd already drained a large bottle of Woodpecker cider while readying herself in the bedroom she shared with her children, ordering them all to shut up and go to sleep else the bogeyman would come and get them and lock them in a dark cellar and never let them out. Or worse still she'd let their grandmother loose on them. While she preened herself she never heard a murmur from her four terrified offspring. She hadn't bothered rowing with her mother over going out, just slipped out of the front door unobserved while Clarice was glued to the television. There would be hell to pay when she got back but Nadine couldn't give a damn.

She was feeling very pleased with herself. Chas would not know what had hit him tonight, and by the time she had finished with him she was in no doubt they would be planning on moving in together as a prelude to marriage as soon as she was free. No more living a hand-to-mouth existence, worried where the next penny was coming from, and once having entrapped him completely by marriage she would have a permanent babysitter on hand, allowing her to come and go in the evenings doing whatever she liked. And if Chas didn't like that she wouldn't make it at all easy for him to escape her clutches. She meant him to be her meal ticket for life.

She looked down at herself and a warm glow filled her. She was of the opinion that she did not look at all like a mother of four in the tight low-cut mini dress she had acquired via her gifted light fingers this afternoon on a 'shopping trip' in the town, and the new purple platform shoes and yellow handbag courtesy of Freeman, Hardy and Willis looked a treat against the fashionable fluorescent green of the dress.

The only thing that marred her good humour was the fact that her visit to Phil hadn't quite gone the way she had expected it to. She had thought he'd show some sort of reluctance to release her from their marriage, been ready for a fight with him about it, in fact, but instead he'd looked delighted, very eager to agree to her terms for as quick a divorce as they could get. Without even enquiring after the welfare of his children who she'd left with a friend while she did her errand, and before she could tap him for any money which she'd been about to do, he had wished her all the best and disappeared inside the flat, but not before making sure he'd got her key back from her.

Phil was in the past, though, and good riddance to him. Her future was just about to walk through the restaurant door.

She knocked back her drink and ordered another, occupying

her time by studying the menu. As she did so she pulled a disgusted face. It all sounded like muck to her and nothing appealed. What on earth was curry? There seemed to be several varieties of it all with peculiar-sounding names that she could not pronounce. Then she spotted a section offering English dishes. Chicken and chips would suit her nicely.

Nadine knocked back her second drink and glanced at the clock. It was approaching eight-thirty. Where was Chas? The likes of her current husband she would expect to keep her waiting but not the pushover who was her potential second. The waiter appeared and in his broken English asked her if she was ready to order.

She scowled at him. 'I told yer when I came in I was waiting for me boyfriend to come. Does it look like he's arrived, yer thick sod?' she snapped. 'Oi, and don't you dare look down yer nose at me like that,' she retorted angrily after seeing the look the poor man gave her because he could not understand her thick Leicester accent. Nadine was oblivious to the stares that other customers gave her. 'If yer that desperate for summat to do, gerrus another drink,' she demanded, thrusting out her empty glass at him which he took and scurried away. 'Oi!' she called after him. 'And put some proper music on outta the Hit Parade instead of that tinny-sounding stuff.'

'It's Indian sitar,' a man sitting opposite politely informed her.

She sniffed disdainfully. 'I couldn't give a toss whether they stand or sit to listen to it, it still sounds like wailing cats to me and I can't be expected to eat me dinner with that noise blasting in me ears.' She gave a disparaging glance at the dishes of food on his table. 'Christ almighty, looks ter me like dog food! If that's what they eat in foreign parts then they can bloody keep it.'

Her heart then leaped as she heard the outer door opening. About time, she thought. She turned her head only to be disappointed to see a young couple coming in, looking very happy and very much together. That will be me and Chas shortly, she thought smugly.

The waiter arrived back with her drink which Nadine snatched from him. 'Took yer time, didn't yer?' she berated him. Then a thought struck her. 'Has me boyfriend left me a message saying he's going to be late?'

He looked at her non-plussed then gave a shrug. It was obvious he didn't understand her.

'Message? Note? Yer know, letter,' she snapped at him, miming the actions of pen on paper.

He gave another helpless shrug. 'You ready order, please, yes?' he eagerly asked, pad and pencil poised ready to take it.

A look of utter derision on her face, she exhaled loudly. 'I've already bleddy told yer that I'm waiting for me boyfriend. I'll let yer know when I'm ready to order. Now piss off and pester someone else.'

As he hurried away Nadine knocked back her drink and looked over at the clock. The numbers were blurred after her consumption of alcohol but she could just make out that it was after nine. A terrible foreboding began to swirl in her stomach as realisation dawned. Chas wasn't coming. Rage started to boil inside her. How dare he stand her up? Who did he think he was? Chas Tyme was nothing special. Far from it, in fact. It wasn't like he received an invitation to have dinner with a beautiful woman every day, if ever; the least he could do now was turn up. Her first instinct was to rush round to his house, bang down the door and demand an explanation for his non-appearance – and it had better be good.

Then she thought better of it. She knew without a doubt that Chas would have been over the moon that a woman like herself was showing interest in him. This was a man who helped old ladies and never took payment for his good deeds; had taken without retaliation all the abuse she and her brothers had heaped on him when young. Chas Tyme was not a man who would leave a woman sitting in a restaurant waiting for him. Something must have happened to stop him coming. Maybe he had left a message for her but that stupid waiter couldn't comprehend English well enough to pass it on. Maybe the note was back at home. Then another possible reason for his absence occurred to her. Had that snotty cow at Black's actually passed her message on to him at all? There was no way Nadine could find out one way or the other until tomorrow. But that had to be the reason Chas hadn't shown. Her face screwed up with rage. Well, that woman at Black's was certainly going to regret her lapse when Nadine got hold of her.

Then she gave a heavy sigh. It meant she had to go through

this all over again. As it was, the thought of flirting with Chas, pretending to him she thought him the best thing since sliced bread, having sex with him when in fact he repulsed her, had been weighing heavily on her. Okay, she could pretend, pull it off to Oscar standards, but it was such bloody hard work.

She looked great tonight and Chas would have been bowled over by her, honoured to be in her company, and she knew without a doubt so grateful for what she was offering him. But because of that woman at Black's not doing what she'd been asked, he had no idea yet what Nadine had in store for him. Oh, why couldn't it just be as simple as telling him she had decided he was the man for her? Was bestowing on him the honour of being husband to her and father to her kids, affording him the family she knew an oaf like him would never have, and that was that. Life could be very difficult sometimes when it didn't run according to plan.

She was not going to let this set her back. Like hell it would. There was no going back for Nadine. She'd burned her boats as far as Phil was concerned, and the way things were going at home it was only a matter of time before her mother chucked her and her kids out and they were left with no roof over their heads. Chas was the perfect candidate for her particular needs, ripe for the taking. She'd just have to make another booking for dinner tomorrow night, but this time make sure he got the invitation. She'd give it to him personally, waiting for him at Black's premises tomorrow night when he finished his shift.

She made to summon the waiter to tell him she wouldn't be eating tonight but tomorrow instead and book them a table then, when a terrible thought struck her. She might not have had a meal but she'd had plenty to drink and those would need paying for. She hadn't any money on her as Chas would have been settling their bill.

Just then another waiter approached her. He was a big man and by the way he was dressed and held himself she knew without a doubt he was the man in charge. 'Memsahib, you ready order now, yes?'

Memsahib? What the hell was that when it was at home? Time to make my escape, she thought. 'Er . . . yeah, in a minute. I need the lavvy first.' She scraped back her chair, grabbed her handbag off the floor and stood up. 'Where are the lavvies?' she asked him.

He looked at her blankly.

Nadine gave a haughty snort. 'God's sake, do none of you speak English? Lavvies. Bog. Yer know, *the toilet.*'

'Ah, yes, Memsahib. Please, over there.' He pointed in the direction of the corridor at the back of the restaurant.

'I'll be back in a minute so keep me chair warm for me,' she said, giving him a wink and smiling sweetly.

The door leading into the toilet stood next to the coat rack. With a quick glance behind her to make sure no one was watching, which thankfully no one seemed to be, in a flash Nadine had unhooked two coats from the peg nearest to her and disappeared inside the toilet, bolting the door behind her.

The first coat she tried on was far too big and old-fashioned for her liking but the second of the two she'd have bought herself, money permitting, and she was more than pleased with her acquisition. She doubted the woman whose coat she had taken would be as pleased with what she'd been left in exchange.

Nadine's eyes settled on the window at the back of the toilet cubicle. She gave a disdainful click of her tongue. It was on the small side. Getting through it would be a tight squeeze but she'd manage it because the alternative was to race at high speed through the restaurant and possibly be chased down the street by the staff which she didn't fancy in the get up she was wearing, despite the fact she knew she'd escape their clutches because no way would they know all the back alleys and hiding places in these parts like she did, having used them all in the past for similar reasons.

Taking off her shoes, she shut the toilet lid and clambered up on to it. She then pushed up the bottom sash of the window which wasn't easy as it was sticking in places on the fresh paint. Finally it was open as far as it would go. Throwing out her bag, shoes, then the newly acquired coat into the yard outside, she stuck one leg through the window then bent double to manoeuvre her body through after it. In the process she heard a loud rip. It wasn't until she had both feet safely on the yard slabs that she discovered her dress had caught on a jutting nail and a big hole had been ripped in it.

'Fuck,' Nadine muttered under her breath, realising that she couldn't wear this again tomorrow night at wherever she rebooked their meal which meant she'd have to go 'shopping' again tomorrow afternoon.

Picking up her shoulder bag, she donned her shoes, let herself out of the yard then drunkenly swayed her way home. Despite her disappointment that the evening had not gone anything like she'd planned, in her inebriated state she could not help but giggle to herself. She would have given anything to have seen the look on the restaurant staff's faces when they finally broke down the toilet door and found she had absconded.

CHAPTER SEVENTEEN

At four-forty-five the next evening, Chas drew the car to a halt outside a large detached gabled house in the Leicester Forest East area on the outskirts of the city and beeped his horn to let his customer know he'd arrived. He was hoping this was his last job of the night. It hadn't been a particularly busy day considering it was a Saturday. Chas found hanging around for jobs far more tiring than actually being out on them.

As he waited for his customer to arrive his stomach started to rumble. Over four hours had passed since he'd eaten his lunch of potted meat sandwiches and he was ready for his dinner. Saturday night was usually sausage, egg and chips with slices of bread and butter and a dollop of HP brown sauce. He was looking forward to it. After he had helped his mother clear away and had replenished the coal bucket and done any other jobs that needed doing, they would settle down together. While Iris watched the television he would catch up with the daily news via the *Leicester Mercury*. Maybe his mother might fancy a bottle of stout from the off-licence. He could certainly do justice to a bottle of beer himself. Then a thought struck him. Iris hadn't been out in the evening for a while. She might like him to accompany her to the local bingo hall. He wasn't particularly fond of the game himself but his mother was partial now and again. Maybe Freda would like to join them as her husband usually went to the Blackbird for a couple of pints on a Saturday night and meanwhile she was left home on her own. Chas smiled to himself. He could just imagine his driver colleagues' reactions should they hear how he intended to spend his Saturday evening. Well, they might find it hilarious he was accompanying two old ladies to a game of bingo but if it gave his mother and her friend a couple of hours' pleasure then that afforded him as much back.

He turned his head to look at his customer as he got into the back seat.

'Good evening, Mr Graham,' he said, smiling at the old gentleman welcomingly. 'Thurcaston Road is where you want to go, isn't it?' That being the information Ralph had radioed him.

'Yes, please,' he replied. 'Could you make it quick?'

'I'll get you there as fast as I can, sir,' Chas responded politely. Despite the dark night and the limited light from the car's interior lamp he noticed the other man's flushed appearance and the fact that he was rubbing his temple. 'You all right, sir?' he asked in concern.

'Just a headache. I need to get home to take something for it.' As Chas turned around and started the car the old gent continued, 'I'm not surprised I've got one after the tough negotiating I've just had to do. I wasn't expecting it, thought we'd agreed matters and it was just the formalities I'd gone to deal with, but I was proved wrong. I've just sold my business, you see. Rather sad but the time had come. It's been going downhill for a while and was only just supporting me, my wife, my two sons and their familes. A competitor has been after it for a while and it had got to the stage where if I didn't accept his offer, then there soon wouldn't be anything worth offering for. My buyer thought he had me over a barrel and he could beat me down on price at the last minute, but I stuck firm. I'd my family to think of. Now the deal's done I can take care of them. Me and my wife are going to be moving to the coast and my sons are buying a new business between them.'

Chas was of the opinion that there were three types of customer. The first, regardless of their own station in life, nevertheless saw taxi drivers as subservient to them, only speaking to issue instructions. The second was the sort that liked to pass the time of day as they journeyed along and rattled on about nothing in particular. The third type was the sort who viewed a taxi driver as a confidant and spilled out all manner of personal secrets and problems to the back of the driver's head, things they normally would never tell a stranger. This passenger, Chas realised, was the third sort. He politely listened, making suitable comments when he felt he was expected to.

'I expect you can't wait to get home and break the good news to them,' Chas commented as he expertly negotiated the traffic.

'That I can't. My poor long-suffering wife has waited years for this day. I must say, I never thought I'd hear myself say this but I'm ready to take things a lot more easily. No more having to set the alarm. What bliss.'

'Most certainly,' agreed Chas. Getting up when he woke, not when working hours dictated, a luxury he'd years to wait for yet.

He heard the back window being wound down. 'Is it too warm in here for you, sir?' he asked although to him it wasn't unduly so.

'No, it's fine. I'm hoping a blast of cold air might help ease my headache. That's all right with you, driver, isn't it?'

'Yes, of course, sir. You do whatever makes you comfortable.'

The icy draught from the open back window was swirling uncomfortably around Chas's neck but out of courtesy to his passenger he didn't say anything.

His concentration taken up with negotiating the evening traffic as they approached the town centre, it wasn't until he was waiting for a set of traffic lights to change in his favour that he realised his passenger had grown quiet. Chas turned his head to address Mr Graham, meaning to inform him that another fifteen minutes at the most should see him home safely. Instead his jaw dropped open in shock when he saw his passenger slumped against the back seat. Chas didn't need to possess any medical qualifications to know this man was not asleep but unconscious and needed to go to hospital as quickly as possible.

Thankfully the traffic lights had now changed. Chas was able to head straight for Leicester Infirmary Emergency Department.

Forty minutes later a grave-faced doctor came out to speak to Chas who had been sitting patiently in the corridor since the staff had whisked Mr Graham away as soon as they'd arrived. 'I'm sorry but there was nothing we could do. He suffered a massive brain haemorrhage. The police are on their way to inform his family.'

The old man was dead? Chas couldn't believe it. He looked at the doctor, mystified. 'Mr Graham complained of a headache when I first picked him up. Maybe . . .'

'He would have had no idea he was suffering from anything

other than a bad head. There's no reason why you should have realised how ill he was either,' the doctor interjected. He looked at Chas sympathetically. 'Mr Graham suffered from one of those medical conditions that shows no prior symptoms. This is bound to have been a shock to you. Would you like me to ask a nurse to get you a cup of tea, Mr Tyme?'

'Thank you, doctor, but I'm fine. I need to get back to my firm's office and report what's happened.' As it was Chas knew Ralph would be wondering why he couldn't reach him on the radio as the job he knew Chas was on would not have taken him through any blackout areas.

It was a very sad Chas who drove back to base. He felt it most unfair that the old man should pass on just at a time when he had been going to reap the rewards of all his years of hard work and spend time with his wife, doing things they both enjoyed. The incident brought home to Chas the precarious state of health of his boss, the outcome of which was still so finely balanced. It was unclear whether Jack was yet to reap the rewards of all his years of hard labour or whether his wife, like Mrs Graham, was going to find herself a widow. He vehemently prayed Jack Black pulled through.

Meanwhile, back in the office Harrie looked up at the clock and was shocked to see it was nearly six o'clock. She was meant to finish at one on a Saturday but had volunteered to carry on without expecting any overtime in order to settle the outstanding paper-work. There was another reason she had decided to spend her free Saturday afternoon working. She was still finding it difficult not to fill every spare waking moment with planning her wedding.

Since Jeremy's proposal all her free time had been taken up with preparations for their forthcoming nuptials. Now she needed an interval in which to accustom herself to being a free agent again, filling her spare time with the things a single woman did, not an engaged one. She still had no regrets about her decision to end her engagement, but a large part of her felt it wasn't right to resume the old carefree single life-style that she had enjoyed before Jeremy had come on the scene. Not immediately anyway. As a result she had felt that immersing herself in work was a better time-filler than moping around the house, causing her father fresh concern.

Ready for the off, she came out of her office and was surprised to find Ralph still sitting at the radio's-operator's desk. She couldn't help but notice that the old man looked tired. 'Doing anything nice tonight with Mrs Widcombe?' she asked him as she arrived at his desk on her way to the staff entrance.

He gave a despondent sigh. 'Me wife and me usually like to go for a drink down the working men's club on a Sat'day night, they generally have a good turn on, but by the time Marlene decides to turn up and relieve me, I doubt there'll be much of the evening left. I don't think that gel can tell the time, if you want my opinion. In normal circumstances I'd feel obliged to tell Mrs Black about her lax behaviour, but then we ain't in normal circumstances, are we?

'Besides, I ain't too long in the tooth not to realise that Marlene is taking liberties because she knows we have too much regard for what Mrs Black's going through to bother her with work-related problems. If you want the truth, though, lovey, if I'd known how long Mr Black was going to be off ill, I would have thought twice about offering to come out of retirement to help out. Not that I blame him. It's not his fault, is it? It's just that I'm finding this all too much now at my age. The extra money has come in handy, there's no denying it ain't, but we were managing fine without it on me savings and the bit of pension I get from the government. Me wife grumbled like hell when I first retired about me getting under her feet. Now she's moaning like hell about the fact I ain't there for her to boss about, and all the jobs I did for her aren't getting done 'cos I'm too tired when I get home.'

Harrie smiled kindly at him. 'Well, hopefully Mr Black will be back soon, Ralph, and then your wife will get you back again. And Marlene will be in shortly then you can get off home.'

'And pigs might fly,' he grunted. 'Look, can you hold the fort for a minute while I make a visit to spend a penny?'

'Yes, of course I can.'

Since she had commenced her temporary employment with Black's, Harrie had been itching to have a go on the radio. She didn't need to ask how it was operated. She had picked it up purely by observation on her visits to Ralph with queries he could help with. As she sat herself down on his chair she willed the telephone to ring so she could take details to radio through to a driver. To prepare herself to contact the nearest car to the customer she hoped would ring in, she began to study the book logging their pick ups and eventual destinations, and the relevant timings, so she could quickly calculate which driver was best positioned to fulfil any job that came in.

So engrossed was Harrie that she didn't hear someone come in through the outer door.

'Oi, you!'

Harrie's head jerked up. She saw a woman leaning on the counter, her face murderous with rage. Recognition dawned. It was the same woman who had called in yesterday asking her to deliver a message to Chas, the one she had passed on to Marlene. Harrie rose to her feet. As she walked across to the counter she asked politely, 'Can I help you?'

Nadine grunted, 'Like yer did yesterday, yer mean? I asked yer to pass a message on ter Chas.'

'Yes, I . . .'

'I ain't got time to listen to yer lies, lady,' Nadine cut in, wagging a finger warningly. 'You just thank God there's a counter between us else yer'd have no hair left on yer head. And be warned. Next time I ask for a message to be passed on to me boyfriend and it ain't, you won't live to regret it.'

With that she turned and stalked out. The outer door banged loudly behind her.

Harrie stared after her. Whether Marlene had or hadn't passed the message on to Chas was something Harrie would have to bring up with her when she saw her. She still couldn't understand how such a nice man as Chas had come to land himself with the likes of that woman. Obviously he saw good points in her that Harrie herself just couldn't. What did get her thinking, though, was why exactly Chas Tyme's choice of girlfriend should bother her so much?

On arriving back at the firm's premises Chas drove his car straight into the compound for security overnight. The very sad demise of Mr Graham was still weighing on him. The last thing he felt like doing was cleaning out the inside of the car and washing it down ready for work first thing Monday morning. The death of that old man had brought home to him how precious life was. He felt an overwhelming need to get home and see his mother, tell her he loved her and sincerely hope she took up his offer of a trip to the bingo hall. If Terry wasn't too busy, maybe he would clean out Chas's car, same as he did for the other drivers. That would save some time.

As he got out of the car Chas took a quick look around the yard in search of the maintenance man but couldn't see him. There was no light shining from the wooden hut in the corner of the compound where Terry conducted his business so it didn't seem he'd arrived for work yet. He could be in the office for some reason, Chas thought. He was just about to lock up his car and go in search when he felt a tap on his shoulder and jumped in alarm, spinning around to come face to face with Nadine.

She was grinning at him. 'Surprise!' she cried.

She'd more than surprised him, creeping up on him like that. Shocked him even. 'Nadine, what . . . what are you doing here?' he asked her, wondering why she looked so excited.

'Come to give you a message yer should've got last night only that silly office cow forgot ter give it to yer. But I've sorted her out so don't you worry, she won't be forgetting to do it again. Anyway, I've better things to talk about than about *her*. I've booked us a table at the Berni Inn for tonight at eight. Don't be late, I'll be waiting for yer. Now I've got to dash, I want to make meself beautiful.'

His heart sank. This was just the situation he had been desperate to avoid. His mind raced for a way to tell her that he couldn't accept her invitation without insulting or hurting her. He caught her by the arm. 'Nadine, look . . . er . . . I don't mean to hurt your feelings but as I've told you already there's no need to repay me for any help I've given you.'

'But I want to repay you, yer daft ha'p'orth. See you at eight.'

She was trying to pull her arm free from his grasp but he clung on tight, fearing she would leave before he'd resolved this situation. 'Nadine, I appreciate your offer, I really do, but I can't come out with you tonight. I've got other arrangements.'

She stopped struggling to free her arm and looked at him, stunned. 'Other arrangements? But you can't have! Who'd wanna go out with you?' Realising what she'd said, she hurriedly added, 'Well, I mean, I do of course. But you ain't got a girl-friend, have yer, so who else can yer be going out with?'

'My mother.'

'*Your mother!*'

'I'm taking her to bingo.'

Nadine's face twisted in astonishment. 'You're giving up the chance of a night out with *me* to take your *mother* out?'

Releasing his hold on her arm, Chas nodded. 'I appreciate your offer, Nadine, but I'm sure you won't have any trouble finding someone else to go with.'

'But I don't want no one else to go with me, I want you. So you tell your mother you'll take her to bingo another night and I'll see you at eight.'

Chas couldn't believe that she wasn't prepared to take no for an answer. 'I won't be there, Nadine. I've told you, I'm taking my mother out. Besides, she'll already have cooked my dinner.'

The woman was staring at him, astounded. She couldn't believe he was refusing her. Before she could stop it her temper flared and she blurted, 'Are you fucking thick or what? Can't yer see what I'm offering you, you flaming idiot? This meal ain't to say thanks for helping me with the rat trap or for when me mother brained herself, it's a date.'

He looked taken aback. 'A date?'

'I expect this date with me is the first you've ever been on but yer do know what a date is, don't yer, Quas . . . Chas?' She gave him a long lingering look while running her tongue over her top lip. 'I'm going to make sure I give you a date you'll never, ever forget and it'll be the first of many for us.' She lowered her voice to a seductive whisper. 'I'm sure yer not so thick you don't know what I mean, Chas?' She kissed the ends of her fingers then placed them on his lips.

A look of utter disgust crossed his face. Hastily he wiped his lips with the back of his hand. His voice was resolute when he said, 'I don't want to go out on a date with you, Nadine. I apologise if there's anything I've ever said or done to make you think I did.'

She seemed stupefied. 'You're turning me down! And when the flaming hell do you think the likes of you is ever going to be offered again what I'm offering you now?'

Chas could take no more of this unwelcome conversation. He couldn't understand what Nadine was playing at. What had got into her to make her think he would ever want a romantic attachment to her? There was nothing about her that attracted him and he'd never given her any reason to think in such a way. She must be drunk, there was no other explanation. 'Please excuse me, Nadine. I have to go into the office and report an incident that happened this afternoon.'

She grabbed his arm and frenziedly cried, 'I know yer want me, I know yer do!'

He peeled her hand away. 'Nadine, stop this nonsense. You're making yourself look stupid. I don't know what's got into you, I'm sure. Now go home, please.'

'Me making meself look stupid? It's you that's stupid! You're just a . . . a . . . you're weird, that's what you are. You're one of them queers, ain't yer?' she spat at him furiously. 'Yeah, yer'd have to be, turning a woman like me down,' she cried.

He looked at her sadly, shaking his head, and without another word walked away.

Dumbstruck she watched him go, powerless to do anything to stop him. All her dreams of a secure future for herself and her children were going with him. What on earth was she going to do now? A great rush of anger and frustration swelled within her. Spinning round to face the car she stood next to, she started hammering her fists on it. Blast the man! Fuck him! I hope he dies a horrible death, her mind was screaming.

Terry, who was just arriving for work through the compound gates, couldn't believe his eyes, seeing a woman standing there beating hell out of one of the firm's cars. He ran over to her. 'You all right?' he demanded.

Nadine spun to face him, fists raised as though to beat him instead of the car. 'Do I look all right, yer blind clot?'

'Er . . . well, no. You shouldn't be doing what yer are, though. You could damage the car.'

'Do I look as though I give a shit?' she hurled back. Then the thought of the police being called and herself carted off to jail made her drop her arms and unclench her fists. 'Who the hell are you anyway?'

'I'm the firm's mechanic.' That's what Terry told everyone who enquired about his job as it sounded far more important than maintenance man. He quickly scanned the woman before him. She was a good-looking piece, no denying it. 'Who are you?' he asked her back.

Nadine's temper was subsiding to be replaced by a sense of real fear of what the future held for her now her dream of a golden life with Chas, free from monetary worries, was lost. She gave a miserable sniff. 'I'm a woman who's just been dumped by me boyfriend.'

He was pleased to hear that, but then she wasn't the type who'd look in his direction so there was no point in getting his hopes up. 'And yer've come in here to take it out on one of Black's cars? You do know yer trespassing, don't yer?'

'I'm not. Me boyfriend works here.'

Curiosity got the better of him. 'Who would that be then?'

'That great big oaf Chas Tyme. Well, I thought he was me boyfriend but it seems he ain't now. I can't believe he's turned me down.'

Terry couldn't either. The man must be mad. 'Well, he's got to be blind, that's all I can say.'

Nadine looked at him hard. He wasn't what she'd deem a good-looking sort, but he wasn't exactly ugly either. With the lights down low he could pass for Brian Jones from the Rolling Stones – well, just. He'd got a job which was a big plus as far as she was concerned. The possibilities of this man were certainly worth further investigation. She flicked her hand through her blonde tresses and flashed her eyelashes at him. 'Do yer reckon?'

He nodded. 'I don't think much of Chas Tyme meself, if that's any consolation.'

'Oh, why?'

Terry did not have the grace to bat an eyelid when he lied. 'He did me out of a job. That cabby's job he's got should have been mine by rights.'

'Oh, well, that gives us summat in common then, don't it? Chas Tyme's done the dirty on both of us. We should get our heads together, see what we can come up with by way of payback. You married?'

He shook his head.

'Attached at all?'

He shook it again.

Maybe her future wasn't as black as she had thought a few moments ago. 'Then is your lucky night.' Nadine was just about to ask his name when the heavens suddenly opened. 'Shit,' she spat, 'that's all I need tonight.'

Instinctively Terry tried the car door next to him. It was locked. He stepped across and tried the one Nadine was standing by. The back door opened. Without needing to be told she scrambled inside and he followed.

Close together on the back seat, the sound of heavy rain beating on the roof, she turned to face him. 'Now ain't this cosy? So how d'yer fancy taking me out for a meal tonight then we can discuss ways to get back at that bastard for what he's done to us both?'

He couldn't believe his luck that such a good-looking woman wanted to go out with him. Chas might not want her but Terry certainly did. 'I'd love to, yer don't know how much, but I can't tonight. I'm working. It's me night off tomorrow, though. They do chicken in the basket at the Crow's Nest on Hinckley Road. Or yer could have scampi, if yer fancy?'

'I'm a girl who's used to rather more upmarket places but chicken in the basket at the Crow's Nest will do for a first date, I suppose.' Nadine moved up to snuggle against him and give him a kiss, something to remember her by until tomorrow evening. Her foot struck something on the floor by her feet. 'What's this?' she said, leaning over to retrieve it. She picked the object up to rest on her lap and opened it.

They both stared at the contents incredulously.

Chas arrived in the office just as Ralph was returning to relieve Harrie.

'Oh, there you are, Chas,' Ralph said to him, retaking his seat. 'I tried to get you on the radio a couple of times a while back but got no response from you. Car radio's working all right, ain't it?'

Chas looked apologetic. 'Yes, it's working fine. I switched it off. I should have told you before I did but, you see . . .' He proceeded to explain the details of what had transpired.

'Oh, dear,' said a grave-faced Harrie after he had finished. 'That must have been a terrible shock for you, a customer dying in the back of your cab. Are you all right yourself, Chas?' she asked with deep concern.

'It's Mr Graham's family I feel for. They've probably a meal ready waiting to celebrate their new future on his return. Instead they're going to get a knock on the door and find a policeman on the other side with bad news. I can't imagine what that's going to be like for them.'

Harrie's already favourable opinion of Chas rose even higher. After what he had just gone through most men would be wallowing in self-pity, encouraging everyone else to sympathise. This man's only concern was for others. She suddenly felt an urge to throw her arms around him and give him a comforting hug. She might have done if others hadn't been present. Instead she asked, 'Would you like me to make you a cup of tea?'

Chas smiled at her. 'I appreciate your offer but . . . well, this might sound pathetic . . . I just want to get home and see my mam.'

She returned his smile. 'I can appreciate your need to do that. It's made me want to rush home and check my dad's all right too. I feel this great urge to tell him how much I love him. Things like this happening make you realise how precious life is, don't they?'

'They certainly do,' agreed Ralph, looking pensive, privately wondering how much longer he and his wife had together. She might get on his nerves sometimes but he'd be lost without her.

Just then Marlene breezed in. As she began taking off her coat, revealing a ridiculously short skirt that hardly covered her underwear and a tight top accentuating her well-rounded bosom, she cast a glance at them all. 'Oh, a welcome committee. How nice. Darren's not signed out yet, has he?'

'He's on his way back from a run to Market Harborough,' Ralph told her.

She looked highly delighted by that news. 'Oh, good, then me tarting meself up ain't bin wasted.'

'Aren't you supposed to relieve Ralph at six, Marlene?' Harrie said to her.

'Me watch says it is six,' she snapped back defensively.

'Well, your watch is either slow or it's broken and you need a new one. It's getting on for twenty-past.'

Marlene scowled at her. 'Ronald Tyler is never on time to relieve me for the night shift and no one says anything about that, do they?'

Ralph and Harrie knew this was not true as Ronald was a meticulous timekeeper, known for arriving early to start his shift. There'd been a more than adequate excuse for the handful of times he'd been even a few minutes late over the years he'd been employed by Black's as their night-shift radio operator, starting at ten and working through the night until Ralph returned in the morning.

'And you've suddenly appointed yerself in charge, have yer, to be telling me I'm late?' Marlene continued. 'As far as I'm aware you're just the temporary office help with no authority here. If Mrs Black's gorra problem with me timekeeping then she can tell me herself. Shift, then,' she addressed Ralph.

He got up and she plonked herself down on the chair he'd vacated. The telephone started ringing but Marlene ignored it as she was busy taking a magazine and some cigarettes out of her handbag.

'Are you going to answer that, Marlene?' Ralph asked her.

'God's sake, give me a minute,' she retorted sharply. She lit a cigarette before she picked up the telephone receiver. 'Yeah?'

Harrie and Chas looked at one other with raised eyebrows.

'That girl really does take the biscuit,' said Ralph, joining them. 'All I can think is that she lied through her back teeth about having radio-operating experience when Mrs Black interviewed her. Soon as she gives us the nod that Jack's starting to rally I'm gonna say something, else I feel Marlene could single-handedly ruin his business and then he'll have nothing to return to.' Then it struck him that despite Marlene's receiving a call from a customer, he still had not heard her relay anything over the radio to a night-shift driver. 'Marlene, do you intend to alert a driver to pick up that fare or do you want me to call them back and tell them they might be quicker catching a bus?'

She was flicking through her copy of *Jackie* which was actually aimed at the thirteen-to-sixteen-year-old age group. Without lifting her head she said, 'What fare?'

Ralph signed. 'The one that's just rung in?'

'That weren't a fare.'

'Then who was it?'

'Mrs Black.'

'What did she want, Marlene?' Harrie asked her.

'She didn't want anything.'

'Why did she telephone then?' Chas asked.

'Eh? Oh, just to say that Mr Black died this afternoon.'

They all gasped in shock.

'Weren't you even going to tell us?' Ralph snapped at her.

She dragged her eyes away from her magazine reluctantly. 'Mrs Black never asked me to. She just said she was letting me know Mr Black passed away this afternoon.'

Despite reeling from this shocking news they were all looking at her incredulously.

'Did you offer her our condolences?' Harrie demanded.

The girl gave her a blank look. 'Our what?'

Harrie responded with an irritated sigh. 'Did you tell Mrs Black how sorry we all are to hear her bad news?'

'Well, how could I? I didn't know that you was all sorry.' And she added matter-of-factly, 'I never even met Mr Black so I don't feel nothing one way or the other meself.'

'What must Mrs Black be thinking of us all?' a worried Ralph asked Harrie and Chas. 'Do you think we should go round and see her? Ask her if there's anything we can do for her?' His face was drawn with grief. 'I can't believe Jack's gone. He is . . . was the sort of bloke you think will go on for ever. He was no pushover, wasn't Jack, a bit unconventional in his ways, but if you treated him fair, he treated you fair back.'

Chas laid a hand on his arm. 'The best way we can serve Mr Black's memory and help his wife, Ralph, is by making sure we do our best to keep this place going. Not go giving Mrs Black any reason to worry, so she can concentrate on what she has to do next.'

'Chas is right, Ralph,' Harrie agreed with him. 'We could have a collection on Monday, have some flowers delivered to her, and that way she'll know all our thoughts are with her.'

'That's a nice idea,' Chas agreed, smiling warmly at her. Harrie was very thoughtful, he thought, unlike Marlene who seemed to have no thought for anyone other than herself and Darren.

'I'll radio through and tell the night-shift drivers what's happened. We can't tell the others 'til Monday now,' said Ralph.

He left them to go over to the radio-operator's desk.

Something occurred to Harrie then. 'Oh, Chas, I believe I owe you an apology.'

He looked at her askance. 'You do?'

'Your girlfriend gave me a message to give you yesterday evening. I understand you never got it?'

'Oh, I see, yes. Well . . . Nadine had her wires crossed, she is *not* my girlfriend. It's all right, we've sorted it out.'

So that woman and Chas weren't an item? Harrie was surprised to realise how pleased she was to hear this. 'Well, I suppose there's nothing else for us to do here so we might as well go home.' She looked at him expectantly, hoping he'd suggest he should walk with her as they went the same way, although she lived several streets further along the Blackbird Road than he did. She would welcome his company, though. Maybe as they walked along she could get to know him better which was what she really wanted to do.

Chas knew they went in the same direction and was conscious it was now very dark outside. His natural instinct to offer to see her home was swiftly quashed when it struck him she might think he was acting too familiarly. He wouldn't want her to think badly of him. It was Saturday night and she was probably in a rush to get home and ready herself to go out with friends – despite his knowing from his mother that she had just broken off an engagement, he presumed an attractive woman like Harrie would have many more admirers waiting in the wings ready to show their hand when she let it be known she was available again. He'd seen for himself that Darren was most certainly interested in her. Was Harrie interested in return? Chas felt a stab of jealousy at the thought that she might be.

'Have a nice weekend, Harrie,' he said breezily.

He thought it was just his imagination that a look of disappointment crossed her face before she said, 'Oh, you too. See you Monday then, Chas. Goodnight, Ralph. Marlene,' she added as an afterthought, and wasn't surprised that the girl did not respond.

Ralph came across to Chas.

'Well, that's the night drivers told the news. They're all very shocked and said they'd happily give something towards some flowers for Mrs Black and a wreath for Jack. The others will be in agreement when we tell them on Monday, I know they will.' He gave a deep sigh. 'It's the end of an era. I've retired so it's not really of any consequence to me but I wonder what the future holds for Black's Taxis now?'

What indeed? thought Chas.

CHAPTER EIGHTEEN

Chas was surprised to find no sign of dinner on the go when he arrived home, but instead his mother dozing in the armchair by a low-burning fire. This was the second time in a few days he'd caught her asleep when he got home from work. He tiptoed across and knelt down before her, looking at her tenderly, worry building within him. Surely this was a sign that age was beginning to take its toll on her? Looking after this house and himself was obviously getting to be too much.

He felt positive the answer was a modern house with more labour-saving devices. In his savings account was just over two thousand pounds, an amount it had taken him the last ten years to accumulate. Would that be enough to cover the costs of buying a house, the legal fees, and whatever they needed to move into it? Trouble was, though, that with Jack Black's demise, Chas's employment was up in the air. Whether his job was safe or he'd be looking for another depended entirely on what Muriel Black decided to do next. He made up his mind, though, that once matters were settled on the job front, he'd speak to Iris and not give up until he'd made her see that a move was the best thing for her.

Iris suddenly roused herself. Sleep-fuddled, she stared at him blindly for a moment before recognition struck. 'Oh, my God, son, is that the time?' she exclaimed, struggling to right herself in her chair. 'I only sat down for a minute and I must have dozed off. You must be famished. It won't take me long . . .'

He put a hand on her shoulder. 'Forget cooking tonight, Mam. I'll pop out and get us some fish and chips.'

'Oh, would yer, lovey? I had planned to do us sausage and chips but the sausages will keep for another night. I quite fancy a bit of cod. I'll get the plates warmed through and some bread and butter cut and a pot of tea mashed while yer away.'

'I'll just stoke up the fire then I'll be off.'

After replenishing the fire he made to depart for the chip shop then stopped, to look back at her. 'I wondered if you'd like me to take you to bingo tonight? You could ask Freda to come as well, if you fancied?'

'Oh, that's a nice suggestion, son, but I've had quite enough excitement for one day as it is. Maybe next Saturday, eh? *The Rag Trade* is on later with that funny Sheila Hancock and Reg Varney, I'm really looking forward to watching it. Are you going to nip for a pint later? Look, why don't you, Chas? You'll never find a nice woman sitting by the telly with yer old mother, now will you?'

His mother was desperate for him to settle down and he daren't tell her she'd nearly got her wish today, if Nadine had got her way. He doubted she would ever approve of Nadine as a daughter-in-law, though. He still couldn't understand what had got into Nadine to made her act as she had, and doubted he ever would. The woman who did interest him he had no doubt Iris would most definitely approve of, but unfortunately the woman in question wasn't the kind to be interested in Chas.

A couple of pints and a chat with the locals he was acquainted with sounded just the ticket after the day he had had, but overriding that was his need to be with his mother tonight. Maybe not so much by his words but certainly by his actions he'd let her know how much he loved her. He'd surprise her by bringing her back a bottle of stout to accompany her fish and chips; he knew she'd enjoy that.

'The only woman I'm interesting in spending time with is you, Mam. A night by the telly with you is all I need tonight.' Chas suddenly looked at her quizzically as something she'd said earlier came back to him. 'What did you mean by saying you've had enough excitement for one day? What excitement?'

She looked at him for a moment and he got the distinct impression she was about to tell him something then she gave a nonchalant shrug. 'You must have misheard me,' she said dismissively.

He knew fine well he had not misheard her and made to probe further when she stopped him by saying, 'I haven't asked you yet what kind of day you've had?'

He sighed. 'I'll tell you about my day when I get back with the fish and chips.'

*　　*　　*

When Harrie arrived home that night she was most surprised to be greeted by the record player blaring 'The Blue Danube' by Johann Strauss, but even more surprised to find her seventy-year-old father had pushed the furniture back in the living room and was dancing around the space he'd created, using a sweeping brush for a partner.

The unexpected sight was such a comical one that she couldn't stop herself from laughing.

As Percy spun around he jumped on spotting her and immediately dropped the brush. He rushed over and lifted the needle arm off the record, plunging the room into silence. Hands on hips, a twinkle in his eyes, he said, 'You find the sight of yer old dad having a dance funny then, do yer?'

'Not at all but I do your choice of partner.'

He bent down to pick up the brush and patted its head. 'Oh, she's not a bad sort is Gertie. She doesn't complain when I tread on her toes. I suppose she could do with a visit to a decent hairdresser, though.'

Harrie giggled then asked, 'What's this all about, Dad?'

He looked at her for a moment and it seemed to Harrie he was about to tell her something. Instead he gave a shrug and said, 'If you remember, me and yer mam used to love old-time dancing when she was alive and ... well ... the mood just took me. I thought, why not see if I still had what it took?'

'And from what I saw you have, Dad. So why not ask me to partner you?'

He beamed at her. 'You mean it?'

'I can't promise to be as uncomplaining as Gertie when you tread on my toes but I'd like nothing better than a spin around with you.'

Ten minutes later, Percy bowed to his daughter and she curtsied to him. 'Well, I really enjoyed that, thank you,' he said. 'I never knew you could do the waltz.'

'I learned at school. I'm surprised I remembered all the steps because I haven't done one since.'

'You youngsters do all that jiggy stuff these days, don't you? That's not proper dancing. Anyway, waltzing is like riding a bike, lovey. Once yer learn, yer never forget.'

'Tell you what, Dad, when we've had our dinner, we could dance a bit more, if you like?'

'Oh, but aren't you going out? It's Saturday night, a night for you young things to be enjoying yourselves. It'll do you good to get out and have some fun with your friends, Harrie, after what you've been through recently. It'll help you get over it.'

'I appreciate what you're saying, Dad, but I fancy staying in tonight and enjoying myself with you.'

He looked at her in delight. 'D'yer mean that, ducky? Oh, I'd love that. I'm glad I never got rid of me old collection of records after yer mother died now. You stopped me, didn't you? I remember you telling me that I might be saying I'd never play them again now yer mother was no longer here to share them with me, but one day I might regret parting with them, once I'd got over her death. You was right and I'm glad I listened to you now.' A thought suddenly struck him and he exclaimed, 'Oh, yer dinner. By God, yer must be famished, our Harrie. I'd planned to have sausage and chips on the go for you. I must admit I was worried when I got home this afternoon and found you'd not eaten the sandwich I'd made you. Thought you finished at one on Saturday?'

'I didn't know you were planning to go out today, Dad. Where did you go?'

'Oh . . . just down the allotment, lovey, like I normally do. Anyway, I assumed you'd gone into town, but then when yer wasn't home on the four-thirty bus like you normally are when you go into town on a Saturday afternoon with Marion, well, I thought to meself, I bet she's stayed at work.'

'You were right, Dad. I wanted to get some more entering done in the account books to get them properly up to date for when . . .'

As her voice trailed off he saw the look on her face and asked, 'What's wrong, lovey?'

'Mr Black has died, Dad,' she said sadly. 'We got news just before I left tonight.'

'Oh, dear. Oh, I am sorry to hear that. What does that mean for you, Harrie?'

'I don't know yet. I don't suppose Mrs Black knows herself what she intends to do with the business with everything else she'll have on her mind. I've only been at Black's a week, Dad, but I really like it. I suppose I'll be kept on at least another week until after Mr Black's funeral. What happens to me then depends on what Mrs Black decides to do.'

'Well, by that time you might be ready to resume your secretarial work in a solicitor's office. That's what you're trained for, isn't it?'

'Yes, but now I've had a taste of something different, I'm not sure whether I want to go back into that. Secretarial work was interesting, Dad, but I didn't have the variety of work I have to do at Black's in running the office single-handed.'

'Ah, well, let's see what the future brings, eh, lovey? For what it's worth, yer mam always used to say there's no point in worrying about things that ain't happened yet. In the meantime, that dancing has made me famished. Tell yer what, how d'yer fancy fish and chips? The sausages will keep for another night.'

'Sounds good to me. I'll fetch them while you warm the plates and mash the tea.'

Harrie had expected the fish and chip shop to be packed, it being early on a Saturday evening, and that she'd have a long wait ahead. Instead she was surprised to find only a couple of customers in front of her.

'You've timed it just right, Harrie lovey,' Jim Waddall the owner greeted her when her turn came around. 'Half-hour ago you'd have been joining the queue outside.'

She looked relieved. 'Glad I didn't come half an hour ago then. But you had the queue because you sell the best fish and chips for miles around.'

'Kind of you to say so, ducky, and I happen to agree with you. Oh, did yer dad have a good time today?'

'Sorry?'

'At wherever he was off to when I seen him this morning. He was all spruced up in his best suit so I assumed he was off to a wedding or summat? I called across to him but he didn't hear me.'

'It couldn't have been my dad. He was down the allotment this morning and he certainly wouldn't be wearing his best suit to go down there.'

'Oh, well, it couldn't have bin him I saw then. Funny, I could have sworn it was, though. So what can I do you for today?' Jim asked her.

Several minutes later, with her order ready, she prepared to hurry home. She felt something squelch beneath her shoe and before she could stop herself was losing her balance and heading rapidly towards the floor. Clinging protectively to her parcel, which she had no intention of losing, she automatically tensed herself for a heavy landing, but got the shock of her life instead to have her fall broken by a pair of strong arms that encircled her and held her tight.

'Oh, thank you,' Harrie exclaimed, looking up gratefully into the face of her saviour and getting the shock of her life when recognition struck.

She was no more surprised than Chas was to see just who he'd rescued.

Encircled in his protective arms, eyes fixed on his kindly gaze, Harrie suddenly felt a surge of emotion swamp her. It was like nothing she had ever experienced before. She knew instinctively that she belonged inside these arms, belonged with the man whose arms were holding her so protectively. She had never been so sure of anything in her life before. The shock of it shook her rigid. But what also struck her was the way he was looking back at her. He was feeling the same as she was, it was so plain to see.

Chas had never held a woman in such an intimate way. On the occasions he had wondered what such closeness felt like, he had never envisaged for a moment that it would feel like this. This woman felt so good in his arms, like she belonged there, and he felt a desperate need to scoop her up and run away with her. Then the shock in her eyes registered. She was clearly embarrassed by the way he was holding her, worried anyone should see them and get the wrong idea. He dropped his arms and sprang away from her.

'You're all right now?' he blustered matter-of-factly. Then gave a nervous laugh. 'I couldn't believe my eyes when I entered the shop to see someone careering towards me. Glad I was on hand to save you from causing yourself damage. It was a chip you slipped on. Right, I'd . . . better get my order in as my mother's waiting. Goodnight then.'

With that Chas made his way to the counter and placed his order.

Harrie stared after him, stunned by his brusqueness. She hadn't mistaken that look in his eyes when he had been holding her, so why was he acting all distant with her now? Her mind a jumble of thoughts, she left the shop and made her way home.

As she arrived at the entrance that split the Harrises' house from the one next-door, Marion charged up to her.

'Oh, I was just coming to see you,' she breathlessly announced.

A distracted Harrie looked at her blankly for a moment before saying, 'Oh, why?'

'Well, yer could look more pleased to see me, Harrie,' her friend said, hurt.

'I am glad to see you, Marion, of course I am. I thought you were going out for a drink with Allen tonight so I'm surprised, that's all.'

'We are going for a drink but I've come to ask if you'd like to come with us? It'll do you good, Harrie, please say you will? You need to start getting yourself out and about, that's the best way to put the past behind you. Oh, and I found out today that Gillian Innes has split up with her boyfriend same as you have with Jeremy, only for different reasons. She found out he was seeing someone else behind her back and she's devastated, poor gel, but she'll get over it. But this means you won't be stuck for another single woman to pal around with, doesn't it? I quite envy you both in a way, being free and single, having fun going dancing and wondering who you might end up with if yer lucky at the end of the night. Eh, but don't tell Allen I told you that.'

'Thanks for the offer, Marion, but I'm having a night in with my dad tonight and I'm looking forward to it. We're going to be old-time dancing.'

Marion didn't look impressed. 'Oh, well, each to their own, I suppose. Next Saturday though, eh?' She suddenly stared at Harrie quizzically and grabbed her, dragging her over to stand under the street lamp and staring at her hard. 'What's happened?' she demanded.

'Sorry?'

'Summat's happened. You've got a sort of shocked look on your face and you're most certainly acting like you've summat important on your mind.'

Harrie sighed long and loudly. 'You're right, I have just had a shock. A bloody big one, let me tell you.' She eyed her friend earnestly. 'Marion, would it be so bad of me, considering I've only just broken off things with Jeremy and I thought I loved him, didn't I? Only I know now I didn't. I most certainly know now I didn't after . . . well, after what's just happened.'

'Harrie, you're babbling. Why would I consider you bad? For what reason? What did just happen?' Marion demanded. She looked at the parcel in Harrie's arms. 'What *could* have happened on a visit to the chip shop?'

'Well, I knew I liked him but this . . . well . . . Oh, Marion, I think I've fallen in love. In fact, I know I have. Real love this time. He's the man for me, I know he is. He's such a kind man, the sort you feel safe with, and I know he'll be good company to be with, I just know it.' A look of pure rapture flooded Harrie's face. 'Oh, and when he held me in his arms . . . well, I've never felt so . . . so . . . Oh, Marion, I knew when I met him he was going to mean a lot to me, and you suspected he could be the great love of my life though I didn't believe you, but he is, Marion, *he is*!'

Marion was staring at her. 'I take it you're talking about your cuddly bear man at work? Crikey, this is a turn up for the books. That clairvoyant was right, wasn't she? So when are you seeing him? Oh, I can't wait to meet him myself. We could arrange a foursome.'

'Slow down, Marion, he hasn't asked me out yet. That's if he ever does. You see, I'm not sure how he feels about me.'

'Oh, you must have some idea. We women just know when a man has the hots for us, don't we?'

'Well, I did get the impression he was feeling the same as I was when he was holding me in his arms after saving me from slipping. But afterwards, Marion, he acted like touching me had given him a nasty disease or something. I don't understand it, it's really confusing.'

'I'm sure you're imagining things. He saved you from slipping, did he? Oh, how romantic. Tell me what happened!' she enthused.

Harrie did.

After she had finished Marion pulled a knowing face. 'He was just shocked like you were. Poor chap was reeling from what had just hit him.'

'Do you think so, Marion?'

'I'm positive. I bet he asks you out the first opportunity he gets. Oh, I wonder where he'll take you?'

'I don't care. I don't mind if we sit on the park swings, swigging pop from bottles, I just want to be with him. I've never wanted to be with someone so much in all my life. I can't believe this has happened to me.' She paused and looked worriedly at her friend. 'It isn't wrong of me, is it, to be feeling like this for another man so soon after breaking up with Jeremy?'

'Hey, gel, this is Mother Nature you're dealing with. You can't fight her. At least you and Jeremy had broken up before you fell for someone else. I know women who are still with their blokes while hankering after someone else or actually seeing them behind their blokes' backs. For all you know Jeremy has someone else already taking your place. Oh, I can't wait to hear the next instalment! You must promise to come and see me as soon as you leave work on Monday night. You do promise, don't you?'

'You're always the first to know when anything happens to me, aren't you?'

'Look, I'd better be off as Allen is waiting for me. I hope your dad likes cold chips.'

'Pardon? Oh, goodness, I'd forgotten about these,' she exclaimed. 'I'd better hurry too.'

CHAPTER NINETEEN

Despite enjoying the rest of the weekend in her father's company, Monday could not come quick enough for Harrie. She couldn't wait to see Chas again. Couldn't understand how she could be feeling as if every minute she spent away from him was a minute wasted. All she prayed was that Marion's interpretation of his reaction after he'd saved her was right and it had been caused solely by shock upon realising his feelings for her.

The atmosphere in Black's office on Monday morning was sombre. Each employee in turn learned the sad news of their employer's death, and most had private concerns about what the future held for them job-wise. They had no choice but to carry on with business as usual in the meantime and wait until Mrs Black made her decision after the funeral.

Chas was not around at all when Harrie arrived for work but out on a job. It was well after nine-thirty and she was busy in the office checking recorded mileage against petrol receipts when she heard Ralph say, 'Oh, hello, Chas. Glad you got your last job finished sharpish. Glenfield General has just called. They want a package picking up from the Haematology department at ten-thirty and delivered to the Pathology Lab at the Royal Infirmary. You've time for a coffee before you go.' And he added tongue-in-cheek, 'You might as well make one for me while yer at it.'

Grabbing a handful of petrol receipts, her prearranged excuse to go and see Ralph, Harrie shot out of her office and over to his desk just in time to catch Chas making his way to the drivers' rest room.

'Good morning, Chas,' she called brightly across to him.

He still assumed he had embarrassed her by his actions on Saturday night, and had been meaning to apologise to her for doing so. But this was not the right moment for him to pick as Ralph was within earshot. Instead he turned and looked back at her awkwardly, flashed her a brief smile and said a brusque, 'Morning.' Then he hurried into the rest room.

Harrie was stunned by his shortness with her. Then she reasoned with herself that he was unlikely to ask her out with others around. Chas was not the brash, full of himself sort like Darren whose conquests he liked to make common knowledge. She knew she wasn't wrong in her assumption that Chas would wish anything that transpired between them to be their business.

'Did yer want me for summat, Harrie?' Ralph asked her.

'Pardon? Oh, yes, I just wanted to know if you've any petrol receipts out here you haven't given me? I seem to have a couple missing, that's all.'

'Since you've started, the drivers put them on your desk themselves. Any excuse to come in and see you, Harrie.'

She smiled at him. 'The ones I'm missing have probably got hidden under the other paperwork on my desk. Sorry to have disturbed you, Ralph.'

'You can disturb me anytime,' he said, winking at her cheekily.

Just then the outer door opened and a man came in.

'I'll deal with him for you,' Harrie offered. 'Can I help you, sir?' she asked the new arrival, going across to the counter.

'I'd like to speak to one of your drivers if he's available. Mr Tyme?'

'Yes, you're lucky, he's just arrived back in. May I ask your name so I can tell him?'

'Geoffrey Graham. It's about my father.'

'Oh, yes, I was here on Saturday when Chas came back and told us what had happened. We're all so sorry about your loss. I'll get Mr Tyme for you.'

She made her way to the drivers' rest room and poked her head round the door. The room was empty except for Chas who was busy making two cups of coffee.

Harrie went across to him. 'Chas, there's a man at the counter asking to see you. It's Mr Graham's son. He's obviously come to thank you for what you did for his father.'

'Considerate of him to put himself out with all he's having to face at the moment. Thank you for coming to tell me.' He looked at her awkwardly for a moment before fixing his eyes on his hands. 'Er . . . Harrie?'

Excitement raced within her. He was going to ask her out. 'Yes, Chas?'

'I . . . er . . . apologise if I embarrassed you in any way on Saturday night. It wasn't my intention. Right, better not keep Mr Graham's son waiting.'

She stared after him as he hurried out of the room. What on earth made him think he had embarrassed her on Saturday night when in truth it was just the opposite? She racked her brain for any reason she might have given him for thinking such a thing. She couldn't think of anything. In her urgent need to put him straight she rushed after him but he was already addressing the man at the counter so Harrie returned to her office, meaning to do the deed as soon as she got an opportunity.

Chas held his hand out in greeting to Geoffrey Graham. He looked like a pleasant man, in his mid-thirties and clean-cut, but it was very obvious he was suffering from deep distress. 'I'm sorry we meet in such circumstances,' Chas said sincerely.

Geoffrey gave a drawn smile. 'I represent the family. We'd like to express our gratitude for what you did for my father.'

Chas sighed deeply. 'I only wish I could have done more. If it's any consolation, as we drove along before . . . well, before he took ill . . . your father talked very highly of you and your brother, and said he was looking forward to spending more time with your mother on his retirement.'

Geoffrey gulped back a lump in his throat. 'We were very close. He'll be greatly missed. I'm glad I got to see you person-ally and thank you, I was concerned you might be out on a job. Anyway, I must get off. I've to see the funeral director at Ginns and Gutteridge at ten-thirty. So if I could just collect Dad's belongings?'

Chas looked at him, puzzled. 'His belongings?'

'The briefcase that was left in the back of your cab.'

Chas frowned thoughtfully. 'I don't remember any briefcase. I was sitting in the cab when your father got in so I never saw if he was actually carrying anything. I don't remember seeing any of the hospital staff taking a briefcase off with them when they took your father out of the back of my cab, but then at the time it was all quite frantic as I suppose you can appreciate.'

'My father definitely had it with him when you picked him up. It wasn't at the hospital when we went to identify him and collect his things so it must have been left in the back of your cab.' The man's face clouded over worriedly. 'Could your next passenger have picked it up, do you think?'

Chas paused momentarily to think back over events after he'd left the hospital before saying, 'Your father was my last job that night, the firm doesn't operate on a Sunday, and I've only had one job so far this morning and that was an old lady I took into town. She sat in the front with me. If I'd found it when I cleaned out the cab on Saturday night I would have put it in the lost property box which is here in the office. We get all sorts left in cabs as you can imagine. Most people remember eventually and come in to collect them. We keep stuff for six months.' A memory struck him. 'Ah, wait a minute. What happened to your father ... well, it did knock me for six and I signed out on Saturday night without cleaning out my cab. I just wanted to get home, you see. The case will still be in the back.' He lifted the counter flap and joined Geoffrey Graham on the other side. 'Come with me and I'll take you to get it. My car's parked on the road outside.'

Minutes later Chas looked helplessly at Geoffrey Graham. 'As you can see for yourself, the case isn't here. Your father couldn't have had it on him when he got into my cab or else it's in the hospital somewhere.'

Geoffrey's face was paling rapidly. 'But they've checked everywhere it could be and it's definitely not at the hospital. My father left Mr Timminson's house in Leicester Forest East where you picked him up with his case in his hand. Mr Timminson's solicitor was there at the time and is a reliable witness. Mr Tyme, there was six thousand pounds in that case.'

Chas's eyes widened in shock. 'What?'

'It was the proceeds of the sale of his business. It's all we have in the world to secure our future.'

'Yes, your father told me he'd just completed the sale.'

A look of accusation filled Geoffrey Graham's eyes then. 'So you knew he had money on him?'

Chas flinched. 'Mr Graham, no, I most certainly did not know your father was carrying the proceeds of the sale on him. He just told me he had completed negotiations.'

A look of remorse crossed the other man's face. 'Look, Mr Tyme, you can understand . . .'

'Yes, I can,' Chas cut in. 'I am the obvious suspect, aren't I? Well, I can only give you my word that I knew nothing about the briefcase and say again that if your father got in my cab with it, it would still be here. You need to get the police involved. I'll willingly be interviewed by them and tell them all I know.'

As the implications of the case's absence sank in, Geoffrey Graham stared at Chas blindly for several long moments before his shoulders sagged despairingly and he uttered, 'I'll go and see them as soon as I've dealt with the funeral arrangements. I have to find that case.' He held out his hand towards Chas. 'Thank you, Mr Tyme.'

He accepted the gesture and they shook hands. 'I'm sure the police will turn it up,' Chas said, sincerely hoping they would but deep down wondering if there was a dishonest member of the hospital staff who was now revelling in their good fortune.

'You don't know how much I hope they do! It's bad enough coping with losing Dad. Without the money . . .' The man took a deep breath. 'Good day, Mr Tyme.'

A solemn Chas watched as he walked away towards the bus stop.

Harrie was coming out of her office to ask Ralph's help in deciphering Marlene's scrawl on a job she had logged into the book the previous Saturday evening and could not help noticing the gravity of Chas's expression when he returned inside the office. It was obvious to her that something had transpired between him and Mr Graham's son that had upset Chas badly.

She walked across to waylay him, the intended offer of support not just made towards the man who had won her affections but something she would have offered any work colleague in similar circumstances. 'Chas, could you spare me a moment in my office, please?' Without waiting for a response from him she made her way there.

As he joined her, thinking she needed to see him regarding the paperwork, he asked, 'What can I do for you, Harrie?'

'It's what I can do for you, Chas. Please sit down,' she said, indicating a chair to the front of her desk.

She was aware that he seemed very ill at ease but hoped it was because he realised he had strong feelings for her and didn't know how to proceed while they were both officially working. Wasn't she herself feeling all jangly inside in anticipation of what was to come? All it needed was for him to make a move so they could embark on the wonderful relationship she knew without a doubt they were going to share together. But at the moment it was clear Chas had other things on his mind.

She smiled warmly at him. 'It's obvious to me you're upset about something. I wondered if I could be of any help?'

He looked startled at that. He was confused as to why she had apparently been embarrassed by his actions on Saturday night, but now was offering him help as if she cared about him? Then he realised the intimate moment on Saturday had taken place in public where people could easily misconstrue the relationship between them, whereas now they were in a work environment and her concern was strictly that of one colleague for another. In that light he appreciated her offer and proceeded to tell her what had just transpired.

Harrie had no doubt at all that Chas was telling the absolute truth when he said he had no idea where the briefcase was. When he had finished, she said, 'I'm positive Mr Graham does not believe you've anything to do with the missing case, Chas, please put your mind at rest on that. People only have to talk to you to see how honest you are. I hate to think it, but if Mr Graham Senior definitely had the case on him when he got into your car then it has to have been taken by a member of staff at the hospital. The police will find out the truth.'

'I just hope someone comes across it slipped inside a cupboard somewhere. That money is crucial to the Grahams' future survival. I dread to think what's going to happen to them if they don't find it. If the police come to interview me when I'm out on a job, will you please make sure I'm radioed to come straight in so I can tell them all I know as soon as possible and they can get on with their investigations?'

'Yes, of course I will.' Here was the ideal opportunity to put him straight about thinking he'd embarrassed her by his actions on Saturday night. 'Er . . . Chas, about . . .'

Her words were interrupted by Darren breezing in to perch on the edge of her desk. A suggestive look on his face, he leaned over towards her and said, 'Hello, gorgeous. I've a couple of petrol receipts for you.' He fished them out of his pocket and held them out to her. 'Cream are doing a gig at the Ilrondo night club tonight and I've two tickets. How about you and me tripping the light fantastic together?'

Convinced he was in the way of Harrie and Darren making arrangements to go out for the evening, Chas got up. 'I've the hospital job and I'll be late if I don't get a move on. Thanks for your help, I appreciate it, Harrie. Darren,' he said, nodding at the other man.

Without giving Harrie a chance to stop him, he left.

She glared at Darren, annoyed at his intrusion on her private conversation. She had been denied her chance to put Chas right and had also hoped that with that out of the way he might have taken the opportunity to ask her out. Darren's untimely arrival had put paid to that.

'Thank you for the receipts,' she said to him shortly. 'You will excuse me, I've a mountain of things to do.'

'Yeah, 'course I'll let you get on.' He got up off the desk. 'That's a yes for tonight then, is it?' he said confidently. 'I'll meet you at eight, shall I, in the Stag and Pheasant and we can have a drink first?'

'No, that isn't a yes for tonight, and no, I will not meet you at eight. But whoever you take, I hope you have a good time.'

He gave a nonchalant shrug. 'Okay, maybe not tonight then, but you won't be able to resist my charms for long,' he said, giving her a confident smile. 'No woman can.'

With that he breezed out of the office.

Harrie couldn't believe his conceitedness but was more concerned that Chas would think there was something going on between herself and Darren. She planned to get Chas on one side as soon as she could but for the rest of the day he was busy on jobs.

Harrie had barely finished washing the dinner dishes that evening when Marion arrived.

'I couldn't wait to find out what happened today,' she said excitedly. 'I'm not stopping as I've Allen's dinner to get. So come on then, spill the beans. When yer seeing him? Where's he taking you? What yer wearing?'

As she dried her hands, Harrie realised her father was looking at her quizzically from the back room doorway. 'Women's talk, Dad,' she said to him.

'Oh, I see,' Percy said knowingly. 'I'll leave yer to it then.' He departed into the back room shutting the kitchen door behind him, affording his daughter and her friend privacy.

Harrie sighed heavily. 'Today went nothing like I was hoping it would, Marion. In fact, it turned into a complete nightmare.'

'Oh!'

She sighed again. 'Not only is Chas under the impression he embarrassed me on Saturday night, though I can't understand at all why he should think so, he's also under the impression there's something going on between me and Darren.'

Harrie told her friend exactly what had transpired that day.

'He seems to think he's God's gift, does that Darren,' Marion said when Harrie had finished. 'I wish I was working at Black's so I could bring him down a peg or two. You've got to let Chas know he didn't upset you on Saturday night, just the opposite in fact, and that there's nothing going on between you and Darren.'

'That's easier said than done, Marion. Chas and I might work at the same place but we don't come into contact that often. He's mostly out on jobs, and then actually catching him when he does come in with no one else around is another matter.'

'Well, he ain't going to ask you out until you do put him right on both counts, so it's up to you to keep yer beady eyes peeled and grab him at your first opportunity.'

Harrie just hoped that such an opportunity didn't take too long presenting itself. But then she reminded herself of the saying: If something is worth having, it's worth waiting for. She had no doubt whatsoever that Chas Tyme was.

CHAPTER TWENTY

Jack Black's funeral took place that Thursday morning. It was a well-attended affair, the small church packed to bursting with family, friends, acquaintances and employees. A spread had been laid on in the church hall afterwards. Out of respect for Jack and for those employees who wanted to attend, the firm was closed during the morning but open again that afternoon to serve the clientele Jack had built up over his twenty years in business.

Harrie hadn't come into contact with Chas on a one-to-one basis since their chat in the office which had been abruptly cut short by Darren, a situation that was frustrating the hell out of her.

She was in close proximity to him during the funeral but had to quash her overwhelming desire to seize the opportunity. This was not the time or place to be thinking of her own personal problems. They were all gathered to pay their respects to Jack Black and be a support to his grieving widow.

During the service Chas had been very aware of Harrie and feared she was finding the sad occasion a strain. He had desperately wanted to offer her comfort but did not want a repetition of the incident in the chip shop. Besides, any offer of support should surely come from Darren as he presumed they were an item, though he couldn't understand why Harrie seemed to be shunning Darren's attentions recently.

Two noticeable absences from the gathering of employees at their boss's funeral had been Marlene and Terry. No one seemed surprised that Marlene hadn't shown herself. Terry hadn't shown up for his shifts at all this week and no word had been received from him as to the reason. It was presumed he was ill enough to be bedridden. Everyone hoped that his recovery would be swift as there was no one to cover his job. Thankfully no car had suffered serious mechanical problems while he'd been off, and any minor repairs the drivers had attended to themselves.

When they all returned to the office the telephone was ringing. Like the other drivers, Chas had immediately been despatched on a job while Harrie got stuck into her office work. They were all conscious, though, that it was only a matter of time now before Mrs Black informed them of her intentions regarding the business, and they were all secretly worried as to what the future could hold for them.

Harrie was leaving the office that night and just saying her goodbyes to Ralph when Marlene sauntered in.

She glanced Ralph over and cocked an eyebrow sardonically. 'What's with the suit?' Then she looked Harrie over. 'Posh coat for work, in't it?' Then, stripping off her own, she said, laughing, 'Ain't both bin to a funeral, have yer?'

'Well, actually, yes, we have,' said Ralph, and added stonily, 'As it happens, your boss's.'

'Oh, yeah, I forgot that that was today,' she said casually. 'Oh, did anyone bring any goodies back from the funeral lunch?' She was casting her eyes down the signing in book to see if Darren had already left.

Ralph was just about to respond suitably to her flippant remark when Darren came in to sign out and, seeming oblivious to the way Marlene's face lit up at his entrance, immediately accosted Harrie.

No one spotted Chas enter seconds after Darren along with several other drivers who had also come in to sign out for the night.

'Hello, gorgeous,' Darren said to Harrie, his tone very suggestive. 'I saw yer looking at me at the funeral. Mind you, I can't blame yer, I was the best-looking bloke there.'

Before Harrie knew what was happening to her, someone had her pinned up against the wall and was screaming at her, 'You bitch, I fucking knew you were after my man!'

It was Marlene.

'I can assure you, I have no interest in Darren whatsoever,' Harrie retorted, desperately trying to push her away.

'Liar!' Marlene spat ferociously 'You were eyeing him up at the funeral, I just heard Darren say so. You know he's mine, everyone does.'

She started beating Harrie hard with her fists. Harrie, eyes closed, had her arms over her face to try and protect herself while crying out, 'Marlene, stop it! Stop it, will you? You've got it wrong, I've no interest in Darren.' The blows suddenly ceased and she heard Marlene screaming, 'Get off me, will yer? Get off me!' Harrie lowered her arms and opened her eyes to see that Chas had Marlene in a bear-like grip around her waist and was holding her away from him while she was kicking out her legs and screaming abuse at him. 'Put me down, you bastard. Let me get back at her to give her the pasting she deserves. Bleddy tart she is! Put me down, I said.'

Darren was looking on at proceedings with great amusement. He gave Ralph, standing next to him, a nudge in his ribs. 'Yer've gotta be summat, ain't yer, when yer've got two women fighting over yer?'

From the doorway a stern voice boomed, 'Marlene, I'd like to speak to you in the office *now*.'

Chas dropped Marlene and all the occupants of the room turned to see Mrs Black standing in the doorway. She did not look happy. A distinguished-looking man carrying a briefcase stood by her side. He looked appalled.

'It was her what started it, Mrs Black,' Marlene cried accusingly, pointing at Harrie. 'She attacked me 'cos I found out she was trying to get my man off me.'

'I'm not *your* man and never will be,' Darren spoke up, looking at her with a sneer. 'I wouldn't be seen dead with the likes of you, yer dozy cow!'

'That's enough,' the man with Mrs Black snapped. 'Show some respect, can't you? Mrs Black has buried her husband today who, may I remind you, was your boss.' He fixed his eyes on Marlene. 'Mrs Black asked you, young lady, for a private word in the office. And don't bother with any more lies as we were both witness to exactly what transpired. The rest of you, please wait here. Mrs Black would like to address you.'

Marlene, her face thunderous, slunk off into the office and Muriel Black followed, shutting the door behind her. The rest of them all milled round waiting for their employer to come back out. No one needed to wonder what she was going to speak to them about.

Chas was standing on his own by the drivers' rest room door

when Harrie took the opportunity to go across and speak to him.

Her voice low so that no one else would hear, she said, 'I can't imagine what Mrs Black must be thinking of us.'

'Neither can I. I don't like to speak ill of anyone but I fear Marlene is about to get what she deserves. I couldn't believe it when I saw her launch herself like that at you, and unprovoked.' He looked at her closely. 'Are you all right? She didn't hurt you, did she?'

His concern was so genuine that Harrie smiled warmly at him. 'I've a feeling I've a couple of nice bruises on my arm but nothing that a dab of witch hazel won't sort out. My injuries could have been much worse if you hadn't stepped in so quickly. Thank you for coming to my rescue again, Chas.'

'Oh, if it hadn't been me who got in first, one of the other men would have,' he said matter-of-factly.

'But you did, Chas, and I'm glad it was you.' Harrie was feeling a prickling sensation all over to be standing so close to this man she desperately wanted the chance to get to know better. She was positive that once she did she had a wonderful future with him. She took a deep breath. 'Chas, it's important to me you know there is nothing between me and Darren and never will be. Also, I don't know how you got the idea I was embarrassed when you saved me from falling in the chip shop. I wasn't, far from it.'

He felt a sudden rush of joy that nothing was going on between Harrie and Darren, then it evaporated as it struck him that it didn't matter whether there was or wasn't as far as her looking in his direction was concerned. He couldn't understand why Harrie should feel it was important he should hear these things. He really wished she wouldn't look at him in that way. If he didn't know better he would be under the impression she fancied him. But he *did* know better. If good-looking, outgoing Darren was getting nowhere with her, then Chas stood absolutely no chance. He'd been such a fool in the chip shop, believing for those few seconds that she'd not scream in protest if he'd followed his mindless desire and scooped her up in his arms and run off with her.

'Well, I . . . er . . . appreciate you telling me, Harrie.'

She waited with bated breath, hoping that now he'd been put

straight he'd suggest their going out together. To her disappointment he didn't. Then she remembered that despite not quite being in earshot of anyone they weren't exactly on their own at present. Chas had a sense of decorum, unlike Darren who seemed to possess none whatsoever. That thought only made her respect Chas more. She fought for something to say to keep conversation flowing between them and remembered she did have something to ask him about. 'How did your interview with the police go, Chas?'

'Oh, thanks for asking, yes, they seemed to be happy with everything I told them. I said I was available any time if they needed to question me further. I really do hope for the Grahams' sake that they find that case. I think the police suspect as I do that it's in the hospital somewhere.'

Just then the office door was thrust open and Marlene came storming out, shouting at the top of her voice, 'Who d'yer think you are, telling me it doesn't make any difference whether I felt provoked by that temporary office bitch or not? It's a poxy job anyway and you can stick it up yer arse!' She stuck two fingers up at Mrs Black who was coming out of the office herself, before grabbing her coat and shoulder bag from where she had left them on the radio-operator's desk when she had first come in.

As she reached the staff entrance she turned to look back at Darren, sneering at him. 'You say you wouldn't be seen dead with me, eh? Well, that's not what yer said when you was giving me one across the desk the other night when yer passed by on yer way home from the pub. I was good enough for yer then, wasn't I, yer bastard?' She stared across at Harrie. 'You're welcome to my cast-off 'cos I wouldn't have him now if he was the last man on earth. Oh, and in case yer don't know yet he's got a little dick and no idea what to do with it. Like me, you'll have to pretend yer enjoying it to feed his ego.' She cast an amused eye over them all. 'I shan't hold me breath for a leaving present and I can't tell a lie and say I'll miss you all. Ta-ra.'

With that she slung her coat over her shoulder and stalked off the premises.

They all stared after her for a moment speechless before Darren broke the silence by blurting, 'It's not true what Marlene said about me having a little d—'

'I'm sure none of us believed her,' cut in the distinguished-looking man who'd accompanied Mrs Black. He turned to look at her. 'Would you like me to speak to the staff on your behalf?'

Muriel shook her head. 'Thank you but it's only right I do this.' She faced the gathering. They all knew the smile on her face was forced. Jack Black's widow was grieving deeply for the man she had loved for the last forty years. The situation she'd just had to deal with couldn't have helped either.

She took a deep breath. Clasping her hands in front of her, she began: 'As you can appreciate this has been a very sad day for me. Mr Grogin, Jack's . . . my . . . solicitor who's come with me today wanted me to leave what I have to tell you for another occasion, but I felt it only fair that you should know my decision about the firm as soon as I'd made it. First, though, I want to thank all those of you who came to the funeral today. Jack would have appreciated it. As you know, he lived and breathed his business and I always said that one day it would be the death of him. Hard work never killed anyone, it's said, but that's a lie 'cos it certainly did him no favours.'

She paused momentarily before continuing. 'I've decided to sell up. I've no head myself for business and under my charge it would more than likely end up bankrupt. And to be honest I've no heart for it now even if I had the necessary skills to run it.' They could all clearly see she was fighting to keep control of her emotions as she spoke. 'I've no idea how long it will take to find a buyer but I hope whoever does take this place will keep you all on. Be assured I'll tell whoever it is what a loyal and trustworthy bunch you are. Until then I know I can trust you to see that it's business as usual.

Ralph, you were kind enough to come out of retirement when Jack first took ill and help out. I hope you'll stay on in the meantime? You too, Harrie. I'm more than happy with the grand job you're doing. I have no doubt many firms would like to snap you up, offering better pay and conditions than you're getting here, and it's probably a cheek of me to hope you'll consider staying like Ralph until . . . until . . .'

It all became too much for her then. She fumbled in her handbag for a handkerchief to wipe away the tears.

Mr Grogin took her arm. 'Let's get you home.' He flashed a brief smile at the gathering before he led her out.

'Well,' said Ralph, sighing sadly, 'that's that then. We can only wait and see what happens next. Like Mrs Black said, though, until the business is sold we carry on as usual.'

'Why does something like this always happen so near Christmas?' one of the drivers grumbled.

'Yer can't blame Jack for that,' responded another.

Chas could tell that discord was beginning to manifest itself and in order to defuse the situation said, 'At least we know we do have a job over Christmas and maybe for some time after that. It'll take a while surely for a buyer to be found and the deal to go through.'

'Yeah, I grant yer that, Chas, but I'm keeping me eyes and ears open in case summat more permanent comes along,' said Brian Kirk, one of the night-shift drivers.

Several other drivers mumbled their agreement.

'Well, that's everyone's right,' said Chas. 'But while we're employed by Black's it's only fair we're as loyal as we've ever been.'

'Chas is right,' piped up Harrie. 'And think about it this way. If a buyer sees how well this place is operating then he won't feel the need to make changes, will he, and your jobs will be safe.'

They saw the wisdom in what she was saying and nodded approvingly.

'We do have another more pressing problem,' Harrie continued. 'Now that Marlene has gone there's no evening-shift radio operator.'

Caught up with the announcement of the selling of Black's they'd forgotten about that problem.

'Well, I can't say I'm sorry to see the back of that little madam but Mrs Black obviously hasn't realised we need someone tonight. Then, it ain't surprising with all she's had on her mind,' said Ralph. 'It's going to take a few days to advertise and inter- view and then get someone started. I could stay on and cover for tonight, I suppose, although me wife ain't gonna like it.'

Chas smiled at the old man. 'No disrespect, Ralph, but you've been on your feet ten hours as it is and that's enough for anyone of your age. I'll cover for tonight. Jim, could you pop into my house on your way home and tell my mother what's happening or she'll worry?' he asked one of the other drivers.

'Yeah, 'course, mate,' agreed Jim.

'And I'll do tomorrow night,' said Harrie. 'I've watched you, Ralph, and know how the radio operates.'

Chas looked at her in surprise that she should offer. But then the better he was getting to know Harrie, the more he realised she wasn't the type to stand back when someone needed help. She really was a woman in a million. He so envied the man she'd choose to share her life with.

'I don't mind doing my bit 'til yer get someone in permanent as I could do with the extra towards Christmas,' said a driver.

'Count me in too,' said another. And another after that.

Harrie smiled. 'I'll sort out a roster tomorrow.'

As she made her way home she felt terrible in the circumstances for the sense of disappointment she was experiencing. If Chas hadn't volunteered to cover this evening's shift he might possibly have suggested they walk partway home together and maybe by now, should things have gone the way she so vehemently hoped, they would have been planning an evening out together, the first of many.

She found her father bustling around the kitchen. It struck her that just lately Percy seemed to have found an extra zest for living, though she couldn't for the life of her think what could be the cause of it. Maybe it was because he'd had a reprieve, she wasn't leaving him to cope on his own now she was not getting married to Jeremy.

'You're a bit later than usual tonight, lovey,' he said, planting a kiss on her cheek. 'I hope the funeral went well.'

She told him about it and the reason for her lateness.

'Oh, dear, Mrs Black's selling up then, is she? Well, I suppose it's the only thing she can do, her having no head for business. Good thing you'll have a job there until the sale goes through at least. Yer never know, whoever takes it on might offer you the office job permanently. You've enjoyed it from the start, but the longer yer there the more yer getting to like it, lovey, I can tell.'

Harrie privately wondered if the fact Chas worked there was what really made her enjoy the job as much as she did.

'I've made us a cheese and potato pie for our dinner,' Percy announced proudly.

'Oh, is that what I could smell when I came in? I have to say, it smells good, Dad.' Despite her immense feeling of pride in him for what he was undertaking, nevertheless she said, 'You're taking this cooking lark seriously, aren't you? But you don't need to really, it's not like I'm leaving you to fend for yourself now.'

'Oh, yes, well, er . . . you will one day and I need to be prepared.' Percy's face lit up and he began, 'And I am so enjoying meself with . . .' before suddenly he stopped.

She frowned at him quizzically. 'Enjoying yourself with what, Dad?'

'Eh? Oh, with what I'm doing learning to cook and having a meal ready for you when you come home, instead of you having to do it.'

A warm glow filled Harrie. She had a wonderful father. Most men of his age and in his position would be sitting back, letting their offspring run after them, but not her father.

As he tucked into his pie Percy said to Harrie, 'All right, is it?'

It was rather bland for her liking, felt like it needed more seasoning, and she would never have dreamed of adding diced carrots, peas and chopped Savoy cabbage to it. She wondered what had made her father think of doing so. Nevertheless Harrie enthused, 'It's very good, Dad.'

CHAPTER TWENTY-ONE

After covering the radio-operator's position until ten, and considering he'd already done a ten-hour shift, Chas was almost falling asleep on his feet by the time he got home. He glanced down blankly at the plate of food his mother had just set before him. It looked very dried up but he couldn't blame her for that. When she had prepared it she would have had no idea it was going to be four hours after his normal home-time before he would be eating it. He guessed the white-looking stuff on his plate to be mashed potato with cheese mixed through it, and recognised the exposed peas and florets of broccoli, but he did not know what the white-ish chunks were. He had thought at first they were potato lumps as his mother wasn't the best at mashing potatoes but then he realised they weren't. Now it struck him these chunks were in fact diced parsnips.

'What yer staring at yer dinner like that for? It ain't gonna bite yer. Now tuck in, son, before it gets cold,' Iris told him, sitting down opposite cradling a cup of tea. Before he put his fork in his mouth, she said, 'I hope Mr Black's funeral went all right?'

'Yes, it did, Mam. Well, as well as funerals go, I suppose. There was a really good turn out. Mrs Black came into the office tonight to tell us all she's decided to sell up.'

The response he received to this news wasn't quite what he was expecting. 'Oh, really!' Iris enthused, putting down her cup and looking at him excitedly.

'You seem pleased, Mam. You do realise that I could end up looking for another job if whoever buys it decides not to keep some of us on. They could bring in their own staff instead.' And, he thought, one not so near to home so he wouldn't be conveniently on hand should his mother have need of him.

'Yes, I realise that and that's how I come to have the answer to make sure you do keep yer job. I thought of this a while ago and wanted to tell you my idea but I never got around to it.'

'So what is this answer you've come up with?' he asked her.

'Well, it's really quite simple, son. You should buy Black's.'

He looked astounded. 'Me!'

'Yes, why not?'

'Why not? Well, for a start, what do I know about running a business?'

'What did Jack Black know before he started up, and he did all right for himself. And anyway, it won't be like starting from scratch for you. Everything's already in place for you to take over. You might even come up with some ways to make the business better and more profitable.'

His mother was showing a faith in his abilities he wasn't sure he possessed himself. 'But aren't you forgetting one big obstacle, Mam? Where am I supposed to get the money from to buy Black's with?'

'Oh, that's easy. You've yer savings and the rest you borrow from a bank.'

'You've thought this through, haven't you, Mam?'

Iris scowled at him. 'Don't look so surprised. I might only be a housewife but that doesn't mean to say I ain't a brain in me head.'

'I'm sorry, Mam, I didn't mean to imply that you haven't. But my savings are intended to buy you a new house that'll be nicer for you to live in and much easier to keep.'

'I keep telling yer, son, and I wish you'd listen to me: I'm happy where I am. If you buy that house and all these labour-saving machines you keep on about, you'll be moving into it and using the machines on your own. Now please, let that be the last of it. About buying Black's . . .'

'Mam, please, there's no point in discussing this because . . . because . . .'

'Because what? Oh, you don't need to tell me. I know. It's because you don't think you're capable of running a business.' Her face screwed up angrily. 'Those Dewhurst kids have so much to answer for, knocking your confidence right out of the window with their nasty antics when you was a kid. You *do* have it in you to do whatever you want to, Chas, and make a great success of it. What will it take for you to realise that? You're a good man, one who'd make a great boss people would be happy to work for and be loyal to. There wasn't much I could do when you was young to stop those Dewhursts plaguing the life out of yer. They were such sneaky little so-and-so's that catching 'em at it was nigh on impossible, but what I can do now is stop you from passing up such a good opportunity. One which might never come your way again.'

She eyed him tenderly. 'For what it's worth, son, I love you too much ever to suggest you do anything you ain't capable of tackling. I know you ain't the type to want to seek revenge on anyone, but wouldn't it just be a kick in the teeth to those Dewhursts, eh, to show them that the boy they constantly taunted as being useless had grown up to be a businessman while they . . . well, we all know how *they've* turned out.' She could tell he still wasn't convinced of his ability to aim higher. 'All right, I'll make you a deal. When yer make yer first clear profit that's enough to buy me one of them posh houses with all those labour-saving gadgets you keep threatening me with, *then* I'll move into it.'

His mother was blackmailing him. He knew she was well aware that his greatest desire was to make her life as easy as he could and that he was willing to do anything to achieve that. Chas wasn't the type, though, to go headlong into doing something without checking it out thoroughly first. 'All right, Mam,' he sighed. 'I suppose it wouldn't hurt to make some enquiries.'

A grin of delight split her face. 'That's the ticket, son. Now the first thing you should do is approach young Harrie to give you an idea what sort of profit the firm makes. As she's updating the books, she will be in the know. Then before you approach the bank you need to find out how much Mrs Black is expecting for the firm.'

Chas shook his head at her. 'You make it sound so easy, Mam.' He eyed her quizzically. 'How did you know Harrie was updating the books?'

'Eh? You told me she was.'

'I don't remember telling you anything of the kind. In fact, I don't remember discussing Harrie with you at all.'

'Well, you must have or how else would I know? So you'll get on to it first thing in the morning? No sense in wasting time or yer risk someone else beating you to it. Now eat yer dinner before it gets cold,' Iris ordered him. 'You're going to need all your energy in future when you're a boss.'

As he tucked in Chas's thoughts were whirling. It was madness his considering taking over Black's Taxis even if the bank would lend him the money. But then, what if he did? If the business did make a reasonable profit under his ownership, not only would he fulfil his ambition to make his mother's life better, he could also do his best to keep the other drivers and staff in work, maybe even pay them a little more in their wage packets to give them a better standard of living. He only had his mother and himself to keep on his wage. They might not live frugally but neither were they spendthrifts by any stretch of the imagination. How the other drivers coped with the costs involved in supporting themselves plus wives and children he'd no idea, even though he knew some of the men upped their wage by illegal means. He was also well aware what long hours taxi drivers had to work to earn their money, leaving them little time to be with their families. Maybe he could find a way to improve their lot.

As all these thoughts and ideas were going around in his head, not once did Chas think of the rewards that would come his way as the owner of a business. He thought only of what it would bring to others.

CHAPTER TWENTY-TWO

Chas didn't get the chance to approach Harrie until after eleven the next day. He'd slept badly the previous night, tossing and turning, going over in his mind the enormous undertaking his mother seemed to be absolutely certain he had every chance of making a success of, and battling all the time with his own terrible lack of self-confidence which was telling him the opposite. When he got up that morning, Iris had made him promise he wouldn't come home that night until he had at least approached Harrie and obtained some facts and figures, ascertained whether it was worth proceeding further.

Sincerely hoping that Harrie wouldn't mind his taking up her time on what he felt was more than likely a fool's errand, Chas tapped on her office door. On hearing her response, he popped his head round. 'Would it be convenient to have a private word, Harrie?'

Her heart pounded. At last. It looked like he was nervous and she didn't need to ask why. 'Yes, of course, Chas. Please come in,' she said enthusiastically. As he sat down on the chair in front of her desk she saw a look of discomfiture momentarily cross his face. 'Are you all right? she asked.

He rubbed his chest. 'I've indigestion. My mother made cheese and potato pie for my dinner last night and it's sitting heavy on me.'

'Oh, what a coincidence! My father made the same for my dinner last night. Mind you, I don't know where he got the recipe from as I've never had cheese and potato pie with an assortment of other vegetables in it before.'

'Isn't cheese and potato pie supposed to have an assortment of vegetables in it then?'

'No. Just cheese and potatoes, that's why it's called cheese and potato pie, Chas. Why did you ask that?'

'Oh, well, it's just my mother always puts vegetables in hers so I wouldn't be any the wiser.'

Harrie was desperate for him to get to the point. 'You wanted a private word with me?' she gently prompted him.

'Oh, yes, I did.' He scraped his hand through his hair. 'I don't know where to start really. I don't want you to think I'm mad even to be considering it . . .'

'I would never think such a thing of you, Chas,' she cut him short to reassure him. 'Now just ask me what you want to ask me?' she urged.

He took a breath. 'All right. Look, this isn't my idea but my mother's.'

His mother's! She would have preferred it to have been his idea but supposed she was pleased to hear that Chas's mother approved enough of her to suggest he ask her out. She had taken a liking to Iris when the woman had come to her and her father's rescue at the bus stop and had spent a pleasant hour afterwards in the café listening to her chatter. It was mostly about the son she was obviously proud of, and Harrie herself now knew that pride in him to be more than justified.

'Well, I would never have thought of it myself, you see.'

She looked taken aback. 'You wouldn't?'

'Oh, no. I can see her point, I suppose, about not letting this opportunity pass me by when I might not get another like it but . . . well, I don't know whether I'm up to it, you see, as I've no experience really.'

She liked the thought he hadn't been with many girls, it made her feel special, but she did wonder why he was telling her as usually men liked to brag about their experience not the lack of it. But then Chas wasn't most men and that was why she had fallen in love with him. 'Experience doesn't matter, Chas,' she reassured him.

'Do you think? That's a relief to hear. I thought it would be very important, you see, so as to make a success of it. If I do go ahead with this I want to do my best to make a success of it.'

She was so pleased to hear that. Her mind started to wander to what she would wear for their first date. Depending, of course, on where he took her. She didn't mind really but a meal would be nice then they could chat and get to know each other. There was so much she wanted to know about him and obviously he'd want the same. She wished though he'd stop going around the houses and just ask her for a date. 'Just ask me what you want to ask me, Chas?' she prompted.

'Oh, yes, I apologise for taking up your time. I do appreciate you're very busy. Is it making a profit?'

Harrie looked at him stupefied. 'Sorry?'

'Well, there's no point in me going any further with this if it's not in profit. I presume it is or else Jack would have thrown in the towel long ago but I need to know how much for when I approach the bank. Then I can be sure I can repay the loan comfortably as well as everything else. Provided, of course, they will lend me what money I need and Mrs Black isn't asking more than I can afford for the business.'

She gawped at him, stunned. 'Oh, so you want my opinion as to whether the firm is viable as I do the books and you're considering buying it?'

Now Chas looked confused. 'Yes, that's right.' His face clouded over. 'Do you think this is a hare-brained idea for me even to be considering?'

Harrie fought to hide the acute disappointment she was experiencing. 'No, not at all. It's just this isn't what I was expecting you to ask . . . er . . . Look, I'm sure Mrs Black won't have any objection to me divulging this information in the circumstances. I've just about got the books up-to-date and a regular profit is showing. This sort of business can have its ups and downs, but overall takings average out at five hundred pounds a week, give or take. Not huge by some firms' standards, and you need to work out how much the weekly repayment on the loan would be plus wages, rent on the premises, etcetera. But what you'd be left with, I feel, would be more than you're earning as an employee. I do know how much it is as I do the wages. It's certainly better to be your own boss than work for someone else, if you get the chance.' Harrie looked at him searchingly. 'I think your mother's right to tell you to consider buying the firm if you can. It's a wonderful idea. You'd make a great boss, Chas.'

'You think so?'

She nodded. 'I'd work for you.' I'd more than work for you if you'd give me the chance, she thought.

'Would you?'

She was surprised that he seemed so shocked to hear it. 'If anything goes ahead, would you consider keeping me on as your office staff?'

He couldn't envisage this office without her in it. 'If I'm successful in getting the business then consider the job yours, Harrie. I hope the other staff feel they'd like to work for me too. If this does come off, I was thinking that maybe I could shorten their hours or rearrange them somehow so they can spend more time with their families. I also hope it might be possible to pay them a bit more on the hourly rate so they can have a better standard of living.'

Oh, Chas, she thought, what a lovely, lovely man you are. How could you possibly doubt anyone would want to work for you? Yet he did, and she couldn't understand why he should have such a lack of confidence in himself.

'I have to say, I'm worried I'm about to bite off more than I can chew,' he said, looking undecided.

'I bet Mr Ford thought just that when he started planning his first production line to make cars.'

'Mmm, yes, I suppose. But are you sure it's not important to have experience?'

When she had said that she'd thought he was talking about something else! 'Well, maybe you haven't the office experience but that's what you'd pay me to handle for you, and it's not like you don't know how a taxi firm operates, is it? You're a cabby yourself so you must have a good idea.'

'Maybe not all the ins and outs but I have a good knowledge of the basics.'

'More than some people have when they start up a business. I bet you know more than you think you do, and what you don't know you can soon learn. Anyway, it's not like you're starting this business up from scratch, is it? Everything is already in place so really you'd just be taking it over.'

'That's what my mother said.'

'Well, we can't both be wrong, can we?' Harrie paused thoughtfully for a moment before saying, 'Tyme's Taxis. It's got a good ring to it. Oh, a good slogan would be: *On Tyme Taxis*.' She grabbed a piece of paper and wrote it down then showed it to him. 'I can just picture that on the side of the cabs.'

Chas looked impressed. 'That's very clever, you thinking of

that. You really think I should seriously consider taking this further then?'

Harrie was pleased he liked her slogan and valued her opinion. 'I most certainly do, Chas. I think you should approach Mrs Black immediately to find out how much she wants for the place. In the meantime I'll see if one of the drivers will swap the radio-operator's shift with me tonight and then work late to get the books bang up to date so you'll be able to show the bank the figures should the price Mrs Black is expecting not prove too extortionate.'

How thoughtful of her to offer to do that for him, he thought. But then he guessed she would offer to do it for anyone. And, after all, she had shown a deep interest in working here permanently so all she was really doing was her bit towards securing a position for herself.

'You could go in your lunch hour to see Mrs Black,' Harrie suggested to him. 'No point in wasting time, Chas. You can be damn' sure if you dilly-dally on something like this, someone will jump in and beat you to it.'

And if I do dilly-dally it will give me time to think more deeply about what I'm going to do and there is a danger I will lose my nerve, he thought. He wondered if Harrie realised how much encouragement she had given him. Once again he was finding how easy he found her to talk to. She hadn't made him feel inadequate for considering doing something most people of his ilk wouldn't even contemplate. Once again he deeply envied the man who won her affections as Harrie seemed to him a rarity amongst women, certainly the women of around her age he had come across anyway.

He stood up. 'Thank you, Harrie.'

'My pleasure to help a friend, Chas.'

She considered him a friend? He felt a blush of embarrassment creeping up his neck, wondering what he'd done to deserve such an accolade. But he could do with a friend to help him through this if he was to proceed, especially one like Harrie. He felt privileged to have her.

Mixed emotions raced through Harrie as she watched Chas leave her office. She was pleased he had turned to her for help and advice regarding the enormous undertaking he was embarking on. But she was also greatly disappointed that he hadn't taken the opportunity to ask her out. Then she told herself that she was being unreasonable, expecting him to start a relationship with her while his mind was consumed by such important matters. Men were not like women who could easily handle several things at once. She needed to have patience, allow him to deal with buying the business, then once that was settled one way or the other, hopefully he would turn his attention to her.

CHAPTER TWENTY-THREE

Anyone witnessing the tall, well-made, smartly suited man walking purposefully up the Humberstone Gate the following Tuesday morning would have been very surprised to know of his inner turmoil. Armed with the facts and figures on Black's which Harrie had neatly typed out for him, Chas was on his way to attend an appointment with the bank manager.

Muriel Black had been astonished to find Chas on her doorstep a few days before. After apologising for disturbing her at such an emotional time, he'd awkwardly informed her of his interest in buying her late husband's business. To Chas's surprise she took his enquiry seriously and ushered him inside to discuss details over tea and Garibaldi biscuits. She was delighted, she told him, that someone like him would be considering taking over the business her dear late husband had given his life to. She'd much sooner that than it be swallowed up by a larger town-run firm who would possibly close it down because in truth they were just after the licence plates to expand their own fleet.

The sum of fifteen thousand pounds which she told him she was expecting from the sale sounded an absolute fortune to Chas. Fifteen thousand pounds would buy his mother three, or possibly four, four-bedroomed detached houses, complete with labour-saving devices, and have change left over to pay the wages of live-in help for at least five years at today's rates of ten shillings an hour including board and keep. Regardless of his savings of two thousand pounds, a sum it had taken him years to accumulate bit by bit, the bank would never advance him the rest, he was positive they wouldn't. He could picture the bank manager laughing at him for even considering such a thing. Beside that, how would he sleep at night with such a huge debt hanging over him?

Thanking Muriel Black for her time, and sorry that he had wasted it, Chas had returned to the office and given Harrie the disappointing news, also hoping his mother wouldn't be too distressed when he told her later that evening.

To his surprise Harrie had told him she didn't think the price Mrs Black wanted extortionate at all taking into consideration the fact that the sum asked was for the purchase of fifteen cars, not new admittedly but in good condition and none showing signs of major mechanical faults; plus the much-coveted fifteen licence plates authorising the carrying of passengers as well as the goodwill Jack Black had built up over twenty years. She was surprised herself that Muriel Black wasn't asking for more.

'You think I should still pursue this and approach the bank?' Chas had asked her.

'Well, of course that is your decision. You mustn't assume they'll turn you down, they could do the opposite. They'll look at you favourably because you told me you'd banked with them for years and they'll see from their records that you consistently saved each week. It might only have been small amounts but still regular savings, and that will stand you in good stead, show you're a reliable person. If they do agree to advance you the money, you still have the choice as to whether to go ahead or not.'

He knew his mother would be saying the same as Harrie, and was reminded of the reasons he'd bowed to Iris's blackmail attempt in the first place. He meant not only to improve her lot but also that of his colleagues who'd become his employees if this went through. 'All right, I'll make an appointment to see the bank manager and let Mrs Black know that I am interested after all.'

'Right, Chas, that's you sorted. Now I need to ask your advice.'

'Oh?'

'I don't know what to do about the fact that Terry Briggs seems to have disappeared off the face of the earth. Several of the drivers have complained there's no one to do their minor repairs for them and also no security guard watching over the compound at night in case vandals or thieves show an interest. It's over a week now that he's been off and he's not notified us of any reason for his absence. What do you think I should do about it?'

He scratched his chin. 'Well, I don't think we should worry Mrs Black unnecessarily with this, considering what she's going through, do you?'

'No, I agree we shouldn't.'

'Well then, we should give Terry the benefit of the doubt a little longer. I'm sure his excuse for being off is a good one. The men are capable of doing the minor repairs themselves in the meantime, and anything they can't they'll just have to get the garage to do. I know a little about engines as I had to make temporary repairs when I was on the road as a lorry driver, I can always see what I can do to help. Maybe we should ask Ronald Tyler, the night-shift operator, to keep an eye on the compound regularly during the night too. Hopefully we can manage this way until Terry does return to work.'

And you doubt your abilities to make a good boss, she thought. She wondered if Chas realised that he had just shown all the qualities a good leader should possess: compassion towards his fellow human beings, and well thought out solutions to counteract possible problems.

'You're spending a lot of time in Harrie's office just lately,' Ralph commented as Chas came out.

'Oh, er . . . just a query over mileage I'd logged against petrol receipts that needed clearing up.' He did not like lying to Ralph but what he was considering had better not become common knowledge yet.

Ralph quite rightly looked unconvinced by Chas's explanation. 'Huh, you sure there's n'ote going on between you two romantically?'

Chas stared at him stolidly. 'I can assure you there isn't, Ralph, and please don't let Harrie hear you talk like that. She could be insulted by the idea people would think such a thing.'

Ralph might be getting on in years but his eyesight had not diminished that much. He had witnessed the way Harrie looked at Chas when she wasn't aware anyone was observing her and he knew she would definitely not be upset should anyone think they were an item. He'd seen the way Chas looked at Harrie when no one was observing him and knew the man had more than a passing fancy for her, whether he knew it himself or not. If the purpose of Chas's response had been to throw off the scent, then Chas was badly mistaken because Ralph was even

211

more convinced now that something was going on between them.

On the morning of his appointment with the bank Iris had driven Chas mad with her continual offers of motherly advice as to how to conduct himself with the bank official, as well as fussing over his attire to make sure he was as well turned out for his interview as she could make him. His best suit had been sponged and hung up to air so no smell of mothballs lingered; his best shirt pressed several times to make sure not one minute crease remained; his shoes polished to a glass-like finish so Chas could see his face in them. After telling him he was as good as any other person asking the bank to advance them money, Iris waved her son off and sat down to drink endless cups of tea before he returned.

He had just alighted from the bus in town and was weaving his way through the throng of Christmas shoppers, passing by Lewis's department store towards the Midland Bank on the corner of Gallowtree Gate, when an expensively dressed woman, laden down with heavy shopping bags, caught his eye. It was Nadine.

He watched her flounce off to become enveloped by the crowds of shoppers. He found himself wondering where she'd suddenly found the money from to buy her expensive clothes and whatever else was in her shopping bags. Maybe she had found herself a well-off man and he was funding her? Nadine might be coarse of mouth and spiteful of nature but she was a good-looking woman for a mother of four, he couldn't deny that. Then it struck him that it was a well-known fact how the Dewhursts had financed themselves in the past. There was a good possibility that was how she was doing it now, and if so she obviously hadn't lost her touch.

His own reason for being in the town then occurred to him and he continued on to his appointment.

Two hours later a very distracted Chas walked into Black's office.

Ralph looked at him, perplexed. 'Harrie told me you sent word in you were ill in bed. Yer don't look ill to me. So where yer bin, all dressed up like a dog's dinner?'

Harrie, who had been keeping her eyes peeled, ears alert for the first sign of Chas's appearance, came charging out of her office then to grab hold of his arm and pull him back inside, shutting the door behind them. Ralph sat staring at the door open-mouthed. It was obvious to him something was going on.

'How did it go?' she demanded. The stupefied expression on his face registered then and her own fell in dismay. 'Oh, they turned you down? Oh, Chas, I'm so sorry.'

'Eh? Oh, Harrie, no, they didn't. I'm still having trouble believing it. I'm in shock, if you want the truth, because I was fully convinced I'd be sent packing without a by your leave but the bank manager was very interested in what I put to him. You were right, the fact I'd banked with them for years went very much in my favour. He studied the figures you gave me and asked me to tell him as much as I could about the business and how I intended to run it. Well, I have to say I was a bit flum-moxed by that as I hadn't really thought how I am going to run it yet. The same as it is now, I told him. It's doing all right and hopefully I can come up with some improvements to up the profits. I was honest with him, though, told him I was keener to improve the drivers' lot before the profits. I said you were managing all the office side, and how experienced you were and good at what you did and that you'd asked to be made perma-nent if I was successful in taking over. He seemed impressed I had a sizeable deposit. Told me he would put all this to the board when they next met and let me know their decision then.'

'Oh, Chas, that's great, just great,' she enthused excitedly. 'If the bank manager didn't think it was a good proposal he wouldn't be passing it to the board for approval. Were you given any indication how long we'd have to wait until we hear the outcome?'

He noticed she'd said *we* as if she was part of this, and didn't quite know what to make of that. Maybe it had been a slip of the tongue on her part. 'I didn't like to ask, Harrie.'

'Oh, it could be days or weeks, depends how often the board sits. Oh, Lord, the waiting is going to be terrible.'

'Well, there's nothing we can do but carry on as normal until then. I'd better get home and tell my mam what's what. She'll have my guts for garters if she finds out I called in here first. Thanks again for all your help, Harrie, I couldn't have come this far without it.' He felt a sudden overwhelming urge to grab her in his arms and kiss her by way of thanking her for all she'd done for him but hurriedly quashed it, knowing such an intimate display could well ruin the friendship that was growing between them, which was the last thing he wanted. 'I'll get changed and be back to work this afternoon. See you later, Harrie.'

A warm glow filled her at the knowledge that he had called in to tell her first what had transpired at the bank before he had gone home to tell his mother. But again she couldn't help but feel disappointed that no mention of their going out together had been made. But then, she couldn't expect him to be thinking of social matters when he had so much more important things to occupy his mind.

CHAPTER TWENTY-FOUR

Two weeks later Chas arrived home to find his mother dozing in her armchair. He stood looking down at her worriedly. Several times now he had found her like this. She had never been one for napping before so what had changed in her life to make her feel the need to do it now? Then he frowned as a thought struck him. The first time he had caught her was the Saturday evening of the incident in the chip shop with Harrie, but he felt sure each time since had been a Wednesday, the same as today. He wasn't sure whether there was any significance to that fact. Then he noticed his mother's best dress hanging on the door that led into the narrow passage where the front door and stairs were.

He realised she had woken and smiled down at her. 'All right, Mam, are you?'

She yawned. 'Yes, ducky, I'm fine, ta. Couldn't be better.'

'You sure, Mam?'

Giving a stretch, Iris looked up at him quizzically. 'What d'yer mean?'

'Well, it's just I've caught you asleep several times now and I'm getting concerned about it.'

'Caught me? You make it sound like I've done summat wrong.'

'No, I'm not saying that, Mam, you know I'm not.'

'I'm glad to hear it. There's no law against having a cat nap now and again, is there, son?'

'No, not at all. I just wondered, though, why it's always a Wednesday that I find you doing it?'

'Maybe I just get tired on a Wednesday. You keeping tabs on me?'

'Don't be daft, Mam, 'course I'm not. I just wondered if there's something you do on a Wednesday that tires you out then maybe I could do it for you, that's all.'

She wagged a finger at him. 'I know yer heart's in the right place, son, but you've got more important things to worry about than me having a snooze in the afternoon now and again. Heard 'ote yet?'

Chas shook his head. 'No.'

Iris gave a loud sigh. 'I can't stand this,' she grumbled. 'The suspense is killing me. How long does that bank need to make its decision whether to loan you the money or not?'

'They'll inform me as soon as they've made it, Mam, and not before. I'm not the only person applying for help from them and they have other business to deal with too.' A worried expression filled Chas's face then and he started to rub his chin distractedly.

Iris knew he was still having doubts he was capable of running a business and making a success of it, fearing not for himself but about letting others down. That was typical of her son and what she loved most about him, that he genuinely cared for others above himself. Iris nursed a deep grudge against the Dewhurst children for the damage they had done him through their nasty remarks and mindless pranks in the past, but if it had in turn brought out the tender caring traits in his nature, to make him the man he was now, then for that and only that she was glad.

'Eh, don't you dare be thinking you ain't got what it takes to pull this off,' she scolded him. 'You can do this, son. If I wasn't sure of that I wouldn't have encouraged you to go ahead with it.'

Chas sighed, hoping she was right. He daren't tell her he'd not slept properly since he'd approached the bank, knowing that should they approve the loan he could not disappoint her by not going ahead when she was showing such faith in him. His eyes fell on her dress hanging on the door. 'Have you been out somewhere nice today?' he asked her.

Iris looked at him sharply. 'What made you ask that?' It was more of a demand than a question.

'I just noticed your best dress hanging up on the door. You only bring that particular one out for high days and holidays and as far as I know there are none of those in the offing.'

She looked across at it and Chas couldn't understand why a fleeting look of horror crossed her face before she said, 'Oh . . .

er . . . I meant to take that upstairs. I must have forgot.' She looked blankly at him for a minute before explaining, 'I took it down to give it an airing. I was hoping we might have something to celebrate and then I'd need summat posh to put on.'

'Don't build your hopes up, Mam. I'd hate you to be disa—' He stopped mid-flow as the sound of screaming children erupted outside. 'What on earth is that noise?'

'It's them bleddy Dewhurst grandkids causing mayhem. The older ones have been causing havoc since Nadine moved back, especially these past few weeks. They're giving us neighbours a hell of a time, just like when their mam was little and running amok with her brothers. Sounds to me like they're running riot out front,' Ivy said, getting out of her chair. 'I can't think what she's thinking of letting 'em out this time of night in this cold.'

They both went to the front door to have a look at what was going on and were stunned to see most of the other neighbours standing on their doorsteps, everyone's attention fixed keenly on what was going on outside the Dewhursts' house.

An authoritative man and woman were struggling to get Nadine's four hysterical children inside a parked car. Leaning on her walking stick in her own doorway, Clarice was shouting at the poor mites to do as they were told.

Freda came up to them. 'Clarice Dewhurst is handing her grandkids over to the authorities to take care of. It seems Nadine's done a bunk. Been weeks now since Clarice has seen her apparently.'

Chas was just about to inform his mother and Freda that he'd actually seen Nadine a couple of weeks ago on the day of his bank appointment when he was interrupted by Clarice shouting at the gathering.

'What you lot gawping at? Expect me to look after four brats, do yer, with my ailments? I'd like to see you fucking lot try! And none of you offered to help me, did yer? Like hell yer did. All yer did was keep knocking on me door complaining about the racket the kids were making and blaming the older ones for causing mischief yer own kids had done. Call yerselves neighbourly? Huh!' she sneered.

The children were in the car now and the doors were locked so they couldn't escape. The woman and man got in and the car roared off.

217

Simultaneously an expensively dressed Nadine, struggling to carry a heavy-looking suitcase, arrived on the scene. She looked around at the gathering of neighbours and then at her mother. 'What's going on, Mam? Who was that going off in that car just now?'

'Yer bleddy kids, that's who,' her mother loudly informed her. 'I've handed 'em over to the authorities,' she said proudly.

Nadine stared at her before screaming, 'YOU'VE WHAT?'

Clarice reared back her head. 'Well, what did you expect me to do?' she spat. 'I ain't heard a word from you for weeks.'

'Two weeks, Mam,' Nadine thundered back.

'Four. Can't yer count, where you've bin? You've told me more times than I care to remember what a lousy mother I've bin to yer but one thing I never did was abandon me own kids.'

'I never abandoned my kids. I left them with you.'

Leaning on the door-frame for support, Clarice lifted her walking stick and waved it menacingly at her errant daughter. 'Listen here, lady, I didn't know whether you was alive or dead or ever coming back. So why have you suddenly turned up? Chucked yer out, did he, whoever you've been with? Seen what yer was really like, I bet, and got out while the going was good. It always amazed me yer kept yer husband in yer bed for as long as yer did, but then you pair was the same kind. Lazy good-for-nothings, neither of yer giving a shit about anyone else but yerselves.'

Clarice glared at her murderously. 'If you think yer stepping over this doorstep again, then yer've another think coming. You're no daughter of mine. I never liked yer anyway. I hate yer now. I can't stand them bawling brats of yours but they didn't deserve what you did to them. That Saturday night you disappeared, you said you was popping out to the corner shop for a packet of fags. Not a peep have I heard from yer since.

'Then you swan back here with yer fancy clothes and what-ever is in that case, like yer've done nothing wrong. Sugar Daddy buy you all that stuff, has he, or did yer get it by yer usual methods? Don't bother telling me, I ain't interested. I bet there ain't nothing in that case for me or your kids, just stuff for you. While yer've been off enjoying yerself wherever it is yer've bin, did yer give a thought to how I was managing or for yer kids crying for their mammy? They're better off where they're going and I hope the authorities have the sense never to let you set eyes on 'em again.'

'You bitch, our Mam,' Nadine screamed out. 'You can't do this. They're my kids. You'd no right.'

'Oh, I see. *I* had no right to do what I felt was best for them kids, but *you* had a right to bugger off and leave 'em 'cos the fancy took yer? You want your kids back, you'll have to fight the authorities for 'em. First you'll have to prove to 'em yer've a roof to put over them kiddies' heads but don't bother giving this address 'cos I'll deny all knowledge of yer. Now get out me sight and don't dare bother darkening my door again.'

Clarice looked around the silent gathering. 'Give yer a good show, have we? I missed a good opportunity, didn't I? I should have sold tickets.'

With that she stepped back inside her house and slammed shut the door.

Nadine was shaking violently with rage. She launched herself at the door and hammered on it repeatedly. 'Let me in, Mother, you hear me? LET ME IN.' Getting no response she kicked the door hard, chipping the already flaking paintwork. Then she swung around and glared daggers at Chas standing several feet away from her. 'This is your fault, you bastard,' she screamed at him accusingly. 'If you hadn't turned me down this wouldn't have happened. I've lost me kids through you and now I've nowhere to live.'

Snatching up her case, she threw back her head and struggled off down the street to disappear around the corner.

Chas was staring after her dumbstruck. What she had said to him was preying on his mind. How on earth could she blame him for what had happened to her? Then the truth hit him. The date she had made for them in the restaurant had been meant as a prelude to their getting together. She had seriously believed he would jump at the chance of taking on her and her children, and providing for them. Did she think he was that desperate for a woman that he'd settle for one who had until very recently not wasted any opportunity to show revulsion for him? Now he saw why she had started to act kindly towards him. It had been purely to provide herself with a meal ticket, replacing the one she had lost with the break up of her marriage and, from what he had heard of her husband and how they had been living, securing a far better one for herself. Were there no depths that woman wouldn't stoop to to get what she wanted? Nevertheless he felt a twinge of pity for Nadine. She might not have proved to be the best of mothers and her children were probably better off being adopted by parents who would care for them properly, but it was obvious by her reaction to what her mother had done that Nadine did care for them.

Iris was yanking at his arm. 'What was she going on about, blaming you for what's happened?'

'Yeah,' said Freda, looking at him inquisitively. 'What did she mean?'

Chas thought it better Iris did not know what Nadine had planned for him. 'I've no idea,' he lied. 'I can only guess she had to blame someone for what happened and she picked me.'

Iris's face contorted angrily. 'You'd have thought that trollop would've had her belly full of picking on you and target someone else for a change. I can't believe she left her kids all that time with no word. I can't imagine what those poor mites have gone through. Nadine knows fine well her mother ain't fit to care for four lively youngsters. She weren't fit to look after her own before the illness struck her. Nadine's kids are better off where they're going if that's how she treats 'em. And good riddance to her! I for one won't lose any sleep if we never hear from her again.

'I didn't like the way she started calling on you, son, to help her out. Knowing her ways as I do from past experience, I couldn't help but worry she'd a hidden agenda. Thank God it seems she hadn't.' Iris gave a shiver. 'It's parky out here, I'm off back inside to get yer dinner. It's tripe and onions tonight only I ran out of onions so I'll do yer a fried egg to go with it. Ta-ra, Freda,' she called after her friend as she hurried back inside.

Chas cringed. He had never had the heart to tell his mother that he detested tripe. The way she cooked it made it reminiscent of rubber. And a fried egg wasn't really the best accompaniment. But as usual he would eat it and tell her it'd been grand. He realised Freda was speaking to him and looked down at her, smiling. 'Sorry, Mrs Lumley?'

'I was just asking, lovey, if yer'd take a look at Nell Hill's tap for her when yer've got a minute? It's drip, drip, drip, and driving her mad.'

'Of course I will, Mrs Lumley.'

'I said yer would. Yer a good lad, yer really are, Chas. I don't know what us old ducks would do without you helping us out, I don't. Now after all that excitement, I need a drop of whisky in me tea. Clarice was right, she should have sold tickets for that performance. It was better than some plays you see on the telly. Good night then, Chas.'

'Good night, Mrs Lumley.' Then he remembered he'd something to ask her. 'Oh, Mrs Lumley?'

She stopped and turned back to face him. 'You want me, lovey?'

He stepped across to her. 'I'm thinking of getting me mam one of those soap sets for Christmas. I know her favourite scent is Lily of the Valley but I can't remember her favourite brand and I thought you would, being's you're her best friend.'

'Yardley, ducky, same as mine is. My preference is Lavender, in case yer wondering.'

He hid a smile. 'I'll remember that. Thank you. Oh, Mrs Lumley, is me mam all right?'

She looked at him suspiciously. 'Why d'yer ask?'

'Well, I don't want to make too much of it but it's just I've caught her asleep for the last three or four Wednesday nights when I've come home from work and wondered if she does anything on a Wednesday that tires her out. Something I could help her with. You know what a stubborn so-and-so she is. She won't admit she's getting on and can't do as much as she used to.'

Freda clicked her tongue at him. 'Good Lord, Chas, when yer get to me and yer mam's age it's a poor shame if yer can't have a snooze now and again in the afternoon. Now listen to me, lad, stop worrying about yer mam. She's fine, never been better, believe me. Why, it's so excit— She suddenly stopped talking and seemed to check herself before blurting, 'Oh, is that my Henry calling me? Best go. Goodnight, Chas.'

He responded accordingly. Watching her hurry off down the entry, he frowned. He hadn't heard Freda's husband calling out for her and there was nothing wrong with Chas's hearing. It fleetingly crossed his mind that Freda had used that ruse to get away from him, to stop him from questioning her further over his concerns for his mother. Was there something they didn't want him to know? Then he gave himself a mental shake. He was making far too much of the fact he'd caught his mother several times cat napping. Its being a Wednesday each time was just coincidence. Freda was right, there was nothing wrong with anyone of their advancing years having a snooze in the afternoon. Didn't he himself do it after his dinner on a Sunday, and he was less than half his mother's age.

The very next night Terry turned up to resume his post, offering no explanation for his four-week absence. It was Harrie who noticed the lights on in the hut where he carried out his duties when she was leaving for the night via the back staff entrance. Wondering if Terry had indeed returned or an intruder was inside, she crept across to investigate. Terry was donning his overalls and stared at her in shock when he saw her standing in the entrance.

'Oh, it's you, Terry,' she said, relieved. 'Thank goodness, I thought we could have burglars on the premises. You're fully recovered, I hope? Well, I assume you've been off sick. We were wondering what was going on as we hadn't heard a word from you for four weeks.'

He looked awkwardly at her. 'Yeah, well, it's me gran. It's her that's been really sick. I've had to nurse her day and night 'cos we ain't got no one else, see.'

'I'm so sorry to hear that. I hope she's fully recovered,' Harrie said solicitously.

'Yeah, she is, thanks.'

'You should have let us know what was going on. We didn't know whether you were sick, had left, if you were coming back or if we'd need to find someone else for your job.'

He looked alarmed. 'You ain't gave someone else me job, have yer?'

'No, but you're lucky as I was about to ask Mrs Black what she wanted to do about the situation. So next time you need time off, even a day, you will call in to let us know?'

'Yeah, 'course. Look, I'd better get on. I see there's a pile of jobs marked down in the maintenance book for me to do on the cars.'

'I'll leave you to it then. I'll let everyone know you're back.'

Despite Terry's explanation for his absence seeming perfectly plausible, something about his manner towards Harrie gave her the impression his whole tale had been a complete fabrication. She couldn't pinpoint exactly why. Well, the main thing was he was back, Mrs Black was saved the bother of looking for someone else during her mourning period and the men had a mechanic on hand again to deal with the niggling jobs. Terry could count himself lucky that everyone was too affected by the boss's death to enquire further as to what exactly he'd been doing.

CHAPTER TWENTY-FIVE

Chas blinked rapidly as the bright flash from a camera bulb temporarily blinded him.

'See, that wasn't painful, was it?' Harrie said to him. 'It's fantastic getting the *Leicester Mercury* here to do a piece on the changeover. Hopefully it's going to go into tonight's edition. Great publicity, and free.'

Harrie was right but Chas didn't like it one bit being in the spotlight, and would have much preferred to let the rest of the staff be in the photograph and leave him out of it. The reporter had insisted, though. Tyme's Taxis was the name over the door now and on the side of the vehicles, so it was only right Mr Tyme himself should take pride of place in the photograph accompanying the write up. Not many people found themselves in a position to take over the firm they were previously working for and *Mercury* readers would be inspired to learn of a local lad made good and be rooting for his success.

Chas was still reeling from how quickly all this had come about. Only just over two weeks had passed since the bank had approved the loan and deposited the money into his new business account, contracts between Muriel Black and himself been exchanged, and the organising and carrying out of the repainting of the sign over the premises and the alteration of the vehicles' logos had been carried out, all in time for them to take advantage of the busy Christmas period which was on them in three days. It had been Muriel herself who had pushed it through so quickly, wanting the burden of the business off her shoulders so she could concentrate on rebuilding a future without her husband in it.

The reactions of his colleagues had absolutely shocked Chas. He hadn't known quite what to expect when they had all been gathered and informed of the change in ownership. They had looked momentarily shocked before expressions of approval started to be heard. It was obvious they were more than delighted to find out who their new boss was, and the slaps of congratulation on Chas's back had resulted in a few minor bruises.

When he had broken the news that the bank would back him to his mother, she had not said a word, for the first time ever struck speechless, but the look on her face told him all he needed to know. 'Proud' was not a strong enough word to describe the glow that emanated from Iris.

It was one thing, though, having his mother's faith in him but Chas could not have done all this without Harrie's encouragement too. She had willingly tackled for him things he would never have had a clue how to go about. He had a lot to thank her for. He was feeling the pressure of the financial commitment he had taken on in order to buy the business, but somehow, with Harrie on board, his burden didn't quite feel so great. It felt like everything would be all right as long as she was around.

One morning a couple of weeks ago he had come in from a job to see her desk was empty and no sign of her. For Chas it felt as if the heart had gone out of the office. Then she had come back, having been out to fetch fresh supplies of tea, coffee and sugar to replenish the empty containers in the newly cleaned rest room. Harriet had undertaken to clean this herself. After hours of hard labour it was now a much more inviting environment for the men to take refuge in than the dirty, smelly room it had previously been. As she walked back in, the office had instantly come alive again for Chas. It felt as if the sun had come out from behind a cloud and bathed his world in its warm enveloping rays.

He knew he was setting himself up for disappointment but Harrie had a warmth and allure that drew him to her.

'Hopefully this article will alert local people to Tyme's Taxis,' she was saying to him now.

Chas smiled gratefully at her. 'I have you to thank for getting that reporter and photographer here.'

Harrie wanted to say that she would do anything for him but it was not the time or the place. Now the business was in Chas's hands, though, she fervently hoped he would turn his attention to doing something about establishing a relationship between them, at least ask her out on a first date. What she did say was,

'Well, it's in my own interest to do all I can towards making your business prosper, now I work here permanently.'

Yes, of course it was, he realised with a twinge of disappointment.

The *Mercury* having finished, the staff all trooped back into the office. The interior looked very festive as Harrie had put up paper decorations and sprigs of plastic holly.

Ralph had stayed behind to man the telephone while everyone else had been outside for the photo shoot. As they all arrived back he called Chas over. 'As soon as I've seen the lads out on some jobs that have come in, could I have a word, please, boss?'

Chas still found it strange being called 'boss' but knew he had to get used to it. 'Yes, of course.' He had a feeling he knew what Ralph wanted to speak to him about and had been dreading this moment. He couldn't blame Ralph for wanting to resume his retirement, though. He'd stayed on far longer than the couple of weeks he'd initially thought he'd be doing when Jack Black was first taken ill. Chas was grateful to the old man for staying at his post until the new boss was safely on board, and planned to reward his loyalty by paying for a weekend trip to the seaside for him and his wife. Ralph's departure, though, presented Chas with the problem of finding a replacement radio operator which wasn't going to be easy at this time of year. Then he was reminded that in actual fact it was two operators he needed as the evening-shift post had not been filled while the change of ownership was going through.

'You don't want to consider doing the job yourself? The day shift at any rate,' Harrie suggested to Chas a while later when he had gone into her office to inform her of Ralph's desire to leave as soon as possible.

He looked horrified at the thought. 'I don't have to, do I?'

Harrie laughed. 'Chas, you're the boss. You can do whatever you like.'

He looked relieved. 'I like being out on the road. I wouldn't be any good at radio operating.'

'Well, you seem to do all right when you take your share of the evening cover,' she said encouragingly. She wasn't overdoing her praise. All the drivers who had volunteered their services had done their best to log everything down clear and concisely, but her expert eye could tell that Chas had been extra-meticulous.

She knew it wasn't just because he was aware that very shortly this would be his business; it reflected the sort of person he was, one who wanted to do the best job he could whatever he tackled.

Chas, not one to heap praise on himself, felt he had muddled through all right, but then the evenings weren't quite as hectic as during the day with so many drivers to organise. 'I think it's best I stick to what I know and let someone more experienced take care of that.' He paused thoughtfully for a moment. 'I found out about the vacancy for a driver through overhearing talk in the pub. I wasn't eavesdropping,' he added hurriedly, 'I wouldn't want you to think that. But maybe if we tell the lads to spread word we're looking for staff when they are out and about, someone might come forward.'

'I think that's a great idea,' Harrie agreed. 'It'll save money on advertising in the *Mercury*, but that's something we'll have to consider eventually if nothing comes up by word of mouth. Thankfully Ralph has said he will stay on until we do get someone and I'm sure everyone who volunteered to cover the evening shift will continue to do so until we get someone else. They're grateful for the extra money they're earning, especially at this time of year.'

'I'm lucky I've inherited a good bunch of people,' Chas said.

But Harrie had her suspicions about that. Because of little snippets of conversation she had overheard in the drivers' rest room when she had been making drinks, and also the way a couple of drivers clammed up whenever she was within earshot of them, she believed not all the drivers were as conscientious as Chas trusted them to be. It hurt her to think that because of his kindly, trusting nature they were able to pull the wool over his eyes. But then, Chas was far from stupid and she knew he would wise up eventually and deal with the situation in the best way he could. From what she had deduced Jack had been a fair boss but not quite as thoughtful towards his staff as she knew Chas was going to prove. In truth, she felt it was they who were the lucky ones in having him as their boss now. None of them had any notion yet that he was planning to review their working hours and see if he could up their hourly rate a little, as soon as he had a clearer idea how the business was doing under his ownership.

She knew he was worried about making a success of this venture and that this worry wasn't for himself but the prospect of letting his workers down, maybe even having to lay some of them off should business slacken for any reason. She was very aware from doing the books that the couple of months after Christmas was the firm's leanest time as people watched their money after the festive season. She wasn't sure if Chas was aware of that fact due to his lack of experience and didn't want to bring it to his attention now for fear of spoiling Christmas for him.

He was badly in need of at least one day's rest. He looked tired, a man who obviously had much on his mind. She was desperate to put her arms around him and help allay his fears that he hadn't taken on more than he could handle. As matters stood, though, that gesture would be far too intimate between employer and member of staff. Hopefully, though, her desire for a closer relationship between them would come to fruition sooner rather than later and then she wouldn't have to hold back from showing affection towards him. She did wish he would hurry up now as her yearning to be close to him was causing her sleepless nights.

She suddenly thought it extremely unfair that the accepted code of conduct meant that a woman had to wait for a man to ask her out unless she wanted to be branded forward. Why was it that most things in life were undertaken on men's terms? It really was an anachronism. It was about time that code of conduct was changed and favoured women a little more. This was the Swinging Sixties after all. Not that Harrie was free and easy herself but women nowadays had the contraceptive pill available to them so they could indulge in sexual encounters without fear of pregnancy. Institutions that had been closed to them previously were now welcoming women through their doors. They were even being considered for the police force, an institution that had until recently been completely dominated by men. Other trades too, albeit slowly, were starting to include women in their ranks.

Her mind started to drift. Christmas was such a good time for making headway with someone you cared for. All that goodwill towards your fellow man, kissing under the mistletoe . . . She couldn't wait to feel Chas's lips on hers. She knew instinctively that his kisses would be gentle but passionate. In her mind's eye she pictured herself enveloped in his manly arms, crushed to his chest. Before she could stop herself she had let out a loud sigh.

'Are you all right, Harrie?'

She mentally shook herself, seeing Chas looking at her with obvious concern. Harrie was horrified to realise what she had done without realising it. How could she explain herself without embarrassing them both?

'I'm ... er ... er ...' she said the first thing that entered her head '... suffering from indigestion. It's Dad's cooking. I don't know where he's getting his ideas for meals from but they leave much to be desired. I don't like to say anything, he's trying so hard and I wouldn't want to put a dampener on what he's trying to do.' What she had said was absolutely true if not strictly an account of the reason for her sighing.

Chas could appreciate what she was saying as his mother's cooking was similarly erratic. He found it a strange coincidence they each had a parent whose cooking skills left much to be desired.

Suddenly Harrie thought of a way she could prod Chas into asking her out and get the ball rolling between them without appearing unduly forward. She could have kicked herself for not having thought of it before.

'Chas, you haven't toasted the success of the business yet. Be a shame not to.'

He looked at her aghast. 'Oh, no, I haven't, have I? With everything else on my mind I never gave it a thought. I can't imagine what the lads must be thinking of me. I expect they've been waiting for some sort of knees up. I'll see about taking them for a drink after work tonight. Christmas Eve they'll be wanting to get home to their families, won't they, so tonight's the best bet. I could get some bottles of beer for the lads on the night shift to take home with them. That should please everyone, shouldn't it?' He would have liked nothing better than to ask Harrie to join them, then worried she might feel insulted about being asked to join a bunch of men for a pint in the local. But might she not be equally insulted if he didn't ask her? What a dilemma. He decided to let her say for herself whether she wanted to join them or not.

It was me on my own I wanted you to take out, not the rest of them, Harrie wanted to shout at him. She didn't, though, begrudge the rest of the staff having a celebration drink with their new boss. She waited breathlessly for Chas to ask her to join them. When he didn't a terrible disappointment struck her. But she supposed he was thinking that everyone but her would be male, and when a gang of males had a drink in them they got rowdy and weren't exactly careful what came out of their mouths. Chas was being protective of her, that was all. She wanted to hug him for his thoughtfulness. Once he'd treated the men she was sure it would be her turn.

The next morning at just after ten Chas was about to leave on a job when a man came in. He looked clean-shaven and well-presented. Ralph was busy on the telephone so Chas went over to take his booking.

'Can I help you?' he asked politely. He thought this man looked vaguely familiar but couldn't remember ever meeting him before.

'Could I see the boss?' the man asked.

'I'll see if he's . . .' Chas stopped himself, feeling stupid. He was the boss now, wasn't he? 'That's me. What can I do for you?'

'My name's Stanley Slater and I'm after a job. Anything will do. I've plenty of experience as a taxi driver. Was one for years with a firm in Coalville. I can give you their number so you can check me out, if you like. I had to move to Leicester so my wife could be near her family as her mother's not well. I've been round all the other firms and they have nothing. I've tried getting work in a factory but the pay's terrible unless you've certain skills which I've not. I've put my name down for the Corporation buses and the Midland Red but they've stopped taking on until well after the Christmas period. I'm really desperate, Mr Tyme. So desperate I'd take anything you had to offer. I'm really hoping you've got something?'

The man's plight touched Chas deeply. He rubbed his hand across the back of his neck thoughtfully. 'Well, my licences are all covered, I'm afraid, and I can't see anything coming up in the near future for a driver as I've no reason to believe any of my men are thinking of moving on.' Then a picture of this man's family swam before him. Chas could just see Stanley Slater returning home and his wife's disappointed expression when he informed her he hadn't found work. He saw them sitting around an empty grate on Christmas Day, table bare, no presents in the children's stockings. Chas could not send this desperate man away, not when he was able to help. He just hoped that as a driver the man wouldn't be insulted by what he was about to offer. 'If it's of any interest to you, I do happen to have a radio-operator's job going.'

Stanley Slater's face was a delight to behold. 'Oh, Mr Tyme, you have and you'll consider me? Oh, you don't know what this means to me. Radio operating is what I'd really like, absolutely it is. I'm experienced at it too. I covered the radio on loads of occasions when the firm I worked for were desperate. I was good at it. In fact, I'd sooner have that job, Mr Tyme.'

'You would? Well, that suits me just fine.' This man turning up out of the blue was really the answer to Chas's problem of finding a suitable replacement for Ralph. He seemed genuine enough. Articulate. Well-presented. Chas couldn't believe his luck. 'All right, you can start tomorrow, eight o'clock sharp. We'll sort out pay and conditions then, but don't worry, I pay a fair rate for a job well done. And ... er ... I suspect you're strapped for cash so I'll advance you some of your wages to tide you over Christmas.'

At his offer a look crossed Stanley Slater's face that Chas couldn't quite fathom. It was as if an offer to help this man provide Christmas for his family was the last thing he'd expected of Chas. Then he thought he must have been mistaken and it was just the shock of landing himself work that was written on Slater's face.

By now Stanley was holding out his hand to Chas. He accepted it and they shook to seal their deal.

Chas watched the other man leave. It felt so rewarding to be able to help someone out at this time of year. Slater could return home with good news. His family's Christmas was going to be far happier than it had promised to be earlier today.

Just as Harrie was leaving that night, Darren popped his head round her office door, waving a sprig of mistletoe at her. 'Me

232

and you under this tonight, georgeous. Good of the boss, isn't it, taking us all out for a drink?'

Continuing her task of tidying her desk Harrie said, 'I'm sure you won't have any trouble finding someone to share your mistletoe with, Darren, but it won't be me. I'm not going. Mr Tyme is taking you men out to celebrate his acquisition of the business.'

His face fell in disappointment. 'I see. Oh, well, shame to waste this,' he said, a lustful expression on his face as he advanced on her. Before she could stop him he had grabbed her in his arms and puckered up his lips.

She struggled to evade them. 'Darren, control yourself!' she commanded, turning her face away so his lips missed hers.

Just then Chas walked in dressed for the off. Witnessing Harrie in the arms of Darren froze him rigid. Seeing another man embracing her in such an intimate way tore the very soul out of him. The man holding Harrie should be him. Darren had no right even to lay a finger on her. He fought a strong desire to grab the driver by the scruff of his neck and throw him out bodily, warning him severely that should he ever touch Harrie again Chas wouldn't be responsible for his actions. He knew then that he loved this woman, loved her with all his being, so much so he would lie down and die for her. Before he could check himself he'd thundered, 'Darren, shouldn't you be off home to get ready for tonight?'

Not having realised his boss had entered the office, Darren sprang away from Harrie. 'Just getting a Christmas kiss from our luscious Harrie, boss. No harm in that, is there?' It was then he noticed the murderous expression on Chas's face. The driver flashed a glance at Harrie, noticing the look of mortification on hers that Chas had caught her in such a compromising situation, and the truth dawned on him. Something was going on between Harrie and Chas. In fact, he'd go so far as to say they were in love with each other. But Darren knew better than to voice his discovery. He reminded himself that Chas was no longer just another of his colleagues to rib but his boss, in a position to fire him should he speak or act out of turn. But no wonder Harrie had spurned him! Chas was hardly the better-looking man by any stretch of the imagination but he certainly had far more than Darren could offer her. He would never have put her in the gold-digger category, had nursed high hopes of himself and the very fanciable Harrie getting together, but it was crystal clear to Darren he was wasting his time.

'I'll be off then. Good night, Harrie. See yer later, boss.'

With that Darren walked out.

Chas was staring awkwardly at Harrie. Realising the depth of his feelings for her had shocked him to the core, but those feelings were one-sided, hers for him no more than the friendship of an employee for her employer. He had no right whatsoever to interfere in her private life, should never have displayed such anger towards Darren. He vehemently hoped that Harrie had been too preoccupied at the time to have noticed his rage, Darren too. In future, unless he wanted to lose her friendship and risk her leaving his employment, he must never display his emotions in such a way again.

'I'm off then, Harrie,' Chas said briskly. 'Don't want to be late for meeting the lads tonight. See you tomorrow. Good night.'

In fact, Harrie had missed nothing. Chas's jealousy upon catching her in a compromising position with Darren had been very obvious to her. He had displayed all the emotion of a man in love, she had no doubt of it. So why didn't he ask her out? What on earth was he waiting for?

CHAPTER TWENTY-SIX

Harrie stole a glance at her father, her brow furrowed. Percy's newfound zest for life seemed to have dissipated today for some reason. There was a distracted air about him. She couldn't pinpoint why. He had seemed overjoyed with the presents she had bought him: cardigan and slippers, socks, and a box of his favourite chocolate-covered Brazil nuts. He'd devoured his dinner with relish, enthusiastically complimenting her on her efforts, and he'd enjoyed himself carrying out his usual Christmas Day ritual of popping in to see several neighbours, wishing them good cheer and readily accepting the tot of whisky they pressed on him in return.

Now he was relaxing comfortably in his armchair, eyes fixed on the television screen, seemingly engrossed in the Queen's speech. But, knowing him as well as she did, Harrie knew his mind wasn't fully on it. Why was he so preoccupied? Her father had no work problems to worry him. The allotment was resting over winter so he hadn't any concerns for failed crops. He was on friendly terms with all the neighbours he associated with so no disputes there that she was aware of could be concerning him. Then it struck her. Of course. For some reason this year he must be missing her mother more than usual. It was six years since her death and Harrie was missing her too, but it had to be worse for her father as they had been partners, and very happy ones at that. Her heart went out to him. He must be so lonely. How she wished he could meet someone special to be a companion to him during his last remaining years. That wasn't likely, though, as he hardly went out socialising, saying he was too old for all that sort of thing now and happy as he was. But Harrie had a feeling that today he wasn't entirely happy though she didn't quite know what to do about it apart from making sure he was comfortable and well cared for.

'Can I get you anything else, Dad?'

He blew out his cheeks and loudly exhaled. 'Me darling, if I have anything else just now I'll burst,' he said, patting his stomach. 'You made a grand job of the dinner.'

'You helped too so I can't take all the praise. Er . . . Dad, just where did you come across that recipe for the stuffing for the chicken?'

'Well . . . er . . . a friend gave it to me. They said they were good at cooking, you see, and when I said I was teaching meself they offered to give me some of their recipes. Only I'm realising now, after following some of them, that they're not as good a cook as they think they are. I'd never hurt them by telling them, though. I might suggest instead they could try some of yours.'

She was honoured her father thought some of her recipes worth passing on, but then they had been her mother's originally. 'Who is this friend, Dad?' Harrie asked, interested.

'Oh, just someone I know,' Percy said dismissively. 'You usually pop round to see Marion after dinner on Christmas Day, don't you?'

Yes, she did, so the best friends could exchange presents and give their best wishes to each other. But this year because of Percy's show of melancholy she wasn't comfortable about leaving her father on his own, even for an hour. 'Well, I might give it a miss this year. See Marion tomorrow instead.'

'Why?'

'Because I prefer to stop here with you, Dad.'

He peered closely at his daughter. Harrie seemed like her usual cheery self, had done her utmost to make this day as special as she could for them both, but he knew her very well and there was something on her mind that was bothering her, although she was doing her best to hide it from him. He wondered what it was. She couldn't possibly be regretting her decision to break things off with Jeremy, could she? Percy set that notion aside. She had been emphatic that he was not the right man for her and had given him no reason since the break up to think she had changed her mind. So what then? Couldn't be her new job as she was really enthusiastic about how much she loved working there, really felt she was contributing to the firm. She had loved her job at the solicitor's but didn't derive from it quite the same satisfaction she did from running the office for Tyme's taxi firm. Had she met a new man and didn't know how to tell him? No, that couldn't be it. Harrie would have told him if she'd started seeing someone new, she always had done in the past.

Then he realised what the matter was. Not that she didn't usually miss her mother, but today of all days she was missing her more than she normally did and wasn't voicing her emotions for fear of upsetting him. That had to be it. What a dear thoughtful daughter he had.

He eyed her tenderly. 'Don't you think you've spent enough time with this old fuddy-duddy today, me darlin'? You get yerself off out and be in company of yer own age for a while, it'll do you good. Marion will be looking forward to seeing you. I can have a snooze while you're gone and look forward to our supper later on.'

Marion was delighted to see her and welcomed her in with a big hug.

'Merry Christmas, Harrie. Where's me present then?' she demanded impatiently.

Marion was thrilled with the latest Walker Brothers LP, delighted that Harrie had remembered her strong hint that that was what she wanted, Harrie equally as delighted with the latest Jimi Hendrix LP Marion had bought for her.

They sat down at the kitchen table with a pot of tea and plate of mince pies, though neither could face eating again after just having dinner.

'Allen's snoring his head off in the armchair so we won't be disturbed for a bit and we can have a good catch up,' Marion said. 'Being married does have its drawbacks, yer know, Harrie. We've just had a massive dinner at his mam's, and we've a massive tea at my mam's to look forward to in . . .' she lifted her eyes and glanced at the kitchen wall clock '. . . a couple of hours. Oh, bloody hell, I hope I've managed to make room by then. I shall be glad when tomorrow comes so I can give me stomach a rest.' She paused long enough to pour out cups of tea and pass Harrie's to her. Sipping on her own, she looked keenly over the rim at Harrie. 'Right, let's cut the chat and get to the nitty-gritty. What's the latest on you and Chas?'

Harrie gave a despondent sigh. 'There is no latest, Marion. He's still not asked me out and I can't understand it. Nothing's changed, in fact, since the last time I saw you. Oh, except for something that happened in the office a couple of nights ago.' She told Marion about Chas catching Darren trying to kiss her under the mistletoe and the look on his face when he'd reprimanded the driver.

'Yes, he certainly didn't like catching you in another man's arms, did he?' said Marion, pulling a knowing face. 'Definitely jealous. The man's in love with you, isn't he?'

'I have no doubt he is,' Harrie replied with conviction. 'I've never been so sure of anything in all my life. So why hasn't he asked me out yet, Marion?'

She stared at Harrie thoughtfully for a moment before she said, 'It's just a thought, but I wonder if he's afraid you're going to reject him if he does and that's what's holding him back? Yes, that could be the reason, yer know. He might not be quite sure you like him enough to go out with him, and you did say you'd got a good friendship developing between you. Well, he could be worried that by asking you out and being turned down he could ruin that friendship. Then things would be very awkward between you, especially as you work together.'

Harrie gave a despondent sigh. 'Well, I feel I've made very plain to him how I feel about him.'

'Not plain enough obviously.'

'Well, apart from telling him outright of my feelings, what do I do to let him know?'

Marion gave a disdainful tut. 'Men drive you mad, don't they? We women drop all the hints we can to them but nine times out of ten we end up having to spell it out to them letter by letter before they finally cotton on. Let me think . . .' She sipped tea for a moment as she did so. Then, after putting her cup down in its saucer, she folded her arms, leaned on the table and fixed Harrie with her eyes. 'Well, it seems to me you've two choices. Either you just have patience and wait for him to pluck up the courage, however long that takes, or else it's got to be you who asks him out.'

Harrie sighed loudly. 'I've already tried that, Marion. I suggested a drink to celebrate his taking over the business but Chas took it as meaning he should take all the staff out. He didn't even ask me to go along, though I do understand why.

He was being thoughtful, not wanting me to be in a bunch of drunken men's company all night.'

'Yes, that was nice of him. Wish my Allen was as considerate. He actually thinks I do enjoy being in rowdy male company and encourages me to come along when he's meeting his mates down the pub.'

'Well, Allen's right, you do. When you've had a drink you're more raucous than the men are.'

'Yeah, well, maybe I am,' Marion grudgingly admitted, knowing she did make her presence known when she had a few drinks inside her, though she was never coarse or vulgar like some women were. Marion's eyes suddenly lit up as an idea struck her. 'I've got it! Get Chas to take you to the pictures. America put a man on the moon in July this year, surely you can do a simple thing like get him to take you to the flicks! There's loads of good films on just now. *Midnight Cowboy, Easy Rider, The Love Bug* . . . No, maybe not that film, it's funny but more for kids. Oh, I know! *Butch Cassidy and the Sundance Kid.*' Her eyes glazed over dreamily. 'Paul Newman makes my toes curl with them blue eyes of his, but then Robert Redford . . . boy, is he sexy! I know you'd like the film and I'm sure Chas would too, it's got plenty of action in it. Use all your womanly wiles to get him to take you, Harrie.'

She pursed her lips thoughtfully. 'Mmm, it's worth a try. Actually, I really do fancy seeing that film. I suggested it to Jeremy when I was with him but somehow we never did go.'

'Yes, well, we both know now that he wasn't the sort to sit in the back row sharing a bag of sweets and having a good giggle over a *Carry On* film. You're well out of that, Harrie, as you well know. Anyway, you could sort of bring up the subject casually with Chas, let him know you really want to see the film but have no one to go with. He can't not take a hint like that, surely. And he can't suggest taking the whole firm to the pictures either. If he does then you're flogging a dead horse, Harrie.'

She knew she wasn't. Marion's suggestion was a good one. She'd give it a try at the first opportunity.

She hadn't been able to get Chas out of her mind all day. Whatever she'd been doing, a picture of him kept popping up in her mind's eye and she hadn't been able to stop her thoughts from dwelling on him, wondering what he was doing. Was he having a good Christmas Day? What presents had he been given? The fact was she'd have liked to have given one to him herself, something personal that he would treasure. If Chas had taken the plunge and asked her out before Christmas Day she could have had that pleasure. She wondered gloomily if this time next year she'd still desperately be waiting for him to do the deed. Now Marion had opened her eyes – and her friend was good at doing that – to one possibility why he was procrastinating. If Marion was right and he was not sure of Harrie's feelings for him, stalling because he feared she'd reject his advances, then he wasn't going to be left in any doubt for much longer. Chas and she were meant for each other, Harrie had absolutely no doubt about that, and all her instincts told her he felt the same. She just prayed she wasn't wrong or else she was about to make one hell of a fool of herself.

Meanwhile in the Tyme household Chas was feeling stuffed to bursting after his huge Christmas dinner. Having helped his mother clear away, he was relaxing in the armchair, feet stretched out on the hearth being warmed by a blazing fire, watching *The Perry Como Christmas Show* on the television. It wasn't his preferred viewing but his mother liked these variety shows, and if she was happy so was he.

Trouble was, he wasn't sure if his mother *was* entirely happy. Oh, not that she hadn't shown great delight with the presents he had given her: a new pink candlewick dressing gown with a pair of matching slippers, a Yardley Lily of the Valley soap and bath-cube gift set, and a pound box of Terry's All Gold chocolates. She had bustled cheerily around the kitchen preparing the dinner and enthusiastically welcomed in Freda for their ritual glass of sherry mid-morning, toasting each other's good health and exchanging token gifts. Freda was delighted with the soap set Chas had bought her, remembering her favourite fragrance was Lavender. It was just that, knowing his mother as well as he did, she seemed a little distracted today, as if part of her mind was elsewhere. He wondered if she was suffering from some ailment she wasn't telling him about because she didn't want to worry him. But then she didn't appear to be ill at all. The picture of health, in fact. She and Freda were on the best of terms as he'd witnessed this morning so no disputes there for her to be worrying over. Although, he did wonder what they had been whispering about when Iris had first greeted Freda at the door. He had witnessed Freda wagging a stern finger at his mother before they had both started giggling like naughty schoolgirls sharing a secret. When he had asked to be let in on the joke, they had stared at him like they had been caught doing something they shouldn't, before Iris had accused him of being nosey, and of being a bad host and not offering her a festive drink. After Freda had left, his mother's mood had returned and it wasn't until during the Queen's speech, when Her Majesty had told her subjects she hoped this day was uniting families across her domain, that he realised the truth behind his mother's pre-occupation. For some reason this year she had been thinking of past Christmases when his father had been alive and of the happy times she had shared with him before his untimely death. Chas's heart went out to her. She obviously still missed him terribly, even after all these years. Iris had many friends as she was well liked and respected but she must be lonely for companionship of the male variety. It was such a pity she couldn't meet someone she got on well with, someone who liked her back and would share her remaining years. She wasn't exactly a regular participant at social events, much preferring her own fireside these days, but neither was she a hermit. Chas was hopeful that one day she'd meet someone who took her fancy while she was out and about.

But then his mother wasn't the only one whose mind wasn't entirely focused on what was going on around her. Try as he might Chas himself could not stop a vision of Harrie from continually coming to mind. It was only yesterday evening that he had wished her goodnight and a Happy Christmas but those intervening few hours seemed an age to him. He couldn't wait to witness her smile when he saw her again at work the day after Boxing Day. The rest of the workforce was in tomorrow as Christmas Day and New Year's Day were the only days of the year taxi firms did not provide their services to the public. Despite knowing he'd miss her Chas had generously given Harrie the extra day off as she had worked so hard since she'd joined the firm, been invaluable to him while the takeover was going through. She more than deserved a good break and any office matters could wait to be dealt with until she returned.

He was very aware that he was heading for a painful time if he continued to allow himself to harbour secret desires for a woman who would never be his, but try as he might to stem his feelings, he just couldn't. Stupid, he knew, but he felt Harrie was part of him, as if he'd only been half-functioning for all the years before they met, and her arrival in his life had made him whole. All he could do was try and prepare himself for the devastating hurt he knew was coming his way when she met the man she would marry, which was going to happen sooner or later considering the sort of woman she was. He just hoped that by that time he had managed to get his feelings for her into perspective, so he could wish her well and truly mean it.

He gave himself a mental shake as he realised his mother was speaking to him and looked up to see her holding out a plate of mince pies. 'Oh, no, thanks, Mam. After that wonderful dinner I doubt I'll eat for another week,' he said, patting his stomach. His mother really had excelled herself for once. The chicken hadn't been dry at all but maybe that was because he hadn't put it in the oven when she had asked him, hiding it in the pantry instead and waiting until an hour later which thankfully she hadn't noticed. But whatever had possessed her to substitute salted peanuts for walnuts in the new recipe for stuffing that she said she had taken down from a cookery programme on the television? Either she had misunderstood the ingredients when the television chef had been relaying them or she had decided that nuts were nuts and any would do, which seemed quite likely, knowing Iris. He'd had to force down the peculiar-tasting stuffing and pretend he was enjoying it, which in fact was far from true.

'Well, I'm glad you enjoyed it all,' Iris said proudly. 'I'll put these pies on the table and you can help yerself if yer change yer mind.' She settled herself down in the armchair opposite and looked at Chas. Her son didn't seem quite with it today, his mind was elsewhere and she worried that something was troubling him. 'What's on yer mind, son?' she asked.

'What made you ask that, Mam?'

'Oh, it was just that you seem a bit distant today and I wondered why?'

He would like nothing better than to discuss the truth, reveal to her that he'd been stupid enough to allow himself to fall in love with a woman he knew would never return his feelings, ask her advice on how to handle what he was going through. But he knew that to learn the truth would be so worrying for her, he couldn't bear to put her through that. This was something he had to deal with on his own.

'I'm fine, Mam, really,' Chas said lightly. 'Nothing is bothering me.'

He wasn't being truthful with her and Iris wondered why. She knew instinctively he was fighting some inner turmoil and wished he'd open up to her so she could help him deal with it. While he was growing up he had kept from her many painful incidents so as not to upset her. Those incidents had eventually come to light through neighbours' gossip but too late for Iris to do anything about them. Chas was an adult now, and though still gentle by nature would hardly stand by and do nothing when someone was causing him grief.

She knew he must still be grappling with his change in status from employee to owner of a business. That must be what was on his mind. She had no regrets about spurring him on to do what he had. Iris just wished he'd have a little more faith in himself, and hoped that would come in time when the facts and figures proved to him the business was thriving even more under his ownership than it had under Jack Black's.

'You told me you'd set a new bloke on as radio operator to replace Ralph Widcombe. You don't have any worries over him, do you?' Iris probed. 'He was rather a Godsend, turning up like that just when yer needed someone.'

Chas's mind flew back to two days ago when he had spoken privately to Ralph, asking his opinion of his replacement. The two men had sat side by side for an introductory day before Ralph left to resume his retirement.

'Well, if yer want me honest opinion then I have to say the man's claim to be experienced in this business is highly exaggerated,' Ralph had said candidly. 'Most taxi firms operate in more or less the same way, so after what you told me about him I was surprised I needed to go through everything with him from start to finish. I can't see how he can say he's experienced, meself. Having said that, he's keen, I'll say that for him, and he picked things up quick and asked me lots of questions about all the ins and outs which I did me best to answer. I'm sure he'll do fine, boss. He's competent enough now to manage by himself. Give him a few days at it and he'll be handling the radio as well as I do, with all my years of experience.'

Chas was appreciative of Ralph's honest opinion, if a bit concerned that he'd set a man on who maybe hadn't been entirely truthful with him about his knowhow. But then, it had been very apparent how desperate Stanley Slater was for work. If Chas had found himself in such circumstances, Christmas upon him, no money coming in and a wife and family to keep, then wouldn't he have done anything to secure himself a job, just like Stanley had?

Chas had been expecting Ralph to be quite emotional when it came time for them to part company but the old man seemed very relieved that his stint back at work was now at an end. He was, though, deeply touched by Chas's generous gift of twenty pounds extra in his final pay packet to pay for his wife and him taking a weekend together at the seaside.

Chas was aware that along with the extra he'd given Ralph as well as the ten-pound bonus he'd paid all the drivers, with the same for Harrie as he felt it was only fair to treat her equally, he was leaving himself just about able to pay the firm's bills, rent and incidentals, and cover his first loan instalment to the bank as well as seeing his mother right for housekeeping. He just prayed that takings kept up to the level they had been under Jack and did not dip for any reason or he'd find himself in financial trouble. Regardless he did not regret at all what he'd done to help make his staff's Christmas a better one.

'Yes, he was a real Godsend, Mam, and he's doing fine as far as I can tell. What's really surprised me is that he's offered to work evenings as well. I pointed out to him that it would mean doing a sixteen-hour shift, six days a week, but he said he needed the money and was more than happy to do it. I have to say it saves me finding someone else so I've agreed as long as he tells me straightaway if he's finding it too much.'

'Well, yer can't blame a man for taking on extra work to provide for his family. Then everything so far at work is fine, I'm glad to hear. So what is bothering yer, son? Summat is, I know. Don't forget yer can talk to me about anything and I'll do me best to help you in whatever way I can.'

His mother cared so much for him and wouldn't give up until

she had wheedled it out of him, but he had no intention of telling her what was really on his mind. He needed to change the subject. 'Actually, I was trying to think of ways to drum up new business, Mam.' Despite his lack of business acumen, he was aware that to sit on his laurels and assume that Jack's clients would remain for the duration of his ownership was an attitude that courted disaster. He'd need to start thinking of the future now the firm was in his hands.

She eyed him, impressed. 'You'll come up with ways of bringing in new business, I've no doubt, and damned good ones, too. Ready for a piece of Christmas cake?'

He groaned. The cake did look good. She had peaked the icing, creating a snow scene with little plastic Christmas figures dotted here and there, and a thick red ribbon was tied around the side. Whether the mixture was made up of the usual Christmas cake ingredients or his mother had added extras remained to be seen.

CHAPTER TWENTY-SEVEN

Harrie's first opportunity to manoeuvre Chas into asking her out came after a frustrating morning back at work once Christmas was over. Her ears were pricked for the sound of his arrival on the premises, and she was having terrible difficulty concentrating on the pile of work she had to do. The constant stream of jobs coming in meant that Chas and the other drivers were kept busy out on the road, and while she knew she shouldn't be annoyed, she wished today could have been one of their slacker days instead of one of their busier, so that she could do what she had to do and, hopefully, have an evening with Chas to look forward to.

It was Wally Bender's voice that she heard first filtering through her open office door and her heart leaped as she realised who he was speaking to.

'Some morning that was, Boss. Non-stop for me, at any rate. I ain't had time to stop for a bite of lunch yet and it's after two.'

She heard Chas's reply. 'Take the opportunity now, Wally, and if anything comes in I'll take it on.'

'Yer a decent boss, Chas, I'll give yer that. I don't mean to speak ill of the dead, but Jack Black wouldn't have been so considerate. I'll just take long enough to eat me sandwiches then I'll report back for duty.'

The telephone started ringing and Harrie heard Stanley answer it. She pretended to be immersed in her work but secretly willed Chas to come into her office. Her wish was cruelly dashed when she heard Stanley say, 'Boss, that was Fred Owens calling from a telephone box. He's had a slight accident that has knocked his radio out and he needs someone to go and give him a push to get the car started.'

A while later, Chas surveyed the scene before him in dismay. Fred's slight accident had been an understatement. The front of his car was embedded in a low, front-garden wall and, apart from the obvious dents, Chas would only know the full extent of the damage once the car had been towed into the garage. It seemed that no other vehicle had been involved and he wondered how this could have happened on such a quiet road. Chas's first concern, though, was for Fred's wellbeing. 'Any harm to you, Fred?' he asked the middle-aged, wiry man, whose sparse head of greying hair and lived-in face, that other drivers likened to a pickled walnut, had earned him the nickname Nutty.

'No, Boss, well, just a bruise to me head where I hit the windscreen when I came to a halt. Oh, and me neck hurts a bit,' he said rubbing it.

'Well, maybe I ought to take you down to the hospital and get you checked out.'

'No, I'm fine, Boss, honest. A couple of Aspro will sort me out.'

'If you're sure. How did this happen, Fred?'

The man looked awkwardly at him. 'Well, er . . . it were like this, Boss. I'd picked up a woman at a house up the top end of Narborough Road as Stan had radioed through to me. Posh house 'un all, and I was thinking to meself that anyone living there was bound to tip well. But when she came out she was . . . well, she weren't as well dressed as I thought she'd be. I realise now just what she was and why she was in a house like that. Anyway, she asked me to take her to a street up the Clarendon Park area. She insisted on sitting up front next to me, as she liked to chat, she said. Well, she rattled on about n'ote in particular and, to be honest, I wasn't really listening. Then suddenly she asks if I'd like a special sort of payment for the fare instead of the usual kind. Before I knew it she had her hand on me . . . me . . . well, me credentials and . . . well, yer know . . . I was so shocked I lost control of the car and you can see for yourself what happened, Boss. The woman scarpered before I could stop her so she can't have been hurt.' His face then puckered into a frown. 'Eh, listen, Boss, this mustn't get back to me wife. She's a jealous woman is my Edna and there's no telling what she'd do if she found out just who that woman was. Murder, believe me.'

If the situation hadn't been so serious and potentially life threatening to Fred, Chas would have laughed out loud at the comical vision in his mind. He wondered what the insurance company would make of this tale when Chas put in the claim. 'We'll keep this to ourselves, Fred, you have my word. As far as I'm concerned you swerved to avoid a dog.'

'Ah, thanks, Boss,' he said gratefully. His face then screwed up worriedly. 'This means I'm gonna be off the road while the car is repaired. I ain't gonna have no wage coming in. Oh, bloody hell and just after all the expense of Christmas.'

Fred wasn't the only one who would lose out because the car was off the road. Chas's own predicament, though, was over-ridden by Fred's worry about not being able to pay his bills. 'Well, let's hope the garage can do the repairs as quickly as possible once the insurance company give us the go ahead and, in the meantime, you can use my car so you won't lose out money-wise.'

Fred looked at him gob-smacked. 'You really are a gent, Boss. God, we're lucky it was you who took over and not some money-grabbing so-and-so who doesn't care a jot for the staff.'

Satisfied that Fred was fit enough to drive, Chas sent him back to the firm's premises in his own car for a much-needed cup of tea. He stayed with the damaged vehicle to see it safely stowed on the back of the garage tow truck, knowing they'd accommodate a lift for him. Fred was to ask Harrie to organise it all as soon as he arrived back. He also had the foresight to put a note through the door of the house whose wall had been crushed, apologising for what had happened and promising to repair it. As he had sat waiting for the tow truck to arrive a policeman had approached him wanting to know what had gone on. Thankfully, he had accepted Chas's version of events, particularly as no one had been injured, and he went on his way.

As a result, Chas did not return to the office until well after Harrie had left for the night. She had stayed much later than normal, but had become fearful of arousing suspicions amongst the remaining workers as to why she was hanging around for the boss to come back.

Her wish to talk to him privately, though, was granted just after she arrived for work the next morning. She had just begun to update the account books when Chas tapped on the door and walked in.

'Sorry to disturb you, Harrie, but I wanted to thank you for organising the tow truck yesterday. Fred's car's in the garage and they'll telephone you with an estimate of the repair costs as soon as they can, so you can fill in the insurance claim forms and we can get their go ahead so it's not off the road longer than necessary.'

Harrie had already overheard two drivers discussing Chas's generosity in handing over the use of his car to Fred while his was off the road. From what was said it was obvious that they hadn't noticed her arrival.

'Nutty was lucky not to write himself off let alone the car,' said Dan Peters, a thick-set man in his forties, who'd been a taxi driver for several other firms before landing a job at Black's five years ago. 'I'd have run the bleddy dog over instead of smashing into a wall.'

'Oh, come on. Things like that happen so quickly yer can't predict what yer'd do in the circumstances,' replied Sonny James. 'I nearly had a cyclist off his bike the other day when he careered at break-neck speed around a corner and it was only his good fortune that I happened to be looking his way and saw him in time.'

Dan Peters rubbed his hands, a look of glee in his eyes. 'Yeah, well, one thing this has proved to me is that our new boss is a soft touch. He's gotta be ain't he to give over his own car to a driver who's caused damage to his own. Jack Black weren't a bad boss in the big scheme of things, but I doubt he'd have done that. I've learned a few ways to make extra money during my time, but Jack knew all the scams better than we did, and we knew better than to risk doing 'em for fear of the sack. Well, our Mr Tyme ain't bin in this game long enough to know what ter look for, has he?'

As Harrie listened to the two men, an anger burned inside her. Before she could stop herself, she spun round to face the two men and called over, 'It would be a mistake to interpret Mr Tyme's generosity as him being soft. Mr Tyme might not have had years in this business but his eye is on the ball, let me tell you, and if he got a whiff that any of you drivers was up to anything you'd be out. I count myself extremely lucky that I have a kind and considerate boss like Mr Tyme who puts his employees' welfare before his own. You should count yourself fortunate too instead of planning ways to fleece him to line your own pockets.'

Dan Peters' face fell. 'Now, look here, Harrie, lovey, I didn't know you was there and I was only having a bit of fun with Sonny. Wasn't I, Sonny? I didn't mean none of what I said, honest, Harrie. I don't really know any scams, I was just trying to impress Sonny. That right, Sonny?'

She knew Dan was lying but hoped her words had put a stop to anything untoward. Chas was so trusting she doubted it'd crossed his mind that any of his staff would do anything to harm him. He had enough on his plate worrying about keeping the business afloat without her heaping this on him. She decided to keep her eyes peeled, on his behalf. She would try and work out herself what scams could be worked and do her best to prevent them.

She fixed her eyes on Dan. ''Course I know you were having a joke. I know you're not a stupid man, Dan, who'd risk his job for a few extra shillings.'

Now, as she looked at Chas, her stomach was turning somersaults. Should anyone or anything interrupt them this time she would personally lock and bolt her office door until she had fulfilled her quest. She smiled warmly at him. 'I'll do my best to chivvy the insurance company along once I get the repair figures from the garage. I understand you've handed over your own car to Fred while his is in for repair, so what will you do in the meantime?'

'Oh, I'll find something to keep me busy. You did a grand job of cleaning up the drivers' rest room, so I thought I'd give it a fresh coat of paint to make it look better. Plus the sink in the toilet is hanging off the wall . . . Oh, well, I could keep myself occupied for at least a month with the repair jobs that the landlord should take care of but never seems to get around to doing. I thought I could also give Terry a hand with some of the minor repairs that have piled up while he's been off looking after his sick gran. Also, I need to give a lot of thought to ways of bringing in new trade. If I do come up with any ideas, do you mind if I run them past you?'

'Oh, I'd be delighted to give you my opinion, Chas. Now I've the books up to date and am managing to keep them that way, I've more or less got the office work under control, so I'll put my thinking cap on too and see if I can come up with anything.'

Harrie knew he was about to make his excuses and leave. Now was the time to put her plan into operation. She suddenly felt very nervous that she'd mistaken his feelings for her and was about to make the biggest fool of herself. But then she told herself there was no way she had mistaken the look in his eyes when he had held her in his arms in the chip shop and neither was she mistaken over his jealousy when he had caught Darren trying to kiss her under the mistletoe.

Pulling a copy of the previous Friday's *Leicester Mercury* towards her, she said, 'Oh, there's an article in last night's paper that I thought would be of interest to you and, not knowing if you read the *Mercury*, I bought it in for you to have a look at.' Not giving him time to respond, she opened the newspaper out at a page she had already marked as the one she wanted to open it at and then swung the paper around so he could look down at it.

He scanned the page quizzically. 'I can't see any articles on this page, it's the cinema page you've shown me.'

She planted a puzzled look on her face and spun the newspaper back around to face her. 'Oh, so it is. Oh, damn, I've picked up the wrong newspaper as this is last Friday's and the article was in last night's.' She then exclaimed, 'Oh, just look what's showing at the Fosse Picture House: *Butch Cassidy and the Sundance Kid*. I so badly want to see that film. It's supposed to be really good.' She looked forlorn. 'But I've no one to go with me. All my friends are either courting or married.' She then looked as though a thought had just struck her. 'Have you seen the film yourself yet, Chas?'

He wondered why she wanted to know. 'Er ... no, no, I haven't.'

Oh, she was so relieved to hear that. 'Oh, then you wouldn't take me, would you?' She then added meaningfully, 'I really would like to go with you, Chas.' There. She couldn't have been plainer, could she? Even the dimmest of men would know from what she had said and how she had said it she was asking for a date with him because she liked him, liked him very much.

Chas was thinking that Harrie really must be desperate to see the film if she was asking him to accompany her. She had no idea what she was asking of him though. Apart from the fact he'd never been to the pictures with a woman before and this would be a whole new experience for him, knowing how he felt about her, it was going to be so difficult for him to act the perfect escort, when all the time he would be fighting to stop himself from scooping her up in his arms, to proclaim his love for her, then to kiss her so passionately she would need to beg him to stop. He wished she wouldn't look at him the way she was doing. If he didn't know better, he would swear she liked him far more than just the work friends that they were.

'Well, I could take you, I suppose.'

'Tonight?' she said eagerly.

Goodness she was keen to see the film. He'd nothing else planned to do that evening 'Well, yes, I could.'

'I'll meet you then at seven thirty, outside the Fosse Picture House.' She noticed the anxiety on his face. 'Have I said something wrong, Chas?'

'Oh, no, no, it's just that it's very dark now at that time of night and . . . well, if you're entrusting me to make sure you get there and back safely wouldn't it be better if I called for you at your house?' As soon as he suggested it, he realised Harrie maybe didn't want to be seen walking along with him. 'But, if you prefer we meet outside the pictures, then that's fine with me.'

Not many men these days would put themselves out to offer what he had. More and more she was being convinced that this man was the man for her. 'I'd like very much if you'd call for me. Shall we say seven?'

Her request for him to call for her shocked him as he hadn't expected her to want that. 'Oh, right, seven it is then? Er . . . just what was the article about that you thought I'd be interested in?

'Oh, er . . . do you know, I can't remember now. I'll rack my brains and, if I remember, I'll tell you later.'

As Chas walked out of Harrie's office he kept reminding himself that this definitely wasn't a date. He was just accompanying her to the pictures because she had no one else to go with.

As he left the office, Harrie wanted to clap her hands and jump up and down with glee. She had done it. She'd finally got Chas to take her out. Their relationship had begun and she had never felt so excited at the prospect of a date with a man in all her life.

As Chas left the office he noticed a smartly dressed man waiting at the counter. He looked irritated.

'Can I help you, sir?' Chas asked him as he arrived at the counter.

'Finally, I get service?' the man snapped. 'I've been waiting at least two minutes. I want to speak to Harriet Harris. Hurry up, man, I haven't got all day.'

Chas did not like this man's attitude and wondered what he wanted with Harrie. He was a very good-looking man and appeared well set up to Chas. 'Who shall I say wants her?' he asked politely.

'Just fetch her, man, I've already told you I haven't got all day.'

Chas popped his head round the office door. 'There's a man at the counter wanting to see you, Harrie.'

She looked askance. 'Who, Chas?'

'He wouldn't say.'

As soon as Harrie saw who had summoned her, her heart plummeted. She had thought she had seen the last of Jeremy. Before she could ask him what he wanted with her, he requested she accompany him outside.

In front of the premises of Black's now he looked at her mystified. 'I couldn't believe it when I saw the article in the newspaper about this place and saw you in the picture amongst the staff. Harriet, what on earth are you playing at, reducing yourself to working in a place like this? Anyway, that's by the by. I've given you ample time to come to your senses and enough is enough. I realise that you must be feeling rather stupid for acting so childishly, therefore, against my better nature, I've come to see you so we can get this over with and get on with our wedding preparations. Mother has persuaded the Belmont to rearrange our wedding date . . .'

Harrie was staring at him dumbstruck. She couldn't believe that he had not taken on board at all what she had said to him but had continued to believe that during their separation she was still suffering from pre-wedding nerves. 'Jeremy,' she interjected. 'I meant what I said to you. Our relationship is over. I know I'm not right for you and you're not right for me. I don't like hurting you more than I have already but I can't marry you just to make you happy. There is someone else for you, Jeremy, who will make you the sort of wife you want, but that woman is not me. Now, please, leave me alone, Jeremy, and I mean that.'

Before he could stop her, she had spun on her heels and disappeared back inside the firm's premises.

During her absence, Chas had been hovering inside the office, wondering who this man was and why he'd taken Harrie outside to speak to her. As soon as she came back in he went across to her and asked, 'Everything all right, Harrie?' He could tell by her face all was not well.

She looked upset and Chas wasn't fooled by the smile she planted on her face when she responded, 'Oh, yes, thanks, Chas, everything is fine. That was just a friend who I'd lost touch with who'd seen the article in the paper about Black's and saw me in the photograph and came to ask how I was. I'd better get on with my work.'

He stared after her as she returned to her office. He had a feeling that the man was more than just a friend. Several possibilities sprang to mind as to who he was, some of them evoking jealousy within Chas. Regardless, though, one thing did strike Chas: Harrie was acquainted with men like him and possibly others of his ilk and, in that respect, the likes of himself stood no chance whatsoever with her in a romantic way and he was stupid to even dream otherwise.

CHAPTER TWENTY-EIGHT

'You're home sharpish tonight, son,' Iris said to Chas as he walked through the back door just after six that evening. 'Good job yer dinner's all ready. It's shepherd's pie. Go and sit yerself down and I'll bring it through. Work's not slack, is it? Hope that's not why yer home earlier than normal.'

'No, Mam, I'm glad to say it's not. That article in the *Mercury* that was printed the day before Christmas Eve has brought more customers in. Harrie said it would do and she was right. I'm just hoping they're all pleased with our services and will continue to use us when they need a taxi.'

'You're pleased with what Harrie's doing in the office, ain't yer, son?'

'If you want the truth, Mam, I couldn't manage without her.' He happened to catch the look on her face as he lifted his fork to his mouth and said, 'We just work well together so don't get any ideas, Mam. And don't say you weren't because I know you were.'

'Well, I really took to her when we met. She's such a nice girl and you're such a nice man and . . .'

He eyed her sharply. 'Mam, I know you really want nothing more than to see me happily settled but stop getting your hopes up that it could be with Harrie because I'm not her sort and I'm certainly not stupid enough to think I am,' he said, remembering the calibre of the man who had visited Harrie in the office earlier. He frowned quizzically then. 'Er . . . just what have you done to this shepherd's pie?'

Iris looked worried. 'Why, what's wrong with it?'

'Nothing, it's delicious.'

'So yer saying my other ones weren't, even though you said at the time they were?'

'Er . . . well, they weren't as tasty as this, Mam,' he said diplomatically. 'Have you done something different to it?'

'I've used a new recipe I was given by a friend.'

'Oh, Freda?'

'Er . . . yes, that's right. Well, if it's so delicious I'd better stick to using that one in future instead of me own. And here was me thinking mine was best.'

'Oh, but Mam, I didn't mean . . .'

'It's all right, son,' Iris cut in. 'Sometimes even I have to admit that someone else's recipe is better. I've some more pie left in the dish, if you want it?'

'Well, I'll pass if you don't mind, Mam. I'm going out tonight and I'm in a bit of a rush to get ready.'

Her eyes lit up. 'You're going out? Good, I'm glad to hear it. Who with?' she asked keenly.

She was clearly hoping he was going to tell her he'd a date with a woman. Well, he was going out with a woman but it was definitely not a date and in order not to get his mother's hopes up he felt it would be better to tell her he was going by himself.

'I'm going to the pictures on my own, Mam, because there's a film I want to see.'

'Oh? Well, you might meet someone nice there that's gone on their own too, mightn't you? Eh, and if you do and she shows interest in you, don't you dare think you're not good enough and miss an opportunity.'

Chas pushed away his empty plate. 'You don't mind if I don't give you a hand with the dishes tonight?'

'No, 'course I don't, son. It's not often you decide to go out for some enjoyment even if it is on yer own. About time you did. I know there's a nice woman out there waiting for you to come along, son, but you won't meet her unless you go out and find her, will yer?'

Percy was pleased to hear his daughter was going out for an evening's entertainment with a friend who he assumed to be female. She had hardly been out socially since her break up with Jeremy and he felt it was about time she did. She wouldn't find the man of her dreams sitting in a chair by the fireside.

Harrie had decided to let him assume that it was a female friend she was going out with as she had already made one mistake in going out with a boss and didn't want her father worrying she might be making another with Chas until their

258

relationship was on a firm footing. Then she could bring Chas round to meet him and Percy could see for himself that this time she definitely was not making a mistake.

Before she left, though, Percy made her promise to be very careful when she walked home that night as he'd read a report in the *Mercury* that evening about two women on separate occasions having their handbag snatched from their hand by an assailant who then jumped into a car which sped away. Harrie promised him she would be very diligent and felt a little guilty for not putting his mind at rest by saying her escort was a man who definitely would not let any harm come to her while she was with him.

Immediately Chas knocked on the door of the address Harrie had given him it was pulled open and Harrie stood beaming at him.

The sight of her dressed very becomingly in an ankle-length peasant-style dress in soft pastel colours, over which she was wearing a long black maxi coat with fake fur around its collar, almost knocked him for six. She'd looped her hair up at the back and tendrils framed her lovely face. He couldn't believe that this beautiful woman had requested his company when she could have any man she wanted. Even more surprising, she was looking very pleased to see him.

Harrie was thinking how handsome Chas looked in his black polo-necked jumper, over which he wore a smart navy blue blazer. He wore blue casual trousers which she was pleased to note were not the flared type that were all the rage just now as they were more for stick-thin dandy-type men which Chas certainly wasn't and would not suit his more well-proportioned manly shape. How proud she was going to feel, walking down the road with him by her side.

'Right on time just like I knew you'd be,' Harrie said to him. She turned her head and called back down the passageway, 'I'm off now, Dad, won't be too late.' Then, joining Chas on the pavement, she closed the door and again surprised him by hooking her arm through his. Smiling up at him, she said, 'Shall we go then?'

At just after eleven o'clock that night they stood facing each other once more on the doorstep. Harrie had had a wonderful evening, just as she'd known she would. She had learned much more about Chas as they chatted easily on the way to and from the picture house. She had heard about his great love of music, the huge collection of records he regularly played, and was thrilled to find out that some of his preferred artists were hers as well. She hadn't met a man before who admitted he enjoyed reading, and after his enthusiastic accounts of several of his favourite novels she wanted to read them too.

He had insisted on paying for the tickets so she had offered to treat them both to an assortment of sweets. Despite the film's being riveting, usually the type she would have lost herself in, Harrie had remained very conscious of the man sitting next to her. Throughout the performance she willed him to hold her hand or put his arm around her and was disappointed that he never attempted any intimate gesture towards her whatsoever. But maybe he didn't want to push his attentions on her too quickly. After all it was their first date. Maybe on their next one he would be bolder and show more affection towards her.

Chas had had a wonderful evening too. Harrie was very good company, very easy to talk to, and seemed so interested in his likes and dislikes. It surprised him to learn they had quite a lot in common in their musical tastes and both liked reading, and although she'd never been to speedway before she said she certainly would after Chas had made it sound so exciting. It had been difficult for him as they sat side by side to keep his hands clasped firmly in his lap except to accept a sweet from the bag when she regularly offered it to him. He was desperate to hold her hand, or even better put his arm around her and pull her close to him. But once again he was reminded of the man who'd visited Harrie and that he wasn't of her calibre.

'I've had a wonderful evening, Chas, and thank you so much for taking me,' Harrie said, back on her own doorstep.

'I've enjoyed it too. It was a pleasure.'

Harrie fully expected him at least to kiss her cheek or prefer-ably her lips before suggesting another date soon. What he did next stunned her speechless.

He held out his hand to her, which she automatically shook. 'Well you're home safely so good night then, Harrie. I'll see you at work tomorrow.'

She watched in astonishment as he marched off down the road.

She felt sick with disappointment. How could she have been so badly mistaken about Chas's feelings for her? Obviously after his actions of tonight she most definitely had been. She hadn't held back over allowing him to see how she felt about him and had given him more than ample opportunity to take their relationship further should he want to. Whatever type of woman Chas preferred, Harrie was without doubt not his sort. A great sense of loss filled her. She felt bereft. She had no choice but to accept Chas's rejection of her, see that she was no more to him than an employee he got on well with. But whoever she met in the future and settled for, she would always know deep down that Chas Tyme was the man she should really be with.

Marion was stunned when next evening Harrie told her what had transpired.

'I can't believe it, Harrie, I really can't. He showed no signs of fancying you at all?'

Miserably she shook her head. 'Treated me like a friend, that's it.'

Marion affectionately patted her hand. 'Well, yer can't win 'em all, gel. Plenty more fish in the sea. You won't be on yer own for long,' she said by way of cheering Harrie up. It was obvious she was heartbroken that she hadn't after all got the man she'd been sure she was meant to spend the rest of her life with. 'How did you manage today at work, Harrie? It must have been awful for you?'

'Oh, Marion, it was, I can't tell you how awful. As Chas is not out on the road at the moment until a damaged car gets fixed, but on the premises all the time. As soon as I arrived I saw him looking over the log book to see what jobs had been done the previous night. I wanted to leap into his arms and demand to know what was so wrong with me that he didn't feel attracted to me. How I managed it I'll never know but I just acted towards him like any employee would to her boss and he was the same to me as he always is. But what I can't understand, Marion, is why his eyes looked the way they did those times if he hasn't got strong feelings for me?'

She shrugged. 'Search me, Harrie. Maybe you wanted to see what you thought you did.'

'Imagined it, you mean? Yes, seems I did, doesn't it?'

'Look, Harrie, wouldn't it be best if you got yourself another job? That way you'd get over the man quicker.'

That thought had crossed her mind as she lay tossing and turning the night before, so devastated by her disappointment she couldn't sleep. 'It would be the sensible thing to do but I love my job, Marion. I feel as if I'm more than earning my money, and Chas does pay me a decent wage for what I do. And I want to do what I can to help him make a success of his business. He really needs someone with my office experience to run that side for him, he's not up to doing it himself yet. It'd be childish of me to give up a job I really enjoy just because the boss doesn't like me the way I like him, don't you think? Best thing I can do is throw myself into my work and accept that you're right, Marion, you can't win them all. As much as I would so love to have won this one.'

But when it came to Chas, Harrie knew this would be a lot easier said than done.

CHAPTER TWENTY-NINE

True to her word Harrie threw herself into her work, doing her best to submerge her feelings for Chas and hide them away. It was far from easy. She would be glad when Fred's car was ready to be picked up from the garage and Chas got his own back, then he wouldn't be physically on the premises so often and she not constantly coming into contact with him.

If her father had noticed she was not quite her usual self then he had elected not to say anything to her, for which she was grateful. She had noticed, though, that the extra spark Percy had had about him recently, and which he seemed to have lost on Christmas Day, was back again. What was causing this newfound energy and joy within him she had no idea.

On New Year's Eve Marion had begged Harrie to join her and Allen, his mates and the rest of the revellers, at the Blackbird pub which had laid on entertainment: a group who specialised in playing chart-topping music and a comedian renowned for having his audience rolling in the aisles. Harrie knew it wasn't going to do her any good sitting at home moping and wondering how Chas was celebrating the start of the seventies so she agreed she'd join them.

To Harrie's surprise she did manage to enjoy herself, though she constantly found herself scouring the crowds, hoping for a glimpse of Chas. She knew this pub to be the one he used when he did venture out for a drink and was disappointed when he didn't appear. She told herself off for that. It wasn't as if she could rush up to him, throw her arms around him and kiss him for New Year. Now she knew he didn't care for her in the way she wanted him to care, she was best off putting all romantic thoughts of him from her mind. She was glad when the evening's frivolities were over and she could make her way home with the rest of the crowd, most of them extremely inebriated.

On the first Friday morning in January Harrie was tackling the wages when she realised she hadn't got the details of Stanley Slater's tax code or National Insurance number so she could add him to the payroll. Unable to proceed further without them, she went out to see him.

Stanley was on the telephone taking details of a job from a customer. As she stood waiting to speak to him slightly behind him, she noted he was jotting the details down on a piece of paper which struck her as odd. All jobs were usually first logged in the book lying on the desk in front of him. Having concluded the call, he put the telephone back into the receiver and the piece of paper in his jacket pocket.

He must have sensed her presence then as he jumped and turned his head to look at her. 'Oh, blimey, you gave me a scare, Harrie. I didn't know you were there.'

'I'm sorry, Stanley, I didn't mean to but you were taking down details of a job and I didn't want to disturb you. I need to speak to you but I don't mind waiting until you've radioed that job through to a driver.'

'Eh? Oh, it's not for today but tomorrow. I can do it later. What did you want to speak to me about?'

'Just to ask if you'd brought your P45 in yet like I asked you to do when you first started. I need your details to make up your wages.'

'Ah, well, I haven't got a P45. You see, my last firm insisted on all their staff being self-employed. It saved them the bother of paying tax and National Insurance for their employees as we were responsible for paying our own. It'd be easier for you if I continued as self-employed. Save me a lot of bother, too, getting my status changed at the tax office and having to wait weeks for my code to come through while paying full-rate tax on every penny I earn. I know you get the overpaid tax back eventually but in the meantime I'd have to pay out and I can't afford to, what with my wife not being able to work while she looks after her sick mother. So it's all right with you then, is it, Harrie, if I stay self-employed?'

It would make her life easier, not having to calculate and

deduct his dues each week, plus Chas would be saving his employer's contribution. 'If it's all right with you then it's fine with me,' she confirmed.

Stanley seemed very relieved by this.

'Are you still happy to be working all hours, Stanley, now you've been doing them for a week?' she asked. 'A sixteen-hour shift, six days a week, is a tall order for anyone.'

'Oh, I'm more than happy,' he insisted. 'I need the money.'

'Well, remember what the boss said to you when you first asked to be allowed to do it. If you do find it getting too much for you, then don't hesitate to say so and we'll get another operator in to cover the evening shift.'

As Harrie made her way back to her office to resume her own work she thought this man must be desperate indeed for money, to be prepared to work such long hours to earn it. Still, she did admire Stanley for what he was prepared to do in order to provide for his family.

A little later that morning she was making herself a drink in the rest room. While the kettle was boiling she took a look at a copy of last night's *Mercury* which someone had left on the table. The front-page article immediately caught her eye and she was reminded of something her father had warned her about on the night of her ill-fated outing with Chas. BAG-SNATCHING EPIDEMIC, screamed the headline. It seemed from the article that six women now had had their handbag stolen as they walked home alone late at night, all it seemed by a person dressed from head to toe in black, head covered by a balaclava, who immediately after snatching the handbags from the surprised victims ran off down the road to where a parked car was waiting. As soon as the thief was safely inside it sped off. As yet all the victims had been far too stunned by the speed of events to have had time to take down the vehicle's number for the police to trace.

She realised someone had entered the rest room and lifted her head to see who it was. It was Chas. Despite fighting hard to play down her feelings for him, the sight of Chas still managed to set her heart racing and her thoughts pondering miserably what might have been.

Harrie planted a smile on her face. 'Hello,' she said brightly. 'Get the sink in the toilets fixed?'

'Finally,' Chas replied. 'It's now firmly back against the wall and I hope it stays that way.' He took a glance around. 'I can make a start on freshening the walls in here now I've done all the smaller jobs.'

'You're enjoying yourself doing all the odd jobs around here, aren't you?'

'I have to say I am, though I'd prefer to be out on the road earning the firm some money. Any news yet from the garage?'

'Oh, yes, they called a few minutes ago. As soon as I'd made my drink I was coming to tell you about it. Fred's car will be ready on Monday. The insurance company has pushed through the claim and will settle the bill as soon as the garage sends it to them.'

'Oh, that is good news,' said Chas, relieved. 'Thanks, Harrie. I know it's through your hard work this has all gone through so quickly. Well, seems my stint of odd jobbing is at an end. I'll have to come in on Sundays to paint this room up. One Sunday might even do it if I start early and don't finish until it's done.'

'Maybe one of the drivers will offer to help you?'

'Oh, I wouldn't expect them to give up their day off after working hard all week.'

No thought for himself after all the hard work he'd put in all week, she noticed. 'Coffee?' she asked, moving across to the table as the kettle started singing to announce it had boiled.

'Tea if you don't mind, please, Harrie.'

She didn't mind. Despite her devastation on learning he didn't return her feelings she'd still do anything for Chas, would make him a hundred cups if that's what he wanted.

Chas's eyes fell on the article Harrie had been reading. 'Oh, dear, those poor women must have been terrified, having their handbags stolen from them as they walked home. A couple of them were carrying as much as twenty pounds on them at the time. God, that's a lot of money to have stolen! I hope they find the culprits soon before many more women are attacked like that. Oh, thank you, Harrie,' he said as he accepted his mug of tea gratefully from her. He couldn't bear the thought of anything like this happening to her and, before he could check himself, asked, 'You do take care when you're out late at night, don't you, Harrie? Especially with people like this on the loose at the moment.'

She had learned to her cost not to misconstrue his show of concern for anything more than it was, a boss worried for the welfare of a female member of staff. 'I'm not often out in the evening on my own these days so don't worry about me, Chas. But all the same, thank you for doing so.' She hardly went out in the evenings nowadays, except to call on Marion, not feeling in the mood for socialising at the moment while still struggling to accept the fact that the man she knew to be perfect for her would never be hers.

From what she said Chas interpreted this as meaning that when Harrie did go out she had the protection of a male companion. A boyfriend most likely. He had warned himself not to expect that a woman like her would be unattached for long. Nevertheless, he hadn't envisaged the news hurting as much as it actually did. He felt like his guts had been ripped open. 'Well, that's good to hear,' he said matter-of-factly. 'I'll leave you to it then.'

Harrie watched him go, feeling utterly dejected.

As the weeks passed, try as she might, Harrie's feelings for Chas did not diminish in the slightest. Well, she would just have to learn to live with them. She was in love with him and true love did not die. She dreaded the day she would learn that he had found a woman who suited him, vehemently hoping she could sound convincing when she wished them both well for the future.

CHAPTER THIRTY

One morning at the start of April found Harrie staring into space, her brow creased into a worried frown. She had just finished updating the end-of-month figures in the accounts book. Since the beginning of January Tymc's had taken approximately fifty pounds a week less than Jack Black had done. Harrie could not understand this state of affairs. It seemed to her they should have been making more profit than Jack had due to several changes in the way the firm operated that had been made over the last three months, as well as the article in the *Mercury* that had been published the night before Christmas Eve and had brought many new customers walking through the door.

Besides all that, Harrie had also put her brain into overdrive and come up with several new ideas to improve profits. Chas had been delighted to hear them and she in turn delighted he'd put them into operation.

On Chas's behalf she had negotiated with the local garage a penny a gallon discount, which over a year added up to quite a saving on their fuel costs.

The customer waiting area had also been made a much more pleasant environment than it had been in Jack's day in the hope that people would choose to spend extra on a taxi rather than catch a bus. The walls in the waiting section at the front of the premises were now painted an inviting bright yellow and potted plants stood on the window ledge. More comfortable chairs had been provided to sit on, along with an assortment of magazines to read. Facilities to make a cup of tea or coffee while people waited had also been made available and were proving very popular.

To improve the overall image of the firm to the customer, all drivers had been issued with smart new navy blue jackets and matching trousers so none had any excuse for presenting a scruffy appearance as they had previously tended to do.

Harrie had also worked out a possible way the drivers could be lining their own pockets. Fares were calculated by drivers on arrival at the destination. They would log the actual mileage then double it to include the return to base. The total mileage was then multiplied by the mileage rate which at the moment was a shilling a mile. Unless a very astute customer logged the vehicle's mileage when they first got into the taxi and again when they arrived at journey's end, which she doubted many would consider doing, Harrie could see that drivers could very easily charge customers for an extra half-mile or mile on that trip, the passenger being none the wiser. The driver could pocket the extra shilling or so charged, along with his tip, and over a week, even only carrying out this scam on half the allotted jobs, a substantial sum could be made by defrauding the customer and Chas who bore the cost of the vehicle and petrol.

Fair-minded Chas hated the thought that any of his drivers could be up to no good, preferring to give them the benefit of the doubt, but Harrie had finally convinced him that this was a business he was running. If a way to undermine that business presented itself then he had no choice but to take action to protect his own livelihood.

The solution to this particular situation was simple, Harrie explained. Each driver would be issued with two separate, carbon-copy, numbered receipt books. At the end of each job a receipt must be written out for the cost of the journey, the top copy being given to the customer in exchange for their fare, the carbon to remain in the receipt book. Each night that day's receipt book would be handed in to Harrie by the driver along with their takings. The next day they would take the other receipt book out with them. Harrie would keep a separate account book for each driver. In that book she would log the details on each receipt, checking the numbers ran consecutively and none were missing or she'd want to know why, and also make sure the takings handed in tallied with the total mileage recorded. Due consideration was given to wrong change being given due to human error but a rule was put in place that for any shortages over ten shillings a week, the driver would have to be responsible. In order to ensure drivers furnished every customer with a receipt, they were informed that regular random checks with customers would be done by the management, not only to verify that they had been given a receipt but also to clarify that the service they had received from Tyme's Taxis had been first class.

Harrie pointed out to Chas that implementing this system would prove one way or another if any of their drivers were up to something. If they were, and were not happy that their way of making extra for themselves had been ended, they were quite at liberty to terminate their employment with Tyme's Taxis and take up a position elsewhere.

After the system was introduced in the middle of February, Chas was delighted that none of his drivers resigned their post. After pondering this, Harrie herself could only conclude that the firm must have lost more customers than it had gained through the article in the *Mercury* and the changes they had since implemented. The reason why customers had possibly chosen to leave them and use other cab firms remained a mystery to her. Surely Tyme's offered the best service in the area?

Harrie knew Chas was desperately worried about the fall in profits, feeling that under his ownership the company was failing despite Harrie's own assurances to him that he was proving to be a more than exemplary boss, well respected by his staff. She knew it also grieved him that if this trend continued it could reach a stage where he'd have to start laying off men instead of upping their hourly rate to compensate for the shorter shifts he had planned to introduce: three shifts of eight hours each instead of the two at twelve they worked now, affording the drivers more leisure time to spend with their families. Chas also had the added burden of repaying the bank loan. If he failed to do that each week the bank would have no choice but to foreclose on him.

Harrie strongly felt that it would be a crying shame if the business did go under. Chas had done everything in his power during the short time he'd owned it to make it a success. Tyme's Taxis was a slicker operation by far than ever Jack had run. Whatever lay behind their loss of custom, Harrie knew it was nothing to do with Chas's management of the business. All she could hope, like him, was that those lost customers would come back and the profits rise again.

Harrie rubbed her hands wearily over her face and gave a deep sigh. Having now updated the accounts book to show the figures for March, she knew she was going to be adding to Chas's worries. She closed the books and placed them on the shelf above her desk, ready to show Chas when he came in as he knew she was closing the balance on the month of March figures that morning. She felt a great need for a cup of coffee before she began her next task. She was just coming out of her room when her attention was drawn to the outer office. She saw two rain-coated men entering. Glancing across the room to see that Stanley was busy on the telephone, she went over to deal with them herself.

She was stunned when the older of the two men introduced them.

'We're police officers,' he said. 'I'm Detective Wright and this is Detective Newman. We'd like to speak privately to the owner.'

'He's not in,' she told them. 'We've a contract with Marconi to supply taxis as and when required. Mr Tyme personally has taken one of the staff down to Marconi's office in Basildon. I don't know when he'll get back. My name is Harriet Harris and I'm in charge of the office. Can I help you or would you like me to ask Mr Tyme to contact you when he comes back?'

'Well, perhaps you can give us the information we're after. Could we go somewhere private?'

Inside her office with the door closed, Harriet looked at them expectantly.

'I don't know if you're aware of the spate of bag-snatching that's been going on recently?' Detective Wright began.

'Yes, I am. I read an update about it in the paper last week It said twelve women had now had their handbags stolen from them while walking home late at night.'

'Yes, that's right, only now it's fourteen. Two more were attacked last night.'

Harrie gasped. 'Oh, that's terrible!' Then she looked at the detectives quizzically. 'But what has this to do with us?'

'Well, that's what we're here to clarify – whether it is or it isn't anything to do with Tyme's Taxis. The last victim has been able to give us more details than any of the others up to now. She gathered her wits about her quicker than the rest and gave chase to her attacker. She witnessed him getting into a car which then sped away but she noticed that the car in question had writing on the side of it, like private-hire taxis have, although she couldn't make out the name, unfortunately.

'If this information is correct then it appears for that particular incident at any rate, a taxi driver and his accomplice are the likely culprits. We're visiting all the taxi firms in Leicester to find out what vehicles they had operating that night, and what areas they were in at the time of the crime so we can rule that firm out. The incident we're checking out took place last night at around ten-forty-five on Latimer Street soon after the victim had left the Crow's Nest public house. You can give us information about your drivers' whereabouts at that time, I trust?'

'Yes. We have three drivers covering the night shift which runs from six in the evening until six in the morning. The jobs they do are all logged in the night-shift job book. But, officer, none of our three drivers would be involved in anything like this, I know they wouldn't,' she said with conviction. 'They're all decent family men. In fact, Sam Little is a grandfather.'

'Could we have a look at the book, Miss Harris?'

'Oh, yes, of course. I'll fetch it.'

Back in her office Harrie opened the book at the relevant page and scanned down it. The drivers had been kept busy that night but at the time in question it seemed all three men were in the office, waiting for work to come in, so they could vouch for each other. She relayed this information to the policemen then clarified her statement by showing them the log book.

Satisfied no driver from Tyme's Taxis could be involved in the incident the previous night, they thanked her and she politely accompanied them to the counter to see them off the premises.

No sooner had they walked out than a smartly dressed, matronly woman walked in. Harrie flashed a glance across at Stanley to see him once again busy on the telephone. Turning back to face the woman, she smiled welcomingly and asked if she could help her.

'Yes, you can, dear,' the woman said in a baritone voice. 'I tried to telephone earlier but the line was continually busy. As I had to come this way, I decided to call in personally. I've arranged for a taxi for Thursday at nine o'clock to take me to see my daughter in Coventry. Unfortunately my arrangements have been changed and I won't now be going tomorrow but on Friday instead. My name is Mrs Jackson, 33 Anstey Lane. If you could make new arrangements for me at the same pick-up time, I'd be grateful.'

When Harrie arrived at Stanley's desk he was busy radioing through a job to a driver and it seemed he was having difficulty as the driver's radio kept cutting out. Sooner than wait for Stanley to finish, which could take a while she guessed from what she was overhearing, Harrie thought she'd help him out by doing it herself.

Sliding the book from in front of him, she turned the page to show the next day's jobs. Details of several pre-booked fares had been written down and she quickly scanned them, searching for Mrs Jackson's booking. It wasn't there. Thinking she had missed it, she scanned the page again. No, she hadn't been wrong, there was no booking for a Mrs Jackson, nor even a name that could be mistaken for Jackson or an address anywhere near the one she had given to Harrie.

Stanley had by now managed to get the information he needed to the driver and had snapped off the radio-mic.

'A radio-operator's job isn't an easy one, is it, when you get situations like that, Stanley?' Harrie said to him. 'I enjoyed my stint before you started with us but I don't think I'd like to do it all the hours you do, six days a week.'

'Well, when you need the money you can't turn down the chance to earn it, can you?'

'No, you can't,' she agreed, knowing that if she was in Stanley's situation she would be doing just what he was to look after her family. 'Anyway, can you help me? A Mrs Jackson has just called in to the office. You were busy at the time so I dealt with her for you. She says she pre-booked a taxi for tomorrow to go to Coventry but her arrangements have changed and now she wants to rearrange her booking for Friday. I can't find an entry for her at all in the book tomorrow, though.'

He stared blankly at her. 'Oh, I see. Yes, well . . . she couldn't have booked it with us then.'

'She seemed so positive she had a taxi booked with us for Thursday.'

'Well, maybe she came in here thinking we were another taxi firm? The one she had in fact booked with. It's an easy mistake to make.'

'But we're the only firm in this area. Oh, we could be trying to work out what's happened for the rest of the day but as far as Mrs Jackson is concerned she's cancelled her taxi for tomorrow and rearranged it for Friday so we have no alternative but to send her one. I suppose it's only fair I should call all the other taxi firms to find out which one she booked it through and then cancel it . . . this is naughty, I know, but I won't tell them we're now providing her taxi and hopefully Mrs Jackson will be so pleased with our services she'll use us for all her future business.'

'Well, as I know you're busy, Harrie, give me Mrs Jackson's details and I'll log down the job and call round the other firms for you.'

'But you're busy too, Stanley. Have you had a break at all today? You know I've told you I'll cover the telephone and radio for you whenever you need relieving, if no one else is around to take over. You've only called on me a couple of times since you started here, Stanley, and that was just while you nipped out to spend a penny. Anyone would think you and the desk were part of each other.'

'Well, I may as well sit here and work than idle my time away reading a newspaper in the rest room.'

Harrie smiled at him. 'We were lucky to get you, Stanley. Not many men are as willing and conscientious in their job as you are.' She handed him the piece of paper on which she had taken down Mrs Jackson's details. 'I'll leave you to it then.'

Harrie was right, Chas was visibly distressed on learning that the profits were down for the third month in a row. This big, wonderful man she loved so much it physically hurt had looked so tired when he arrived in the office after his long journey to Basildon and back. Receiving this news on top of it seemed to drain the life from him. Harrie desperately wanted to give him a comforting hug but he had made his lack of feelings for her very plain on the night of their outing to the cinema and she felt he wouldn't welcome the gesture.

Rubbing one big hand wearily over his face, Chas gave a deep sigh and said, 'I'm going to end up bankrupt at this rate. I've tossed and turned for nights over this and decided that if the profits were down again at the end of March then I'd no alter-native but to throw in the towel. I'm obviously not cut out to be the owner of a business.'

'Oh, but you are,' she insisted. 'You have got what it takes. You have.'

He forced a smile. 'I know you're trying to make me feel better, Harrie, and I appreciate your efforts but it's obvious by the fall in profits that I've not. I haven't got what the likes of Jack had to make my own business a success, it's as simple as that. If I put the firm up for sale now, hopefully someone will buy it who has the know how to make a go of it. That way the men's jobs and yours will be saved and hopefully I'll get enough to pay off the bank loan. I might even be lucky enough to get a job from whoever buys it.'

'Oh, Chas, please can't I change your mind?' she begged. 'At least give it a little longer. I'm sure next month will see a rise in the profits. Look, I could be wrong about the reason for the fall being down to customers using another firm. It could be we're going through a longer post-Christmas lull than usual. Maybe other taxi firms too are going through it. I could try and find out.'

'Harrie, please, there's no point. Look, I might not have a business brain but I have enough sense to realise that if I give it another month and the profits take another fall then the firm will be worth even less. I'm not worried for myself, Harrie, it's the staff that concern me. I have to do my best for all. And there's also my mother to consider. If I'm back on a wage and still repaying what I owe the bank, I might not be able to give her all she needs for her housekeeping. It's not right that she be reduced to living on the breadline at her age, not if I can help it.'

Chas stood up. 'Thank you for staying behind to tell me the end-of-March figures. I know I don't need to ask you to keep my decision to sell to yourself, Harrie. I don't want the men worrying over possibly losing their jobs for as long as I can keep this from them. Well, I'd better get off home and find the right moment to break this news to my mother.'

Then a thought struck him. It was Wednesday so his mother would be having her usual snooze. In all these months he'd never got to the bottom of why exactly Wednesdays affected her in this way. He felt sure it was because on that day she went to town and tired herself out looking around the shops, and didn't want to come clean to him because she knew he wasn't happy about her going far on her own.

When he reached home and saw his mother, peacefully asleep

in her chair, Chas couldn't bring himself to tell her the distressing news. He didn't want to worry her any sooner than necessary, and he also knew she was going to be very disappointed. He felt he had let down her faith in him and that was the hardest thing to bear.

The next day he informed Harrie that he'd an appointment the following Tuesday afternoon with a firm that handled the sale of businesses. He'd need the account books to take with him so they could give him an idea what they felt the company was worth. They would then find a buyer for him, and the quicker the better, so he could get this over and done with.

CHAPTER THIRTY-ONE

It was a very subdued Harrie who next Monday morning sat logging the details of the previous Friday's individual drivers' receipts in their separate log books and checking that their takings balanced with the total amounts written on the receipts. When she had finished, only three of the drivers had shortages in their money for that day and then only by a matter of pennies. Harrie got out her purse and made the balance up herself.

As she made to start on Saturday's receipt-logging, she remembered that tomorrow afternoon Chas had an appointment to begin proceedings to sell the firm and it reminded her of the day he went to the bank all smart in his suit to ask them for a loan to buy the business. He would be smart in his suit again tomorrow but how far removed the appointments were. How ironic it would be, she thought, if things should start picking up suddenly, those lost customers start using them again, and people like Mrs Jackson be so pleased with their services that they used Tyme's in future instead of whoever they had before.

Then a memory stirred. Mrs Jackson had been going to Coventry on Friday but Harrie couldn't remember a receipt made out for that fare in any of the drivers' receipt books when she had logged them all earlier. Had the driver who had done the job for Mrs Jackson forgotten for some reason to give her a receipt? Yet the takings had tallied with the amounts on the receipts apart from by a few coppers. Harrie gnawed her bottom lip anxiously, not at all liking what seemed to be glaringly obvious. Did this mean that one of the drivers was on the fiddle? Had Mrs Jackson not been given a receipt for her fare because the driver had pocketed the money and taken a chance that Mrs Jackson would not be one of the customers randomly checked by management? Harrie just couldn't believe that any of the drivers would do this to Chas, after he'd more than proved himself to them to be such a considerate boss, always putting his staff's welfare above his own.

Anger rose within her. Chas of all people didn't deserve this. She wouldn't let whoever this driver was get away with what he'd done. She would find out who it was then confront him and make him pay back the fare he'd pocketed. She'd speak to Chas about it as soon as she could and see what he wanted to do with the culprit. She felt, though, that he would have no choice but to sack whoever it was, as how could he continue working for them when they knew he was dishonest? What a foolish man to risk his job for the sake of a few pounds!

She'd find out who Stanley had allocated the job to via the job-logging book. He had just finished relaying details of a new job to a driver over the radio when Harrie went over.

'Can I just check with you which driver you allocated to Mrs Jackson's job on Friday, please, Stanley? If you remember, she's the lady who mistook us for another firm and you were left with all the rigmarole of calling round all the others to find out which one she'd really booked her taxi with.'

He looked blankly at her for a moment then said, 'Oh, yes, Mrs Jackson. Oh, er . . . but she telephoned in a while later to apologise as she realised she'd mixed us up with another firm, like we thought she had. Thankfully it was before I'd wasted my time calling round the others.'

'She did? Oh!' So Harrie was wrong and a driver hadn't fiddled the fare after all. Mrs Jackson's job had never taken place. She felt terrible for mentally accusing one of their men of doing something she now realised he hadn't.

'There isn't a problem, is there?' Stanley asked.

'Oh, no, no,' she said hurriedly. 'After logging the drivers' receipts for last Friday, I remembered Mrs Jackson and wondered why I hadn't come across a receipt in her name. Now I know why.'

Neither of them had noticed that a woman had come in and was standing at the counter until they heard her call, ''Scuse me, I'm sorry to interrupt, but can I get some service? I'm in a hurry.'

Stanley shot up out of his chair and hurried across to deal with her.

Harrie was halfway back to her office when the telephone started to ring. With Stanley already busy at the counter, she turned back to deal with the caller before they gave up and rang off.

'Good morning, Tyme's Taxis. How can I help you?'

A deep baritone voice boomed back at her. 'Mrs Jackson here. I left a scarf in the back of the taxi on Friday. I can manage without it so no point me making a special trip down to fetch it but if you have a driver passing my way sometime soon, I'd be obliged if you could drop it off to me.'

'Oh, er . . . Mrs Jackson, this is Tyme's Taxis you've called.'

'Yes, I'm well aware of that.'

'But you cancelled your taxi with us for Friday.'

'I most certainly did *not* cancel my taxi for Friday. If I did, why did one with your name on the side come and pick me up? It's you that's muddled, dear. Please have my scarf sent round for me as soon as you can, it was a gift from my late husband. Thank you.'

With that she rang off.

Harrie stared blankly at the receiver in her hand. So Stanley had lied to her about Mrs Jackson's cancellation. But why would he?

As he approached the desk to resume his seat after dealing with the woman at the counter's requirements, he noticed the confused expression on Harrie's face and asked her, 'Anything wrong?'

Something obviously was but she wasn't quite sure what. She needed to get back to her office and think about all this. One thing she mustn't do was alert him to the fact that she suspected he was up to something until she was sure one way or the other. 'Pardon? Oh, no, nothing at all, Stanley.'

Once seated back behind her desk, her head in her hands, Harrie's mind was racing. What reason could Stanley have for lying to her about Mrs Jackson's booking? Mrs Jackson was adamant that a Tyme's taxi had arrived to pick her up and take her to her destination and that she had left her scarf in the back of it. Why then hadn't Harrie come across a receipt for Friday with Mrs Jackson's name on it? She sat for a moment puzzling over this problem. Then a terrible thought struck her. Was it possible that Stanley and a driver were in league together and had split Mrs Jackson's fare between them? All the facts seemed to be pointing that way.

If she was right this was terrible. She couldn't believe it of him. Stanley seemed such a pleasant, trustworthy man. Chas had given him a job when he was desperate for work. Had advanced him money on his wages to tide him over Christmas. Allowed him to earn himself extra by agreeing to let him cover the evening shift as well as the days. Now she realised why he was so keen to do that, it was not just for the extra income. That way he could pick and choose all the plum fares to share with his accomplice, during the evening as well as during the day.

Then another memory stirred. A vision rose before her of witnessing Stanley writing details of a job he was taking over the telephone on a piece of paper instead of straight into the book. He'd put that piece of paper into his pocket and told her he was going to deal with it later. Oh, he was going to be dealing with it later all right – by handing those details to his partner-in-crime, whoever that was. But she had witnessed the incident weeks ago. Stanley and his accomplice had probably been operating this scam for a while. It could well be the reason for the fall in profits over the months since Christmas. There was still one question that bothered Harrie, though. How was the mileage on the firm's cars being falsified to cover these jobs? Maybe the culprits when brought to book would answer this question, Harrie couldn't fathom it.

She still couldn't work out which driver could possibly be in league with Stanley. They all appeared to be such decent men. But then, so did Stanley himself.

Her first instinct was to tackle him with her suspicions right now and see what he had to say in his own defence. But she knew that as owner of the business it was up to Chas to tackle him. This was going to devastate him, she just knew it was. But would her findings be enough to change his mind about selling the business? She supposed that depended on how much Stanley and his accomplice had been getting away with.

It was a nerve-racking time for Harrie, trying to carry on as normal in front of Stanley until Chas arrived back and she could divulge her grave suspicions.

Time ticked past and there was still no sign of him. She was desperate to get this matter resolved, very conscious that while Stanley was left at liberty behind the radio-operator's desk, under the impression he was getting away with things, he could be plotting another scam. But she had no alternative but to sit it out until Chas came in.

Harrie's leaving time came and went and still he hadn't returned. Tonight of all nights a job had kept him out late. The day-shift drivers had all signed out, the three night ones had taken over. It was after eight o'clock by now and she knew her father would be wondering where she was. Stanley too must be wondering why she was working so late.

She jumped as the man himself popped his head round her door. 'Oh, er . . . hello, Stanley. What can I do for you?'

'I just wondered if you'd like a cup of coffee as I'm about to make myself one? You don't usually work this late, Harrie. Well, you haven't since I've been working here.'

She hoped she sounded convincing when she told him, 'Oh, I'm just finishing off a job and thought I might as well stay until I'd done it. Give me a clear desk in the morning so to speak. I'd love a cup of coffee, thanks. Er . . . I noticed the boss's been out all day and hasn't come back yet?'

'Oh, yeah. I radioed him this morning to pick a man up and take him to the station to catch the train to London. Chas radioed me back a while later to say the chap had changed his mind about catching the train and wanted Chas to drive him instead. By my reckoning he should be back anytime now.' The telephone started ringing. 'Oh, better go. I'll bring that coffee through as soon as I get chance to make it.'

CHAPTER THIRTY-TWO

Chas finally arrived back at nine-thirty that night. He was surprised to see the light still on in Harrie's office and made his way straight in to ask what she was still doing at work at that time of night.

As soon as he came into the room, she leaped up from her desk, went over to the door and shut it behind him, conscious that he was staring at her in bewilderment.

'Harrie, what's going on?'

'I need to talk to you, Chas, without Stanley overhearing us. I think you'd better sit down,' she advised him.

Several minutes later he was staring at her, looking astounded. 'I can't believe this . . . You've got to be wrong, Harrie.'

'I'm not, Chas. Mrs Jackson is adamant a Tyme's taxi took her to Coventry on Friday. She said she left her scarf in the back and wants us to have it taken round to her. She was quite put out when I asked her if she'd called the wrong firm, mistaken us for another. She didn't come across to me as the type of woman who'd easily make a mistake. Don't forget she called into the office when she rearranged her taxi. That would mean she'd mistaken us for another firm twice, and I find that hard to believe.'

'I'd better get Stanley in and find out what he's got to say about all this.'

The radio operator entered, smiling at them both. With his eyes on Chas, he said, 'Yes, Boss, what can I do for you?'

Chas invited him to sit down and began, 'Well, it's just that we have a mystery on our hands, Stanley, one we hope you can clear up for us. You see, a customer called Mrs Jackson is adamant that she left her scarf in the back of one of our taxis after it took her to Coventry on Friday, only there's no record of her having ordered a car in the book and neither is there a driver's receipt

285

for such a trip. I'm not accusing you of anything, Stanley, I'd just like to clear the matter up, that's all.'

He gave a shrug. 'Well, it's as I told Harrie, Boss. Mrs Jackson cancelled her taxi so she couldn't have left her scarf behind in it because she never had one from us. She's got our firm muddled with another, that's what she's done.'

Chas flashed a look at Harrie as though to say, I have no alternative but to accept this man's version of events. It's Mrs Jackson's word against his that she actually had a taxi from Tyme's.

Stanley got up. 'Well, if that's all you wanted to see me about, I'd better get back to my post.'

Harrie watched him closely as he turned and made to walk out. She knew Mrs Jackson had been telling the truth and that she had had a taxi on Friday from Tyme's. Stanley was lying. But how could she prove it? Then an idea suddenly struck her.

'Stanley?' she called after him.

He stopped and turned back to face her. 'Yes, Harrie?'

'Would you mind turning out your pockets, please?'

Chas glared at her. 'Harrie! What on earth is possessing you to ask Stanley to do that? What's in his pockets is personal to him, surely?'

'I'm not so sure about that, Chas, and I need my suspicions confirmed. If Stanley has nothing to hide he will do as I ask.'

The man stared at them both frozen for what seemed like an age. Then his shoulders sagged and he blurted out, 'You know what's in my pockets, don't you, Harrie? It's details of jobs. You've sussed me, haven't you? But me and my brother were only getting back what was *ours*. As soon as we had all the money back that would have been it. We're not thieves.' He glared at Chas accusingly. 'It's *you* that's the thief, Mr Tyme, isn't it? It was you who took my dead father's case and then used what was inside it to start up your own business. Did you give a thought to the state you left my mother in, and me and my brother and our families? That money was to provide for us all. You go around pretending to everyone you're such a nice man and they have no idea what you're really like, have they? No idea at all.'

Chas was staring at him, astounded. 'You're Mr Graham's son? You think *I* took his briefcase? You're wrong, Stan— Mr

286

Graham, you're so wrong. I didn't use your father's money to start this business. It was my own savings I used, along with a large loan from the bank. I've hocked myself up to the eyeballs, can easily prove everything I say. I have no idea who took your father's money, Mr Graham, but it wasn't me. I told the truth when the police interviewed me.'

Harrie, who couldn't believe what she was hearing, nevertheless shot to Chas's defence. 'I can confirm all he is telling you. You're badly mistaken, branding him a thief as you have.'

Graham stared at Chas, horrified. 'You didn't steal it then? Didn't use our money to buy this place?' He sank down on the chair in front of Harrie's desk, cradling his head in his hands. 'Oh, no, no. We were positive it had to be you after seeing the article about you buying this place in the *Mercury*. Oh, God, I . . . I don't know what to say. I'm so afraid we've made a terrible mistake. It's not you who's the thief, it's me and my brother, isn't it? Oh, dear God, dear God.'

Chas was looking confused. 'Would you care to tell me just what exactly has been going on here, Mr Graham?'

The other man raised his head and looked at him guiltily. 'Yes, you deserve to know what my brother and I have been doing and then I'll leave it to you to decide what to do next. But you have to believe me, we thought we were justified in what we were doing. Thought we were taking back what was rightfully ours.' Clasping his hands, he took a deep breath. 'My name is Gordon Graham – you've met my brother Geoffrey. You know how Dad died, and Geoffrey told you about the money in his briefcase. When the police had exhausted their investigations and couldn't find any trace of the case, they concluded that it must have been taken out of the back of your taxi by an opportunist thief at the hospital while you and the staff were concentrating on getting my father inside.

'As if it wasn't bad enough for all of us losing him, our future depended on what was in that case. The shop hadn't been doing well for a long time and so my brother and I persuaded Dad that he had no choice but to accept a cash offer for the business from a competitor.

'Mum and Dad were going to be selling the house they'd lived in all their married life and using that money to buy a bungalow on the coast, something they'd always wanted to do. With two thousand of the money from the sale of the business to help eke out their government pensions, Dad was giving me and my brother the other four thousand between us to put down as a deposit on a newsagency and work there to support both families.

'When the police told us three weeks after Dad's death that they'd drawn a blank on what had happened to the case, my brother and I had no choice but to give up our plan to buy a business and get ourselves whatever jobs we could, trying to help Mother out between us as well as looking after our own families. I found myself a job as an electrician in a factory and my brother worked as a machine operator. We just hoped that whoever had taken our money was proud of themselves for ruining the futures of those they'd stolen from. We felt it best to try and forget it and get on with making the best future we could for ourselves.

'Then the night before Christmas Eve I read the article in the paper about you buying this business. I went straight round to see my brother and showed it to him. It just seemed such a co-incidence to us that one day you were a taxi driver and the next you'd bought this business. Well, we could only draw one conclusion – you must have done it with our money. We felt there was no point in going to the police as they'd already interviewed you and were happy with your statement. We also thought that if you were clever enough to convince the police it wasn't you who had taken our money, then you'd be clever enough to have a story ready as to how you got hold of the capital for the business.

'We were faced with two choices. Either we let you get away with what we thought you had done or else we tried to get what was ours back from you.

'We hadn't a clue how but felt if one of us could get a job with you and be on the inside, so to speak, that would be a good place to start. Neither of us is what you'd call criminally minded but we both felt that to achieve what we wanted, we had to start thinking that way. It was decided it would be me who tried to get work with you as you'd already met my brother when he came here to ask after the case. Our first hurdle, though, was for me to get a job with your firm.

'I couldn't believe my luck when you believed my sob story

and took me on starting immediately. I was prepared to take anything just to get set on, and when you offered me the radio-operator's job I just hoped I could make a stab at it. I'd arranged with my brother what to do if you wanted references. The number I'd given was actually my brother's telephone number and he was all geared up to pretend he was my past employer and give me a glowing reference. You did shock me, I have to say, when you offered to advance me some money on my wages to tide me over Christmas. I couldn't understand how a man who had done what you had could show such compassion . . . Then I thought it was just an act you were putting on, wanting to make everyone believe you were a kind man when in truth you were the opposite.

'When I told my brother what job I'd been given he was over the moon because he said that, unbeknown to you, you'd given me the best job you could have for us to stand a chance of getting back what was ours. Radio operators had control over what jobs were given to the drivers. If he became a Tyme's driver then as radio operator I could make sure all the good jobs went his way.'

Chas was looking puzzled. 'But I haven't taken on any new drivers since I bought the business, how could he have become one of Tyme's men?'

'It was unofficial. You didn't know my brother was working for you. We used our own car, had two magnetic signs made up that we stuck to the side-front doors each time the car was being used as a taxi. We took them off when it wasn't being used illic-itly. When you issued the men with their new trousers and jackets for work, my brother bought himself a set too. The signs and working outfit were the only outlay involved for us. All we had to hope was that you didn't cotton on that some of the jobs coming in weren't being done by your official drivers. We did realise you could become concerned about any fall in your profits, but if so much as a whiff about that was heard in the office then I would made a quick exit.

'I was very relieved when you, Harrie, accepted my request to work as self-employed because it meant I didn't need to keep finding an excuse to fob you off for not giving you my P45. Well, I couldn't because you would have known then I wasn't Stanley Slater. The home address I gave you when I first started obviously isn't my real one.

'I was terrified that you'd suspected I was up to something when you saw me writing those job details down, Harrie. I was so relieved that you seemed to believe the excuse I gave you. I was managing on average to pass over to my brother jobs that brought us in about two hundred pounds a week. Out of that money, of course, he had to fund the petrol for all the jobs he did and pay maintenance for the car but we put the rest of it aside to accumulate. We wanted to keep things going until we'd made all of Dad's six thousand back, or as much as we could of it. We'd all moved in with my mother and tried as best we could to survive on my wages from here. It's been tight for us but it was worth it. It seemed the only chance we were going to get of regaining Dad's money and buying our own business. As time passed and no one here seemed to have any idea what was going on, I really thought we'd pull it off. Until today, that is. When I passed that original booking of Mrs Jackson's over to my brother I had no idea it would end up . . . well, proving to be the thing that would be our downfall.'

He gave a deep sigh. 'Well, now you have it, Chas. You have to believe me that since we thought you'd stolen from us, we felt justified in our actions. It didn't seem like a crime to us. My brother will be beside himself when he learns all this. We will give you the money we've made back, every penny of it. You have my word on that, for what it's worth. Obviously what you decide to do with us is your decision.'

Harrie spoke up first. 'I don't know what to say about all this, I really don't. I feel I ought to ring the police and have you and your brother arrested, but then I also feel you were right to try and get back what was yours when you thought Chas had stolen it from you. Oh, what a mess.'

Chas slowly slid to his feet from where he'd been sitting on the edge of Harrie's desk. He walked across to the door and stood facing it for several long moments before turning back to look at Gordon. 'The money you and your brother made from me . . . I don't want it back.'

Gordon stared at him in utter shock. 'You don't? But I don't understand . . .'

Chas sighed. 'The case was stolen from my car and I have to take some responsibility for that fact. I want you to put what you've made towards doing what your father intended.'

The other man couldn't believe what he was hearing.

'You mean that?'

'Yes, I do.'

'Well, I . . . don't know what to say.'

'There's nothing to say.' Chas held out his hand to Gordon who slowly shook it. 'Goodbye, Mr Graham.' He held the door open for Gordon to leave.

Only Chas would have done what he just had, Harrie thought to herself. Chas Tyme was the most generous man she had ever come across or was ever likely to.

He was looking at her gratefully. 'Once again I have a lot to thank you for, Harrie. I don't know how I can ever express my feelings.'

In fact, he could think of one way last doubted she'd welcome it.

I know how I'd like you to thank me, Harrie thought. By grabbing me in your arms, kissing me passionately and telling me you love me. But you won't, Chas, will you, because you don't love me. She planted a smile on her face. 'There's no need for thanks, you pay me for what I do, Chas. I'm just glad we got to the bottom of this. I wonder who did take that case?' she mused.

'Well, like Gordon Graham said, I hope whoever did it is proud of themselves.'

'They probably are,' she said dryly. 'Proud they got away with it, I mean. And I hope that money brings them nothing but misery. But, Chas, you know what this means, don't you? Gordon said that he and his brother were making themselves about two hundred pounds a week. Your profits haven't been declining after all but going up – and by a lot. This changes everything, doesn't it?'

He smiled at her. 'Yes, it seems it does. I'm not quite the failure I thought I was, am I?'

'I always knew you weren't. So you'll be cancelling your appointment tomorrow?'

'Well, I won't have time to go, I'll be too busy trying to find replacements for Gordon, won't I? But one thing I have learned from all this is that before I take on anyone else for such a responsible position, we must check them out thoroughly first. Until we find replacements, I'll have to do my best to cover the job.'

'I'll help where I can, and I'm sure the other drivers will pitch in when they can until the vacancies are filled. Best we tell all the staff that Gordon, or Stanley as he's known to them, just decided he'd had enough and left, don't you think, Chas?'

'Oh, yes, I certainly agree with that.'

Harrie was suddenly very conscious of the time. 'I really ought to be getting off home,' she said, moving around her desk to unhook her coat from the nail on the wall that she used as a makeshift coat hook. 'It's getting on for eleven and my dad is probably frantic, wondering where I am.'

'Oh, goodness, yes, me too,' Chas exclaimed. 'My mother will probably have called the police out by now and half the Leicester force will be searching for me. I'll drive you home, Harrie, it's too late for you to be walking alone at this time of night.'

'Oh, I couldn't put you to all the trouble of getting your car out of the compound.'

Nothing was too much trouble when it came to Harrie. Didn't she have any idea he would do anything for her? 'It's not in the compound, it's parked around the corner. When I arrived back tonight I found some kind soul had blocked our entrance by parking a van across it. Hopefully they've gone by now. I've got to move the car anyway. To be honest, Harrie, I don't fancy the walk home myself so after dropping you off I intend driving home and for once leaving the car parked outside my house. Come on then.'

CHAPTER THIRTY-THREE

Moments later Chas turned to face Harrie who was seated beside him. 'Comfortable?' he asked.

She smiled at him. 'Yes, thank you.'

'Good. I'll have you home in a jiffy then.'

Starting the car, he drove it the short distance to the junction with the main Blackbird Road where he needed to turn right. A car was approaching, travelling in the same direction that Chas needed to go in, and he waited for it pass. As it did he had a clear view of what was painted boldly on the side of it.

Harrie had seen it too and commented, 'One of the night drivers off to do a pick up?'

Chas frowned. 'All the drivers were out when we left just now. Anyway, I caught a glimpse of the first couple of letters of the number plate and that's the car allocated during the day to Harry Gibbons. That car isn't being used by any of the night drivers this week.'

She looked at him quizzically. 'Well, if the night drivers are all spoken for, and that car isn't one of theirs, then it shouldn't be out at all but parked securely in the compound.' She gasped as a thought struck her. 'Oh, Chas, do you think it's being stolen?'

'Oh, hell, that's the only explanation, Harrie. God, that's all we need after what we've just been through. What a day this is turning out to be! And I pay Terry to keep that compound secure as part of his job . . . Oh, no time to think about what I'll be saying to that young man. Harrie, I'm sorry . . .'

'Shut up, Chas, and just get after it.'

'Hold tight then,' he warned her.

They were so consumed by their need to chase after the car that neither of them gave a thought to radioing through to Ronald Tyler and telling him to alert the police to what was going on, enlisting their help in the chase to reclaim the stolen car.

Flashing a quick glance up and down the road to see that his way was clear, Chas pressed his foot hard down on the accelerator and swung the car expertly out into the main Blackbird Road, setting the tyres screeching.

Harrie was eagerly scanning the road ahead, looking for the car. She couldn't see it. Then she spotted its back end disappearing around a corner ahead of them.

'I see it,' said Chas, pre-empting her.

'What are you going to do when we catch up with it?'

'I don't know. Stop them somehow before they cause any damage to it.'

'Drunks, do you think, having fun?'

'More than likely. Obviously a drunk who knows how to hot wire, though.'

'Sorry?'

'Now's not the time to explain what it means, Harrie, not while I'm trying to concentrate. Where has the car gone now?'

Harrie's eyes darted. 'There it is, look! It's just turned down the Loughborough Road. I wonder where they're headed?'

'I just hope it's not a patch of waste ground to be abandoned after they've set it alight. We've just had an insurance claim for Fred's car after his accident and with another coming so soon afterwards . . . well, the insurance company could start getting suspicious about us.'

Harrie clung on tight to the edge of her seat as Chas spun the car expertly into the Loughborough Road and then along its curving length, eventually leading on to the Belgrave Road. Chas slowed right down to manoeuvre a tight bend just after they had passed by the busy Checkett's public house. The road ahead straightened out. There was no sign of the car they'd been following.

Chas drew his car to the side of the road, taking his hands off the wheel and holding them up in bewilderment. 'Well, where did they go, Harrie?' he exclaimed.

She looked mystified. 'Not ahead, we'd see them as we weren't that far behind. They must have turned off on one of these side streets. But which one? We'll lose them for sure if we don't try and look. Go down that one,' she suggested, pointing in the direction of a tree-lined street just slightly ahead and to the right of them.

Knowing the area well through his job as a cabby, Chas said, 'But that only leads to another maze of streets. There's no waste ground down there to my knowledge. Oh, we'll lose them by sitting here! Okay, let's try the street you suggested.'

Moving off again, he turned right into the street and set off down it.

It was Harrie who spotted the woman half-lying on the pavement. 'That woman, Chas, she looks like she's had an accident!'

He looked across and spotted her. Being the man he was, he automatically slammed his foot on the brakes, pulling the car to a halt at the kerbside by the prostrate woman. Leaping out of the car, he dashed over to her and squatted down beside her. He could smell drink on her. One of her stockings was ripped and blood was pouring from a deep graze on her knee.

Before he could ask what help he could give her, she cried, 'He got me handbag! It all happened so quick. I'd just left the pub and was on my way home when I was attacked. All in black the man was, one of them balaclavas pulled down over his head. He ran off before I could stop him. But I saw him getting into a car parked just down there,' she said, pointing ahead of her. 'It was a dark car and as it turned the corner at the end of the street I saw it had white writing on the side. Don't mind about me, I need me handbag back. It's got all me stuff and money in it. Get after them and get it back. Go on,' she urgently cried. 'Go on!'

Chas jumped up and dashed back to the car. He hurriedly clambered inside, slamming the door shut behind him, just in time to stop Harrie from getting out to come and offer her help to the woman. 'Shut the door, Harrie,' he ordered her, revving the engine.

Doing as he said, she spun to face him, looking stunned. 'What about that woman . . .'

'Harrie, whoever's stolen our taxi has just snatched her bag. We've got to try and catch those bastards who did this to her and get her bag back. Now we know why they wanted a vehicle . . . it certainly wasn't to ride around in for a bit of fun. Is this a coincidence, do you think, or are these the same people who've been doing this to women for the last few months? Hold on tight, Harrie.'

She just had time to cling on to the edge of her seat before he sped off in the direction the woman had indicated.

Harrie had never seen Chas angry or heard him swear before in her company but she felt it to be well justified in the circumstances. A memory struck her then. 'Oh, Chas, I forgot to tell you after everything else that's happened today . . . two policemen turned up this morning to see you. Two more women were attacked last night and it seems one of them saw the getaway car. She said it had writing on the side, like a taxi. The gang are obviously stealing taxis to do their dirty work from, Chas.'

'And tonight it was our turn,' he hissed. 'Well, let's hope their choice of our car was a bad one for them, eh, Harrie?'

They caught sight of the stolen taxi a little way ahead of them as they turned the next corner.

'There it is!' she cried. 'Put your foot down, Chas, and catch up with it.' She was surprised, though, when he actually did just the opposite. 'You're slowing down, Chas. Why?'

'Well, if they get an inkling they're being followed they could try and lose us. If they succeed we've achieved nothing and they're at liberty to keep on doing this. I've a suspicion they'll abandon the car soon and then we can follow them on foot. Hopefully they'll lead us to an address. We can give that to the police and let them take it from there.'

Harrie looked impressed. 'Oh, good thinking. Look, they've turned right to head back down the Loughborough Road.'

Following a safe distance behind, it soon became apparent to them both that the car was heading back towards the Blackbird Road.

'This doesn't make sense,' said Harrie, confused. 'They seem to be going back towards our premises. You don't think . . . no, they can't be . . . but they do seem to be taking the car back to our compound.'

'I have a feeling you're right but we'll soon see,' he responded gravely.

Moments later Chas drew his car to a stop a short distance from the office. They sat in bewildered silence as they watched the car entering through the open gates to the compound. It drew to a halt in a space next to several other vehicles parked for the night. Immediately the driver's door opened and a man's figure got out and hurried across towards the hut at the back of the compound where Terry did his jobs. It disappeared inside. Seconds later they saw the driver's-side back door inch open just wide enough for another figure to emerge. It was dressed from head to toe in black, head completely encased in a bala-clava-type hood. It slipped out and ran across to the hut, carrying something over its arm. The shed door closed behind it.

The onlookers stared at each other mystified, neither having a clue what was going on.

Chas opened his door and prepared to get out. 'Harrie, go and telephone for the police,' he ordered her. 'Tell them to hurry.'

'Where are you going?' she demanded.

'There are two robbers on my premises, Harrie. What they're doing in there I have no idea but there's no time to try and work it out as they could make a getaway. There's also Terry to consider. I'm worried they could have harmed him so they could get away with stealing that car.'

Her face paled. 'But those men could attack you. It's two against one, Chas. I'm coming with you!' She made to open her door and leap out to accompany him, but he grabbed her arm to stop her. 'Harrie, do as I say,' he ordered her. 'Go and tele-phone the police. I can look after myself.'

'But, Chas . . .'

He had already got out of the car and was making his way across the road towards the compound whose gates were still open.

Harrie's heart started thudding painfully. Fear for Chas's safety flooded through her. She was torn. To go and telephone the police was the sensible thing to do, but the man she loved with all her being could be heading towards danger. Those men in the shed were capable of attacking a defenceless woman and robbing her of her handbag, might also have hurt Terry so they could steal the car, so there was no telling what they would do to Chas when he confronted them. She could not abandon him to face two criminals alone. As soon as she was certain he was in no danger she would summon the police.

As stealthily as his large frame would allow, Chas arrived outside the shed. Stopping just long enough to steel himself, he pushed open the door and stepped over the threshold.

He hadn't known quite what to expect but certainly hadn't expected to see Terry perched on a stool in front of his work bench, rifling through a woman's handbag.

To the side of him the person dressed all in black was in the process of pulling their balaclava off while saying, 'Another success, eh, Terry? God, we're getting good at this. Well, me really, as I do all the hard work while you have the easy bit. Yer should have seen that woman's face tonight when I surprised her. God, was she scared!'

Chas didn't need the balaclava to be fully removed to know whose face was concealed under it. He'd know that voice anywhere, having been at the receiving end of its nasty comments often enough in the past.

The balaclava fully off now, Nadine shook her head and ran her fingers through her hair. As she did so her eyes caught sight of the figure filling the doorway and her face froze in shock for a moment only to relax into a broad beaming smile as recognition struck.

'Well, look what's crawled in out the woodwork. If it isn't Quasimodo. Whoops, sorry, I shouldn't be so disrespectful to yer boss, should I, Terry? Yer don't mind, do yer, Terry's boss, that I've popped in to see me boyfriend for a minute while he's working?'

One hand still inside the woman's handbag, Terry was staring at Chas, wild-eyed. 'Oh, er . . . Boss. Yeah, Nadine's just popped in to see me. Yer don't mind, do yer? Er . . . what brings you here at this time of night? Summat I can help yer with?' His hand was out of the bag now and he was desperately trying to hide it under a piece of oily rag.

Outside the shed Harrie stood behind the open door, riveted by what was going on inside. She was stunned rigid that Terry appeared to be one of the robbers but who his woman accomplice was she didn't know, although her voice and manner did seem familiar. The woman obviously knew Chas, though. Harrie did not like the way she was addressing him. She was still torn as to whether to obey Chas's orders for her to fetch the police or wait and see if he was in danger. She decided to wait just a little longer, to make sure he had the situation under control.

Inside the shed Chas's face was a blank mask. 'I wouldn't normally have any objection to a friend or relative dropping in on my staff while they're at work, but I do object to your presence here, Nadine. I know what you've both been up to.'

Nadine gave a mocking sneer. 'So yer caught us taking one of the cars out for a spin. Well, so what? Terry don't get any other perks in this poxy job of his. Anyway I'm glad you're here, Quassie, 'cos it gives me chance to thank you. We've got a lot to thank your boss for, ain't we, Terry?'

'Nadine,' he hissed at her warningly.

'Oh, shut up, you,' she shot back at him. 'Chas has a right to know what he did for us. It certainly helped to make up for the way he turned me down. You've got a fucking nerve turning me down,' she spat at him. 'Who d'yer think yer are, eh? I told yer what he done to me, didn't I, Terry? Led me on to believe he'd give me the world, only to toss me aside when he changed his mind. And you ain't exactly his best friend neither, are yer, Terry, him taking that cabby's job off yer like he did.' She narrowed her eyes and glared at Chas murderously. 'And after me lowering meself even to consider giving an ugly git like you a chance.' Then her face lightened. 'But I forgive you, see, because if you hadn't done what yer did that night, we would never've found it, would we, Terry?'

'Nadine!' he stormed at her. 'Will yer shut yer trap before yer say summat yer shouldn't?'

She shot a glance at him. 'No, I won't shut up. He can't do anything, no one can, 'cos they can't prove we ever had it. Have yer forgotten, we spent all the evidence and got rid of what we found it in, in the canal? Now will you stop yer whittling, I want Quassie to know that through him we had so much fun. Best holiday I've ever had. First holiday I've ever had. And money no object. Boy, did I enjoy spending it.

'When we found it, we couldn't believe our eyes, could we, Terry? More money than either of us had ever seen in our lives.' She gave a wicked grin. 'Surprising what yer can find in the back of a taxi when yer sheltering from the rain.'

Chas gasped as realisation struck. 'It was you who stole the case?'

She looked mortally wounded. 'Stole? We never stole nothing,' she erupted. 'We found that case, and as far as I'm concerned, finders is keepers.'

'But you had no right to that money, Nadine, and you knew

you hadn't,' Chas accused her. 'The man who owned that case had just died and what was in it belonged . . .'

'Oh, well, he had no use for it then where he was going. Someone else might as well put it to good use,' she interjected before Chas could finish. 'Oh, and we certainly did put it to good use, didn't we, Terry? We booked ourselves into the Grand Hotel that night in the best room they'd got and spent a great week blasting the shops. Then I thought to meself, I've never been out of this hole of a city, now's me chance. So we caught a train to London and booked ourselves into one of them posh hotels, The Dorchester, I think it was called, and we shopped 'til we dropped. We ate in lots of fancy restaurants too where waiters dress like penguins. Got chucked out of a couple an' all, didn't we, Terry?' she guffawed. 'Anyway, I got quite a taste for the high life. Took to it like a duck to water, I did. Shame, though, when yer living like that, money don't go far, does it? So we had to come back until we'd decided on our next money-making scheme.'

'You blew the whole lot?' Chas exclaimed, horrified.

Terry was by now cradling his head in his hands, deeply regretting the day he'd happened across Nadine out in the compound and got involved with her. Little did he know then what this woman had been about to lead him into.

'Too bloody right we did!' Nadine shot at Chas as though he was stupid. 'So Terry had no choice but to come back to work for you. At least that way we had some money coming in until something better turned up. He moved back in with his grand-mother and I went back to my mother's meantime. Only I found out that the bitch had turned me kids over to the authorities and wouldn't let me back in her house.'

Terry's head jerked up. 'Kids! You never told me you had kids, Nadine!'

'Well, yer know now, don't yer? And you'll make 'em a lovely dad when I get them back. We're working hard at being able to afford our own place, ain't we, Terry? After me mam chucked me out I had nowhere to go, see, so I had no choice but to move in with Terry and his gran. Well, I thought *I* had it bad with the mother I'd been cursed with but, as God's my witness, I ain't never heard anyone nag like his grandmother does. That's why I been popping down here at night to see him now and again, so I can get away from her.' She flashed Terry a sweet smile. 'Anyway, best be off, darling, and leave you to it. I'll keep the bed warm for yer for when yer get home in the morning. Don't work too hard now, keep some strength for me.'

Chas held up his hand in a warning gesture. 'You're not going anywhere, Nadine, except down to the police station.'

'And why would I want to go down there?' she snapped.

'Taking the car out for a spin wasn't really what you were doing tonight. We found the woman you attacked and whose handbag Terry is trying to hide in front of him. It's my guess she's not the first you've done this to. How many is it, Nadine?'

She sneered at him. 'You ain't got n'ote on me. You ain't found me with no handbag on me tonight, and the police can come around to his gran's and search the place from top to bottom but they won't find n'ote in my belongings 'cos I'm too clever to hang on to incriminating evidence.' She wagged a finger at Terry. 'It's him you saw with his hand inside that woman's bag when yer came in, not me. I'm just an innocent bystander and as far as I'm concerned the police can lock him up and throw away the key, 'cos I'm fed up with him anyway. Plenty more where he came from and I'm off to find meself one.'

She made to get past Chas but he blocked her route. 'I told you, Nadine, you're going nowhere. Neither of you. I might not be able to prove that you stole that briefcase or that you'd any involvement in those other bag snatches, but I can prove this one tonight as you've still got the evidence. The police will be here any minute.'

'And I told you, yer thick cretin, I ain't going to no police station tonight or any other night.' Glancing around her, Nadine grabbed up a monkey wrench and waved it menacingly at him. 'I'll brain you if you don't get out of my way, you big ugly bastard!'

Before she could take a swing at Chas, he had lunged forward to grab her arm and shake the wrench from it. With her arms pinned to her sides, he grabbed her around the waist in a bear hug.

They were all surprised by the figure that then burst through the door, crying, 'You lay a finger on him and I'll swing for you!'

Chas was alarmed to see Harrie. 'What are you doing here?

301

I told you to call the police and wait for me in the office. I don't want you involved in this.'

'I was worried you were in danger, Chas.'

He was desperately trying not to mind the painful kicks his shins were receiving from Nadine's heels as she thrashed wildly against him. 'You can see I'm not. Now please fetch the police. In fact, when you leave the shed, lock us all in,' he commanded.

'But, Chas . . .'

'Do it, Harrie.'

A long time later Chas came back into the office. He'd just seen a policeman off the premises after he'd taken Chas's and Harrie's statements. Terry and Nadine were already down at the police station, being charged by the police. Apparently they'd found a safety deposit key in Nadine's handbag and it looked to be hopeful that at least some of Mr Graham's missing money would be recovered, though Terry seemed stunned to hear it.

Harrie rushed over to him and took hold of his hand to examine the painful-looking bite he'd received from Nadine as she'd tried to free herself from his clutches in a vain attempt to make a getaway before Harrie locked them all in the shed.

'That needs medical attention, Chas.'

'It's fine, Harrie. I'll bathe it with TCP when I get home.'

'But I noticed you limping too. What else did that woman do to you after you made me lock you inside the shed and fetch the police? You shouldn't have made me do that, Chas. I was frantic while we waited for them to arrive, knowing you were in the shed with those two, hearing that woman screaming abuse at you. Such nasty things she was saying, evil woman that she is.'

It was after two in the morning and Chas was desperately tired, still reeling from the shock of all that had happened that day. His usually placid nature was stretched to breaking. Before he could check himself, he snapped, 'Harrie, please stop fussing.'

After all that had happened to her that day, Harrie too was feeling the strain. 'Fussing!' she exclaimed. 'How dare you accuse me of fussing? You have no idea how I felt when you were in that shed. I was imagining all sorts. Waiting for the police to arrive to rescue you and march those two off to jail was the worst wait of my life.'

'I don't know why you're getting yourself so het up, Harrie. I . . .'

'You don't know why I'm getting so het up?' she interjected. And before she could stop herself blurted, 'Because I was terrified you'd be seriously hurt and I couldn't bear the thought of you getting hurt because . . . because . . . I care. I care because I bloody well love you, that's why.' It then struck her just what she had divulged and horror flooded though her. 'Now, on top of everything else today, you've made me go and make an idiot of myself. But don't you dare feel sorry for me. I realised a long time ago that you didn't have the same feelings for me as I do for you and I've accepted it. Right, I'm going home now. And, no, I don't want a lift. I'll walk, thank you.'

She made to storm past him but he grabbed her arm and pulled her to a halt in front of him, looking deep into her eyes, his face mystified. 'Did I hear you right, Harrie? You love me? But how can someone like you be in love with me?'

She looked up at him wide-eyed. 'What do you mean, how can I love you?'

'Well, I'm not handsome, I know that, and I'm big and . . .'

'Just the most wonderful, kind, considerate, compassionate man I've ever met in my life! I'd marry you tomorrow if you asked me to.'

He couldn't believe what he was hearing. 'What?'

'You heard me. Now I really *have* made a fool of myself and I want to go home. In fact, right this minute I wish the ground would open and swallow me up. If I've embarrassed you . . .'

'Embarrassed me? Oh, Harrie, you could never embarrass me. I've worshipped the ground you walk on almost from the moment I set eyes on you. I just never thought for a minute you would ever feel that way about me. I never dared dream you would. That man who came in to see you in the office, well, I might be mistaken, but I got the impression he was more than a friend looking you up as he happened to be passing. That's the sort of man you attract, Harrie. My sort . . . well . . .'

'Oh, Chas,' she interjected sharply. 'You are my sort. Fine clothes don't make a man, Chas, it's what's inside that counts. You're right, that man wasn't just a friend. He was my ex-fiancé who wouldn't accept that our relationship was over. But he wasn't for me, nor was I for him. Jeremy will find another woman who will suit him far better than I ever would, I've no doubt of that. And he will be much happier with her than he would ever have been with me. We weren't suited. Not like you and I are suited. Oh, Chas, all this time we've been wasting.' She looked at him expectantly. 'Would you please do something for me?'

'Oh, anything, Harrie. Name it?'

'Just kiss me.'

It was everything they had dared hoped it would be and more. Neither of them wanted that kiss to end.

It was a breathless Harrie who pulled away first but only because she had a crick in her neck as Chas was so much taller than she was.

Eyes beaming with love, she looked up at him and said, 'Saturday then?'

He looked disappointed. 'Oh, have I to wait that long? But if it's the soonest you can manage, that's fine by me. Where would you like to go? To the pictures again?'

'No, maybe another time. On Saturday I want you to take me to the church to get married.'

Laughing loudly, he scooped her up in his arms and crushed her to him.

CHAPTER THIRTY-FOUR

An exhilarated Chas drew his car to a halt outside the neat-looking semi-detached house. He was having great trouble behaving with his usual calmness when in reality all he wanted to do was stand on a soap box in a crowded area and proclaim to anyone who'd listen that he was loved by the most beautiful woman in the world, and as soon as they could arrange it they were going to get married.

Before he and Harrie had reluctantly parted the previous night they had made firm arrangements to take the afternoon off work the next day, first paying a visit to a jeweller so Chas could buy her an engagement ring, then seeing Iris to break their wonderful news to her, and then Percy. Hopefully both parents would join their respective son and daughter for a celebration meal that night. Parents dealt with, next stop was the vicar.

Before an excited Chas could go and collect an equally excited Harrie back at the office, though, he still had to finish dealing with the customer in the back of his car.

'Well, here we are safe and sound. I hope you've had a comfortable journey with Tyme's Taxis. That will be seven and six, please.'

A ten-shilling note was pressed into his hand. 'Thank you. Please keep the change. Yes, I have had a very comfortable journey, Chas. It is Chas, isn't it?'

He manoeuvred his body around so he could take a proper look at the smartly dressed woman seated in the back. He didn't recognise her. 'Yes, it is,' he said quizzically.

She smiled at him. 'I can see you don't remember me. My name is Sylvia Vines. Well, Sylvia Blaydon now as I'm married, you see. I used to live with my parents in the shop on the corner near where you lived. I often think of you, Chas. I wish you knew the number of times I've prayed to have a chance to say how sorry I am for how badly I treated you that night.

'I did love you, Chas. You were my first love. I'd loved you for a long time before you even noticed me. But I never dreamed for a moment a handsome boy like you would look at a thin ugly thing like me. When I realised you liked me back, well, I couldn't believe it. I was so excited when you plucked up the courage to ask me to meet you in the entry that evening because I knew you were going to ask me out.'

Her face fell then. 'Trouble was, somehow Nadine Dewhurst found out about our arrangement. I don't know how she did but then Nadine always had a knack for finding out things that could be of use to her. Before I met you that evening, she collared me and threatened that if I didn't do exactly what she said, she and her brothers would set fire to my parents' shop. Well, you can imagine what a situation I was in. I so much wanted to go out with you, Chas, but I was worried for my parents. The shop was their livelihood and I had no doubt Nadine and her brothers would do what they said if I didn't do what she told me. I had no choice. But I can't tell you how much it grieved me to say what I did to you. I assure you they were Nadine's words, not mine. For weeks afterwards I cried myself to sleep, knowing that what I'd done must have hurt you terribly. But I couldn't risk putting you right because if Nadine and her brothers found out they would have carried out their threat.

'The Dewhursts never treated any of us kids well, terrorised us all in truth, but I could never understand why they hated you so much more, Chas, what it was they had against you. I know you'd never have done anything bad to them. Then one day I found out what the reason was. My mother had sent me round to deliver a loaf of bread to Mrs Dewhurst and when I arrived at the back door I could hear this almighty row going on inside. Nadine was screaming at her, "*Why couldn't we have a mother like Chas's got? Why did we have to get you?*" Well, then I realised exactly why Nadine and her brothers hated you so much. You had something they hadn't and would never have. They were jealous of you, Chas. You had the one thing they couldn't steal or extort through their threatening ways, like they got everything else they wanted. You had a good mother.'

Sylvia took a deep breath and flashed him a bright smile. 'You don't know how good it feels to get that off my chest. Well, it's been lovely to meet you again. I don't need to ask you how well you're doing as the company's in your name, I see. I have no doubt there's a lovely woman waiting at home for you. Now I'm going to go and cook my lovely husband his dinner. Goodbye, Chas.'

With that she slipped out of the car and hurried inside her house.

A stunned Chas sat for a while going over all Sylvia Vines had said to him. He had never understood why Nadine and her brothers had picked on him in particular to be the brunt of their endless tormenting. Now he knew. He didn't need this final piece of information, though, to lift the great burden of self-doubt the Dewhurst offspring had left him with over their years of abuse because Harrie had already done so the previous night.

CHAPTER THIRTY-FIVE

Later that afternoon Chas opened the back door of his house and politely stood aside to allow Harrie to go before him. Closing the back door behind them, as pre-arranged Chas went ahead to warn his mother he had someone with him so she could prepare herself to greet their visitor.

As he walked into the back room his mouth dropped open in shock to see his mother sitting side by side on the settee with an elderly man. They were holding hands and chatting and laughing very intimately together. On the table before them was a tray of tea things and a plate of biscuits.

Sensing another presence in the room, Iris turned her head to see who had come in. When she saw who it was her face drained and she dropped the man's hands, jumping up from her seat like a scalded cat.

The man too jumped out of his seat and stood next to her, putting one arm around her protectively.

Thinking that by now Chas would have prepared his mother for her visitor, Harrie walked in to join them.

On seeing her, Iris's face turned even paler and she exclaimed, 'Oh, my God, Percy, we've been sprung!' Her eyes darted backwards and forwards between Harrie and Chas, panic-stricken. 'We were going to tell you both about us. We were, honest,' she blurted.

'Yes, we were,' insisted Percy, pulling Iris closer to him. 'We just didn't know how to, that's all. We didn't know how yer'd both take it. We were bothered you'd think us too old to be wanting to get married again. And the last thing we wanted either of you to think was that just because we'd found each other we cared less for the dear departed. And we worried that you two worked together. I mean, we knew you got on well from what yer both said, but we didn't know how yer'd feel about us two being together. But we couldn't help falling in love, could we, me darlin'?' he said, looking tenderly at Iris.

'No, we couldn't,' she agreed, looking tenderly back.

'Look, it's all my fault,' explained Percy. 'It was me who asked Iris to meet me again in the café after the day we first met. I couldn't help meself, you see. There was just something about this lovely lady that struck a chord with me. I felt comfortable with her. I was so chuffed when she agreed to see me again.'

'And I was just as chuffed that you'd asked me,' said Iris to him. 'If you hadn't, I would have asked you meself 'cos I knew yer liked me.'

'Did you?'

'Oh, yes. We women know these things. And we've had such fun together since, ain't we, ducky?'

'Oh, yes, we most certainly have. We've been for walks in the park, and up the town together, and after you finding out I loved dancing, I've been teaching you to dance ever since at the old-time dancing on a Wednesday afternoon.'

'Yes, and I'm getting really good at it now. And I've been teaching you to cook, ain't I, when you told me you wanted to learn to help yer daughter out.'

'Er . . . yes, you certainly have, my dear.'

'What d'yer mean by that?'

'Nothing, me darlin'. But let's just say I know what I'm buying you as a wedding present and I'm going to make sure you stick to the recipes written in it to the letter because your days of slinging whatever you think fit together are over.' Percy glanced at Harrie and Chas who both seemed staggered. 'Now, look here, I don't know how you found out about us but I'm glad it's all out in the open and we don't have to sneak around any more.'

'I'm so glad too,' agreed Iris. 'Freda's the only one who knew about us. Well, I had to tell her as she's me best friend and I needed someone to talk to. But I was getting sick to death of you asking me why I was having a snooze on a Wednesday evening, son. Now you know. It's 'cos I was bushed after dancing me feet off all afternoon.' She looked warily at Chas. 'Are you angry with me?'

'Are you with me?' Percy asked Harrie.

'Oh, no, most definitely not,' they both answered in unison.

A delighted beam lighting her face, Harrie held her arms wide and rushed over to her father, hugging him tightly. 'Oh, I'm so pleased for you, Dad, really I am.' She let go of him then to envelop Iris in her arms. 'I couldn't wish for anyone better for Dad than you,' she said sincerely, kissing her cheek. 'Would you mind if I call you Mum when you're married?'

'Oh, ducky,' Iris said, tears of happiness filling her eyes. Then she looked at Chas. 'What about you, son? Are you happy for us too?'

He had been desperately trying to swallow down the lump in his throat. He came towards her and hugged her fiercely. 'I'm more than happy for you, Mam.' Releasing her, he held out his hand to Percy and they shook. 'If Harrie is being allowed to say Mum, have I your permission to call you Dad?'

'With pleasure, son,' said Percy, beaming proudly.

'So how did you suss us?' Iris asked.

'We didn't,' Harrie answered.

Ivy and Percy looked puzzled.

'Well, what did bring you both here then?' Percy asked, bewildered.

Harrie grinned at them both. 'Well, it's a long story but in a nutshell, how do you fancy a double wedding?' she asked, flashing her solitaire engagement ring at them both.

Iris's eyes darted from Chas to Harrie. Percy's darted from Harrie to Chas.

As the truth dawned on them both the loud eruption of delight had Freda running in to see what had caused such a commotion in the house next-door.